The Price of Magik

THE DESCENDANTS SERIES BOOK 2

SL MCGINNIS

Castle Drum Publishing

Contents

Prologue

KARA

Purple electricity danced along her arms and crackled with her anger. Kara's rage couldn't be contained, and she stared into a single, cold, blue eye. Her heart thudded in her ears like a clock counting down.

Ten, nine, eight...

There were no more options, only this moment. She wouldn't get another chance if she didn't do this. The smell of blood and sulfur filled the air, combining in a deadly scent that made her stomach churn. The screams of the dying ran circles in her head even though the fighting took place a safe distance. The curses of those fighting for a lost cause kept her grounded in the present.

Seven, six, five...

Kara pressed her blade to the man's thick neck and gulped, trying to control her trembling. It wasn't hard to take a life, but the price was something that would sit on her soul like an ugly scar. Someone told her that once, or maybe she read it. She didn't want to be a murderer. Did she? *It's not murder if he deserves it.* He didn't deserve mercy because he never offered it to those he viewed beneath him. Kara could bring justice to every person this man hurt with a simple slide of the knife across his soft flesh. Souls that never had closure could finally rest in peace. She would be hailed a hero... *This isn't the way you want to do it.*

Four, three, two...

The sound of a gunshot pierced the air, and she turned her head toward the sky. Her hand was slick with blood, and she could feel it getting tacky against the cold metal handle of the weapon. Her raven hair stuck to her forehead pressed there with sweat and grime from the battle. Her electric blue eyes sought out the sound, but all she heard was a deafening silence. There was a war raging because of men like this, and until people like him were held accountable, there would always be suffering. Kara smiled wildly until her cheeks burned from the strain.

The man gulped, making the bead of blood bob like a fish.

One...

They were out of time – *no, he's out of time.*

Good Days and Bad

KARA

Three Months Earlier:

The sickly, sweet stench of burning flesh invaded her nostrils. Screams resonated through the air, catching in the wind and bouncing around her head like the balls her brother used to make with rubber bands. The howling pain as those around her turned to ash was worse than that of howling animals late at night. Goose-bumps rose along her arms as the tension built a solid wall of fear around her. Her heart shredding to pieces as she watched people's flesh turn red like the sun before melting off their bones, leaving nothing behind. How many people suffered at her hands, and how many families had she destroyed – Kara couldn't remember.

A presence as soft as a feather touched the edges of her mind, breaking the trance the past held. Kara's eyes snapped open at the unexpected intrusion and found herself staring into Justin's scarred, milky-white gaze. His face was inches from hers as he studied her energy, trying to determine what led her down the path of darkness. The question was evident in his careful, sightless eyes, but his lips didn't move. His salt and pepper hair lay in his face instead of being pulled back. His stubbly face was rough and weathered like he lived a thousand years despite him being the same age as her missing parents.

"What color do you see?" he asked, though his voice sounded muf-fled, thanks to the screams fighting for dominance inside her head.

Kara stared blankly, knowing he wouldn't be able to read her expression, only her aura, thanks to a fight he had with Angel years ago. Her hands trembled on her knees even though she squeezed the bony structures. This was the present, and she had nothing to fear because all that horrible stuff was in the past. The screaming grew louder as she tried to force herself out of it, and Kara flinched, not daring to take her eyes off Justin - her anchor in the dark storm that left her breathless.

"Kara, color," Justin said firmly, letting her know her response was not optional.

The feather in her mind pressed against her mental walls like a gentle hand, asking for entrance to her innermost thoughts. With a slow exhale, she let Justin's energy wrap around her like a warm hug. Her shoulders relaxed, leaving a dull ache as the tension eased up. The wind caressed her face, leaving cold patches where tears had streaked down her pale skin.

"Green," she said before she could lose herself in her thoughts. "I see green."

"What's green?" he asked.

This is stupid. "The grass," she said despite her iron-like tongue.

A ghost of a smile caressed Justin's thin lips. "Good," he said. "What else?"

She looked over his shoulder into the forest past Haven's borders, where magik shimmered between her new "home" and the rest of the world. "The leaves," she said.

Large oaks, pines, and maples extended as far as the eye could see. They were lush and green, but some maple leaves were a golden-yellow hue, and she knew it wouldn't be long before the seasons changed.

"What do the leaves look like?" Justin asked.

"They're wilting," Kara said, giving the conversation little thought. Wilting was a poor way to describe the change of time.

Time continued, changing the world around her despite the people she loved not being there. The surge of anger that came with that knowledge struck her like a sledgehammer, and her breath caught as her vision blurred with unshed tears.

"Wilting?" Justin asked as his bushy black brows furrowed.

The prickly grass stabbed her calves and thighs when she shifted, thanks to the large hand-me-down shorts riding up. She tried to make herself more comfortable, tugging them down with an absent hand and organizing her thoughts to describe it better.

"They are turning yellow and aren't as firm," she said, hesitating on the last word.

"Firm," Justin spit the word as if it were sour. He chuckled after a little more thought. "How's a leaf firm?"

Kara scowled and crossed her arms against her chest. The screaming finally subsided enough that he didn't sound like he was mumbling. *So, I'm not a poet; sue me.*

Justin smirked as if reading her mind. "How about we call it a day?" he asked, slapping his knees and standing.

Kara wouldn't complain if it meant he would leave her alone. She followed suit and stood, stretching her back and legs with a low groan. One could only sit crisscross for so long without feeling the effects, even one as young as herself. She rolled her neck in slow circles, sighed, and wiped her hands on the coarse, black shorts.

She never dreamed she could have this life before escaping from Angel's city. Her eyes roamed the unfamiliar place's gardens, trees, and land. Kara desperately tried to familiarize herself with some part of the outside world but found it challenging. She hoped that Haven would feel like a home and less of a nasty smudge on the fabric of her memory, but it had yet to happen.

"Hey." Ryan appeared before her, holding a dull-edged rusty sword before Justin could fully exit. He turned the pommel toward her and raised an eyebrow when she didn't move to take it.

Sweat dripped from the sandy-blonde strands of his hair, and his sun-bronzed skin was tinted red with sunburn and exertion. Brown-flecked green eyes studied her carefully. He wore a loose-fitting tank that showed off a black mark on his bicep that resembled a fuzzy ball of fire, and a red ring around the mark.

As Kara learned, the red ring was only something she could see. Each of the marks the Descendants had were a distinct color, and she could see it since she was a Descendant of Energy. It was like a secret painting that was only for herm, and while it was tantalizing and intriguing, she closed her eyes to it, trying to ignore what she had become.

Justin ruffled her hair as he walked past, muttering about playing nice. He made his way to the porch without using his walking stick, and Kara looked back at Ryan when the front door shut behind the man—another training session. Swords, daggers, and knives were things she didn't like using. When the blade was unsheathed, it couldn't be satiated without its weight in blood. Her throat constricted when she finally reached out to take the blade, and the moment her hand closed around the hilt, bitter bile rose in the back of her throat.

"Come on," Ryan said as he released it. His voice wasn't unkind but dull and apathetic, quite unlike the boisterous energy she was used to hearing from him.

He disappeared around the side of the house toward the training grounds. It was the only area in the yard that Nicholas allowed them to spar, thanks to the absence of grass and trees. Sometimes, she caught Nicholas and Justin practicing amongst themselves, though she never saw them cast spells like Killian and Ryan when they were embroiled in a fight.

The older brothers often danced around each other in swirls of blues, greens, browns, and silvers. Sometimes, Nicholas practiced with a sword and tried to hit his brother, but Justin would always find a way to be just out of range, making Nicholas rely on the earth's vibrations to determine where Justin would land. Other times, Justin shot arrows at the erected logs, using only his bare hands and energy to construct the arrows – a secret he had yet to share with any of them.

Kara stood rooted to the spot as if she had become a tree. She squeezed the sword's leather pommel until she was sure the straps would leave an imprint on her palm. When she determined the world wouldn't end, Kara followed Ryan with a frown. She could manage one more lesson; how bad could it be? *You could have a meltdown and electrocute someone.* And while that wasn't inherently bad, she hoped it was Ryan she shocked instead of someone innocent.

The grass tickled her bare toes, and she wiggled them as she walked—a gentle reminder that she was still in the present. She stepped on a pebble, and pain shot through her foot, making her wince. Kara paused and put all her weight on the rock until the pain stopped.

Nicholas said the more she went out without shoes, the tougher her feet soles would become. He rarely wore shoes, and she sometimes saw him running the woods at night like a deer – or, more appropriately, a deranged animal who saw by moonlight alone.

Kara hurried to the training grounds and met Ryan at one of the posts buried deep in the ground. The logs were large, too large for her to wrap her arms around, and littered with cuts and scorch marks. There were even arrowheads embedded in the bark that she sometimes tried to pick out of the wood when she was bored. The bark was coarse and dry, cracking in some places, leaving the log cratered like a face full of acne.

Ryan stood at the most damaged of the logs with his eyes closed and his hand pressed against it. He didn't look up when she approached and took her spot beside him. "Same thing as yesterday," he said.

Kara waited for him to remove his hand so she could proceed with her slashing, but Ryan didn't move. She grabbed his wrist, and his eyes snapped open. He went still when she physically tried to remove his hand, and like a statue, he was impossible to move.

"Today is about aim. You're going to work around me," he said. His eyes flicked to hers with the most serious expression she had ever seen.

It reminded her of her Physics teacher's face when he told Kara she was failing his class. Which, in a way, is what started this entire mess.

"No," she said without hesitation.

Ryan smiled, though it wasn't warm. He shook his head with a low chuckle. "It's a dull blade. You've got nothing to worry about," he said.

"How many broken fingers would you like?" she asked, though it came out more of a low growl.

"You won't hurt me. I'm using a shield, so the sword will bounce off." His voice was a smidge lighter.

Irritation swept through her veins because he was amused that she was concerned about his stupid fingers. Kara grabbed the sword with both hands and lifted it. *Break them. Leave his hand swollen and bruised.*

Ryan tapped her left wrist and shook his head before she could act on her violent thoughts. "You don't need two hands. It's a short sword. The point is to build your strength," he said.

Kara scowled. She was always sore after these sessions because the sword was too heavy. "What would you know?"

He didn't move as he raised a slender eyebrow in question. "I use two short swords. Would you like to argue more?"

Nicholas trained the boys in something he called their Descendant's disguise. Before arriving in Haven, she had only ever seen Killian's because of the night he almost bled out in her driveway after a nasty fight with Tory. When she dropped her left hand, her right struggled to keep the sword pointed straight.

"Would it be easier if it were a gun?" Ryan asked.

Kara didn't think. She turned the sword in her hand and slammed the pommel into his stomach with as much force as possible. It resonated with a dull thud, and a sadistic smile flickered on her lips when Ryan doubled over with a loud 'oof.'

Ryan clutched his stomach and groaned. "I deserved that."

"I would say it's well overdue." Killian walked over, kicking at the sand and smirking as he studied his doubled-over brother. "Next time, step into the attack. Gives you more power," he said. His voice was deeper than Ryan's, but they were virtually identical.

They had the same sandy-blonde hair that nearly fell into emerald eyes, with sun-bronzed skin and matching bad attitudes. While Killian was more observational and analytical, Ryan was quick to fight and the first to lose his temper. In the beginning, Nicholas struggled to tell them apart, but he figured out how to read the twins thanks to their differing energies. It was curious, but Justin had never seemed to have a problem telling who was who when it came to the boys.

Kara nodded and dropped the weapon, wiping her hands on her shirt. "I'm done," she said.

Killian stepped in front of her, cutting off her escape. "You've got to do something productive with your energy. House rules." His voice was neither cold nor angry. He was stating a fact in the same monotonous tone he used when addressing anyone but his twin.

She bared her teeth like an angry cat and turned to the forest, deciding she would go around. There was no way she was going to get an ounce of peace in this damn place. "Fine, I'm going for a run." And her only hope that they wouldn't follow was that neither twin liked running.

The forest was always silent and let her think without asking her a million questions.

"You might want to grab your shoes if you're gonna do that," Killian called before she could cross Justin's shields and spell lines.

She flipped him off and walked wordlessly across the wards. Her skin tingled and burned with the pure unchecked magik that spread like spiderwebs across his land. She took a moment to let her head stop spinning when she was past the most concentrated spots.

Barriers were odd bits of magik that Kara didn't fully understand. They were powerful pieces of magik that deflected most attacks and other energies. In Justin's case, the barrier was placed around his land, making it impossible for humans to see what was beyond the shimmering wall. It was almost like an illusion that confused and wiped the memory of whoever stumbled across it, yet, somehow, it was classified as a barrier instead of an illusion.

Justin assured her the effects of his intense energy would eventually fade as she grew accustomed to magik, but she didn't believe him. She couldn't imagine a world that would feel normal to her involving this mess lying dormant under her skin. Feeling Ryan and Killian's eyes on her back, Kara faked a quick ten-second stretch and ran.

The twigs and rocks cut into her feet, but the pain wasn't enough to make her stop – not with eyes on her, waiting for her to break. *Take a picture; it'll last longer.*

Kara was sick of being told what to do, how to do it, and when. It was more exhausting than sitting and waiting for Angel to execute someone or arrest her parents for treason. She took a couple of deep breaths to calm her heart and stop the screaming from returning. So long as she kept her mind busy, the past couldn't bother her. She listened to tiny scampering paws and let the sounds of the forest consume her senses as she filled her lungs with the pollen-sweet air.

Birds cackled and cawed in the distance, provoking one another from their nests to start fights. Chipmunks and squirrels ran through the bushes, tearing after each other and storing their nuts for the winter months. Leaves flitted to the forest floor, landing in soft, breathy sighs as the wind cushioned their landing. The first months of fall were always calm and quiet, with the occasional thunderstorm. Kara figured she would enjoy it while she could since the fall and winter would be easy compared to the heat of summer.

Justin had told her horrible stories of hundred-degree days where not even the chill of the lake was cold enough to cool his bones.

"If it isn't broken glass girl," a low voice drawled, tearing Kara from her thoughts.

She blinked in surprise as she looked around, her eyes darting through the trees. Nick told her ages ago to be careful in the forest alone because of bandits, but Kara had never found a reason to believe him.

There was a short, sharp whistle, and her eyes widened when she saw him.

He was up in the trees, standing on a branch at least ten feet above her head. He was a tall, dark-haired hunter with beady black eyes lit up like hot coals in his excitement. His hair was floppy and fluffy on top but shaved around the sides and long in the back.

Kara wrinkled her nose distrustfully but recognized him after a few seconds. "Avery..." she said, testing the name. It sounded right, and when he threw his head back in a bellowing laugh, she assumed she was right, or at the very least, close.

Avery jumped from the branch and landed on the forest floor, absorbing the fall with his hands and feet like a wild cat. "You remembered," he said, his voice nearly a purr. His hair fell in his eyes, casting shadows across his face and making him look more intimidating than last time.

Kara crossed her arms and frowned. "No need to show off," she said, unable to stop herself.

Avery chuckled and twirled his bow in circles with one hand before laying it across his shoulders. "No, that's showin' off," he said, stopping a few feet away. "Now, what are you doin' around here? Are you havin' more existential crises?" he asked. He walked toward her, his footsteps steady but with purpose. Leaves crunched under thick-soled boots, and Kara fought the desire to cringe with every 'crack' and 'crunch.'

What was his purpose in appearing before her? Kara didn't know, but she had no desire to find out when Justin was miles from hearing her scream. She eyed the young man warily but didn't move. Doing so would have shown weakness, and Ryan had told her never to show weakness to strangers in case they took advantage of it. Then again, should she be taking advice from someone who often got into fistfights and lost?

Avery smirked and popped his hands on his hips like the superheroes in the books Kara used to read to her brother. Her throat tightened at the thought, and she tried to wipe the emotion from her face. "I was going for a run," she said. *Not that it's any of your business.*

"You kinda have to run to be goin' for a run," Avery said, his smirk widening.

Kara's muscles tensed as she waited for something horrible to happen. Her eyes flicked around the space Avery stood, and she shook her head. As a Descendant of Energy, she could see everyone's energy, and all things had it– whether gray and dull or colorful and vibrant, there was an un-hideable energy. Avery was a blank slate. Since arriving in Haven, Kara had seen color and auras everywhere, but everything went silent the minute he stepped into her space.

The colors were muted and dull, and Kara had to work hard to see anything magikal.

"I didn't kill your wolf friend. He's been hanging around," Avery said, moving the conversation along. A smile warmed his face as if he were trying to reassure her. "Have you spent time with him?"

Kara shrugged. "I don't leave the house," she said. Her voice was well-controlled, but her hands shook against her biceps, so she tightened her grip until her knuckles went white.

Avery paced, not taking his eyes off her. His steps crunched against the dirt and dragged twigs and leaves around as he shuffled from one tree to the next. "Your magik is more controlled. I can hear a change."

She tried not to gape at his words. Avery was the first person she encountered after Dawson's death, and he had seen her at her absolute worst. That was before she could do anything with her magik, so she didn't know any better, but she hadn't anticipated that he was a Descendant himself.

"Yes, I know what you are." Avery chuckled at her look of confusion.

Knowing he knew about magik was more unnerving because she still couldn't see the energy that should be around another Descendant. She pointed at him and took a step back. *"You're* a Descendant?"

He nodded and furrowed his brow, noticing her sudden retreat.. "Of water," he said quietly.

Her heart jumped. Tory was a Descendant of Water and a good person, so that meant most of them should be, right? Kara wracked her brain for anything to say but found herself short when she remembered Nicholas' original lecture. Magik wasn't good or bad; it depended on who wielded it. She opened her mouth to share what was going through her head but closed it because who's to say Avery was a good person? She didn't know anything about him.

"You are as much of a mess now as you were then," Avery said, shaking his head with a tsk. "I thought maybe you would've gotten over it."

She frowned, unable to stop herself from asking, "Over what?"

"That irrational fear." His words didn't do much to answer her question, but Kara didn't get a chance to ask for clarification.

A second, smaller voice called out in a language she didn't recognize. She jumped and stepped back, moving further away before Avery could lead an ambush. It wasn't like she had gems or money, so attacking her would be pointless. Avery sighed and ran a hand through his black hair. He looked away and turned toward the source of the noise, calling back in the same strange language.

Kara's heart pounded, and every nerve told her to run. Most people had a fight-or-flight, but Kara seemed to have gotten the freeze instinct. Something that could get her killed in the wrong situation, yet there she was, immobile and silent. *For God's sake, woman, at least scream.* That, too, seemed impossible as her eyes danced through the tree canopies, looking for a pack of rabid men.

"It's my little hunter in trainin'. You've got nothin' to worry about," Avery said, holding his hands up innocently when her breathing quickened.

Kara stayed rooted to the spot until a small, brown-haired boy climbed out of the brush, giggling wildly. He spoke rapidly in a thick, guttural language that grated on her ears, but Kara couldn't look away.

The boy tugged on the leather strap across Avery's chest, pointed behind him, waved a knife, and giggled like a madman.

Kara was briefly reminded of Dawson the day he figured out what spray paint was and how he could get his hands on it. He had been so excited, and the smile lit up his face, making Kara's worries and fears vanish with the pure joy radiating from his body. She never imagined Dawson would become a vigilante artist and smear Angel's appearance all over the city, but it had happened, and he had loved every second of his life.

Avery pointed to Kara and swatted the boy's hands off the leather strap, holding his quiver in place. The little boy looked at her, and his eyes widened with surprise as if he had just noticed she was there. Avery and the child spoke in the unusual language before Avery grinned back at Kara. "This is Damian," he said, ruffling the boy's hair.

Something clinked along his wrist, and Kara studied the brightly colored bracelets. Avery had five on each wrist, each with perfect round stones that glinted in the sunlight. Each stone was a different color and looked smooth to the touch. Some of the stones were multi-colored, like the white and black ones, which reminded her of mini galaxies. *Beautiful.*

"He's a hunter in training and is shadowing me for the day," he said. "Damian, this is Kara." Avery introduced them as if Kara and he were old friends.

"Nice meet you," the boy said as he composed a few broken words. When he was done, he nodded excitedly, signaling Kara it was her turn.

Kara smiled and waved. Although he looked much younger than her, she could tell by the baby fat on his cheeks that he was still a kid. "What language are you speaking?" she asked.

Ryan and the others only spoke the language she grew up with, and she hadn't met anyone outside the city walls besides Avery. Both times they met, he spoke her language.

"It's called Nivet," Avery said, swaying as Damian tugged on the leather strap again.

Kara frowned. "Nivet." The word was odd and foreign. It didn't roll off her tongue quite the same way as Avery's.

He grinned again and pried Damian's fingers from the strap before walking to her. "Nee-vit," Avery pronounced it slowly and gestured for her to try again.

"Neeveet." Her mouth wouldn't correctly form around the world, sending Avery and Damian into laughter. Her cheeks burned, and she stepped away a little self-consciously. She didn't know there was another language outside of Yorklyn.

"Nice try. It can be difficult," Avery said, clearing his throat and stopping his fits of laughter when her face soured.

A squirrel scurried into sight before stopping between her and Avery. Its tiny nose wiggled, and its brown bushy tail flicked twice before it scampered back into the bush it came.

Avery frowned and looked around. "Now that your life isn't ending as you know it, you don't like me." It was a statement.

I don't know you enough not to like you. Now, ask me if I trust you. She bit her lip and chose not to answer. Ryan and Killian told her all about the horrors of the forest, about the people who preyed on those like her. Kara wasn't about to fall for the trap because some doe-eyed boy had helped her once, and honestly, he hadn't even helped her much.

"Avlua, we take her Rochester," Damian said, grabbing the back of the man's shirt.

Kara frowned, took another step back, and shook her head. "I should go," she said.

Avery chuckled and ruffled Damian's hair. "If you must. Damian and I have some huntin' to do. Maybe next time we meet, you'll be more comfortable."

She didn't know why it mattered if she was comfortable. They didn't know each other, and she had no desire to have another friend when she could barely keep up with the ones she had.

"And maybe you won't be so scared of magik," he said with a wink. He whispered something to Damian, and the boy waved at Kara before returning the way he came.

Kara scowled and pointed at Avery. "I'm not afraid of magik," she said.

He smirked and shrugged before going after the boy. His words lingered in the air, taunting her in a way she couldn't explain.

Kara huffed and wrapped her arms around herself, wiggling her toes in the dirt to ground herself. "I'm not afraid of magik." It didn't matter how many times she said it, though. It didn't feel right.

Miscommunication in the Eye of the Storm

RYAN

"You're not supposed to tell her we're keeping an eye on her," Ryan said when Kara disappeared into the forest. He scooped up Kara's dropped sword and returned it to Nicholas' stash of training weapons behind the house in a rundown old shack.

When he returned, Killian shrugged and turned to the main part of the home, shoving his hands in his pockets. "Secrets aren't my forte," he said.

Ryan glared and grabbed his brother's forearm to keep him from walking away. The response – and an unhinged one at that – was a well-timed punch to the nose. Pain splintered across Ryan's face as Killian's knuckles crunched against the bone and cartilage. Blood streamed from his nose like a faucet, and Ryan let go and clutched his face. Tears blurred his vision, and he scowled between twinges of pain.

Killian shook out his hand, hissing, before wiping Ryan's blood on his pants. "You're getting slow," he muttered, spitting on the ground.

Ryan growled as his irritation spiked. "That isn't how you're supposed to communicate," he snarled, wiping the tears off his face.

Killian chuckled without amusement, his face screwed up in a nice scowl. "Since when?" He stepped toward Ryan with another raised fist.

Ryan backed up until he ran into one of the poles and put his hand against Killian's chest to keep space between them. It wouldn't be ideal to get himself trapped between a rock and a hard place "Stop," he said, trying to sound commanding. In all the years they had fought, Killian had never made him feel as small as he did right now.

Killian knocked his hand away and threw another punch.

Ryan ducked and winced when Killian's hand cracked against the pole.

The skin bruised and tore against the wood, leaving a smear of red across the gnarled trunk.

"Do you not want to try the conversation thing?" Ryan asked, keeping out of arm's length.

"We shouldn't be here!" Killian slapped the pole. "I wanted to leave, but you refuse to leave *that* girl," he said, pointing to the forest.

Ryan gulped. Most days, he didn't mind a good fight, but he knew he was pushing his luck when Killian was this mad. It was a surefire way to make him lose control, and Ryan wanted to avoid that, considering the last time Killian lost it, he went for Cody. That was an act that Justin wouldn't forgive more than once, and Ryan wasn't strong enough to fight Justin off by himself.

"She's lost everything. I can't abandon her," Ryan said, licking his cracked lips.

"You should've listened to me," Killian snarled, pressing his bleeding hand against his thigh.

Ryan's irritation fanned into a roaring fire, and he dug his nails into his palms until pain pricked through them. "Well, I didn't, so, deal or *leave*." The instant the words flew off his tongue, Ryan regretted them.

Pain flashed across Killian's face, and the image seared itself into Ryan's mind. His anger faded only to be replaced with a sickening guilt.

"Maybe I will," Killian said, his voice suddenly soft. He hesitated as if he was waiting for Ryan to say something, but when Ryan didn't, Killian turned and walked away.

Ryan knew his brother wouldn't abandon him because, realistically, neither had anywhere to go besides Haven. A part of him wanted to chase Killian down and beg for forgiveness, but he didn't. Ryan ignored the aching in his face as he dabbed at the blood on his lip and chin. He sighed heavily and dropped his shoulders, heading for the house.

Nicholas appeared on the other side of the lawn as Ryan stomped up the faded white wooden steps to the house. The brunette with a half-shaved head waved his hand wildly when he saw Ryan. "Oi, get over here!"

Ryan narrowed his eyes but didn't budge. The odds of him not losing his temper were dangerously low, and he didn't want to risk another punishment from Nicholas. In the time they had been in Haven, Ryan couldn't count the times Nicholas made him work in the garden or orchard, and he wasn't sure he could handle that level of exertion right now. When the man crossed his arms and tapped his foot like an angry rabbit, Ryan huffed, slumping over to the Descendant of Earth.

Nicholas studied his bruising face and bloody shirt as he approached, undoubtedly looking like the sullen teenager he was. "What the Helwe happened to you?" he asked. Bracelets made of vines and flower stems decorated his tanned wrists and ankles. He wore ratty, muddy clothes except when he was indoors because Justin insisted he wear "appropriate" attire.

"Killian," Ryan grumbled. "What do you want?" He wasn't in the mood to rehash the incident.

Nicholas silently contemplated something before leading him to the vegetable gardens. Although they were vast and took up a good chunk of land, as a Descendant of Earth, Nicholas kept them immaculate. All his vegetables were in neat rows, lush and ripe whenever he asked them to be.

"It's supposed to storm, and I can't let everything drown," Nicholas said, waving Tory down.

Ryan surveyed the scene.

Tory had pulled out tarps and nails, but he didn't look like he knew what to do with them. A few poles towered around the vegetables, and the freshly churned earth had been nicely packed into place to keep them erect.

Ryan walked over to Tory, tiptoeing over plants so he didn't bring Nicholas' wrath down upon him. The man had two loves in the world: Cody and these veggies. "Shouldn't you be able to do something? I mean, it's a garden," he said.

Nicholas frowned. "I'm a Descendant of Earth, not water. Do you know how hard it is to separate water once it seeps into the dirt?"

Ryan shrugged. He had no clue how hard something like that would be, considering he was a fire wielder and could care less about anything to do with water. His eyes flicked purposefully to Tory when he thought it.

Tory narrowed his eyes as if reading Ryan's mind. He leaned forward and lowered his voice so he could talk without Nicholas hearing. "I *will* end you."

A sadistic smirk flicked up the corners of Ryan's mouth. "Is someone not *strong* enough to get some water out of the ground?" His voice was equally soft but a pitch darker.

They held each other's gaze for what felt like centuries when Nicholas stood, grumbling about needing tools. They split apart, each minding their own business, not wanting to let the others in on their dark secret. Whatever timid alliance they created upon Ryan's arrival was non-existent. They tolerated each other in the presence of Kara or the adults, but Ryan and Tory, honestly, wanted nothing to do with one another.

Tory wiped the sweat off his forehead and gestured to Ryan's shirt. "You're bleeding," he said.

Ryan shot him a glare. "You don't say? Thanks for letting me know." *Never said this one had brains.*

"I don't see how a tarp over the top will stop the winds from blowing it over," Tory said. He huffed and lowered the tarp over the top of the sproutlings.

Ryan rubbed the back of his neck. "How long have you been outside Yorklyn? Didn't they have you working the fields in Rochester?" This was everyday survival for anyone outside Angel's walls, yet Tory seemed awkward and uncertain about what he was doing. It almost made Ryan feel sorry for him, but the blonde would be lying if he said he wouldn't enjoy watching Nicholas tear into his "perfect" boyfriend.

"Um no, I... I wasn't very good in the fields. I worked in the schools," Tory admitted, his cheeks turning pink.

"We need to build a wall. Something akin to a dam at the top and bottom of the slope," Ryan said. He checked the surrounding area and nodded. "Shouldn't take long. A few hours at the most." He was sure that was enough for them to stay ahead of the storm.

Tory grabbed an axe off the ground and smirked. "That's what this is for. Nick must've had the same idea," he said, though it was mostly to himself. He jumped up and headed for the forest. "I'll find wood.

You can do the other part." Tory was gone before Ryan could throw something at him.

Ryan rolled his eyes and relished the image of Tory's face when he realized Ryan was pretty good at surviving. He had lived in Rochester until he was ten, and thanks to his attitude problem, he had spent plenty of time working the fields. After these barriers went up, his only plan was to sleep the rest of his life away.

"Where's Tory?" Nicholas asked, returning with hoes and shovels.

"Cutting wood." Ryan didn't need to explain, and Nicholas didn't ask further questions.

Ryan set to work so he didn't have to feign interest in small talk. He removed the tarp from the veggies and tacked them to one of the poles, hoping he stretched it tight enough to prevent collapse. He did this with each section until a pyramid surrounded the saplings.

A little carrot toppled over when he stepped over it, and Ryan scrunched his nose in distaste. He knelt and used a gentle touch to right the little leaves and patted it softly. The little leaves twisted around his small finger as if giving a thankful hug before righting themselves with pride.

"You don't seem like a farmer," Nicholas said.

Ryan looked back and found the man's brown eyes on him. He was leaning on a shovel with his head cocked to the side as he took in Ryan's shorts, sweat-stained shirt, and damp blonde hair. Sure, he lived in the city for seven years, but no way of life could take his early childhood. He cleared his throat and looked away, not sure what he was supposed to say. "How bad is the storm going to be?"

Nicholas looked at the sky, which was quickly darkening. "I don't know, but I can smell it. It's not going to be pretty."

A spike of guilt gnawed Ryan's insides until he wanted to double over in pain. *Is it too young to have a stomach ulcer?*

Killian would be back for dinner. If he weren't, Ryan would find him, no matter the consequences.

Kara stormed across the barriers and onto Haven's land a few minutes after Tory left. The air shimmered around the land's boundaries to indicate a disturbance, and she emerged with twigs in her frizzy mane of black hair. Her cheeks were tinged pink, but he didn't know if it was exertion from her run or a sunburn from meditating earlier.

Ryan was great at using barriers for self-defense, but Justin was on the next level. The man had built a safe place for all magik kind that only they could find. It was like living separately from the rest of the world by a thin veil of magik. It was a skill that Ryan hoped to learn one day.

"Kara, storm's coming. No leaving," Nicholas called, watching her stalk by as if she were on a path that would lead to some long—drawn-out war.

She looked up and flipped them off when her eyes landed on Ryan.

He looked away with a frown. Once, he asked Kara how long the women in her family had held grudges. He was quickly getting the answer.

"Man, what did you do to her?" Tory asked, coming up with an armful of old wood. It was rotting and bugs of all manners crawled across, trying to find an escape.

Ryan shook his head. "What do I always do?" he asked as a black widow crawled out of one of the crevices. He held out his hand and gathered the small spider before depositing it in the grass at their feet.

Tory stared at him like he had grown an extra head. "You shoulda killed it," he mumbled.

"Why?" Ryan asked. He grabbed a couple of pieces of useable wood from Tory's arms. He gestured to the rest and sneered like it had personally offended him. "Don't bring back anything like that. It's rotten."

Tory's eyes were still glued firmly on the place Ryan had released the black spider. "It could kill," he said. His muscles tightened, and Ryan wondered if he would step on the poor thing.

"I could, too."

Tory pulled himself from his bewilderment and met Ryan's eyes. This time, his hazel-blue gaze was curious as he nodded. "I suppose that's true." He dropped the rotting wood to the side and waved as he returned to forage for more wood. "Be back."

Nicholas chuckled when Tory was out of sight. "She appreciated it," he said.

Ryan began sifting through the wood to build mini walls. "Who?"

"The spider. Tory would've killed her, but she was trying to find shelter," he said. "Maybe she won't sneak into the house since you saved her."

Ryan chuckled. He had forgotten that Nicholas could talk to animals. "How is it?" he asked, genuinely curious. "Is it like switching languages?"

Nicholas pursed his lips and thought for a moment. He straightened some of the wood before reaching for more. "Neither. I can't really explain the feeling. It's just... it's like talking to you," he said.

They worked diligently to build walls and protect their source of food. By the time they finished, dark clouds rolled overhead, nearly blotting out the setting sun. Ryan cracked his neck and cringed at his sweat-soaked clothes and dripping hair. *Gross.*

"Your brother won't be gone much longer, will he?" Nicholas asked, pushing himself to his feet.

Lightning streaked across the near-black sky, though the thunder took much longer to reach them. The storm wasn't far off, and dread returned to Ryan's stomach. He blinked at the quickly moving clouds as he chewed the inside of his cheek.

"Do you know where he went?" Nicholas asked.

Tory shook out his chestnut brown hair and grimaced at the droplets of sweat flying off. "I need to shower," he muttered.

"I don't know," Ryan said.

Nicholas followed his gaze and heaved a slow, steady sigh.

When was the last time Killian faced a storm alone? It had to have been years...

Rain pelted the clay roof, and thunder boomed right outside their window. Ryan sat under the blankets with his trembling twin and tried to console him as the boy clung to Ryan's arm with fat tears dripping down his pudgy cheeks. The room was as black as the night, and his cot was itchy and uncomfortable, but Killian wouldn't let him go. His fingers dug into Ryan's arm so tight that a dull pain spread across his bicep where his Descendant mark had appeared.

"It's not so bad, Kilua," Ryan whispered, nudging his brother with his shoulder.

Killian whimpered and clung tighter, squeezing his eyes shut as he sniffled.

Ryan frowned. He shifted under the humid blanket with a groan. "Kilua, can we at least lose the blanket?" he asked with a definitive whine.

A loud crack of thunder shook the clay house. Killian yelped in terror and wrapped his arms around Ryan's middle, crying loudly. His body shook harder than the bending trees outside that bowed to the majesty of the storm.

Ryan sighed and rubbed his brother's back, knowing there wasn't much else he could do. If he could get Killian to stop thinking about the howling wind, it would be possible to help him not be afraid, but, as Ryan learned in seven years of life, that was easier said than done.

Water, moss, and mud mixed to create the perfect, earthy smell that Ryan couldn't enjoy from under the musty blanket he had forgotten in the rain too long yesterday.

"I bet Avery's at the river waiting for it to flood," Ryan said, mostly to himself.

Killian wiped his eyes, and his trembling ceased a little. "Won't he drown?" Killian hiccupped with the force of his sobs.

Ryan grinned and shook his head. "Of course not. When he touches water, he turns into a trout," he said. It was an old argument, but he figured he would let Killian win this time.

Killian bolted upright, throwing the blanket off them and staring hard at his brother like he was trying to determine if he was lying. His dark green eyes were unblinking. "Really?" he asked. When Ryan nodded, keeping his face as serious as he could manage, Killian gasped. "I knew it."

A boom of thunder made Killian yelp, and he dove for cover again.

"I didn't want to spill the beans. He is my best friend, you know?" Ryan said, hiding his smile behind his hand as Killian wrestled with the blankets.

Their bedroom window slid open, and a sopping Avery climbed through, shaking out his hair and spraying water droplets everywhere.

"Trout-man!" Killian abandoned his quest to get under the blanket, which had somehow become firmly lodged under Ryan's legs, to throw a stuffed toy at the black-haired boy.

It bounced off his chest and landed on the floor, where Ryan and Avery burst into laughter until they cried.

"What is all this nonsense then?" Ryan's mom shouted as she stormed into the room.

Her eyes were puffy and red, and she held a lit cigarette between her fingers. The ashes drifted to the floor and snuffed out in a small puddle of water.

Ryan stopped smiling and jumped off the cot, bowing his head. "Sorry, Momma. We were having fun." Any trace of joy and happiness vanished in the shadow of his mother's heated stare.

"At your brother's expense. That's a rotten thing to do, Ryan. You're a naughty child." Her hand closed around Killian's wrist, and she yanked him off the cot and out of the room.

Ryan reached out, wincing when the front door slammed. His fingers closed in the open air.

"Oi', inside. Now!" Nicholas shouted, grabbing the back of Ryan's shirt, ripping him from his memories as a sheet of water fell from the black sky.

He stumbled as Nicholas pulled him along and shoved him onto the porch. Ryan whipped around, but the man's arm blocked his exit, and he pointed to the door.

"But my brother!" He could barely get his words out thanks to the chattering of his teeth. It was incredible how the temperature could go from humid to freezing in seconds.

"I'll go after him," Nicholas said.

Rain swept across the grounds as the howling wind tore leaves and twigs from the treetops. For all he knew, it could have turned into a hurricane, and Killian would be alone. Ryan opened his mouth but shut it quickly as water sprayed his face and chest. *This is your fault.*

Nicholas didn't move. His eyes were hard and firm, and he wanted to keep everyone in the house where they belonged.

Ryan's first instinct was to lash out, but being a Descendant of Fire meant he could not use magik when wet. *I shouldn't have let him leave.*

Tory ran up behind Nicholas and gave him a light shove. "Move it. The lightning's getting worse," he shouted over the wailing wind.

Nicholas shook his head and stepped aside enough to let Tory sidle by, shooting Nicholas a confused glance. "I need you to stay here," he said, keeping his eyes on Ryan like he was trying to bolt past him.

Ryan frowned, and his eyes flicked to the forest.

Nicholas snapped in his face until Ryan's attention was back. "Trust me."

Those were the two words Ryan hated hearing. His first reaction was to recoil or lash out, but Killian was alone in the middle of a massive storm. If someone didn't do something... he let his thoughts trail off, not wanting to imagine the worst.

"We got in a fight," Ryan whispered, not taking his eyes off Nicholas. "Please..." He leaned forward, gripping the porch rail for dear life. His knuckles spasmed as they turned white with tension.

Nicholas nodded and grabbed Tory's elbow. "We've gotta find twin number two."

Tory frowned, but the wind took whatever curse had slipped his lips.

Ryan stared after the two until the storm swallowed them.

A Request for Help Answered

ANGEL

Rebecca smiled dutifully as her mother introduced yet another suitor. This one had a firm, square chin, beady brown eyes, and hair as yellow as hay. He was supposed to rocket them to the top of society, where Rebecca's mother could be sure she would always be financially comfortable. It didn't matter what Rebecca thought because she was a tool—a pawn to use as her mother saw fit.

She picked up her tiny glass cup; mother called them teacups, saying they were a relic from long ago. They were family heirlooms, and nothing could detract from their "importance." Mother's house was full of useless junk she viewed as "important." Rebecca's hand trembled against the cup, making it rattle against a matching plate.

Jessica touched her half-sister's wrist and offered a small smirk hidden in the corner of her mouth. The clattering of glass stopped as their mother raved to the suitor – *what's his name? Lincoln*. Rebecca tried to refocus her attention, but Jessica was distracting. All Rebecca wanted to do was grab her sister and run.

"Lincoln, tell us a bit about yourself," their mother said, waving a hand and encouraging him to talk. Her pudgy cheeks were red and splotchy, giving her a dour look. Thanks to their father's savings, she wore a horrendous green dress fashioned from several different types of cloth.

"I'm the heir to the largest fishing trade in Portlandia," Lincoln said in his thick, airy accent. It was the only attractive thing about him. His beady eyes roamed Rebecca's body as if she were his prize.

She shifted uncomfortably and crossed her legs, hoping to keep his prying eyes from seeing through her.

Jessica turned her head toward the hearth and crackling fire. Her face hardened into a scowl as she mouthed a couple of curses their mother would never approve of. Her honey-brown eyes shimmered beautifully against the pale fabric of her yellow sundress.

Rebecca tried not to compare herself to Jess' smooth dark skin or velvety laugh because they were vastly different. In comparison, Jess made Rebecca look like a child with a flat chest and wide hips.

When Jessica recovered, she cleared her throat and smiled. "Sounds lovely. Do you intend to move to Rochester?" she asked.

Lincoln threw his head back and laughed. His laughter boomed across the room like thunder, and Rebecca set her cup down before she could drop and shatter it. When he was finished, he wiped a tear from his eye and chuckled, his shoulders shaking in amusement. "No, she will be moving to Portlandia with me."

Jessica didn't bother to hide her look of disgust. "Only if she agrees, of course." Her voice was curt and warned the man from trying to insert himself into their lives.

Their mother giggled like a schoolgirl. "Child, what do you think this is? It's their engagement party. Lincoln has already paid a hearty sum."

Jessica jumped off the couch and shook her head. Her hands balled into fists at her side, and a heavy pressure fell across Rebecca's chest as her half-sister's energy got out of control. "Absolutely not," she said.

"Don't cause a scene. Lincoln has a lovely brother for you, too. The plan is for you to join them," their mother said. Her voice was too casual for someone who had just sold her daughters.

Rebecca couldn't breathe. She stared into the flickering flames of the fireplace as Lincoln leaned forward and set a hand on her clammy knee. Her mother couldn't wait to get rid of her at seventeen. She thought she had more time before being forced into a marriage.

Jessica scoffed and crossed her arms. Her hip jutted out sassily, and she shook her beautiful dark curls that framed her elegant, thin face. "Good luck trying. I've been deflowered, you old bat."

Their mother screamed like a banshee and bounced to her feet. It didn't take much for their plump, oversized radish of a mother to move when threatened.

Rebecca's eyes fell on Lincoln, and something possessive flashed behind his dark gaze. She gulped with a shiver. If this was to be her life, she had to ensure Jess stayed far away.

A siren blared through the room, ripping Angel out of the most atrocious dream. Before she was fully awake, most of the dream had faded, but her mood was wrecked. She flicked her wrist and summoned a blinking red, holographic panel. A few alerts popped up on the screen, and Angel scowled. "Cease this noise!"

"Intruder on the roof," her computer system warned, flashing a video across the screen.

Angel groaned and rubbed her eyes when the noise finally quieted. It was probably one of the scouts she requested from Rochester. Since she couldn't leave the city for extended periods, she needed to find someone to track the twins, thanks to Justin's intervention.

An envoy from Rochester shouldn't be on her rooftop. She leaned close to the screen and analyzed the figure standing by the door. Her heart jumped to her throat, and she dashed out of bed and to her closet. Angel tied a plush black robe around herself as she ran out of the room and down the black-marbled halls. Her feet slapped against the floor, but she didn't slow, not even when a couple of her guards caught her half-dressed without any makeup.

Angel stopped before a green pad on the wall and jammed her thumb against it. The black wall swished open, revealing a silver elevator. She bounced on the balls of her feet as she hit the button for the rooftop and closed her eyes. How long had it been since she had seen him?

The doors opened, and Angel's feet carried her onto the burning concrete, though she barely felt the stabbing pain. Her eyes scanned the solar panels, mounds of brick and glass, and empty scaffolds as her heart fell. She shook her head, hurrying to the edge, and stared at her city. People scurried like ants trying to make it to their jobs or school. A couple of cars drove by, honking at the teenagers who walked down the middle of the road.

It made driving difficult because pedestrians overran everything. She sighed and stepped away from the ledge, taking in the massive steel and glass skyscrapers that made up much of the city. She knew better than to hope for more than what she had, but she found it difficult not to.

"You shouldn't stand so close to the edge unless you're plannin' on jumpin'," a deep voice drawled behind her.

Angel whirled around, a spear of ice already in her hands. The clamoring and jabbering of the city below went silent as all her thoughts turned to survival. She pressed the spear tip into the stranger's throat and stopped before she could impale him.

He held his hands up in surrender. His charcoal eyes gleamed mischievously in the sunlight. He was taller, with longer hair and a deeper voice. While he had lost his cute, chubby cheeks, he still resembled the little boy she used to know.

"Cat got your tongue?" he asked as Angel's jaw dropped in shock.

She dropped the spear, and it vanished before it hit the floor as she pressed her hands to her mouth to stifle a shocked sob. "I never thought I'd see you again."

Avery held out his arms and hugged her with a low chuckle. "I suppose I can't stay mad at you forever," he said, swaying as he set his chin on her head.

Angel returned the hug and squeezed for dear life, unable to believe he had returned.

Avery let her have the moment before letting go and shoving his hands in his pockets. "So, what exactly does someone like you need with someone like me? I saw the request come through the merchant's guild, and I had to check it out," he said with an easy smirk.

Angel wiped the tear tracks from her cheeks and smiled. "Do you want to get breakfast?" she asked.

His body tensed, and his eyes flashed angrily, but he didn't give an easy answer, "There's no color in your gorgeous city. Were trees too much of a hassle to program into your computer?"

Angel frowned. They were too problematic, but it also kept the people from wishing for more. Surely, he understood how hard it was to maintain control of an entire city. The less stimulation they had, the easier it was. "Did you not want to eat?"

Avery vanished and reappeared on a large solar panel, looking up at the towering sides of her wall. "The request said you were lookin' for two boys, about seventeen. Guess I had to come ask if you're lookin' for Ryan and Killian," he said. He finally returned his gaze to hers, but it was so overrun with emotion that she couldn't pick out specific feelings.

"You know them?" she asked, not daring to push his boundaries.

Avery chuckled and shook his head. "Long time ago. Didn't know they were back."

Angel stepped toward him and paused when his muscles tightened. "Justin took. I don't know if they would be in Rochester," she said.

Avery smirked and stood to his full height. "I'll check back soon. If you find out anythin', reach out the usual way. If not, you'll hear from me, " he said. His smile still didn't reach his eyes, and his voice was like ice.

Angel held out her hand before he could vanish. "Watch yourself, " she said, trying to make that sound nicer than it came out.

Avery didn't respond. He vanished in a plume of black and purple smoke, and she sighed. Her eyes went to the sky, and she watched the artificial lines draw energy from the outside and use it to power her city. Streaks of static and glitches zinged occasionally, and she took a deep breath.

"Stay safe, my child, " she whispered.

Level Up: New Ability

KILLIAN

No one told him a storm was coming, and that wouldn't be so bad if he had planned to do anything except piss Ryan off. Killian stared pitifully into his quickly dying fire as the wind and rain howled around him like a pack of starving wolves. *Kill me. Who knew the weather could go from humid and sunny to the Gods pissing on everyone.*

Killian let his temper get the best of him yet again. The next time he threw a temper tantrum, he would do it during the spring or summer. It might be hot, but at least he would stay dry.

A gust of bone-chilling wind cut through the clearing and snuffed out what little fire he had. Killian dropped his head to his knees and groaned loudly, but the thunder roared overhead, stealing the sound.

He contemplated returning home with his tail between his legs when a low voice drawled, "You look worse for wear."

Killian didn't look. He summoned a dagger and threw it toward the voice, trusting only his instincts from hunting as a child. His eyes remained on the smoldering ashes of what was once his source of warmth. Smoke ribboned into the sky, twisting and curling before the heavy rain dispersed the rest of it.

When metal clanged against metal, Killian's head snapped up, and he narrowed his eyes. Thick waves of blue energy surrounded a shadowed body in the distance. The last thing he needed was a

Descendant of Water in the middle of a hurricane. "Tory?" he asked, knowing full well it wasn't.

Boots clomped and squelched through the mud toward him, and the rain quieted as the man got closer. The voice didn't sound like Tory's; it was deeper but still familiar. The energy wrapped around them like a bubble, stopping the rain from landing on his already-soaked head.

Killian tensed, pressing his hands into the mud, ready to spring up at a second's notice.

"I don't know a Tory," the voice said with a low chuckle. "But I do know one thing." The leather boots stopped squelching, and a black-haired man knelt, staring at him with charcoal eyes and an amused smile. Even in the dim light, Killian could make out the familiar face. "You look *pathetic*," Avery smirked and leaned on a tree. His eyes didn't leave Killian's.

It took Killian a moment to realize who it was—Ryan's old childhood friend. Killian was none too thrilled to be alone with him now, considering the years they spent torturing each other, vying for Ryan's attention. He shut his mouth and slowly slid a knife from his pocket, daring the man to come closer. *Out of sight, out of mind.*

"Sadly, you've become one of them," Avery said. His eyes closed as he sighed and shook his head like he was chastising Killian. "I thought you were different. After all, you've always told Ryan and I we were too... what was it?"

"Too quick to conform. Do you want to nit-pick things I said when I was eight?" Killian asked. "Because I could do a number on you."

Avery smirked and touched his nose. "I like you. Always have." A flicker of amusement ran through his voice. There was a dark, ominous swarm of tension between them, but his smiling face didn't reflect the danger.

Killian stayed hunched on the ground, clutching his flimsy knife as he waited. Avery wasn't the type to screw around, so if this were going to lead to a fight, it would happen soon.

Avery let out a loud, booming laugh. "And there's that malice you keep locked up deep within. It's only reserved for the best, isn't it?" he asked. His voice dripped with sarcasm and honey. This wasn't the Avery from Killian's childhood. This one acted like a predator with slow, thought-out movements and dangerous, shifty eyes. Eyes that flashed blue before the lightning had a chance to strike.

Avery didn't move as Killian pushed himself to his feet, not wanting to be at a disadvantage. Avery slid his foot through the dirt, making nonsense shapes, but his eyes didn't leave Killian. They burned through him like a wild animal. It took two seconds: a light blue light flickered through his gaze like a candle flame.

Killian clenched his fists as the soft rain droplets on the shield sped up. His heart thudded as he tried to figure Avery out. "Your eyes are blue," he said.

Avery shrugged and looked away. He had an acceptable profile with a sharp nose and firm chin. Conventionally, most people would view this man as attractive, but Killian saw nothing but a wolf in human clothing.

"Nah, I've got black eyes. You should know that with how much time you spend lookin' into them." The man's voice sounded far away as he focused his attention elsewhere.

"They change. Like mine do when I lose control." Killian didn't know why he pushed it; perhaps it was because it was Avery, and they had a lifelong rivalry that they couldn't abandon because of a few years apart.

Avery grabbed his wrist, and Killian jumped. He didn't see the black-haired nuisance move. Avery's smile turned feral. He was nothing but dark eyes and sharp teeth. "The ring isn't cutting it anymore," he said. "I can feel your energy slithering like a snake."

Killian jerked his hand away and scowled. His heart vibrated like the wings of a hummingbird. The forest was dead silent. Even the pounding rain had gone still in the presence of this creature that wasn't entirely human or animal.

"I don't think my life is any of your business, psycho," Killian snarled, trying to keep the tremble from his voice as the shadow within roared, trying to break free to devour the misplaced, aggressive energy.

Avery growled low, a sound that resonated deep from his chest, and he grabbed the front of Killian's shirt.

Killian flinched despite the overwhelming desire to keep his fear in check.

Avery froze, and his snarl faded into a scowl. He pried his fingers from Killian's shirt as if he were stuck with glue. "So testy," Avery whispered.

When Avery reached up, Killian flicked his wrist on instinct and spoke the first spell that came to mind, "Converging tides: Shadow Veil."

A rush of energy poured from his body to put a wall between them, but the ring on his left hand absorbed the energy and spell, reacting to his sour mood. Killian hit the ground with an exhausted grunt and stared at the orange and brown foliage on the forest floor. His vision pulsed, and his chest hurt. It felt like an animal was sitting on top of him – a rather large one. Killian squeezed his eyes shut and gasped out a shaky breath. *I hate this stupid ring.* Ryan had crafted it so carefully to ensure people's safety when he lost control, but what happened when he couldn't protect himself because of it? *Looks like I'm about to find out.* The dirt shifted under his nails as Killian took a deep breath to pull the negative energy from himself. If he did that, he would be free to use magik.

Avery's face softened, and the energy around him calmed. He knelt before Killian and ran a hand across his neck. "Focus on the smallest thing you can see," he said.

Killian grunted and tried to control his breathing. "I don't need your help," he snapped, but it came out breathless, thanks to the impending panic attack.

"Focus. Smallest thing you see." Avery's voice was a little firmer this time, but it was velvety sweet, and Killian couldn't help but comply with his request.

Killian's eyes flicked to the ground. A stick jutted out of the dirt, some maple leaves waving in the wind, a couple of tiny pebbles, and a slithery bug shifting through the mud and darkness. The more things he found, the easier his breath came.

"So that's how it is?" Avery asked.

Killian didn't force himself to look up. It would take too much energy, and the chill that swept through the forest was foreboding enough for him to keep his mouth shut. Whatever Avery had become, he was nothing like Killian remembered. He pulled away from the other when his energy calmed enough for him to think.

"What do you want?" He was tired and unfocused. Right now, all he wanted to do was go home, and just this once, home meant Haven.

Avery's eyes flashed again, and a smile pulled on his lips. "You're still no fun. I didn't think you could get worse, but hey, always gotta prove me wrong."

Killian didn't dare take his eyes off Avery as he stood. His head pounded, and he pressed a palm to his temple with a wince. "What do you want?" he asked again because it was easier not to play the game.

Avery gestured to the growing storm. "I'm bored," he said. His eyes began to harden again, and the smirk became sharper. It was like he didn't want to be there but had no choice.

"Find someone else to mess with," Killian growled.

Avery snapped his fingers as if that were the best idea in the world. "Where's Ryan?" he asked as his eyes narrowed to dangerous slits.

"Screw off."

Avery frowned. He moved as fast as Ryan and grabbed Killian's wrist in a bruising grip. He slid the silver and violet ring off Killian's finger and stepped away, moving across the clearing before Killian could think of reacting.

He stood in frozen shock, staring at the Descendant of Water.

Avery grinned and tossed the ring in the air, catching it with his other hand. "I think I'll take this with me, and you can find it when you decide you want to play nice."

Killian's magik flared like a wildfire catching dry wood. He closed his eyes and took a deep breath when a bucket of water dropped on his head with Avery's disappearance. "Shoot," he whispered.

A hand closed around the back of his neck, and he swung the dagger around when Nicholas yelled in surprise and backed off. The dagger whizzed past his nose, barely missing his face. "Whoa, it's me! Calm down," he shouted over the wind.

Pain shot through his head, and Killian winced, pressing a palm to it. "I'm fine," he snapped, waving Nicholas off.

Ryan's energy poured through his mind like a thick red rope, vibrating with intense fear and guilt, making Killian's stomach ache.

Nicholas' eyes were full of concern and worry as he edged closer, trying to respect Killian's wishes but being close in case he fell.

Killian tried to ward the emotions off, but they grew stronger. He gripped the dagger's hilt until his hand trembled. He opened his mouth to reassure Nicholas hat he was fine when pain tore through his chest. It felt like someone had reached into him and ripped out his still-beating heart. He dropped to his knees, screaming.

"What the Helwe?" Nicholas jumped back in absolute terror as he tried to figure out what injury had befell his young ward.

Ryan's scream resonated through Killian's head, and Killian couldn't help the matching one that slipped past his lips. His throat burned, and tears streamed down his cheeks. Only when the pain dulled a second later could he calm himself and breathe, taking in his surroundings.

Killian flicked his wrist and whispered the spell for one of his portals before darting through it, leaving a bewildered Nicholas behind. He appeared on Haven's lawn, doubled over, clutching his chest but standing. Killian forced himself to move as he stumbled to the porch, barely managing to keep himself upright.

'My fault. It's my fault,' Ryan's voice whispered through his head. It was like his brother was standing right next to him, whispering in his ear. *'I made him leave.'*

Killian gasped and dropped to his knees as another spike of pain tore through his head. He clung to the porch banister, trying to gather himself over the roar of Ryan in his head. "Shut up!" he shouted, willing the voice to leave him alone.

The front door flew open, and light spilled from the cozy home.

Ryan panted in the doorway, staring down, white as a ghost. He ran to Killian and threw his arms around him, burying his face against Killian's collarbone. "I'm sorry," he whispered. "I'm so sorry."

Killian groaned and collapsed against Ryan as the pain settled and cleared.

"It's not normal," someone shouted.

Everything was so quiet. Killian shifted, and his eyes flickered open, burning from the bright light of Haven's living room.

Nicholas and Justin stood before the fire talking animatedly, and Killian had a hunch he was the topic.

"They are identical twins. We don't know anything about normality regarding their abilities," Justin said. His voice was much calmer, and his body more relaxed.

Killian cleared his scratchy throat and pushed himself into a sitting position. The world spun, and Ryan's face swam into view. His dark green eyes were wide with worry, and he was still shaking from whatever moment they had outside. It wasn't often things between him and his brother surprised him.

I feel like I was hit by lightning.

"You weren't," Ryan said, shaking his head.

Killian froze. His vision steadied, and he blinked at his brother, wondering if he had lost his mind or if Ryan had responded to one of his thoughts. *I said it out loud. Maybe...* Except he didn't. He would have known if he had said something out loud, or maybe his brain was still fuzzy from passing out.

Ryan paled and looked away. "Sorry."

Killian fell onto his back and stared at the ceiling. *This isn't happening.* Sharing emotions was one thing, but now he had to deal with someone invading his private thoughts, not just anyone but his brother. When a challenge to make his life a little shittier was issued, obviously, the gods felt the need to take it up.

"Okay, that's a little rough. Maybe you can, you know, tone it down a little," Ryan said, his voice wilting.

Killian thought of every curse word he knew in both languages and hoped Ryan got the message.

Nicholas and Justin stopped talking and looked at them.

Killian didn't speak. *I don't have to.*

"Kill..." Ryan trailed off.

Justin sighed and ran a hand through his hair. "Alright, so there's been a development-"

Killian glared and cut Justin off before he could get into his lecture. "Unless you can fix it, stop talking." His voice was like ice.

A deafening silence fell over the living room. Killian bristled with anger but tried to keep his mind clear so Ryan wouldn't further comment on their messed up situation. When his brother opened his mouth, Killian held up his hand and shook his head.

"This is something we can figure out and study. Once we have a good analysis, we can-"

Killian shot up and got to his feet, snarling at Justin because the man wasn't listening. "I'm *not* a test subject. Do you want your brother reading your thoughts?" When he didn't get a reply, he snorted in mock amusement. "Right, no one does. So, if you don't mind, shut it." He stormed up the stairwell, listening to the clanging and banging of metal before disappearing into his shared bedroom.

Ryan had the sense not to follow.

Killian collapsed on the bed, still in his wet clothes, and screamed into his pillow like a child. This was all a bad dream, and it would all go away when he woke up. After a mini tantrum involving swearing, screaming, and throwing things at the wall, Killian fell into a restless sleep.

"I know you're not happy about this, but I didn't mean to," Ryan said.

Killian stared at his brother across the expanse of stars. They were in a beautiful realm of vast shadows filled with stars and all the colors of the galaxies. He had read about the galaxies once, and as a kid, he had dreamed of seeing them.

"I don't even get my dreams to myself?" he asked.

Ryan sighed and ran a hand down his face. Even in Killian's dream, his brother looked weary and exhausted. His skin was pale, and his eyes dull. "I don't know, Kill," he whispered.

Killian scoffed and flicked his wrist. The shadows rippled and trembled like a sea, ready to suck someone under. "Can we not have this conversation, and you kindly fu-"

Ryan cut him off. "Look, we'll learn. Give me time to figure out how to control it, and I'll teach you just like when we were kids."

A twinkling laugh danced around them, and the ghost of a memory appeared in the vast expanse of the night sky. Ryan and Killian, as young children, danced around each other, playing with their new magik. Visions of red and violet flashed across the expanse like paint splatter.

Killian scowled. "Stop doing that."

"I didn't," Ryan said, holding up his hands in defense.

Killian crossed his arms.

Ryan had the decency to look ashamed but didn't take his eyes off his brother. "I'm sorry. I'd undo this if I could, but I don't even know what happened," he said.

Killian pinched the bridge of his nose and closed his eyes. He could deal with this. They had been through worse, hadn't they? Maybe his thoughts wouldn't be his own for a little while, but Ryan had always come through in the past.

"Thanks. I didn't know you admired me so much," Ryan said with a weak smile as if he were testing the waters.

Killian flipped him off.

Always a Price

KARA

"**A**ll magic has a price, but it isn't obvious until after you cast the spell," Justin said, waving his hand over some grass by his knee.

It was limp, drying after the storm, thanks to the sun that decided to grace them with its presence. Justin expelled a small amount of light blue energy, allowing the grass to return to its soft green. Little purple and blue flowers sprouted by his leg as he "healed" the land after a night of rain.

"There must always be an equal exchange of life." Justin gestured to the apple tree behind him.

The bark began to gray, and leaves dropped to the ground by the handful. Apples fell from the mottled, rotted branches as the tree withered before Kara's eyes.

"Healing is no exception, which means you accept the consequences upon yourself," Justin said with a small smile. "For instance, if you heal a laceration, you will take the pain."

Kara rolled her eyes, not in the mood for a lecture. "How bad could it be? You heal people all the time, and I've never seen you wince," she said. *Might as well humor him, or he won't leave me alone.*

Justin smirked and brushed his greying hair from his face. He had a sharp nose and almond eyes. Once upon a time, he might have been a handsome man. "I don't feel pain like others," he said.

"What, because of war?" she asked. Her voice was more apathetic than intended, and she winced at how insensitive she sounded.

"Not quite," he chuckled in amusement. "I have a unique condition."

She straightened a little and cocked her head to the side. This lecture just got a little more interesting. "I recall you being in pain once. I'm sure of it," she said.

Justin chuckled again. "I can't come off as too much of a freak, now, can I?" he asked, and while there was amusement in his voice, she could hear the tension bubbling under the surface.

Kara went silent and chewed the inside of her cheek. She might have used that word to describe magik users when she arrived in Haven. Kara couldn't say if Tory had told or if Justin overheard, but her cheeks went pink with embarrassment at the thought. Her life had been upended; it wasn't like she had meant it.

Still, she didn't understand why Justin wouldn't utilize an ability like that more often. He could lure an enemy into a false sense of security or use it to teach people not to mess with him. She imagined him catching a sword with his bare hands, blood sliding down the sharpened blade as he smiled at his attacker. *Imagine how intimidating that would be.*

"I'm sure you're imagining something more glorious than what I've got," Justin said, breaking her out of her thoughts.

Kara cleared her throat and straightened her shirt. "You don't sound like you appreciate this condition." She kept her tone polite.

His lips tightened into a thin smile, and he shook his head. "You are imagining something more glorious."

Kara frowned but bit her tongue. *How can it be a bad thing? You don't feel pain. Get over it.* Not able to make herself say anything out loud, she nodded briskly.

"Do you know what it feels like to get stabbed?" he asked, turning his face toward the sun with a soft sigh.

Kara shook her head hesitantly. That sounded like one of those trick questions that would make her sound ignorant.

"Neither do I, and I could bleed out without knowing," Justin said.

She blinked, leaning forward enough to hear what he was saying as his voice got quieter.

"I could break a bone without realizing it, permanently damaging it. As a kid, I couldn't empathize with others because I didn't understand what pain was," Justin said. He shook his head as he turned his face toward her again. "I often hurt others."

They might as well get on with the proper lecture since Justin had to ruin this one. She waved him on, returning to the topic of healing. "Right, so healing sucks. Can I at least save someone from dying?"

"A life must be given for a life to be saved, but unfortunately, you don't get to choose whose life," he said. His response was simple, and he gave her that mischievous smile that looked sad in a way she couldn't describe.

"But it doesn't mean *I* would die," she said.

"Not necessarily, but someone you love might." His eyes flicked to the porch as the front door opened and closed.

Kara followed his gaze and spotted Ryan stretching for his morning session with the others. "I don't see the point in healing if I can't do anything with it," she said.

Justin was quiet as he looked back at her. For a blind man, his stare was oddly unnerving. "The point is that you can make a difference in the lives of those who continue to fight." He slapped his knees and stood, deciding his lecture was over.

Kara relaxed on her palm and played with the grass. She tilted her head up, watching the fluffy white clouds drift by, gently covering much of the pale blue sky. For a moment, she dreamed of being a carefree cloud, blissfully unaware of everything below.

"Are you coming?" Justin asked.

"No," she said when a cool breeze brushed her heated skin.

He sighed when sticks struck against each other in forceful blows.

Kara turned her head as Killian and Ryan practiced with the wooden swords Nicholas made for them. He had said it was due to their inability to handle a real weapon, but she was mostly sure he was afraid the twins would kill each other. The wood clapped, ringing across the lawn, followed by grunts and low curses.

"Do you speak Nivet?" she asked, returning her attention to her mentor before he could walk off.

He stilled. A smile spread across his face when the word sank in. "I'm sorry, but where did you learn that?" Amusement colored his face, and his eyes widened with joy.

Kara wracked her brain for a lie. *Does I need to lie? He doesn't know Avery.* "Some guy," she settled on.

Justin chuckled and waved his hand. He restored the tree, and the grass and flowers died again. "Well then, yes, I do. It's my native language," he said.

"Then why don't I hear you speak it?" she asked.

Ryan and Killian grunted behind her, and she resisted the urge to turn and watch their fight. One of them always lost their tempers and turned to fists. Today, she bet herself that Killian would be the first to lose his temper.

"I wanted Cody to learn the city's language, and since he didn't do well with Nivet, we spoke common," Justin explained. He hesitated and cleared his throat when she didn't respond. "Does it interest you?"

Kara thought for a moment. She had never learned anything she wanted, and all the school programs were strict in math and sciences. She nodded and said, "Yeah."

"I'll gladly help you learn." Justin tapped his fingers to his thigh when the wood stopped echoing across the lawn.

Kara turned to see who threw the first punch. This time it was Ryan. She frowned, glad she hadn't made the bet with anyone. Nicholas shouted something inaudible and threw himself at the twins to split them up.

"It is," she said. "Could you start now?"

Justin beamed. At last, they had found something they could bond over. *Right, because I want to do something stupid like that.* Despite her inner thoughts, she found it difficult to control the flutter of excitement in her chest.

Kara stood over the stove and stirred a pot with a salty, savory aroma. It bubbled lightly as its scent wafted through the small kitchen. Learning to cook had been one of the highlights of her time in Haven. It was possibly the most relaxing thing she had found to keep her mind busy.

"What are you doin'?" Nicholas asked, walking up behind her.

She shrugged. "Did they kill each other today?" She didn't feel like talking about herself.

"They got into a fight. They always fight," Nicholas said, leaning on the wall and grinning, knowing who she was asking about without having to clarify.

She shot him a look over her shoulder and went back to stirring the celery, potatoes, carrots, and sweet onion.

He nodded and put a finger to his lips before beckoning to the pot. "What're you doing?" he asked again.

"It's my night to cook," she said.

Nicholas raised a brow as she turned to focus on her work. "*Your* night?" He sounded confused but amused.

Thanks to his brother, they had arranged a chore schedule. "Yes, we figured that since we were staying here, we would help. Plus, I can't eat any more of that mush Justin makes," she said.

Nicholas chuckled and shook his head. "I hate the mush too. He says it's-"

"Healthy and full of protein for growing children. I like a little flavor with my goop," she said, finishing Nicholas's sentence.

The man laughed out loud and hit the wall in amusement. "Oh man, I'm so glad I'm not the only one who hates my brother's cooking." He clicked his tongue. There was a flash of metal in his mouth.

Kara reached for a knife and slid it from a wooden block. Then, she gathered more vegetables from the pantry and began cutting.

"What are you making?" Nicholas asked.

Kara sliced a potato and then began on a stalk of celery that was starting to wilt. "Vegetable stew. Dawson used to..." the knife cut through her finger when she stalled, and Kara released the handle with a wince.

Blood dripped in a rivulet down her index finger, and pain pulsed through the appendage. She blinked at the crimson staining her skin.

Her breath quickened, and sweat broke out across her back and brow. She didn't move as blood ran down her hand and pooled in her trembling palm.

Dawson lay before her on the cold, gray concrete of Yorklyn City. Blood trickled from his pale lips as life left those gorgeous electric blue eyes like hers.

"Kara." Nicholas grabbed her hand, and the red vanished.

She tore her gaze from her hand and looked into his chocolate gaze. "What?" she asked. Her body shook like a leaf, and her heart did a funny dance in her chest.

"You alright?" he asked. He grabbed a roll of white wrap from his pocket and twisted it around her finger before wiping up the blood. His voice was firm as if he knew she wasn't, but he was giving her something else to focus on.

"Oh, yeah. Sorry," she said.

He shook his head. "Don't apologize." There was unspoken concern in his voice, but she hummed in acknowledgement unable to comment on it. Nicholas set a hand on her shoulder. "I'll finish up," he said.

She nodded and all but ran from the kitchen. Her breaths came in short gasps as she paced the living room, trying to calm down. This wasn't the time for a panic attack.

"Hey, are you alright?"

She whirled around and glared as Tory walked toward her, looking concerned. "Leave me alone!" She shouted, but she couldn't remember when her voice got so loud or why.

Tory stopped when the light shattered on the ceiling and rained glass on his wet hair. His muscles tensed, and he eyed her, eyes wide with surprise and concern.

Nicholas ran into the living room, brandishing a spoon like a broom and shooing Tory off. "Help me in the kitchen," he ordered.

"But she's..."

Kara's eyes narrowed, and the lights flickered. A dull static hum filled her ears, and then they were gone - she was alone.

Nicholas called them all for dinner a half hour after her meltdown.

Kara didn't attend. She sat in her room with her back against the door in case anyone tried to break in. A flash of red ran through her mind, and then Ryan knocked on the door. He was always the first to try.

"You have to eat. Justin said so," he called when she didn't answer.

"Go away," she said.

Ryan grumbled something angrily and knocked again. "Come on, Kara. Will you just come and push food around on your plate like a normal angsty teenager?"

"Go away!" Her voice was louder the second time.

Ryan groaned and turned the knob, pushing it open. She slid across the floor as he shoved past and glared down. "I'm stronger," he said. She glared back in response. "Be rebellious, but Justin says you have to do it downstairs," Ryan said, trying to mimic Justin's voice. He failed epically, and while that would usually make her laugh, she didn't crack a smile.

She snarled and shook her head, "Go away." She watched the air shimmer red and orange around him like a wild flame, and a smile crept across her lips, replacing the sneer.

"Don't," he warned. "Just don't. Come downstairs."

Her bedroom light flickered when her anger threw her energy out of line, but Ryan flicked his wrist, making the energy dissipate. Kara blinked in shock, forgetting to be angry.

"Yeah, I'm stronger and know some tricks. Now, get your butt downstairs," he ordered.

Kara opened her mouth, but he reached for her, and she jumped up before he could make good on his promise. "What trick?" she asked.

"Come downstairs, and I'll show you tomorrow," he said. His voice was strained as if he were fighting his frustration and forcing himself to be nice.

She huffed but went, not wanting to test her boundaries. With her luck, he would carry her down like a screaming child, and she wasn't sure her anxiety would survive something so mortifying. "Swear it," she said.

Ryan quirked a brow, and the red energy around him calmed. "Swear what?"

If they wanted her to play a happy teenager despite not being happy, she would get something out of it. "Swear you'll teach me that trick."

Ryan nodded and held out his hand. "I promise."

She clasped it and sent a jolt of energy through their palms, shocking him.

He hissed and ripped his hand back, shaking it out. "Not cool."

She stuck out her tongue and walked past him, flicking his nose with a huff. No one said she had to be reasonable.

Mars is the Red One

RYAN

"You saw Avery?" Ryan asked as he lay next to his brother.

Killian groaned and rolled onto his side. "Yeah, but something's not right." He kept his voice low despite them being the only two outside.

The grass was still uncomfortably wet, but it was better than being inside as Kara and Justin yelled at each other. Dinner didn't go as planned, and now they were all paying the price.

Ryan hadn't thought about Avery in years, and it wasn't something he was sure he wanted to deal with right now. Pain spasmed through his arm, and he rubbed the spot until it quieted.

"He took the ring," Killian said.

Ryan paused. "Wait, the one with the enchantments?" He propped himself up on his elbow and sighed. It took months to make that darn thing, and now it was gone.

Killian nodded sheepishly.

"Why would he do that?" Ryan asked, trying to understand where his old best friend's mind was.

Killian shrugged. He hadn't been very talkative since their dream conversation, and anytime Ryan tried to initiate a talk, Killian shut him down quite quickly. It had been a struggle to keep their minds separate, but Ryan did his best to do what he promised.

"How's the chaos thing going?" Killian asked.

It was Ryan's turn to shrug. Regarding personal questions, it seemed that not wanting to talk went both ways.

Crickets chirped around them, and bats swooped around the night sky, catching small bugs. Ryan watched the black dots dart in and out of the forest, feasting on whatever they could find.

"Justin said it could be dangerous," Killian reminded him.

Ryan shrugged again. *We're great at communication. Who needs enemies when we're our own?*

They sat silently and watched the night sky twinkling with stars through waves of purple and inky darkness.

Killian pointed at a small red dot and smirked. "Mars."

Ryan cocked his head to the side. "How do you know it's Mars?"

"It was a book. Don't you remember reading it when we were little?" Killian frowned and sat up to study his brother to make sure he was still sane.

"Well, sure, but how do you know Mars is right there? There might be other red planets." Ryan hid his smile by looking away. If he could keep any argument going, it would be better than the thick, awkward silence.

"Dude, it was *your* book." Killian's voice grew more frustrated as he tugged on Ryan's hair.

"Maybe other planets are red. We can't assume Mars is the only one that's red. Humanity hasn't always been smart, so it's possible-"

"Ryan!" Killian cut him off and threw his hands in the air. "I don't care what planet it is."

Ryan chuckled and fell on his back, propping his arms behind his head. This was good. They sat in a new, comfortable silence as Killian fumed silently beside him. They basked in the full moon's glow and admired the stars Ryan had missed while living in Yorklyn.

"It's red. I know it's red. Why do you have to argue about every little thing?" Killian snapped.

Ryan laughed and shrugged, humming to acknowledge him.

"Avery is off. If you go looking for him, be careful," Killian said after a while. His voice was less sharp but full of wariness.

Ryan shrugged. He didn't have time to rekindle old friendships. "Off how?" he asked.

Killian looked down at him, his eyes flashing dangerously. "Don't be too interested. Just trust me."

"He took your ring. I wanna know what he's after," Ryan said. There was no point in lying, not when Killian could read his thoughts. Until he solved their problem, he would have to deal with being honest.

"The ring isn't a big deal. Make another one," Killian said.

Make another one, he says. I think someone's overestimating their brother's abilities.

His brother scoffed in reply and nudged Ryan's arm. "No, I'm underestimating you. The world tends to do that."

"I'm not going after Avery," Ryan promised.

"Liar."

Well, no one could say he didn't try.

"Avery!" Ryan's voice echoed through the forest, and he didn't doubt for two seconds the other would show.

Based on Killian's description of their meeting in the storm Ryan stayed on edge. His muscles were tight and tense, ready for anything that might come. When Ryan had said he wouldn't go after Avery, he didn't say how long he would keep that promise. In this case, he stuck to it until Killian was fast asleep in bed.

"How did I know you'd be shouting my name in less than forty-eight hours?" Avery stepped out of the shadows with a wide smile. He

had big eyes and hungry teeth, meaning Killian was right. There was something off.

Avery's eyes were still smoky black, but his smile wasn't the smile of a child who was happy to see his old best friend. This was a man ready to disembowel him, and Ryan would know that look quite well, considering most of the people in Yorklyn looked at him that way.

"Someone's not excited to see me," Avery said, chuckling as he circled like a vulture. He spoke Nivet, not bothering with Common because he knew Ryan would indulge where Killian probably hadn't.

Ryan stood his ground. The night was ripe with the sound of flapping wings and owls hooting. *"Should I be? We haven't seen each other since we were ten."* The language slid off his tongue like he hadn't taken a ten-year break.

Avery clutched his chest in mock hurt. *"And I thought we were best friends,"* he said. He bent his knees, and his muscles tensed.

It was the only warning Ryan got before Avery charged. He moved faster than any Descendant of Water Ryan had ever seen, but an advantage of being a Descendant of Fire was he was also fast.

Ryan ducked out of the way, the world blurring around them as they danced around each other. Ryan stayed on his toes, speeding around Avery and blocking his punches and kicks. The dark-haired nuisance had gotten more athletic in their time apart, and Ryan struggled to avoid getting another broken nose.

He caught Avery's wrist and twisted his arm behind his back only to earn an elbow to the jaw that splintered pain through his teeth and made his ears ring.

Avery jerked free and slammed his palm into Ryan's sternum. Rigorous coughs wracked his body, and he doubled over with a low groan as a disgusting metallic taste twinged against his tongue.

Avery's chest heaved as he panted. Hopefully, enough of his energy was expended to keep him calm.

"Can we not do another dance of death?" Ryan asked.

Avery stepped forward, his hands fisted at his sides and his face bright red. *"You're the last person I want to see,"* he snarled.

Ryan nodded and attempted to straighten, but his rib cage spasmed, so he stayed doubled over. *"Lately, I've had that effect on people,"* he said.

"Do you know what I had to do because of you? The homestead turned on me!" Avery's thick, warbled accent made it difficult to understand.

Ryan pieced the words together, keeping his distance. For once, he didn't feel like fighting. *"How could I possibly know if I wasn't there?"* His head throbbed with the expended energy he hadn't expected to use.

Avery turned and brushed the hair away from his neck. A deep, jagged scar ran through his Descendant's mark, mottling the skin. It was dark red and looked nothing like the scar on Justin's face.

Ryan's breath caught. He stared at the scar, his brow furrowing in confusion. *"How did a bunch of humans do that?"*

Descendants couldn't scar by regular means, which left nothing but torture, and there's no way a homestead would do that to a child. Avery and Ryan caused their fair share of problems, but it wasn't like Avery was a bad child.

"Like you don't know!" Avery stormed toward him, grabbed the front of Ryan's shirt, and dragged him forward until their noses were almost touching. His fingers trembled, and his eyes burned with a fiery rage that was as cold as ice.

Ryan could diffuse this situation or make it worse. For a split second, he wanted to sling a slew of curses and see how badly Avery beat him, but that was counterproductive to his being out in the middle of the woods at midnight to figure out what Avery wanted from his brother.

"I didn't know what they would do, Avery..." Ryan didn't have any more to say. An apology seemed too little, but groveling was too much.

Avery's hold loosened at the sound of his name, and he froze. His fingers unclenched enough to let Ryan's shirt slide through his fingers, and he just stared. His watery gaze slid across Ryan's face. He must've found whatever he was searching for because he snorted in bitter amusement and turned away.

"I'm sorry," he said. He reached into his pocket and pulled a cigarette out, popping it in between his lips. *"I didn't realize I was that angry."*

Ryan didn't move. He stretched his fingers and looked around, desperately thinking of something to say. Heart-to-hearts were never his forte, and this one was so beyond his comfort zone that he wanted to fall to the depths of Helwe.

"Anyway, what can I do for you, Wilson?" When Avery faced him again, his mask was back in place: a sly smile and twinkling eyes – a force not to be reckoned with.

Ryan opened his mouth and shut it again. How was he supposed to pretend that their conversation didn't happen? There was no closure, no end – Avery just decided they didn't need to finish it.

"Did you suddenly forget how to talk?" Avery asked, holding out the cigarette.

Ryan stared at the thin, poorly wrapped stick and snapped his fingers. A flame appeared above his fingers, and he lit it.

"Maybe if I use common, you'll be more receptive," Avery said, taking a long drag on the smoke.

Ryan shook his thoughts clear and closed his eyes. *"Why... what did you take the fall for?"*

Avery's eyes squinted as he tried to force the smile to remain. "I don't wanna talk about it. I know you don't take cues, so let this be your one warnin'."

Ryan swallowed thickly. He rubbed his sternum and grabbed Avery's wrist when he tried to take another drag. *"Tell me,"* he said.

"I'll hit ya again," Avery said. The darkness crept back into his voice and smoothed his accent to near invisibility.

"Fine, hit me, but tell me." Because being hit was the worst thing that could happen, right? Like Ryan hadn't started fights before he could be hurt first.

Avery's jaw clenched, and his eyes flicked away. The cigarette was still trembling in his hands. "Kevin."

Ryan let him go and vanished. He ran until he was as far from Avery as he could get. His throat constricted, and bile rose, but he couldn't fight it back this time. His stomach emptied itself on Haven's lawn as he grimaced. The name rang through his head like an alarm, and he squeezed his thighs, calming his breathing before he could throw up again.

Killian's thoughts invaded his mind, and Ryan shook them off, struggling to maintain their separation.

Kevin.

With a shuddering gasp, Killian went silent.

Kara walked into their room bright and early the next morning. "You said you'd teach me that thing you did yesterday," she said. Her hand was on her hip, and she stared hard at him as Ryan tried to rouse himself from slumber.

He couldn't remember when he finally dragged himself to bed, but he knew it couldn't have been more than a couple of hours ago.

He blinked in the bright morning light, trying to stop the burning. "What?" he croaked.

"You stopped my magik. I want to know how." Her voice was firm and a little cold. She couldn't still be mad about the gun or dragging or to dinner thing.

Ryan wasn't sure he wanted to teach her anything if she was. It would only end in getting electrocuted and being laid out on the lawn. He was pretty sure he had been attacked enough for forty-eight hours.

'Get her out of the room,' Killian growled through his head.

Ryan groaned and put the pillow over his face. If he applied enough pressure, he might suffocate himself.

"Ryan!"

'Ryan!'

He threw the pillow at his brother across the room and got out of bed. He pointed to the hall and snarled at Kara, "Get out. I'll meet you downstairs." There were too many voices for having just woke up.

She smirked and closed the door as she skipped out.

One of them was going to die during this excersise, and given how arrogant she turned out to be, it might be her.

"Dispel, really?" Killian asked, lifting his head.

Ryan shrugged and pulled a pair of pants on. "I didn't have much to coax her to dinner last night." She didn't end up eating, so technically, their deal was null and void. He paused. Had he not specified that she had to eat? *Push food around on your plate—typical teenager.*

"I hate my life," he grumbled as he walked out the door.

Killian chuckled behind him, but his mind quieted not long after. Obviously, someone was going to take the chance to sleep in. Ryan found himself envying that.

Kara was waiting on the front lawn in her meditation pose. The wind blew through her hair, ruffling the already frizzy strands of black. Her training the last few weeks had slimmed her down but hardened her gaze. This wasn't the same person he knew in Yorklyn, and he didn't know if he could help her return to that person.

"What's the spell?" she asked.

Ryan scoffed. "I have no clue. Spells have never hindered me, so I don't bother remembering them," he said, sitting beside her.

She was quiet again as she stared at the sky, watching the clouds. Her fingers flicked through the long blades of grass, feeling each one before moving to the next as if she were looking for something. Ryan watched her stare into space, though nothing flashed behind her eyes. For once, she was enjoying the peace of the moment.

"You can't teach me then," she said. Her voice dropped a little when the realization washed over her.

He smiled when she finally brought her attention back. Her lips quirked into a sad smile, and her eyes dropped as she found something else to focus on – a tiny ant crawling across his leg. He brushed it away and leaned back on his palms. "No, I can. It'll just take a little work," he said.

Kara's electric blue eyes flicked back to him, and her smile warmed. "Okay, so what do we do?"

There were good and bad days, and today seemed to be good. He wasn't going to waste what good day they had given a lot of the time she hated his guts. A part of him knew she blamed him for her brother, and he couldn't blame her because he did too, but she seemed to care enough about Ryan to try and overlook his stupidity.

"Magik is all about intuition," he said, preparing for a long-winded speech.

He smiled sheepishly at the look on her face. It was a mix of pure hatred and a scowl, daring him to lecture her.

Ryan gave in before she could annihilate him and gave her the footnotes. "You can do anything by channeling your energy into what you see before you. The spell is a dispel, and I use my energy to cancel out yours," he said.

Kara's eyes flicked across his face, and her eyes softened. "Using energy to cancel out others. Can't we do that to Angel?" Her voice was quiet and unsure, but she held his gaze.

Ryan's stomach flipped, and he forced himself to look away before his cheeks started burning. "Your spell will only be as strong as your magik. Unfortunately, I'm not strong enough to do it, but maybe one day, you might be."

'You're sickening. Stop sending me these floaty, happy feelings before I come down there and punch you,' Killian's voice snapped through his head like a leather whip.

Ryan scowled and took his attention off Kara. *Happy moment gone.*

'Good! I'm sick of listening to you pine.' Killian raged, apathetic to his brother's growing rage and embarrassment. *'You should wake up embarrassed.'*

Ryan's frown deepened, and Kara shot him a curious glance. "You alright?"

"Yeah." He didn't hesitate to answer to keep from garnering more suspicion. "Little bit of a headache coming on." The lie came easily, and for half a second, he felt bad, but Killian's snickering made it easy to remember it was a good lie.

"We don't have to do this," Kara said, shrugging. "I don't mind sitting and watching the sky. It's kind of nice being here – with you."

His eyes widened, and he side-eyed her, trying not to look conspicuous. Her cheeks were dusted pink like the splatter of wildflowers in the meadows during the summer. She also made a point not to look at him as her fingers curled around the blades of grass.

He laid back, flopping down like a sack of potatoes, and closed his eyes. "I don't mind that either," he said. A spasm of pain shot through his arm, and he flexed his fingers, trying to ignore it. Ever since that chaos snake bit him, he had been having self-control problems.

It had been on the forefront of his mind to ask Justin what that thing had been, but he always forgot when the man was around. It had been months since he had been bitten and the pain still lingered, which was something he had never experienced before.

Kara fell back beside him and entwined their hands like she used to when they walked to school. It felt like a lifetime ago when she would freely touch him and show affection, and Ryan's heart warmed as her grip remained loose and her thumb brushed the back of his hand in a comforting circular sweep. She stared at the sky, and he opened his eyes to study her profile, taking her in like it was the last time.

"That one looks like a flower," she said, pointing up, ignoring his staring.

Ryan nodded and hummed in acknowledgment but didn't follow her finger.

A smile tugged on the corners of Kara's lips, but she refused to look. They were in the middle of a game of tug of war, and he was determined to win.

"And that one a pillow," she said.

Ryan grinned and tightened his fingers around hers, cementing their hands together. "I'm looking at something better," he whispered.

Her head turned as her eyes widened in surprise, and he knew he had won. The light caught her dazzling blue eyes, making them shine like a thousand stars in the night sky. It reminded him that when all else in the world seemed dark, there was a light if he looked hard enough. She was his light, and he would always fight for her.

"You really are a pathetic, useless child," Angel's voice chided. Right, there was another voice constantly invading his thoughts, and it seemed like she was officially done giving him the silent treatment.

Ryan cursed her himself and tried not to let it ruin his mood.

Women in Power

ANGEL

"We could run away, you know?" Jessica said, running her fingers through Rebecca's curly red mane.

Rebecca sniffled and wiped the tears from her eyes. She agreed to go to Portlandia with Lincoln to shut their mother up. After admitting her relationship with Justin, Jessica was in serious trouble. Rebecca's last desire was to see her sister in a screaming match with their mother or watching her mother throw her sister out.

When her tears stopped falling, she said, "You really shouldn't have told Mom about Justin and you. "

Her sister brushed the tears from her cheeks with a sweet smile. "It was about time she knew. Everyone else does, so it's best I tell her before she hears it around the city."

Rebecca sniffled again and sat up. In a couple of days, she would marry a man she barely knew that made her skin crawl. The least she could do was enjoy the time she had left. "I want to go for a walk. Maybe you can meet with Justin and tell him..."

Jessica cut her off. "Absolutely not. I'm not leaving you. Walk with me because I'm not abandoning you." Her sister's voice was firm, and Jessica crossed her arms. When Rebecca wilted visibly, her sister's shoulders drooped, and she sighed. "But if you want to see Justin, we can."

Rebecca ran her hands up and down her arms where yellow and green bruises marred them. Handprints and fingerprints left behind by her "loving" fiancé when he lost his temper or she was being "too loud."

"You really should forget me, Jess," she whispered. This would be her life, and there was little she could do to change it, but Jessica didn't have to go with her.

Jessica cupped her face gingerly and shook her head. Her brown eyes cut through Rebecca, making her lip wobble and breaking her carefully crafted mask. "I don't want you leaving with this man. He'll kill you, so please, let me help," she pleaded.

Rebecca started to shake her head but was startled by Justin's voice. "You don't have to do this alone."

She looked up under the shade of the oldest pine in the forest and saw him. The sun shone behind him, illuminating his lithe figure. "You shouldn't be here," she said, gesturing to the house where their mother sat for morning tea.

Justin chuckled and shook his head. "Please, she didn't scare me before. She definitely doesn't now." His pitch-black hair flopped into his hazel-brown eyes as he smirked at her.

"But..." she trailed off when Justin outstretched his hand with a goofy smile.

He stood before her like a knight in shining armor with pale white skin and thick, wavy black hair. He was pale, just like her, not sun-tanned or bronzed like the people in Rochester.

Jessica smiled and stood, taking her hand. Rebecca sniffled again and wiped her eyes. "That's right, love, we're in this together. And even if you don't want to go with us, we won't let them take you," she said.

Rebecca pushed the waterfall of fiery red hair out of her eyes and squeezed Justin's hand. Energy zipped through her veins, and she squared her shoulders. "I won't do it," she said. "I won't marry this man."

Justin beamed and adjusted his coarse white shirt. "Then let's go. I've got something you'd like to see."

Jessica pecked her boyfriend on the lips, and the three set off into the forest. Rebecca didn't know what awaited her out there, but she knew what pain and sorrow awaited her here.

Angel opened her eyes and blinked at the black canopy above her bed. Her eyes watered, and her heart stuttered as she took a choked breath, letting the memory wash over her before fading into oblivion. Life was sometimes complicated, especially for a woman of her stature. If more people understood how cold and cruel the world was, they would be more willing to accept their fate. She didn't want the world to end, and Malsumis wasn't the type of God to destroy everything. After all, there would be nothing to admire if everything were wiped from existence, so why couldn't the rest of them understand that this was best?

After this, everyone would be able to live peacefully. She climbed out of bed, trying to quell her growing nausea, and ran a hand through her frizzy hair. The humidity wasn't a good look for her. Angel slipped on a plush robe and rubbed her eyes, stifling a yawn as she walked across the room. A shower would make her feel more like herself, and she could return to being the most powerful woman on the planet.

Angel scrubbed until the memory was a forethought, and then she prepared for her day. With a quick brush of her teeth and pinning the red curls into something presentable, she put on her best outfit and examined herself in the mirror before prodding a couple of crow's feet near her eyes and pursing her lips.

She huffed, smoothed down the pencil-thin black skirt, and fluffed out the white blouse with lacy sleeves. When content with her appearance, she stepped out of the bathroom, and steam billowed out behind her. She inhaled the soft scent of lavender and vanilla before exiting. *Board meetings all day, what fun*, she thought dryly.

No one told her that running a city into the ground would be exhausting. She entered the elevator at the end of her private hall and prepared. It would be a whirlwind of a day, so she wanted to relish this moment to herself for a second more. When the machine dinged, signaling her arrival, her steel-blue eyes opened, and she smiled. The doors swished open, and people flanked her.

Soldiers complained about contraband, teenage attitudes, and a growing concern for thieves in the market district. She was handed report after report, and voices bombarded her from all sides. Angel waved her hands, trying to ease the panic of scientists, soldiers, and board members. Her chest tightened as she signed papers and barked orders to shut some of them up.

Her General walked behind her, hand on his gun as always, but he didn't speak. Of all her creations, he was the finest. Thanks to his painful past as a soldier, he had no free will and no desire for it.

Angel signed papers requesting new supplies and another form requesting a building be demolished. She tried to keep up with the clamoring needs of her advisors, secretaries, and treasurers, but her mind stayed blank as she answered every question with a smile. Someone once told her a smile was the most potent weapon in her arsenal, and while Angel was determined to make the most of it, today, she felt worse for wear, making smiling difficult.

They walked in a group down the hall into one of the main conference rooms. It was the largest, and Angel liked using it for meetings because it was the lowest to the ground, so if someone attacked, she had a quick escape out the wrap-around window behind her. A large rectangular table sat in the middle of the room, and Angel always sat at the furthest end. As soon as she took her seat, everyone else took theirs. The walls were bare and eggshell white. She didn't believe in keeping pictures or art in the city because it allowed too much room for open-mindedness.

"Alright," she said, trying not to let the weariness show. "One at a time." Her fingers trailed along the smooth table as she sat straight, trying to keep her attention on the people around her.

There was a series of murmurs before an odd little man stood. "Ma'am, there are serious talks of rebellion in the residential districts. People aren't happy about murdered children." He passed a white cloth over his squashed, pumpkin-like face as sweat beaded his brow and turned his cheeks an unhealthy shade of red.

Angel watched his hands shake as he dabbed the sweat away before bringing the cloth to his nose and sneezing into it. Her lips curled back in disgust, but she forced herself to mask it as a strained smile. "We've had town meetings about that horrible day," she said. "What more would the parents like from me?" She forced her voice to remain calm despite the rage threatening to boil over.

"A lot of them seem to think you killed those kids," the man whimpered, holding up a stack of papers as a shield between them as if that would save him from her unyielding wrath.

Angel's eyes narrowed, but the smile stayed in place. Her curse was getting harder to maintain. People remembered things they shouldn't and forgot things she wanted them to remember. So much of her energy went into constructing the spell that controlled the thoughts of her citizens that she didn't have it for anything else, such as these mini rebellions beginning to form around the city. She stood and walked the room perimeter with her hands tucked behind her back. Her steps were calculated and spaced evenly to maintain a graceful appearance.

"Why would I do such a horrific thing?" she asked. "Who are these people who accuse me of such acts?"

The man trembled behind his makeshift shield. "Some of the parents who lost children. We don't have names." His voice shook so badly she almost couldn't understand him.

Angel chuckled and pressed her back against the wall. It was cold and solid behind her, and she relished the feeling as she breathed deeply. "Sweetie, if you're going to tell me there's a problem with my people, I expect you to have answers," she said.

The man threw the papers in the air as he let out an agonizing scream.

Her General shot the man before he could get out of his seat.

"Does anyone else have pressing concerns with insufficient information?" Angel asked, looking around the room. Her smile vanished the moment the man got shot. It was time to buckle down on being the terrifying leader everyone knew her to be.

People kept their heads and eyes down. The stench of fear filled her nostrils, and she pushed away from the wall to return to her seat with a short sniff of disdain. *I liked this shirt*, she thought to herself when she noticed a couple of bright red spots on the sleeve.

"The next time there's a problem, I expect a solution," she said, tearing her eyes away from the blood. "I need a new spokesperson for the people." She pointed to a small, thin woman cowering at the far end of the table.

Her dark skin and beautiful curly hair reminded her of Jessica's. The woman's hair flowered around her in all its natural glory, and she wore a pale yellow headband to keep it out of her face.

"What's your name?" Angel asked, pointing to her.

The young woman stood and trembled. "Alicia," she said.

"You just got promoted—woman power. Now, get me answers," Angel said, waving her hand. "I don't have all day."

Alicia ran from the room, tripping over her feet on the way out. The door closed soundlessly behind her, and Angel turned her attention back to the remaining men at her conference table. She snapped her fingers, and energy seeped from her body. "You will all forget what happened to that man. As of now, the man on the floor no longer exists."

There was a tug of resistance before her spell was accepted, and everything returned to normal. Her followers' wide, terrified eyes grew blank and dull, like husks.

She sat heavily in her seat, exhausted by the pull on her energy, and gestured to the body. "Get rid of that," she said to her general. "Everyone else is dismissed," she said, pressing her fingers against her temple to massage it with a slow sigh.

The remaining conference room members filed out like zombies, leaving bags, papers, and briefcases behind. It was not quite the morning she had planned, but she felt quite a bit better after that fuss.

Forging Ahead With New Bonds

KILLIAN

Killian stared into the forest, his eyes boring through the trees as he waited for his prey. Usually, he would have a bow, but considering this was more of a trap than a catch-and-kill.

"You know, if you're gonna try to trap anythin', you need to hide your energy," a voice whispered in his ear.

Killian yelped and jolted on the tree branch he had taken refuge on. He lost his balance and tumbled over the side, crashing ten feet to the floor and groaning as pain prickled across his shoulder and side.

"Oof, yeah," Avery said with a grin.

Killian snarled in reply and pushed himself up, wincing when pain shot down his arm. "I hate you," he said.

"Dully noted. You weren't hopin' to trap little ol' me, were you?" Avery asked innocently.

Killian frowned. He rubbed his shoulder and groaned, trying to keep the pain from showing. "I need the ring back," he said, figuring it was best to get to the point.

With a sly smile, Avery withdrew the purple and black ring from his pocket. He tossed it and caught it, taunting Killian as it caught the sun and glinted brightly. "This?" he asked.

Killian reached up and winced when pain shot through his shoulder. "Damn it," he hissed.

Avery jumped to the ground, landing in a crouch. A mischievous spark ran through his charcoal eyes, and he held out the ring. "Askin' for things is a lot easier than tryin' to trap a hunter," he said.

Killian frowned. He hesitated but reached out and took the ring from Avery's palm. Before he could pull his hand back, the young man grabbed his wrist, holding him tightly. "Looks like you've lost your edge, Kilua."

Killian snarled and tried to jerk his hand back. "Don't call me that," he said, pulling again when unsuccessful the first time.

Avery's fingers tightened around his wrist each time he tried to rip free. "Your brother came lookin' for me. Too bad he didn't have anythin' fun to say."

The trees swayed in a light breeze, and dark clouds moved from the north. If it rained again, Killian would lose his mind. He wasn't going to risk another storm because of a bad decision.

"He mentioned Kevin, so I guess you did, too," Killian said.

Avery smirked. "How many people are you gonna let take the fall for you? Have you grown any, or are you still the selfish little babe mommy has to protect?" His tone was nothing but bitter frustration, and his eyes flashed blue like they did the night of the storm.

Killian spit the first words that came to mind, "Least my mommy's alive." As far as he knew. They did leave her in Angel's clutches the night before a supposed execution.

Avery's fist cracked against his temple before Killian knew anything was happening. When he moved again, Killian stumbled and ducked under another fist, cursing. The ring fell to the forest floor with a soft thump, and a roar of anger tore through Killian's mind. *Kill him!* For once, he wasn't in disagreement with the shadow that controlled his magik.

Killian dove forward, wrapping his arms around Avery's waist and taking him to the ground. Leaves crunched under their weight as they struggled against one another, and Killian took another hit before rolling to the side. His vision pulsed black and white, and his head pounded. Something wet and sticky trickled down his face, and he pressed his palm to the laceration on his cheekbone.

Avery crouched like a cat with bared teeth like the wild animal he was, or, at least, pretended to be.

"Knock it off!" Ryan shouted, appearing between them with a sharp gaze.

Heat swarmed the area, and Killian hissed in pain, doubling over when he tried to get back to his feet.

"Avery, go," Ryan said, glaring at his ex-best friend.

Avery smirked and dabbed the cut on his lip before spitting. "We were just havin' some fun. No need to get your panties in a twist," he said in that low drawl.

"This isn't fun. The minute you draw blood, it's over, just like old times," Ryan said, clenching his jaw as his hands fisted at his sides.

Avery chuckled and leaned back on his palms, not bothering to stand. He let Ryan lord over him like a parent disciplining their child. "I didn't hurt him. He'll live," he said.

Killian tuned their conversation out to focus on the ringing in his ears. He closed his eyes and took a breath, wincing at the surge of pain. All he wanted was the ring, and now he had a concussion and possibly a dislocated shoulder.

Ryan grabbed his brother's arm and hauled him to his feet. "Come on, let's get you to Justin," he said.

Avery scowled as Killian stood and shook the haze from his mind. "Brothers entwined in fate. Too bad for you, that little mark on your arm's gonna seal everythin'," he said.

Killian wanted to ask what he meant but couldn't form a coherent thought. He leaned on Ryan despite his brother going rigid and looking at the Descendant of Water.

"What would you know, Avery?" Ryan mumbled, wrapping an arm around Killian's waist to keep him steady. "You've got no one left."

Killian summoned a portal, and they stepped through without another word. He was mildly surprised he managed a proper portal that took them straight to Haven, given his condition.

Ryan sighed. "Yeah, this is gonna be a great day," he said.

Killian woke later in the dark. The laceration on his cheek was gone, and though he had a mild headache, it didn't feel like he was on a boat anymore.

Ryan snored in the bed across the room, only stopping to turn on his side and grumble something inaudible.

Killian blinked and rubbed his eyes with a low groan. Not only did he not get the ring, but he slept the entire day. *Lovely.* He scrambled out of bed and tiptoed out of their shared bedroom. A hand settled between his shoulder blades as he closed the door behind him.

Killian jumped and whirled around to Justin's smiling face. "I was coming to check on you," he said.

Killian rubbed the back of his neck, embarrassed by how the day turned out. "Oh, thanks for healing or whatever. I kinda got myself into a bind." It was embarrassing, but he owed the man some gratitude.

Justin nodded. "I view it as my job to keep the children under my roof alive."

"I wouldn't have died," Killian said, almost petulantly. He was more offended that Justin would dare call him a child, considering he was nearly eighteen.

"Mind if I check you out to be sure?" Justin asked. Killian shrugged, and the man waved his hand over him before smiling. "It looks like everything's in order. Maybe don't fight your brother unattended next time?"

Killian opened his mouth to argue but hesitated. If Ryan hadn't told them about Avery, maybe there was a reason. *Kevin*. The name ran through his head, and he sighed, closing his eyes. He *was* a selfish prat.

"Yeah, I lost my temper. I'll try to do better," he said.

Justin smiled almost knowingly before stepping aside. "There's dinner on the stove if you're hungry."

Killian nodded and walked past, grimacing when his back was to the man. He would rather die than eat more white salty mush that Justin insisted was good for them. Plus, he wasn't sure he was really hungry after his morning.

"Nicholas made it," Justin said as if he had read his mind.

Killian shivered and hurried down the spiral staircase. He had one person reading his mind; he didn't need another to do the same.

Cody was in the living room, focusing on some strange device on the coffee table and staying warm by the fire. He looked up when Killian walked in. "You're still alive," he said.

"Was that ever in doubt?" Killian asked, collapsing on the couch behind the redhead with a grunt. "I had a mild head injury. Those don't usually kill people."

Cody chuckled and picked up a screwdriver. "Of course not, but I don't know about you." It was supposed to be a thinly veiled compliment, but Killian chose not to comment.

He snorted in amusement and stood. After all, he didn't come down to be roasted by a twelve-year-old.

Cody was Justin's son and a Descendant of Technology, though none of them had seen him use magik. Mostly, the child went to school and spent time in his secret underground laboratory working on different projects. Of all the people in the house, he was the easiest to get along with and, oftentimes, gave the best insight.

Cody had pudgy pink cheeks, a button nose, and eyes as blue as Kara's. His hair was orange and hit the tips of his ears. It curled every which way and frizzed so badly in humidity that it looked like he had a clown wig. His skin was pale like his father's but freckled from his time in the sun. He didn't look like Justin, but Killian figured he looked like his mother, who was no longer alive and whom he had never seen.

Killian watched the boy pull wires from a metal box on the table. When he touched the two wires together, a spark flared to life. He quickly pulled them apart, and a tiny stream of smoke rose.

"You wanna know what's cool about science?" Cody asked, setting the wires aside and writing something down on the paper next to him.

Killian blinked. It took him a moment to realize Cody was talking to him. "What?" he asked.

"I get science, math, chemistry, and physics. It all makes sense in my head." Cody twisted some red plastic off one of the wires and held it out. "This wire and that wire don't get along. I put them together, and they electrocute me. Sometimes, they start a fire," he said.

Killian knew he was about to get a long-winded analogy of something he wouldn't understand, but he bit his tongue and listened intently.

"If I were to connect this wire to one of the others I have hidden inside the machine, they would start it," he said.

Killian frowned. "How could you know that?"

Cody laughed and turned to face him. His cheeks were rose-red, and his hair flopped into his eyes, making him shake it out every few seconds. "It's my magik."

Killian's eyes shone with a challenge. "If you knew what would happen, why did you do it?"

"How else will I know what happens when I connect other parts?" The question was so simple that it took Killian off guard.

All he could do was watch as Cody reinserted the wires into the metal box and turned the invention, so he could pull a panel off the back, revealing more wires, screws, and pieces of equipment that he didn't recognize.

"You said you knew what would happen, so why those two specifically?" Killian asked.

"Because I know how machines work. I know what happens when you cross two electrical currents that don't get along, but because my magik is different, I wanted to make sure it doesn't change how they interact," he said.

It sounded contradictory. Killian held out a hand, and Cody let him take the wire. "You try to put things together just to see how they react? Despite knowing it could blow up?"

"Yeah." Cody beamed as if Killian finally understood.

Killian managed a slanted smile. He couldn't believe he was having this conversation with a pre-teen. "Why?"

"Why do you think I do it?" Cody cocked his head to the side like a curious puppy. His eyes shone with delight as he finally got to spew knowledge that only he understood.

"Because you're weird," Killian said.

Cody grinned from ear to ear. He pushed a small black button on the machine, and it popped before bursting into flames. Killian dropped the wire and recoiled on the couch as black smoke billowed in the air. Cody reached under the table and dumped a cup of water over the flames, snuffing them out and making the machine emit a high-pitched whine before going silent. "How else am I going to learn from my mistakes," he said with a chuckle.

Killian shook his head, trying to understand. "I can see why your dad restricts your magik," he mumbled, waving the smoke from his face. It smelt like old oil and the used cars that sat dead on Yorklyn's roadsides.

Cody chuckled and tossed one of his tools on the table. It clattered noisily before sliding to a stop. "People try to contain what they don't understand," he said. "I take it as a compliment when someone wants to shut me up."

Killian didn't have words to express his feelings, but his eyes flicked to the window near the stairwell. The stars and moon lit the night sky, illuminating the yard in a soft, calming glow. If he let himself, could he also learn from his mistakes?

"Do you really think I'm weird?" Cody asked. His voice was small and quiet, and he refused to meet Killian's eyes.

Killian shook his head and returned his attention to the boy with an unwavering smile. "Nah, you're fine the way you are," he said. He wasn't sure why, but the way Cody smiled was enough to stop him from questioning it further.

Killian walked onto the porch and took a breath. When two objects didn't go together, it meant there was a wrong electrical current between them. He had to understand why Avery instead of trying to fight him for it. especially if he wanted to get his property back.

His eyes glow like mine. There's more to this Descendant of Water. Perhaps Avery would be kind enough to share the secrets of his wisdom, or maybe he would be willing to help Killian learn self-control. Justin wasn't the sole reason Killian wanted to control himself. He looked back toward the house with a small smile. There was a red-haired prodigy that was worth saving.

Killian walked toward the forest, calming his mind and energy. Ryan would be furious if he knew Killian was out again after being injured, but he wouldn't let this devolve into a fight. *Kevin.* The name ran through his head, awash with Ryan's pain the night Avery brought it up.

"How many people you gonna let take the fall for you?" Avery's words rang through his head like a melancholy symphony.

Killian strode across Justin's barriers and into the forest, taking a breath. Avery's energy had been non-existent both times he ran into him, but if Ryan could find him, Killian was sure he could too. At the very least, Avery might find his way to him. He strolled through the trees, taking in the scent of moss and pine and enjoying the sounds of flapping wings and hooting owls. Angel could recreate many things in her city, but the beauty of the real world wasn't one of them.

Killian tapped his fingers to his thigh and spoke a spell, "Energy vision." The world shifted and changed until he saw strands of ethereal magik leading to their respective owners.

His eyes flicked through the red, gold, and orange as he tried to find a trace of the ring he had lost. At the very least, it might lead him to the person determined to keep it. A thin line of violet energy permeated the forest, and Killian touched it. The other colors faded, and he followed the dim light of the ring, not knowing what was waiting at the end of the trail.

The line grew bolder the closer he got, and he was well past the bounds of Haven and Rochester by the time he reached the end. It led through an enclosed wall of thorns, trees, and brush, making him grunt and groan in complaint as Killian struggled to make his way through the barricade. It was an unnatural structure that grew more like a wall than one would see in nature.

Killian stumbled onto a patch of bright green land and froze. Magik washed across his skin, sending tingles and jolts along his arms and legs as a warning. He turned in slow circles, taking everything in. It reminded him much of Haven without the added effect of Justin's watchful eye.

A pile of cut wood was under a shelter near a small wooden house. Spread across the land were fire pits, empty pots, and scorch marks where one had practiced magik.

"I was wonderin' if you'd track me down," Avery said, stepping out of the house with a slow smile. His body was more relaxed than when they last met, and his thumbs were tucked into his pockets as he leaned against one of the posts that kept the shelter up around the wood.

Killian eyed him carefully but didn't move. Sometimes, wires crossed that didn't work well together, but that didn't mean the wires couldn't be fixed. "I wanted to apologize." Even if he had to be the bigger man and take the first step toward friendship, he would. *Though friendship is an awfully strong word.*

Avery frowned, his smile slipping as confusion furrowed his brow. His eyes were dark and stormy, but there was a kindness in them that Killian hadn't seen directed towards him or Ryan since their reunion. "You think butterin' me up will get you the ring back?" He asked though the question wasn't malignant.

"No, I shouldn't have said what I did about your mother. Truth is, I don't know if mine is alive," Killian said. "Last I heard, she was on death row."

Avery nodded and ran a hand down his face. "I made food. You hungry?" This sounded about as close to forgiveness as Killian was going to get. "How'd you find me, by the way?" Avery asked when Killian didn't respond.

Killian shrugged, his mind still processing the offer of food. "I followed the energy of the ring," he said. "It's attuned to mine, so..." he trailed off, realizing he didn't need to explain how magik worked.

Avery nodded and gestured to the house. "Come on, I need to eat. Been a ragin' lunatic all day." He turned to go inside and paused. After a breath of silence, Avery looked over his shoulder, beaming. "I won't touch ya if you come in. Let's call a truce for now." And then he vanished through the crooked wood door, chuckling to himself.

Killian wanted to follow and find out more, but he also wanted to return to Haven, where he knew it was safe. Avery had been set on killing him the last couple of times they met. *Kill might be a little much. He didn't really try to kill you, so let's not be dramatic.* Killian shuffled a little closer to the house and stopped again.

It wasn't like Avery was acting dangerous. He was being pleasant and almost nice, which was a considerable upgrade. It was possible he didn't like leaving his house, so he was only a dick when he had to socialize. *That's why Ryan's a dick.*

"I don't wanna brag, but it's rabbit stew, and I make a mean rabbit stew," Avery said, stepping back outside, holding a steaming bowl of soup.

Meat. It was something with meat that he didn't have to make himself, and while Ryan and Nicholas were vegetarians, Killian wasn't sure he could handle another bowl of oat mush or vegetable soup.

Avery held it out, not moving from his post by the door. "You don't even gotta come inside," he said.

Killian shuffled a little closer and hesitated. "I wanted to talk to you about... magik," he said. He didn't reach for the bowl, but Avery didn't pull it away.

He stood there with an apathetic gaze, waiting for Killian to choose.

"I need help," Killian stuttered over the last word. "And I don't know why I'm coming to you, but..." *We're the same.*

He couldn't stop the thought from shooting through his mind. They *were* the same; he could feel it in Avery's energy when he was near. He saw it the night of the storm and again when Killian pushed him too far in the woods. Avery could control himself, and Killian wanted to be able to do that, too, instead of relying on a stupid piece of metal.

Avery sighed and stepped forward, shoving the bowl into Killian's hands. Obviously, he was tired of waiting for Killian to make the choice. "I can't help you," he said.

"Can't or won't?" Killian asked.

Avery bit his tongue as he thought about it. "You don't even know what you're askin' for," he said. "Why do you think I know anythin' about a Descendant of Shadow?"

Killian opened his mouth and shut it like a gaping fish. He couldn't begin to explain what thoughts were going through his head. "You and Ryan, you're good at magik. Always have been, but I'm not. I - I'm a selfish prat," he said.

Avery hesitated as Killian clutched the bowl to his chest like it was his lifeline. The savory aroma tickled his nose, and he wanted to down it in a single gulp, but not in front of his gracious host.

"I can give you the ring back," Avery said after a while.

"If you didn't want to help, you wouldn't have taken it in the first place. Sure, it might've been out of anger, but you've never been one to do something without reason," Killian said.

"You haven't seen me since we were ten. Do you think people don't change?" Avery asked, his cocky grin returning.

"I don't believe people change to that extent," Killian said, mirroring the smile. His body relaxed, and he brought the bowl to his lips.

When he drank, Avery nodded and ran a hand through his hair. "Well... I'm not much of a teacher, but if you want me to help, there's somethin' I need first," he said.

"And what's that?" Killian asked.

"I'm gonna need you to trust me."

Of course, he would say something like that. Gross.

Forgive, Forget, but Never Let Go

KARA

"I want it to go back to the way it was!" Kara screamed, oblivious for once to the things around her.

Let me return to the city. Wake me from this rotten nightmare. Let my brother be alive. Let my mom and dad find me. Tears streaked her dirty cheeks as she bellowed at whatever god or omnipotent being was listening. How rotten was she – to ignore the suffering of Angel's city to continue so long as she got to go home?

"I'll do whatever you ask. I'll never complain again. Please, make it go back to how it was," her voice softened as a sob erupted.

Justin and Nicholas went to Rochester for supplies and took the boys with them because they didn't trust them to stay home alone. Killian seemed eager enough—maybe he would visit his grandmother—and Cody was more than excited to ask his teacher questions about his homework.

Kara locked herself in her room until she was sure she was alone. When the flickering energy of her comrades vanished through the trees, she made her stand. She stood to fight the gods until they gave her what she asked for.

The happiest she had been in a long time was watching clouds with Ryan when he was supposed to teach her how to use a new spell. They never got around to that, and her joy vanished when she realized she had no right to feel it. How could she possibly let herself be happy after everything that happened with the person who made it happen?

Kara's head swarmed with the screams of the people she killed and her brother's smiling face. Lightning danced along her arms as her rage grew, daring her ever to feel a moment of peace again. *How could you? How could you betray the love of your family for some boy? We don't get to be happy.* She screamed again, and a bolt of lightning struck the ground in front of her.

"Kara!" a familiar voice broke through the haze of anger, but it was hard to pinpoint who through the shroud of emotion she was stuck behind.

A flash of red painted the scene, making it look like something out of a crime novel, and Kara whirled around. *No, not him. Not now. Leave!* Another bolt of lightning struck the ground in front of Ryan, and he froze, not daring to move in case the next one hit. His eyes widened as he held out a hand, the same one she held as they watched the clouds. It had been warm and brought a sense of safety, but that unmistakable flicker of joy would be her downfall.

"I hate you!" she shouted, pointing a threatening finger in his direction. "You ruined everything." Her voice continued to rise until her throat burned from screaming. "I don't want you; I don't want them. None of this was supposed to happen." Her energy zigzagged in lavender streaks around her, crackling with every word she spoke.

Ryan didn't move. His energy remained calm, but it lashed out like a protective animal when hers got too close and disrupted it before it could hurt him. "Kara, it's okay," he lowered his voice, trying to get her to quiet her own.

She laughed without humor. Her mom used to do the same thing, and his manipulation sent a fresh wave of anger through her veins like molten lava. Kara threw her head back and wished she could breathe fire. Surely, that would release the pressure, the pain: anything to stop the nightmares and screams from terrorizing her all night.

"Don't you dare talk down to me like I'm a child," she snarled. The electricity dancing around her snapped like an angry viper, daring Ryan to move a step closer.

"You're acting like a child!" he shouted. His energy flared red hot around him, and he dropped his hands. "There is happiness and beauty in the world, but you want to see nothing but evil." Fire consumed his hands and ran up his arms, making her flinch.

"*Scared of magik,*" Avery's voice flitted through her head like an unwelcome song.

Scared, she wasn't scared. She was a Descendant and had nothing to fear. "Falling light consume my foe," she said the spell before she could stop herself as proof that she wasn't afraid.

Ryan zipped away using the lightning speed he wielded thanks to being a Descendant of Fire as the skies fell upon him in glittering shards of light. Each beam left a smoking crater in its wake, and they were endless. The light pulled on her energy, draining it every time another fell.

Strong arms wrapped around her waist, pulling her out of her thoughts and forcing her out of her trance. The light stopped, and Ryan pinned her to the ground, pushing her hands above her head. His fingers tightened around her wrists, holding her in place as his energy suffocated her. Anytime she tried to use magik, an invisible wall stopped her, leaving the world quiet and still around them.

"Stop," Ryan whispered, dropping his chin to his chest. He knelt over her on all fours, holding her hands in a shaking grip.

His face went in and out of focus as tears clouded her vision.

"Just stop," he pleaded.

Kara didn't think. She kneed him in the nuts, and he rolled to the side, groaning in pain. She ripped her arms away and jumped to her feet, running. It was ridiculous to think she could run from someone who was as fast as he had energy for, but she didn't care. She didn't want to see him, see *them*, because all they were was a nasty reminder of a life she no longer had.

Ryan appeared in front of her before she could cross Justin's barriers. "Stop!" Fire flared and formed a wall on either side of him.

Kara stepped back, panting, feeling the heat of the flames crackling and burning around her. "I hate you!" she shouted again. "You ruined everything."

"Fine, hate me, but you have to stop," Ryan said. His voice bordered on desperation but she barely noticed.

Like a star. She could be like the lights in the sky and burn so bright there would be nothing. Kara panted, feeling the heaviness of her body as the last of her energy left her. Thanks to his stupid spell, she couldn't use her magik even if she wanted to.

"You don't want to move on. If you want to stay miserable, fine. Stay that way, but stop acting like the world around you has ended because it hasn't. Shit things happen, you have to learn to deal like an adult," Ryan said. He dropped the nicetites, seeing as she hadn't responded.

She narrowed her gaze and clenched her hands. "Screw off," she said, not hiding the venom.

He laughed and shook his head.

Her anger burned hotter than any fire. "I wish I'd never met you."

His smile faded, and he looked away with a bitter chuckle. "Well, Princess, it's too bad you did." The fire went out, and Ryan vanished.

He stoked a fire within that wouldn't be put out. Kara stared at the scorched land and turned to face the damage elsewhere. Nicholas was going to be furious.

"You got in a fight? What could have possibly warranted such destruction?"

"This is why I told you to stay in Rochester. It's unacceptable to push one of your friends to this point," Justin said, trying to maintain his calm demeanor.

When they got home, Justin and Nicholas grilled her and Ryan in the living room. Nicholas paced, red-faced, waving hands and making snide remarks. Justin was much calmer, trying to keep his brother from blowing his top.

"Did you see what she did? On my lawn," Nicholas demanded when Justin set a hand on his shoulder for the third time.

Kara scoffed. "Oh, your precious lawn. Who the Helwe cares about your lawn? You're a Descendant of Earth. Grow it back." She stood and moved toward the stairwell, but Justin blocked her exit.

"We need to have a serious conversation about..."

"You can shove it too, old man." She stormed around him and climbed the stairs to her room.

He could've stopped her if he wanted, but they all knew Justin would never force her to do something. He wasn't that kind of mentor.

She felt like she was burning, breaking into a thousand pieces, and she didn't know how to make it disappear. Kara paced her bedroom, swatting papers off her bedside table and slamming her palm into the wall, knowing it hurt her more than anything else.

"She's acting like Ryan," Nicholas shouted. "I didn't sign up for two short-tempered asses."

Justin spoke in low tones, and Kara laughed bitterly. *You haven't seen anything, yet.* Kara collapsed face-first on her bed and screamed into the pillow. It wouldn't be the worst thing in the world if everything burned. Too bad she wasn't a Descendant of Fire.

She woke up sometime later with drool caked to her cheek and chin. Something bounced off her window, and she looked up, blinking the sleep from her eyes. Her muscles were sore from her earlier confrontation with Ryan. She got up and went to the window to look out. Killian stood on the lawn with crossed arms and a dangerous smile. He stayed in the room across the hall, so why didn't he knock on her door like a normal person?

Kara pushed the window open and leaned out. "What?"

"You wanna learn the dispel spell?" he asked, quirking a curious eyebrow.

Her interest was piqued, but she narrowed her eyes. "Why do you want to teach me something?"

Killian wasn't nice on a good day, and she couldn't classify this as a good day. Or maybe he was thrilled someone else went head-to-head with his brother because of the sibling rivalry thing.

"Ryan doesn't want you to learn it, so I want you to," he said.

If it was something that would be used against her, maybe she *should* learn it so she could learn to counter it. Kara nodded and closed the window. She grabbed a sweater on the edge of her bed and headed downstairs.

The night air was thick with humidity, making her feel like she was trudging through a swamp. Her hair stuck to her neck, and she tossed the sweater onto the porch without a second thought. It was odd being this warm at night.

Killian looked up and sighed when she rounded the corner. He smirked and gestured to the scorched ground and grass behind her. "Did I tell you how impressed I was?" he asked.

"Did I mention I didn't care?" Kara wasn't angry at Killian, but she couldn't help her sass as she leaned on the side of the house. The wood was rough and scratchy, and the night air smelt like skunk.

Killian smirked and walked away toward the gravesite where Justin's wife and Kara's little brother were buried. They didn't worry about being quiet or leaving without permission because Justin didn't seem to care where they were or what they were doing so long as they returned.

They walked to the border of the land but didn't cross Justin's barriers. Killian didn't speak as he sat and placed his hands on his knees.

"What are we doing? It's hot and sticky," Kara grumbled, refusing to sit.

Killian shrugged. "I think it's better we do this outside to prevent someone from waking everyone up." He cracked his neck and patted the ground beside him.

Cicadas screeched around them, and the fluttering of tiny wings filled the night with noise. Although it was eerie, Kara almost missed the city's silence. All the random, quiet noises of the forest made it hard to sleep.

"How do you feel?" Killian asked when she refused to budge.

"Angry," she said. "And I was sleeping pretty well until you woke me up."

Killian nodded. "Good, hold onto it. It'll make learning easier." He ignored the last little snip and smirked instead. Of all the people in the house that were easy to piss off, Killian was not one of them unless it was Ryan pushing his buttons.

She scowled. "Aren't you the one who told me to watch my emotions?" she asked, trying not to sound sarcastic.

"I told you your emotions would shape what kind of Descendant you were, yes, but that doesn't mean I can enjoy this any less," Killian said with a shrug. "So, dispel. The technical spell is magik be gone," he said.

"That's dumb." Kara nearly snorted in amusement. She sat and decided to cooperate as long as he tried to help.

He shrugged again. "I don't make the rule; I'm just telling you."

"Okay, so I do what to channel this spell – say the words and hope it works?" she asked.

Killian shook his head. "Imagine your energy, though in your case, you needn't imagine because you can see it. Anyway, imagine your energy absorbing the other and canceling it," he said.

That sounded simple enough. She nodded and sat next to him. "Try it with me." It was always good to have a practice dummy.

Killian sat quietly, and she watched the expanse of his violet and black energy swim around him like fish in a pond.

Kara focused on it and let her energy hang between them. "Magik be gone: dispel," she said. She tried imagining her golden energy swallowing his, but anytime it moved close, Killian's energy recoiled like a wounded animal.

She frowned and pushed her energy toward it again, focusing on the two combining and disappearing. Killian sat perfectly still and closed his eyes, allowing her to play with the spell. A smile quirked across his lips as she groaned in frustration after the third failed attempt.

"You can almost light Ryan on fire but can't diffuse someone's energy. That's funny," he said with a slight chuckle.

She didn't see anything funny about it. Kara growled and punched him in the arm.

He winced and rubbed the spot. "Hey, I'm trying to help, don't get violent," he said.

"You're not helping," she said.

"I can't teach you to cast a spell; that's all on you. All I can do is give you the tools," Killian grumbled. "It's just... do you know how high level of a spell you used to singe the lawn? This should be nothing."

She sighed and hung her head. Everything about this world was complicated, and she missed the simplicity of home. At least the only thing she had to worry about then was getting killed. Now, she had to worry about that on top of killing others.

"Keep practicing," he said, reading her.

Don't stress, he says. Easier said than done. Kara stood and stretched with a shrug. "Fine, yeah. I'll practice," she said. It wouldn't do her any good, but it would give her something to do.

"You really don't hate my brother, do you?" Killian asked as she started back for the house.

Kara paused and stared at the grass in the moon's golden light. Her silence lingered, making the tension thick and uncomfortable. After a while, she sighed and closed her eyes. "I don't know what I hate," she said. *Me.*

Killian hummed in acknowledgment but didn't say anything.

Kara went back to her room.

Piece by Piece

RYAN

"I hate you!"

She hadn't spoken to him since, but Angel had done enough talking for everyone. His dreams varied in the level of bloodshed, and the pain in his arm only got worse. The snake bite had happened before they left Yorklyn – while leaving, but Ryan hadn't noticed it until much later. It was one of those chaos things that wouldn't heal, thanks to Angel's interference. It bound them mentally and emotionally, and now he had to figure out how to block her *and* deal with the connection between Killian and himself.

Something Avery had said the day he pulled Killian off of him was worrying. Her mark was on Ryan, and nothing would help, but that didn't make sense. There was no physical mark, and aside from the random pain, it was easy to forget it had happened. How would Avery know anything about it?

The cup shattered in his hand. Ryan hissed in pain and held it over the sink. Red blood dripped onto the bottom of the basin, but he didn't try to staunch it. A sliver of pain worked its way through his palm until it fanned itself into a burning roar. It was one of the things that kept him from staying in his head. He focused on the pain as it spread, making his wrist ache.

"Ryan!" Killian's voice pulled him out of the slow-spreading peace the cut brought. His brother grabbed a dish towel and pressed it to the laceration. The drip-drip-drip of the blood splattering in the sink stopped, and Ryan frowned.

A dull anger gnawed on the inside of his stomach, but he bit his tongue to keep from lashing out. Killian wouldn't understand his headspace, and Ryan wasn't in the mood to explain it.

"What happened?" Killian asked. His eyes flicked across the broken cup on the floor and counter. "What is it with you and broken glass?"

Ryan smirked. "It's not glass." The last time one of them got cut from a broken item was Killian, and he hadn't let Ryan forget it for months.

"You still managed to cut yourself." Killian removed the towel and winced. "That's deep."

That explained the lingering pain shooting through his wrist. Ryan grabbed the towel and applied pressure. "I guess I should talk to Justin about a healing session," he said.

"You could always ask Kara," Killian suggested, though his voice was the quietest Ryan had ever heard.

Ryan wasn't stupid enough to think Kara would help after their fight.

Kara had spent the last few days in Rochester, so he knew she wasn't alone. He talked to Tory to see if he was going with her, but the man insisted he wasn't. She came home smelling like smoke and pine trees, which didn't bode well because only one person smelt like that. Of course, Ryan wasn't jealous, and he had no right to be, but there was a twinge of something that dug deep into his skin and wouldn't leave him alone.

"You don't want it to get infected," Killian said, letting his wrist go. Ryan smirked.

"A Descendant only gets sick when they're dying," Kara had told him not long ago. She didn't say how she came across the information, but it was amusing that she knew something they didn't.

He had half a mind to repeat the words, but the amusement was gone. It didn't take much for his mood to change these days. Ryan shook his head. "I won't risk that," he said, his voice was softer than usual. He was afraid of talking too loud and not being able to stop himself from going on a rampage.

"You're not managing well," Killian said.

A couple of days ago, Kara told him she hated him. If it were only the words, he might've been able to live with it, but her actions spoke louder. Not only did she invite him to a full-out war, but she avoided him like the plague every second after. *I told you I wouldn't let the darkness take you. I don't know if I can keep that promise.*

Killian set a hand on his back. "It's not your job. Let Kara work her things out and try to focus on what you can do for yourself," he said.

Ryan didn't think. He punched Killian in the stomach and watched him double over with delight. The feeling sent a wave of guilt through him, and he shook the nastiness away. He pressed his good palm to his temple and squeezed his eyes shut. "Sorry, Kill. I'm not in the mood," he muttered, pushing past his brother.

It was getting worse. The waves of anger and moments he couldn't remember. There were spots in his memory, and they were getting more frequent. It was like living a life he didn't know he was living, and that feeling alone was unbearable.

'I can help if you let me,' Killian whispered through his mind. His brother wasn't as effective in reading Ryan's mind unless Ryan let the wall fall between them.

He had to stay busy and distract himself from the things he couldn't change. Ryan stormed down the hall and flung Justin's bedroom door open. His was the first on the right and often smelled of incense. "You said you wanted to help me. Do you still want to?" he asked.

Justin sighed and pinched the bridge of his nose. "Ever heard of knocking?" he asked. He was standing in the middle of his room doing some sort of yoga.

"Do you want to help or not?" Ryan snapped.

Justin waved his hand. "Fine, fine. I'll meet you in the living room," he said.

Ryan considered arguing but decided to take what he could get. He went to the living room and snapped his fingers, starting a fire. Pain surged through his palm, and he sat on the coffee table as heat filled the room.

Justin emerged a few minutes later and sighed. "Why are you bleeding?"

"I'm not." Ryan wasn't in the mood to rehash why he was bleeding or hadn't done anything to stop it.

"I can smell it," Justin said.

Ryan frowned as he pressed his bleeding palm to his thigh. "Accident in the kitchen, no big deal," he said. "That's not what I want to talk about."

Justin decided not to question it further and sat on the couch. "What did you want to learn today?"

Ryan waved his hand in irritation. "Whatever wisdom you wish to impart." There had to be some way to keep his mind so busy that there was no place for Angel.

He was quiet for a while as he contemplated what to teach. "Let's talk about finding respect for your magik."

Ryan hesitated in his snarky response. *I don't know what the Helwe that means.* It was hard to be condescending when he didn't know what the man was saying. "What?"

"If you find mutual respect for your magik, you will have an easier time using it," Justin said. He crossed his legs and settled his hands on his knees with a smile.

"I do respect my magik."

Justin smirked, but it was tight. There was more he wanted to say, but he kept it to himself. "This is going to help you get better." He sounded like a parent saying something to appease their child, who was on the verge of a tantrum, which made Ryan that child. Justin closed his eyes and continued, "Practice this with me. Close your eyes and take some deep breaths," he said.

Ryan knew he was being tricked into a meditation session but rolled his eyes before closing them.

"Fire is all about passion and connection. When you cut yourself off from the world, you lose a part of your magik. There's got to be passion in your life," Justin said.

Ryan didn't care about either of those things. His magik did what he said; that's all that mattered.

As if reading his mind, the Descendant of Wind chuckled. "You don't own magik. It's an entity of its own, and if you disrespect it, it will rid itself of you."

Ryan didn't know what that meant, so he frowned and tried to focus.

"Find the one thing that makes your heart sing," Justin said.

Ryan opened his eyes, stared at the man, and shook his head. That was the weirdest way to phrase it. "My heart doesn't sing for..."

Kara bounced down the stairs, her curly raven hair flouncing around her shoulders.

The minute they made eye contact, her eyes turned stormy, and she hurried away before he could think of saying something. "I hate you," she had said. Did she really?

He didn't realize he was watching her until Justin cleared his throat. When Ryan looked back at him, he was smirking with one of those 'I know what you're thinking' smirks, and Ryan almost got up and walked out.

"I think you've found one thing you might have a little passion for," Justin said.

Ryan's cheeks heated. It wasn't any of his business. "No, she's a friend," he muttered. And right now, she wasn't even that.

"Uh-huh, so the kiss in Rochester was just a friendly peck on the cheek?" Justin asked. "I recall a fight breaking out when you came back."

Ryan frowned. The grooves of the wooden table stung his fingers as he dug them into it. "It was a moment of weakness."

"Let's call passion weakness then," Justin said. There was amusement in his voice.

Ryan was sure this conversation wasn't going anywhere he wanted it to. "Respecting magik. How would I go about it if I was interested?" he asked. "Theoretically, of course." Mainly, he wanted to get off the subject of his non-existent love life.

Justin perked up at the question. "You would meditate, sit with your magik, thank it. Use it correctly and not abuse it," he said.

Correctly using magik. Ryan didn't think he understood that but didn't feel like asking. He was a big boy and could figure it out. He slapped his knees and stood before Justin could get any more comfortable. "Enlightening conversation, thank you," he said.

Justin cleared his throat. "One more thing."

Ryan stopped.

"Your mother is alive. I wanted you to know. It took some work, so I didn't want to say anything prematurely. I had some people who owed me favors do some research," he said with a small smile.

Ryan's heart soared, and he blinked in shock. He didn't know whether he was angry or thrilled, and it was hard to sort through the ongoing emotions in his head.

Killian appeared in front of him, stepping out of a violet portal. A smile split his face as he grabbed Ryan's shoulders. "Mom's alive," he said.

Apparently, shocking news was enough to bring that wall between them down.

"I don't want to share you with the world. You're my special little boy."

Except he wasn't. Ryan stared out the hut window, blinking at the kids running back and forth. Killian was sitting under a tree, whispering to Avery and giggling uncontrollably.

Ryan groaned and set his chin on the window. His mother grabbed his arm and brushed his sleeve up to examine the black mark. She checked thousands of times a day to ensure it hadn't changed. He pulled his arm back and brushed her off with a sigh.

"Come on, we can have just as much fun inside." She beamed at him with the smile that always made him feel warm. Her sandy yellow hair fell in her face, and she tied it back, muttering about nuisances.

Ryan let himself be pulled from the window and the screeching kids outside. They walked to the kitchen, and his mom patted the counter. He climbed onto it and blinked expectantly, his head tilted to the side.

"Help me with dinner. It'll be fun," she said.

Ryan nodded and helped Momma with the food. She let him stir the eggs and rice together before pouring them into the pan over the fire. He giggled excitedly, watching the mixture bubble and pop. She made funny noises and bopped Ryan on the nose with her finger.

"You pick the dessert," she said.

Ryan bit his tongue in deep thought. "Sweetbread?" he asked.

"Sweetbread it is!" Momma said cheerfully.

They laughed and giggled until dinner was done, and Ryan's back straightened. His knee hurt. He rubbed it with a wince and looked over his shoulder toward the window. "Killian," he said.

Momma turned to look at him. "What?" she asked, her smile fading.

"Killian's hurt," he said without thinking.

Momma paled and ran from the kitchen, leaving Ryan on the counter with the fire and goods.

He panicked because fire wasn't supposed to be left unattended by adults. His energy went wild, and the fire leaped to the countertop and into his hands.

"No!" he shouted, flinging it across the room. It caught the hay they used to sit on while they enjoyed dinner and talked about their days.

Smoke billowed through the house, and Ryan jumped off the counter with a panicked yelp. "Momma!"

She was back in a few seconds, holding a weeping Killian. "Ryan!" she flicked her wrist, and a gust of wind rushed through the home, snuffing out the flames and setting everything right again. She set Killian down and grabbed his arms, shaking him. "Why would you do that?" she shouted.

Tears pricked his eyes. "I didn't mean to, Momma, I swear," he said.

"Don't ever play with fire in the house," she said, her voice still loud and her eyes wide with terror.

"I wasn't, ow, you're hurting me," Ryan cried as the tears streaked down his cheeks.

"Never do that again. Never!"

Ryan found himself seeking Avery out.

Killian was beside himself with the news of their mother's survival and couldn't stop talking when Justin told them. They were working on a plan to rescue her, but Ryan couldn't sit and wait.

He wandered the forest and listened to his heart pounding in his ears with the news. His mother was alive, so he should be ecstatic, but it only brought a sense of dread. Was it possible to be happy and terrified at the same time?

"Yo, you look worse for wear," Avery's voice brought him out of his thoughts.

Ryan looked up and nearly ran into him. He stopped walking and shoved his hands in his pockets. *"I don't look any worse than any other day,"* he said. It was easy slipping into his native tongue.

"If this is how you normally look, I feel sorry for your girlfriend," Avery said with a smile. He looked like he was back to his usual self, so maybe their fight had solved their problems.

"Just found out my mom's alive," Ryan said, trying not to sound bitter.

Avery's smile fell. *"Was that ever in question?"* he asked, pulling a cigarette from his pocket.

He offered one to Ryan, but he shook his head. Justin made him quit because it was terrible for his health and a bad influence on Cody. Given everything else, getting back into the habit would be a poor decision.

"We weren't sure about a month ago. Maybe longer," Ryan said, lighting the smoke for his ex-friend – or maybe they were rebuilding that relationship. It was sometimes hard to tell.

"Too bad, well anyway, just came to apologize for trying to beat you up the other night," he said.

Ryan smirked and waved a hand like he often saw Justin do. *"Don't worry about it, 'kay? We used to fight all the time, didn't we?"* Maybe he could let himself forget how miserable he was for the moment.

Avery's smile mirrored Ryan's, and he took a drag on the cigarette. *"So, why haven't you hit me?"* he asked.

"I don't wanna hit you. How about we form a truce for now? I've got bigger things on my plate than dealing with you," Ryan said, trying to sound more amused and less serious.

Avery eyed him suspiciously. *"What's the catch?"* he asked.

"Leave my brother out of whatever game you're playing," Ryan said.

Killian had tried hiding the memories from Ryan, but they shared a dream again, and Avery happened to be in it. Before Ryan could delve too deeply into the thoughts, Killian woke up and cut him off.

Avery threw his head back and laughed. *"You know, you're less fun these days,"* he said. *"So, if I leave Killian alone, you and I return to normal?"*

"I don't care what we go back to. I just want you to leave Killian out of whatever screwed-up game you have," Ryan said. Because Avery and Ryan were almost the same in their messed-up little world, Ryan knew there was more than what he was saying, but so long as he could keep Killian out of it, he was happy.

Avery pursed his lips. *"Good to see you haven't lost that lovely suspicious attitude of yours,"* he said.

Ryan shrugged and started walking again. *"Good to see you're still annoyingly uncomfortable,"* he retorted.

Avery grabbed Ryan's arm, hanging off him like a girlfriend would. *"Me uncomfortable? Now, where would you get a stupid idea like that?"*

Ryan scowled and ripped his arm away. "Oi, knock it off, would you!" He slipped back into common without realizing it.

"I've been waiting for a big, strong man like you to sweep me off my feet with somethin' poignant and romantic," Avery said, throwing himself toward Ryan like a fainting woman.

Ryan stepped to the side and watched Avery hit the ground like a sack of potatoes. Leaves flew into the air at his fall, and he hissed in pain, clutching his head. A slew of curses left his lips, and his cigarette dropped beside him, where Ryan stomped it out.

"That was so cold," Avery murmured in between winces of pain.

"Stop acting like an idiot then," Ryan said with a fake snarl. The smile threatening to fall into place on his face was hard to hide.

Avery rolled onto his stomach and pressed his palms against the ground. Some leaves crunched when he moved, and a particularly irritated chipmunk darted from the bush that Avery's boot struck. He laughed uncontrollably until tears streamed down his face. Avery laughed too hard to say anything. He just shook his head and curled onto his side, clutching his stomach.

"Dude, it wasn't funny. Come on, breathe," Ryan said, giggling in between his stern-sounding words.

And just like that, they were almost back to normal. *Don't worry, Killian. I know I can't do much, but there is one thing I can do. Protecting you.*

Cursed Memories and Cursed Life

ANGEL

She fell in love. It wasn't supposed to happen, but Rebecca fell hard and fast. He was from Kyler Homestead, halfway across the world. Their languages were different but not different enough to make communication impossible. Rebecca walked to the river behind Rochester Homestead. Since she had run off with Jess and Justin, their mother refused to have contact with them.

She found Aryn sitting by the waterside with his hands on his knees and a smile on his soft brown face. His hair was braided and decorated with varying colors of beads, but the brightest were silver and white. They stood out against his dark skin, and he was gorgeous. "Meditate with me," he said in a thick, accented voice that turned her knees to jelly. "Singing birds." He closed his eyes and swayed in place, humming with the bird's tweets.

Rebecca tucked her skirt under her thighs and sat, grinning widely as she looked at the sky. "They sing lovely tunes, don't they?" she asked, taking in their song. It was bright and cheerful, pleasant to her ears as she closed her eyes and wrapped it around her like a blanket.

Aryn nodded and grabbed her hand, squeezing to let her know he was happy. They didn't speak much, but they didn't have to. She could feel his emotions and hear his thoughts with every beat of his heart. They listened to the water gurgle and trout flop in and out of the water. It was nearly breeding season, and soon, the waters would be filled with their offspring.

"You look beautiful," Aryn said, smiling.

Rebecca flushed and pressed her hand to her chest. "I rolled out of bed," she said as she tried to hide her burning cheeks.

He cocked his head to the side, and confusion flashed through his stormy gray eyes. "Rolled? Why did you not get up and walk?" he asked.

She laughed and pressed her face into his shoulder, shaking her head. "It's a saying. I didn't *actually* roll." A fond smile spread across her lips as she took in his warmth.

Aryn brushed his calloused thumb across her cheek, and his smile faded. "I must go back home," he said. "I'd like to come see you."

Rebecca beamed and nodded. "I'd like that." Her voice was light and full of humor, but Aryn didn't crack a smile as he studied her, as if he would never see her again.

"We can write?" he asked.

She nodded and gently kissed his lips. "Yes, we can write," she said.

Aryn left the following day. It wasn't for half a year when she received the first letter:

> I am sorry to inform you that Aryn
> has been killed in the glory of the
> Coliseum. As the sole inheritor of
> his property, per his written de-
> sires, you are entitled to his neck-
> lace, ring, and winnings.

Angel stirred her coffee as she stared at one of the requests for more supplies. It was getting harder to find comfort items to keep her citizens happy. Riots broke out among the lower-class citizens, and many cried about the murders of their children. The chaos she had weaved to keep the people under her thrall was broken and unstable, and Havoc hadn't been seen since the twins were taken.

She groaned and brought the cup to her lips, grimacing at the bitter aroma. She needed something stronger to get through her day, but she had heard it was inappropriate to drink spirits before a specific time. Her feet echoed down the hall as she tried to work up the will to get through the day. She opened her pale white bedroom door and froze when a figure sat sideways in the ornate chair before her fireplace.

"Feel free to summon me anytime you want updates," Avery said, kicking his legs like a child.

There hadn't been any word from him since he accepted the task, and he ignored every invite to dinner. He wasn't in his Descendant's disguise today. He wore a black leather jacket and thick black boots. His black hair hung in his charcoal-black eyes, and she shook her head with a small smile. This time, he looked more like himself, and it was nice to see his broad smile.

Angel huffed in amusement and crossed her arms against her chest. "And how are you this morning? I take it you've been eavesdropping on adult conversations?" she asked. After all, it had only been that morning that she complained about her lack of intel on the twins.

Avery smirked and tapped his chin as the childish glint in his eyes burned. "Oh, please. You don't count me as an adult?"

"The moment you start taking care of yourself, we can call you an adult," she said, walking to him and brushing his hair out of his eyes. He had become a fine young man.

He gave a mock pout, sticking out his lip as he leaned forward. "Come on, I kill, hunt, and maim. Speaking of maiming, I have some information that might interest you," he said, holding out a stack of wrinkled paper.

Angel took the papers and looked at the top page. Avery's handwriting was an untidy scrawl of chicken scratch. He combined the common and native tongue, which made reading difficult, but she always figured it out. There was a lot of detailed information about Ryan and Killian's moods, abilities, and the work Avery was doing, bringing them into a place of trust. It was impressive, but she expected no less from the young man she had trained.

She set the papers aside and gestured for him to follow. "Have you eaten?" she asked. The last invite had been well received, but now that he was acting more like himself, he might accept.

Avery perked up at the mention of food, bounced out of the chair, and walked to the door. "What'd ya have in mind?"

His smile sent a surge of warmth through her chest, and she set her coffee on her dresser without hesitation. "I don't know, let's see what we can find," she said, thinking of the small cafe down the street. There were lots of sweets and overly bright pastries that he might like to try.

"You musta found somethin' good in the stuff I brought you. Which part, so I know more of what to bring?" he asked when she opened the door.

Angel shrugged and led him into the hall. "I like that you're building trust with them. It's a smart move and nothing I would've thought of," she said. Honestly, she didn't care about the report. All she wanted was to spend quality time with him, and if that meant faking light conversation about intel, she would happily do so.

Avery shrugged. "How else am I going to get them to cooperate?" He returned to the main point. They walked down the hall to the elevator, and she pushed the button to call it.

"There's a nice cafe down the street. I think you'll like their food," she said. There was no need to talk about work while they were out in public.

The elevator dinged, and they got on.

Avery observed her as if he were waiting for her to call the joke.

She smirked and twisted her hair into a braid. Angel slipped a pin from her blouse and pinned the red coils atop her head as the machine went down. "What's wrong?" she asked.

Avery shrugged. "Nothin', I just didn't know what you want with them. You vaguely mentioned a curse or somethin', and I just... don't get it," he said.

Angel hummed in acknowledgment but didn't answer. If he got too attached to the children she was trying to collect, it would lead to problems. Until she knew Avery wasn't going to go soft on her, she would only give him vital information.

When the elevator dinged, and the doors opened, they walked through the lobby without saying another word. She tried to stay ahead of him so he couldn't come up with any more questions. It was for the best because no sooner than they reached the door did the building shake like a God was picking it up. Angel froze, and the lights flickered on and off, leaving a strange glow of energy—Havoc.

"By the night's hold, veil us in a shadowy embrace: camouflage." Angel waved her hand over the lobby, and a black dome descended around her and Avery. Anyone looking into the sphere would see her talking with Avery, but they would overlook Havoc. She had to speed this up before someone tried to bother them. It was soundproof until someone knew what they were looking at. She couldn't risk the spell breaking.

The last thing she needed was for her people to associate her with the magik she claimed was evil. Can you imagine the Helwe that would cause?

Havoc walked through the glass doors of the building with a broad smile on his face. He wore his Descendant's disguise proudly. A silver suit with a silver face mask and a metal cane he used due to a bad limp. His eyes were silver, and besides his pale white skin, Angel couldn't see much behind the outfit.

"He'll betray you," Havoc said, pointing to Avery. "Haven't I told you not to let outsiders in?"

Angel stepped in front of Avery and scowled. "He's been more reliable than you," she said.

Havoc threw his head back and laughed. After all this time, he wanted to make an appearance because she was doing something he disagreed with. People said Angel was a control freak, but they didn't know the man behind the darkness. He was the face of evil and everything cruel and terrible in the world, yet she was the bad guy—the one pulling the strings and manipulating. Oh, if only they knew the face of evil wasn't truly evil.

"You think he's your pawn, but you're his. Isn't it odd that he's forgiven you after all these years?" Havoc asked. "He's working for that Descendant of Wind you hate so much."

Angel's throat tightened. She didn't want to - no, she wouldn't believe that.

Avery snarled and stepped around Angel to confront the skeletal man. "Oh please, if I worked for Justin, why would she be my pawn? I'd just kill her."

Havoc roared in anger at his disruption. His energy surged forward to entangle Avery, and Angel yelped in surprise. She had borne the full might of Havoc's energy before, and it was miserable.

The chaos crackled and sparked as it flickered across Avery's skin and clothes. The young man smirked in amusement but didn't budge. A sky-blue ring of light shone around his almost black eyes, and Angel frowned. He didn't falter or bend under Havoc's influence as she had.

Angel tapped her fingers against her thigh. "Energy vision," she whispered the spell to take in his abilities.

The world vanished, replaced by ethereal lines that resembled twine or yarn. Every living thing had some sort of energy that could be followed. Descendants often shed energy of specific colors.

Avery's body was made up of bright blue and purple lines. One color didn't overpower the other but was vibrant and bold. He held his magik in check well for someone as young as he was, but that wasn't the only thing. The chaos, the lines of purple, bled into every fiber of his being. Avery wasn't just emitting energy but was made up of that self-same power.

She let her vision return to normal and bit her lip. How strong was he? It was possible she would never know, but she couldn't risk letting him have too much information. If he did betray her, there was no way she could defeat him, and that thought set her on edge. *Would I even be willing to kill him if he did?*

"He will destroy everything we've worked for!" Havoc roared, turning to look at her. Once he realized he couldn't disarm Avery, his attention turned to someone he thought he could bully.

Angel tapped her chin in mock thought. "He hasn't yet. In fact, he's been a huge help in evaluating Ryan and his brother. Without him, I wouldn't know where to look," she said.

"Mark my words, Angel. This boy will ruin you. He knows what he's doing, and he's become a manipulator," Havoc snarled. "I won't work with someone like him. Either him or me."

She smirked and waved him to the door. "I will always choose my son," she said.

"He's not your son. He's a sex addict whose parents turned their back on him because of the magik you lovingly gave him," Havoc's voice was dangerously low. "And you will do well to remember how you treated him in the past."

Avery growled and clenched his fists.

Angel was a step ahead. She summoned a spear of ice to her hand and rammed it into the man's ribcage, holding back enough to not break the skin. "Avery is *my* child. I don't care who gave birth to him. If you have nothing else to say, be gone."

Havoc's face fell, and he shook his head. "Be careful. When he stabs you in the back, and you have nothing left, you don't get to come to me," he said.

Angel wouldn't go to him if her life depended on it. Havoc vanished in a billowing plume of black smoke, and she coughed as it washed across her face. "So dramatic," she muttered, letting the spear go. It vanished before it touched the floor.

Avery blinked at her like a kicked puppy. "You called me your kid," he whispered.

She put her hands on her hips and nodded. "I suppose I did. Do you still want food?"

Avery forced a smile that didn't quite reach his eyes and nodded. "Yes, please."

Enough is Enough, For You and Me

KILLIAN

Killian held the war strategy book above his head as he lay on the couch downstairs. Ryan was spending more time with Avery. Kara was spending more time being a brat. Tory and Nicholas spent a lot of time behind closed doors, thinking no one heard their extracurricular activities. The thought sent a shiver down his spine, and he forced himself to focus on the words of the book. Justin spent a lot of time walking the house, mumbling about dirt, and then hiding in his room when he wasn't finding new ways to torture them.

Cody was starting to get interesting. Killian ignored the boy for a while, especially after he lost control and attacked him. Cody would occasionally indulge him in a conversation that stuck with Killian for weeks. Those were the days Killian liked best, but Cody had been coming home bruised and quiet for the last week. Even at dinner, the boy wouldn't talk or regale them with stories of what he had done for the day. He often pushed food around on his plate and excused himself with no one asking questions about the boy's state of being. According to Justin, the boy was becoming a teenager and this behavior was normal.

The front door opened and closed, and Killian set the book on his chest with a sigh, praying to whatever God was out there that it wasn't his pissed-off brother. Once Ryan discovered he had taught Kara the spell for dispel, he was furious and went on a walk to cool down. Killian was sure Ryan was just mad that Killian was actually able to teach her something he couldn't.

Cody walked through with a new black eye and split lip. There were splotches of reddish-brown blood dried along his blue shirt collar.

"Good luck hiding that from your uncle," Killian said, folding his arms behind his head and staring at the boy.

Cody wiped a track of dry blood from his chin. Since the bullying started, he wore long sleeves to hide the fingerprints and bruises. "It'll be gone in the morning," he said. "So, I'll stay in my room and do homework."

"Yeah, well, this conversation won't disappear," Killian said.

Cody sighed and waved his hand, slinging his leather bag onto a small, plush chair beside the fireplace. "Fine, tell me what you want. I bet I can get Jay to do whatever," he said.

Killian raised a brow. "Do you think this is blackmail?" His voice went up in confusion, and he had to clear his throat to make himself sound normal again.

"If it's not, come off it. I have a bunch of homework," Cody said. His blue eyes flashed with irritation, and he tried to hurry down the hall.

It wasn't in Killian's personality to stop people from doing what they wanted, but Cody had helped him recently, whether he knew it or not. It was time to repay the favor so Killian could call himself out of this silly made-up debt.

"We're not done talking," Killian said. He stood and grabbed the back of Cody's shirt. "I want to know what's going on."

Cody growled in frustration and ripped himself from Killian's grasp. He turned around and clenched his fists, ignoring the apathetic stare. "You're not my dad, so go away. I can deal with it." Rage masked his adorable, cherub face as he stared Killian down, acting like he was ready for a fight.

"I can see that." Killian gestured to the fresh blood pooling under his nose. "Look, I used to deal with bullies, and I can help."

"Why do you even care?" Cody asked coldly. "All you do is cause problems for the others and make snide comments."

Why do I even care? Kid, if I knew, I would tell you. Killian would've been offended if it was anyone else saying this crap, but he shrugged and ran a hand through his hair. "Look..." That was a good way to start a sentence, but the real success was finishing it.

"I'm not your brother, so you don't owe me anything. I can take care of myself," Cody said. His voice softened, and he turned back to the hall, snagging his bag from the couch.

Killian cleared his throat. "Let me help, or I'll tell Nicholas," he said. It wouldn't be the first time he used the family card. He had done the same thing to Dawson when the boy kept encouraging Ryan's antics, which worked reasonably well then – despite Kara threatening to kill him at one point.

Cody's eyes widened in terror. "What?"

"Let me help, or your uncle will find out about all of this," Killian said.

The boy's voice got shrill, and he stepped back as if he had been physically struck. "No."

Killian crossed his arms and smirked. He knew he had won when the boy's shoulders slumped, and he closed his eyes in defeat.

"Fine. Join me at school, but you'll make it worse," Cody said. He slung his bag over his shoulder and stormed down the hall.

"No, I won't," Killian called after him. "Leave without me in the morning, and I *will* make it worse." That was probably the most adult thing he had ever said, and he hoped never to repeat it.

Killian had no plans of beating up a random child, but if the bully gave him reason... he stopped his train of thought and went back to the couch. There had to be a quick, easy solution before he could move on. Taking his frustrations out on a stranger would be nice for once, instead of having someone use him as a punching back. Namely, Ryan.

Killian hadn't been to the school in Rochester since he was eight. All the "fun" memories surfaced when he walked into the classroom with Cody. His worst fear used to be dealing with kids who wanted to beat them up or make them screw up on tests. Those days seemed faint compared to the worries plaguing them in recent days, like Angel and the end of the world.

The school was one of the larger buildings in the homestead, comfortably accommodating about twenty people. Although classes were held in the forest, students first met in the building to gather their bearings and receive instructions for the day. Students used the building for shorter lessons during the winter and rainy days.

Cody went for a spot in the back as they walked in, ignoring the snickers and stares as other kids talked about him in Nivet. The boy's cheeks turned red, telling Killian he heard it. Killian crossed his arms and sat next to the redhead, watching anyone who walked by, waiting for some tell from the bully.

"You're going to make it worse," Cody whispered.

"How can I make it worse?" They had this argument on their way to school that morning, and neither of them could find a reasonable compromise, so they dropped the subject.

Killian drew symbols in the dirt and kept his awareness around him to avoid drawing much attention. *'Look as inconspicuous as possible,'* Ryan said in his head.

Killian sighed and shook the voice away. Someone delved into his thoughts again and figured out what he was doing.

Ryan's laugh resounded through Killian's head as he spoke in an airy voice, *'To be fair, you initiated it. I was minding my own business.'*

'Aren't you still mad at me?' By the tone of voice and giggles throughout his head, Killian figured out that Ryan was less upset. *'I'm in the middle of something. What do you want?'* Killian asked. He tried to keep his attention on those around them but found it hard with Ryan's judgy thoughts.

'I'm not being judgy,' he said in mock offense.

'Bull. What do you want?'

The teacher was the last to arrive. She had some books and writing utensils, and as soon as her eyes landed on Killian, she smiled. *"We have a new student?"* she asked in Nivet.

'Oh, new student? I wish I could see this,' Ryan said in a deceptively charming voice.

Killian took a breath and tried to build a wall between them. He didn't have the time to deal with his annoying twin in the middle of recon. Like Ryan, he smiled sweetly at the teacher and said, *"I'm Killian."* There was no getting around using his native language here.

"Well, I'm Miriam. Maybe you can stick with Cody, and he can catch you up," she said, raising her eyebrows. When she looked at Cody, she relayed the information in the common tongue, though it was broken.

Killian shot the boy a look and cocked his head to the side. *"You don't speak their language?"* he asked. It was odd, but he couldn't recall either Nicholas or Justin using Nivet, yet it made the most sense for them to speak it fluently because they lived here.

Cody's cheeks burned. "I do, but not well. Jay and Nick taught me, but common was easier." He refused to meet Killian's gaze like this was a super embarrassing secret.

Killian chewed his cheek and leaned back on his palms as Miriam directed everyone's attention to the book in her hands. It was some old poetry that none of these kids would care about. "It's not that bad," he lowered his voice to avoid getting them in trouble.

'Pay attention, Kill.' Ryan was determined not to let Killian forget he was there. *'It's your favorite subject. Boring ass poetry.'*

Cody huffed under his breath and stared hard at his teacher. "It *is* a big deal. I'm the only kid here who can't speak it fluently because I didn't like the language."

Killian looked at the boy, noticing his fisted hands and rigid back. Cody was tense and cold like a statue because he couldn't speak a specific language. "I couldn't speak common the first three years I was there," he whispered.

Cody chanced a look at Killian with a shy gaze. His eyes watered a little, but he sniffed the tears away. "You're super smart, though."

"Yeah, but not all the time. Ryan had to translate everything, and people always made fun of me. Doing the most basic assignments was hard because I didn't understand. Why do you think I use common?" he asked. He traced patterns into the dirt with his fingers and smiled weakly. "I don't want to forget."

A group of boys sitting near the front kept elbowing one another and looking back at them. They all had the same bronzed skin, brown hair, and dark blue eyes, and they took an obvious interest in Cody, which was the first red flag. Killian would have his bullies if he could tick off another box.

Most of the kids had noticed his presence and were snickering and pointing. Cody bristled beside him, fidgeting anytime anyone looked their way. He wrote quick, sloppy notes on paper, but Killian noticed he only wrote the words he was familiar with. He didn't understand a single bit of this poetry.

"Killian, are you familiar with this play by W.S.?" Miriam asked, pulling him out of his thoughts.

No. Move on. He wracked his brain for old stories he knew and who they had been written by.

'You can't hide in that shell of yours forever,' Ryan said. He was enjoying this too much because Killian could feel the waves of joy and amusement through that imaginary red and violet rope that kept them tethered.

Killian closed his eyes and breathed, summoning his energy to avoid losing it. *'If you want to live to see eighteen, you'll shut the Helwe up.'* Killian shook his head when he realized he would have to bite the bullet. "I am not familiar with it," he said. He spoke in common so that Cody didn't feel left out.

There was a series of laughs, and Miriam shushed everyone. *"That's alright."* Her voice was gentle. *"Where were you at in your learning?"*

Killian said, turning away from the wall. He faced the small-minded kids behind him with a firmness he didn't have before. *"I mostly took medical classes,"* he said.

"Oh, you're a healer?" she asked.

"No." He chuckled bitterly.

Cody raised his hand with a sheepish smile. "I can help," he said. At least someone was going to save Killian from this horrendous conversation. "It's a story about two lovers dying from an old family feud."

That's not poetry. Wasn't that an ancient play or something? Killian watched Cody go into an in-depth explanation and smirked when he sat back down. He was smart. A lot smarter than Killian was, and maybe even Ryan.

'He explained a play. Let's see him solve a complex equation in his head,' Ryan whined.

'I'll cut your dick off if you keep butting into my conversation. Is that any more persuasive of a threat?' Killian asked. When Ryan didn't respond, Killian assumed it was.

Cody kept his head down despite the kids who pointed and whispered. It couldn't have been that odd for these kids to hear someone speak a different language.

Killian sat next to him and nudged his shoulder. "You did great," he said.

"They're talking about you," Cody whispered.

"I'm aware. *I* can speak the language." Killian smiled because he didn't know what else to do. "It's little things like how scary I look if that makes you feel better."

Cody's cheeks turned pink, and he looked away again. "Why doesn't it bother you?" he asked.

That was one thing about people that Killian never understood. They were always worried about what their neighbors thought. Killian didn't have the same concerns because they would leave him be if people didn't like him.

"Because I'm never going to see any of these kids again. They can say whatever they want," he said.

They sat silently for the rest of the lesson and did light group reading. Killian didn't mind the reading; as a kid, it had been one of his favorite activities, and he had less time for it now that he was older. When they got outside for archery, Cody groaned. "This is where the day gets bad."

"Why?" Killian asked. "You shoot a bow. How can you mess that up?"

"I'm the only one who can't hit a target," Cody said.

Killian nodded as everyone got their bows and stood before their target. "I'll show you. In return for that book thing."

When Miriam asked for a volunteer, he raised his hand. She blinked. *"Oh? Are you sure?"*

They were in the middle of the forest, with a series of targets set twenty feet from them. Some moderators and arrow gatherers were present, but they were mainly there to ensure no one messed around and hurt each other. If an arrow went astray or too far, they would retrieve it so the kids could focus on proper technique.

Killian forced a charming smile. One of the ones he had seen Ryan use on teachers and adults when he was trying to make a good impression. *"I think so."*

He picked a sturdy redwood longbow from the rack and grabbed three arrows. There were five targets, but he decided he wouldn't show off too much. Killian placed two arrows between his teeth and strung the first, straightening his back. With a soft exhale, he let the arrow loose before grabbing the second, shifting his weight, and letting it go. The third was easier to get off after the warmup, and he only missed one bull's eye.

Killian beckoned at Cody and smiled. This time, it wasn't fake. "Your turn."

Cody stepped over a little timidly and took the bow. "I'm really, really, bad. I shot my last mentor."

Killian thought about that. It had to be hard to shoot someone next to you. "We're going to gloss over that, but I want the full story later," he said. "Hold the bow straight, keep your elbows parallel to the ground. Pull back on the string and take a deep breath as you do." He moved Cody's arm up a little and tilted his head up. "Be confident and breathe out slowly when you let go."

Cody nodded and gulped. His throat bobbed uncertainly as he blinked. "This angle is going to-"

Killian cut him off. "Stop thinking and just shoot. There are no angles and no linear equations. Just shoot," he said.

"But I have-"

Killian cut him off. "Point, aim, and shoot." The redhead sighed and pulled back on the bowstring. He trembled a little, and Killian set his hand in the middle of his shoulder blades. "Relax."

Cody's trembling ceased, and he closed his eyes. When he let out his breath, he let the arrow go, and it hit just above the center ring. "I hit the target!"

Killian chuckled and held up his hand. "Next time, think about keeping your eyes open," he said.

Cody laughed and threw his arms around Killian in a tight hug.

Killian tensed uncomfortably but tried not to make it look too obvious as he patted the boy on the head. "Yeah, yeah, get off," he muttered.

Cody beamed up and giggled, letting him go. "That was awesome."

Killian rolled his eyes but smirked so Cody would know he wasn't annoyed. There was a break between archery and the next class, and Killian sat with Cody near the school. He never strayed far from the building unless it was for an assignment.

"Thanks for helping," Cody said, taking a bite of his sandwich.

Killian leaned against the building and shrugged. "No problem." He hadn't solved the problem he wanted to solve. It wouldn't matter if Cody were still being bullied.

"Do you really not care what people think?" Cody asked. "Because I know people say that, but most don't mean it."

Killian chuckled and shook his head. "You don't think I mean it?"

Cody shrugged and went silent for a few seconds. His head popped up when he thought of another question. "Do you like me?" he asked.

Killian wasn't sure where this conversation was headed. "I wouldn't be here if I didn't." He chose his words carefully, sensing a trap.

Cody nodded and asked, "Do you care what I think about you?"

"No."

The boy huffed and took another bite. "No one's opinion bothers you?"

Killian's mind wandered to Ryan. He shrugged and picked at some of the plush grass. That wasn't entirely true. "Nope."

'Don't be cruel,' Ryan whispered.

Killian flinched and bit his lip. *'I don't care what you think,'* he said. Killian cleared his mind and refused to let himself dwell on the thought. The walls he built weren't as strong as Ryan's, and his brother was quickly able to get into his head when he felt like it.

Ryan went silent.

The boy shrugged and finished his food without any further questions. He leaned against the school building while Killian picked at the grass. So far, the day had been a waste because he hadn't been able to find the bullies.

A young girl with bright blonde hair and sky-blue eyes approached them before class picked up again. She looked nervous as she waved and stopped in front of Cody. "Um, hi," she said.

Cody's back straightened, but he didn't look scared. "Hi, Cherie. Is something wrong?" he asked. His cheeks dusted pink, and his nose wrinkled.

Killian smirked and shook his head. He recognized a crush when he saw one. Spending a couple of years roaming high school walls and watching them fawn over Ryan showed him all he needed to know.

The girl gulped and mentally rearranged some words before saying them aloud. "I need math help." She refused to even look in Killian's direction.

Cody cocked his head to the side. "Sure, but aren't you good at math?" He sounded confused, like maybe there was more to this girl than she was letting on.

This Cherie girl didn't have a problem understanding the language, but when she spoke, it was broken, telling Killian she was still probably learning it. "I moved into older class. I don't know new equations," Cherie said.

Cody smiled the way he always did when someone asked him a favor. A genuine, kind smile that lit up his face and made his blue eyes brighten. "I'd love to help. You can have a seat. I'm done eating."

Cherie clapped and took a step toward him.

She didn't get two feet before a hand grabbed her shoulder, and some older guy sneered at Cody and Killian. *"What's goin' on here?"* the boy asked.

Cody blinked in surprise and scooted back a little. "I'm sorry, you spoke too fast," he said. His voice was softer, and any joy he might've had a moment ago was gone.

Killian nodded, cracked his knuckles, and grinned. *Finally,* it looked like the guys in the front of the class were the right ones to scope out. Three more boys, all around the same age, walked over to Cherie and the one holding her tight. Their blue eyes and facial resemblance made Killian assume they were related—cousins or even siblings.

The boys spoke amongst each other and glared daggers at Cody.

Cherie's face was bright red, and she murmured an apology. She turned to scold the boys for interrupting her, but they weren't interested in listening. They pushed her to the side and advanced on Cody.

Killian stood and wiped his hands on his pants. *"Back off,"* he said, his voice icy.

The boys exchanged glances and pointed at Cody. *"How do you know him?"* they asked.

"It doesn't matter. All that matters is I'll beat your ass if you take another step." Killian preferred to avoid beating around the bush or playing games. The quicker they could get through this, the better.

"He doesn't belong here." The ones behind the lead boy all snickered and high-fived each other.

Cody tugged on Killian's arm and shook his head. "Don't fight."

Killian sighed and bit back the low growl lingering on his tongue. *"What kind of moron can't stand someone being different?"*

Cherie sighed and hung her head. *"My brothers don't want to learn common. They think everyone should know Nivet,"* she said. Cherie was back in front of Cody, hoping to spare him her brother's cruelty.

Go figure. A child who's more mature than those around her. Killian scrunched his nose in irritation. *'How do I fix this, Ryan?'*

'You can't fix stupidity.' Ryan wasn't wrong, but his answer could've been more helpful.

Cherie yelped when one of her brothers dove for him. Violence was the answer today.

Killian stepped out of the way and slammed his elbow between the boy's shoulder blades. In two seconds, he had him pinned with a wicked smile. *"If you're gonna take me, you've gotta be faster. If you touch my brother again, I'll beat you within an inch of your life,"* he promised.

When Killian let him up, the boys took off running. Cody blinked in shock as he tried to process what happened. Killian ruffled his hair. "Come on, let's go inside. It's getting hot." If he didn't get as far from the morons as he could, he might kill one of them.

Cherie stared after them, holding some paper. "I come learn?" she asked.

Killian shot her a look and waved her along. "Come on."

She brightened and followed them inside.

The rest of the day was uneventful. Cherie sat with Cody and Killian and got help with math. Her brothers made sure to stay clear after watching one of their own take a beating. Killian glanced over with a smug smile every so often. Let them try something. He would enjoy the fight.

They exited the room when they were dismissed, and Killian stretched. It would be too soon if he never had to sit through another class. He stopped walking when he saw Avery leaning against a jewelry stall, flirting with some redhead. A cigarette was dangling from his lips, and Killian's eyes narrowed.

"Who's that?" Cody asked.

"No one."

Avery turned and noticed them. He smiled and waved as if he had been expecting to see Killian that afternoon.

Cody chuckled and tugged on his hand. "Doesn't look like no one. Is he a friend?" the boy pushed for more information and elbowed him lightly.

Killian closed his eyes and took a breath. He didn't want Ryan to know about Avery, and since he was feeling intrusive today, he had to find a way to stop that train of thought before it got there.

"Don't tell anyone at home about this, alright?" Killian asked. He knew he shouldn't be keeping secrets from the others, but Avery wasn't something he wanted to tell everyone about. "Distract me before I think the wrong thing," Killian said.

Cody frowned and ran a hand through his curly hair. "Cherie invited me to the river. Should I go?"

"Do you want to go?" he asked, not taking his eyes off Avery.

He had the man's full attention now. Avery exhaled a stream of smoke and winked at Killian seductively. It looked like he was back to himself. "God, he's disgusting," Killian growled. "Do you want to go?" He turned his attention to Cody again.

The boy's cheeks were bright pink. "A little."

"Then you should go," he said.

"What about the brothers?" Cody asked.

Killian smirked. That was easy. He took his eyes off Avery and set a hand on Cody's shoulder. "If they touch you today, they never will again," he promised.

Cody beamed and nodded. He threw his arms around Killian in another hug and ran off, waving. "See you."

Killian walked over to Avery and tried to ignore the shit-eating grin. "Don't say a word."

Avery held out his arms. "Do I get a hug too?"

Killian punched him in the stomach in reply because violence was something he understood.

"Okay, no hugs," Avery wheezed. He walked away from the stand and looked back, dropping the cigarette. "You comin'?" he asked.

Killian hesitated. He hadn't seen Avery since those final words of "trust me." The moment they left his lips, Killian teleported home, leaving behind a stain of stew in the grass.

"What do you want?" Avery asked. When he realized Killian wasn't going to answer, he said, "I don't see you in Rochester often."

This had nothing to do with him this time. Killian opened his mouth to say that, but his brain and mouth were disconnected. "I came to solve a problem."

Trusting Avery was out of the question. His moods shifted too often, but trusting himself was a worse option. If he didn't find a way to control the beast within, he would have a ridiculously hard time keeping the people he cared for safe.

Avery frowned. Leaves crunched underfoot as they got further from the homestead. "Isn't Justin babysittin' you?" he asked.

Killian swallowed thickly and tried to organize his thoughts. How much could he say without giving too much away? "Ryan and I found a new bond... there's this connection between us, and it's taxing." He chose his words carefully in case Ryan was paying attention

"Your brother's wearin' you down?" Avery asked. He gestured for Killian to follow where they could talk about this privately. "Did you think about my offer to help?"

Killian looked back toward the school as he followed Avery through the dusty homestead. Traders and merchants wandered the dirt roads, haggling prices and trying to get the best deals for their goods. The vendors and stalls set up reeked of fish and stale ale, but it wasn't the worst thing Killian had ever smelled. His eyes flicked among the people, waiting for someone to recognize him like they did the last time he dared show up in the homestead, but more people were interested in Avery.

The women and girls smiled and flirted as if they would be the next on his to-do list, while the men waved and smiled in awe at how he quickly captured the hearts of so many. It was odd how well-liked he was, but Killian searched his energy to be sure something fishy wasn't going on and surprised himself. The people genuinely liked Avery. It had nothing to do with his influence over magik, and while that didn't seem odd, Ryan's conversation with Avery a few nights ago contradicted what was happening.

"Do we not have an answer?" Avery asked, startling Killian out of his thoughts.

They were past the gates of Rochester, and apparently, Killian had just been following him like a lost pup. He sighed and kicked a bunch of leaves, scattering them into the air and watching them whisper back to the forest floor. The trees were mostly bare now, meaning there would soon be ice. "I don't know," he said after a while. "I just... I dunno."

Avery chuckled and shook his head. "I'm not askin' much," he said. His voice softened, and he looked around, stopping beside a large oak nearly bare from the change of seasons.

"Fine," Killian ground out. "But this stays between us."

Avery clapped and nodded. "Show me the shadow realm, and we're in business."

Not Afraid Of Magik

"Why is it the lot of you are searchin' me out?" Avery asked as Kara wandered the forest.

She looked up at him as he stood before a massive tree with a silly smile that instantly put her at ease. "I wasn't looking for you," she said. "And what do you mean, the lot of us?"

He shook his head and walked toward her.

"I was afraid of you," she said when he stopped. "Your energy is hard to read."

He smirked. "Well, I am a person to fear. Not that it matters because I don't believe in abusin' women. If I were to go for a fight, it would be with Ryan," he said.

"You've met him?" she asked.

He laughed and beckoned for her to follow as he walked deeper into the woods. "Come to Rochester with me," he said. "I've got a stall to run, and I can share all the sordid stories."

Confusion washed across her face, but she followed, only looking back once before committing. "Sordid stories?" she asked, jogging to catch up, pushing branches out of the way.

"Yeah, we grew up together," he said with that same amused smile. "I can share all the garbage, but only if you admit it."

Admit what? I just told him I was afraid of him. She opened her mouth and shut it before shrugging. "Admit..." she trailed off and waved for him to finish the statement.

Avery stopped and stepped in front of her, blocking her path as he held his hands behind his back like a chastised toddler. "Admit you're afraid of magik," he said.

Kara's heart thudded, but she narrowed her eyes, not letting him know how that statement affected her. "I'm not," she said because if she were going to admit her fear to anyone, it wouldn't be the man she barely knew.

"Oh really? Because I would think someone raised to think all magik was evil would be afraid." There was a hint of knowing in his voice, and his smile tightened like he was fighting to keep it there.

"Why does it matter?" she snapped. *Leave it to boys to ruin a good mood.*

Avery booped her nose and walked away before she could retaliate with a lightning bolt. "I'm just tryin' to help you find yourself."

She cursed him in Nivet and watched his back straighten as he whirled around to face her with excited eyes. "You're learnin'?" he asked.

"A little. Justin taught me a few words, and Killian taught me the fun stuff," she said. *Oh, my gods, fun stuff? Who am I turning into?*

Avery clapped excitedly and dragged her to the homestead. Showing off his fur and leather stall, he bought her a sweet water drink and sweet doughy bread before letting her settle in. It was a small wooden box with furs and animal skins, but there weren't many people out and about. The wood was warped and diveted in places where it looked like kids had been picking. There was a flat counter separating people from the goods, and Avery patted the top. "Hop on, and let's play a game."

Kara nudged the wobbly wood with her foot and frowned when it trembled like an earthquake was passing through. "Will this hold me?" She nibbled the sweet bread, waiting for a response.

Avery nodded and slapped the counter, making the shack wobble again. "You're in good hands! Ol' Betsy here can handle anything." To make his point, he plopped himself in the center of the wood and chuckled.

Kara shrugged and gingerly climbed up next to him. Her only consolation was they were barely four feet off the ground. "What are we playing?" she asked as she settled in and relaxed.

"I want to know why you won't admit you're afraid of magik," Avery said.

She stuck her tongue out and licked the sugar remnants from her lips. "I'm not scared of anything." Except when it was dark, and there were scary sounds outside.

"Right, well. I'll tell you about the twins anyway. What do you wanna know?"

Kara took another nibble of her bread. "How do you know them?"

"We grew up together. They were born here and all but left when we were fairly young," Avery said, leaning back and nearly toppling off the back. The stall shook as he righted himself, clasping a pillar of support to wrench himself up.

A couple of giggling girls walked by and waved to Avery. When he winked, they scattered with excited, high shrieks.

Kara scoffed. "You're just popular with all the gi..." She stopped when a guy with brown hair walked by and blew Avery a kiss. "Everyone."

Avery chuckled again and took a piece of her bread. "*Everyone* is a little over the top. I would say only a good portion."

Kara studied him. Anytime they ran into each other, he was full of life and bubbly. The man always smiled, so it wasn't a surprise he wasn't short of admirers, but she still felt like there was something more to him. "How did you feel when the twins went to the city?"

Avery shrugged, but his smile vanished. He kicked his feet, and his boots thudded against the wall. "It was somethin'. I dunno. We weren't too close."

There had been a falling out, and he didn't want to talk about it. Kara wracked her brain for an innocent question. "Do you have a Descendant's mark of power, too?"

Avery's shoulders slumped further, and his hand went to the back of his neck, but he didn't answer. He stared daggers at the ground and shrugged silently.

Two for two. Way to go. Kara huffed in frustration and tried to move on. "Could you check mine? I can't see it, but it's never taken form." She pointed to her back and turned it to him so he could look.

Avery pulled the collar of her shirt down, and his fingers traced symbols. Diamonds, triangles, and some weird curvy lines that moved to the center of her shoulder blades. She giggled as his feather-light fingers danced across her skin. "It's shapin' up, but I can't really tell what it's supposed to be."

She frowned, hoping it had grown more than when Killian last looked.

He patted her shirt back into place and tugged a strand of her frizzy hair like an older brother terrorizing his sister. "Hey, don't stress it. These things take time." Avery went quiet for a moment but perked up when he remembered something. "Hey! I know. Why don't you and the twins come to Rochester for the special event goin' on in a couple of days."

Kara hesitated. She still hadn't apologized to Ryan for starting a fight and then screaming at him about how much she hated him. Inviting him to an event in Rochester probably wouldn't help their relationship. "Oh, um... Ryan and I had a fight," she said.

"Tell him you want to make up for it. He likes the ceremonies, and you might get points for it," he said.

She cocked her head to the side. "Points?" That wasn't a phrase she was familiar with.

"Yeah, you know, like he'll like it and forget how mad he is," Avery said with a smirk.

Kara wrinkled her nose as she thought about it. Spending time away from Haven with the boys would be fun, but she hadn't done anything with them in a long time. Something that didn't involve training or fighting anyway. After a while, she nodded in agreement. "You know, that could be fun."

After all, what's the worst that could happen?

Can't Handle the Heat

RYAN

"*I'll see you soon, Little Descendant*" Angel's voice always found a way to reach him.

Ryan groaned and dropped his head against the counter, relishing how cool it was against his overheated skin.

"Hey, can you help me with... what're you doing?" Tory stopped in the kitchen entryway.

Ryan turned his head so his cheek was pressed to the counter. "Dying slowly," he said. "What do you want?"

"I need help with some sword thing, but you look busy, so let's go." Tory didn't miss a beat as he grabbed the apple Ryan had been cutting up and bit into it. He shrugged and walked out, crunching on Ryan's snack.

"*Fun and games. Let's have some fun,*" Angel whispered. Her idea of fun wasn't the same as his, and Ryan shivered.

He followed Tory down the hall and out the front door. "You use a great sword. I use short. What exactly do you think I can teach you?" He was looking for a reason out of helping Tory with anything, considering their mutual 'I hate you' vibe was getting worse.

Tory summoned his weapon and swung it onto his shoulders. "You're about speed. I'm about defense. I want to combine our tactics, but I need to figure out how to wield this."

"You want to learn to use the sword faster? Try a different one," Ryan said with a smirk.

Tory chuckled without humor. "You're so funny."

Ryan wasn't sure he had heard someone sound more insincere his entire life. He shrugged as he summoned his swords and twirled them with a flare he didn't know he had, especially after a couple of nights of zero sleep. His Descendant weapons were twin short swords. One was black, and the other was crimson. The few times he used them, they had proven quite helpful, but Nicholas always told him he could be better and do more if he let loose.

"Do you want me to use one or both?" he asked, trying not to sound bored.

Tory grinned. "Don't go easy on me. It's not like you kicked my butt the last time we faced off like this." His voice carried a note of a challenge, and Ryan found his mood rising to the call.

"I believe I won, and you ran like a chicken," he said. Unless he remembered the night Tory stabbed Killian wrong, but he was pretty sure he wasn't.

Tory smirked but didn't have a comeback. He bent his knees and held out his hand, beckoning Ryan closer.

Fine, et's fight. Ryan was always the first to move, and he could never explain why. All he knew was that when there was a fight, his body moved before he could formulate a plan or scope out his actions, so when he surged toward Tory, it was expected.

It made the first couple of blocks easy, and Ryan scowled as Tory smirked with that 'I'm better than you' smile, knowing full well it would piss him off. Ryan swung his swords down, but Tory had his weapon between them in two seconds. From their first fight, Ryan had learned Tory was slow and clumsy, but the man had changed in that time. He was faster and used his weapon more like an extension of his arm instead of a separate object.

The shock must have been evident on his face because Tory smirked as he thrust the sword back and dropped to swipe Ryan's feet out from under him. Ryan jumped back, waving his arms to regain his balance, but Tory slammed his shoulder into Ryan's stomach, toppling him to the ground.

Ryan gasped as he fell flat on his back, wheezing as the air left his lungs in a rush of wind. Tory brought the greatsword over his head in both hands, and Ryan rolled away as it slammed into the ground, pommel first.

That woulda hurt like Helwe. Ryan shook his head as he got back to his feet and calmed his thoughts.

Tory was a competent fighter, but he had apparently become better, which meant Ryan had to pay closer attention to his movements.

"I thought this was a friendly spar. Why are you trying to kill me?" he asked, crossing the swords in an X formation and pushing the weight into his heels.

"What, you can't handle a little heat, Wilson?" Tory asked, smirking dangerously. He knew exactly what he was doing, and for whatever reason, anger surged at the taunt.

Ryan lunged, striking out with one of his swords and ducking under Tory's sword with renewed vigor. As the great blade swished overhead, Ryan looked up and slammed the pommel into Tory's thigh.

Everything moved in slow motion as the brunette dropped to the opposite knee, his face screwed up in pain. Ryan didn't know what happened, but the world went black, and all he could hear was screaming. Angel's laughter cackled around him, and he imagined her throwing her head back in victory as everything around her burned. His blood pumped excitedly through his veins and his vision pulsed like his eyeballs were breathing. A palm flew into his nose, and with a thunderous roar of pain, he flew back into Nicholas' chest, panting like a dehydrated dog.

"What the Helwe's wrong with you?" Tory demanded, clutching his arm with his good hand.

Ryan blinked, and Angel's voice was gone. He looked around in stunned silence as Nicholas rushed past him to check the damage. *What happened?* He had been sparring with Tory, so why was he on the ground, covered in blood? His memory was a black abyss as he reached for the memories leading to the blood and fighting.

"I... I don't know," he stuttered, trying to formulate anything that made sense.

Nicholas looked up, his dark brown eyes sharp and angry. "Go inside," he said. It was a miracle the man maintained a level voice, but Ryan's heart sank despite the calmness.

He had disappointed someone else, and that was a mortifying thought. He dropped his swords, which vanished in red fumes before hitting the grass.

Tory winced as Nicholas forced his fingers away from the deep laceration running the length of his forearm. "It's fine," the young man hissed, trying to wrench his arm away from his boyfriend. "This is nothing." His eyes flicked to Ryan, frustration and concern washing through the blue hazel.

"I'm sorry." Ryan stepped back and held up his hands. There wasn't a scratch on him, and he cursed under his breath, his eyes flicking wildly across the lawn.

"Go away," Nicholas said, wrapping Tory's arm with a white cloth.

Ryan turned and ran into the forest, unable to find words.

Killian giggled and rested his head on Ryan's shoulder, his fingers tugging on the fraying ends of his shirt. "I'm sleepy," he said. His voice was slow and thick, like he had been up all night.

Ryan set his book down and nudged his brother awake with his shoulder. "Don't sleep on me. Go somewhere else," he said.

The forest was quieter than usual, which would have usually been a sign, but Ryan wasn't paying attention because he was engrossed in his book about planetary alignment and stars. It was one of the things the library carried that the scavengers found in their journeys. Ryan loved reading about astronomy, as the scientists called it, because it made him feel like there was more to life.

"What's this one about?" Killian asked, forcing his eyes open when Ryan pushed him. Aliens on Mars?" A lazy smile crossed his lips, making Ryan roll his eyes.

His brother would never understand him. "Yeah," he said to keep the conversation short. The quicker he humored Killian, the quicker he could return to reading.

His brother shrugged and pushed himself to his feet, yawning and stretching. A wave of ice-cold water slapped them both in the face, destroying the book in Ryan's hands and burning across his skin. His breath caught in shock as the ice seeped through his clothes, making his teeth chatter.

Killian snarled, and a surge of dark energy zipped through the air, turning his eyes red and making the shadows tremble. "You'll pay for that, Kevin," Killian said, his rage magnifying his energy as rage tore through Ryan's veins.

Not mine to feel. Not mine to feel. He mentally chanted his mother's words and kept his emotions steady. Ryan didn't see it coming until Killian bolted after the chubby-faced boy with a knife in hand. "Oh no, no, no," he whispered, jumping to his feet and giving chase.

The ruined book thudded to the forest floor and lay open on a smeared page about a planet called Saturn. Ryan wanted to know how it ended and what would happen at the end of the world, but his world would end here if he didn't stop Killian from hurting someone.

"Kilua, stop!" he shouted after the laughing. Ryan ducked under a low-hanging branch and froze. He could hear the echoes of Kevin and his brother's fight, but he couldn't see them anymore. "Kilua!"

If their grandmother found out that Killian hurt someone, she would be furious. Ryan didn't want another punishment because his brother was too hot-headed.

Avery ran over to him and set a hand on his shoulder. "By the lake," he said. "I couldn't separate them."

They tore through the trees and arrived at the lakeside in seconds. That's all it took. Killian had the bloody knife in his hand as he stared down at Kevin's lifeless body. Blood pooled around him like rubies where his throat was slit, decorating the leaves in a daunting red.

Avery grabbed Ryan's shoulder, his fingers digging painfully into the skin with a sharp intake of breath. "We've got to..."

To what? There was nothing they could do at this point, and he knew it. Ryan's hands shook as he took the knife from Killian and wiped some blood from his face. Though dull, his eyes had returned to their usual green sheen as he came out of his stupor.

"Go home," Ryan whispered. "I'll deal with it." He could only take the blame or fix the situation, but this was something he didn't know how to handle. Killian had never actually killed someone before now.

Avery shook his head and grabbed Killian's hand, pulling him away. He led him over to the river and left him there, returning to Ryan as he ran a hand through his hair. "We have to tell someone," he said.

"No, we can't. Go home with him, and I'll deal with it, alright?" Ryan muttered.

Avery put a hand on his shoulder. "What will you do that won't lead to them throwin' you out of here? Your mom's not around to protect you, and this..." he gestured to the cold body with a shiver. "This is bad."

Ryan's stomach twisted, and he fought the urge to throw up. *I don't have a choice. He's my brother. I have to protect my brother.* If he had been paying more attention, he could have avoided this situation, but he had been too busy reading.

"At least tell me the plan," Avery said.

Ryan didn't have one. "I'll make it look like it was me." He forced a smile despite every warning sign going off in his head. If they had to leave for a while, he could manage. Hiding the body would buy him enough time to figure out what to do. Hopefully, he had a concrete plan in a couple of days.

"This is a bad idea," Avery said again.

"I don't have a choice," Ryan hissed. His eyes misted over, and he looked over to where Killian stood, still trapped in whatever trance he was in. "He's my brother."

For Killian, he would become whatever he had to.

Ryan found himself by the river's edge and stared into the rushing water. His mind raced as he tried to figure out what was happening to him, and why he kept forgetting. He beat Tory in a sparring session, but he went way over the top, and he couldn't remember how.

"Hey," Avery's low drawl set him on edge.

Ryan whirled around and held out his hands, begging him to stay back. *"Don't,"* he said. *"I'm dangerous."*

Avery hesitated on the forest's edge, the shadows of the trees hiding his face. One hand was tucked into a pocket, and the other hung loosely at his side.

"Since when have I cared about you bein' dangerous?" Avery asked, stepping into the sunlight. His face was calm and still, though concern and worry flashed through his coal-black eyes.

"I hurt Tory, and I don't... I don't remember doing it, Avery! There's something wrong with me, with my memory. We were sparring. A simple fu-"

Avery stepped forward and flicked his forehead.

Ryan was shocked into silence. He stared at his friend, or ex-friend, or whatever they were, and blinked.

"Calm down. Freakin' out ain't gonna get us anywhere. You wanna try explainin' this rationally?" Avery asked with a yawn as if this conversation was boring.

Ryan blinked again and breathed, letting the panic seep out of his system. He ran a hand through his hair and closed his eyes, ignoring the tremble. *"I'm sorry,"* he said.

"Cool, now, what happened?" Avery asked.

"We were sparring. Tory asked me to help with his technique, and I blacked out. I sliced through his arm," Ryan whispered.

Avery tapped his chin thoughtfully. *"Alright, so... this is the chaos thing?"* he asked. *"And not to diminish your feelings, but an arm laceration is hardly almost killing anyone."*

Ryan shrugged. He didn't know what it was, but he would have said that if he did. *"When Angel marked me..."* he trailed off, remembering Avery's words when they first ran into each other. *"You know something about it."*

"A little. Come," Avery said, tugging his arm. *"I know someone who can help."*

Ryan didn't want to go, so he stayed rooted for a second more before giving in. If he would get answers, he had to trust someone at some point.

They walked through the forest in relative silence. There were chirping birds and scurrying rodents, but otherwise, it was calm and quiet. Ryan knew they were headed West but didn't know the exact destination. It had been years since he had traversed the forest at any great distance, but he wasn't alarmed because Avery was calm.

Avery stopped him when they reached the forest's edge again. This time, it overlooked a rocky outcrop near a cliffside, and Ryan saw a cave mouth not far from the river. He looked Ryan dead in the eye and poked his nose. *"Try to be nice, will you?"* he asked.

Ryan rolled his eyes and swatted Avery's hands away. *"Am I known for my ability to be nice? Also, you're about to lose your touching privileges,"* he said.

"That's why I'm askin' you to try. Let me do most of the talkin'. Don't do anythin' dumb," Avery said.

They walked into the cave, and Ryan crouched. He was a little too tall to stand straight, which didn't make him feel any better. As if sensing his agitation, Avery slipped his hand into Ryan's and gave a slight tug. He was overly touchy for some reason, but it would be a lie if Ryan said he wasn't comforted. It reminded him of all the times they got into trouble as kids, and he knew Avery was right by his side.

"Dante will figure you out," Avery said, nodding. He kept his eyes forward, and their footsteps echoed off the too-close stone walls as they headed into the cave.

Ryan tried to focus on the crackling fire within to calm his nerves, but it didn't help. The cave opened into a ten-foot clearing with high ceilings. A cot, blankets, furs, and bags of dried food were scattered about.

A man sat beside the fire, whittling a piece of dead wood. He was a little older than Justin, with hair that was turning white and soft silver eyes. His hair was mid-back length and stringy. It lay loose and blew in the smallest of breezes. Dante didn't look at the strangers who entered his home without permission.

"Dante, this is Ryan. He has questions about chaos," Avery said as they approached.

"What's a bunch of kids want with chaos?" Dante asked. His voice was a lot deeper than Ryan had imagined.

"Who are you calling a-"

Avery elbowed him hard enough to bring tears to his eyes. *"Ryan's got foot-in-mouth syndrome,"* he said.

Dante chuckled and poked the fire with a large stick, setting his whittling project aside. *"What can I tell you?"*

Ryan looked at Avery but waved him on. *"I was cursed. I need to know what that means,"* he said. He stumbled over his words as he tried to structure things appropriately. The more nervous he got, the harder it was to form coherent sentences.

"It means something different for everyone. How long ago?" Dante asked.

Ryan shrugged. *"More than a month,"* he said. *"I was told if I stayed positive, the thing would wear off."* Maybe. He couldn't be sure that's how the conversation with Justin went.

Dante shot Avery a glance.

Avery shook his head furiously. *"Not me. That would be the Breanin brothers."*

As if that cleared everything up, Dante sighed. *"They always were a bunch of soft-boiled eggs. Never can tell the truth even if it means death,"* he murmured.

Ryan's heart dropped. *"And what's the truth?"* he asked.

"You will be controlled. No, 'if' about it," Dante said.

Ryan sighed and ran a hand through his hair. He knew there was a reason he didn't like doing what Avery told him to. He sat and buried his face in his hands. If he knew it was coming, he could probably find a way to prepare himself.

"Worst case scenario is you don't survive," Dante said with a shrug.

Ryan blinked. He bit back his sarcasm and closed his eyes. "Okay, it's time to go," Ryan muttered, switching back to common.

Avery grabbed his arm and held him in place. "Wait, we need to figure out what to do after that."

Ryan frowned. "After, what do you mean after?"

Dante smirked and poked the fire. *"After you turn,"* he said. He was more in tune with common than he let on.

"After I turn." Ryan hesitated. He didn't want to ask, but when Avery refused to meet his eyes, he had little choice. *"Turn what?"* He looked at Dante.

Dante shot Avery a look and huffed in exasperation.

"I was gonna leave that part out," Avery whispered.

"What are you talking about?" Ryan's heart thundered in his ears.

Avery held up his hands and shook his head. He opened and closed his mouth like a fish. *"I didn't lie. Can't be a lie if I didn't say anythin'."*

"It's a lie by omission," Ryan shouted. He jumped to his feet, and the room spun. He was getting too worked up.

"Ya'll fight like a married couple. Get out of my cave," Dante said.

Ryan shook his head. *"Whoa, whoa, whoa. I need more information about what this turning thing means. You can't kick me out yet."*

"You're going to become a Descendant of Chaos, kid."

Ryan glared at Avery and lunged. "I'm going to what?" his voice echoed off the cave walls.

Avery yelped as Ryan slammed into his chest and knocked him onto the ground. "I wasn't gonna say. It isn't important. You're still you."

Ryan punched him in the face. "That's not all, you stupid son of a..."

Dante pulled them apart and threw a dark violet wall to separate them.

Ryan scowled and shot Avery the middle finger. "He can't protect you forever. Wait till I get you alone. You're dead."

"I was tryin' to protect you, to ease you into it," Avery said, holding his hands.

Ryan ripped out of Dante's grip. "I'm not going to become a Descendant of Chaos. I'm better off dead," he snarled.

"Talk to Justin if you think that way," Avery said.

Ryan froze at the entrance. *Justin.*

It was nearly evening when Ryan returned to Haven, reviewing the conversation in his head. He wanted to ask Justin so many things, but why would he be now if the man wasn't forthcoming with the information? Would he try to lie?

Ryan stopped at the gravesites where Dawson and Justin's wife had been buried.

The man sat before his wife's white marble grave with a cup of water and a book. Ryan didn't understand the book; the man was blind. He hesitated in the trees, keeping himself shrouded as his heart beat against his ribs. This was a bad idea. The more information he had, the worse it would be because he already knew the end game.

"Are you going to come out of hiding anytime soon?" Justin asked. There was a smile in his voice.

Ryan figured he couldn't hide from the man who could see without sight. He walked over to Justin and stared at Dawson's and Jess' graves. "I have a serious question," he said. His voice caught in his throat, and he had to clear it to finish.

Justin took a sip of his water. "No need to ask. I *am* a Descendant of Chaos," he said. Leave it to the man to be a step ahead.

Ryan's heart sank, and he dropped to the ground with it. The grass was cold and moist, but he didn't pay attention. He was going to end up one of them – amonster in a world that hurt others.

"It's not the worst thing," Justin said. I felt like my world was imploding, but I've learned to cope." His eyes didn't leave the gravestone. Having people support you makes it easier."

Ryan swallowed thickly. A cool breeze ruffled his hair, but he didn't move even though it felt nice on his overheated skin. "Why are you hiding it from everyone?" Ryan asked, his voice emotionless. He stared at Dawson's grave and tried to dislodge the lump in his throat.

Justin chuckled bitterly. "I pulled you out of a city terrorized by a woman who controls chaos. None of you would've trusted me if I announced what I was." He held his cup up like he was toasting before taking another drink.

"So, it's better just to pretend you're normal." Ryan didn't think he could pretend like that. He needed to learn what the change entailed and how obvious it would be. His energy would never be the same.

"Magik is viewed as abnormal inherently. It doesn't matter what branch you come from," Justin said.

Ryan pulled his knees to his chest and sucked in a shaking breath. "I'm scared."

"Magik isn't good or evil. It depends on how you use it," Justin said with a small smile. "Descendants of Fire or Water could be just as bad as Angel. It doesn't mean anything, just means you'll have more access to magik."

Ryan grunted. He knew the man was trying to help, but he wasn't. He was honestly making things worse. Before Angel, Ryan didn't even know what chaos was. Seeing what she could do with it made him realize it was a magik no one should possess. It controlled man, and it was awful. He didn't want to tempt himself with such a horrible power.

"I've learned quite a few things. Things that can be used to help and heal. Chaos is a unique branch that can easily be abused," Justin said, confirming his thoughts.

Ryan turned his head to study his profile.

Gray streaked the man's hair, and his skin was pale—paler than any other wilder he had ever met. He was lanky and thin; sometimes, his cheekbones were sunken in, but he looked refreshed today—more so than usual.

"Like what?"

Justin grinned. "You sure you wanna know?"

Ryan nodded and then remembered the man was blind. "Yeah."

"Well, for one, I can do this." He snapped his fingers, and a small flame appeared above his finger.

Ryan blinked. "Wait, how're you..." he didn't finish the question.

"Chaos was long used to catalog weapons, magik, and other Descendants. They were history keepers, and anyone who wanted in-depth training could go to them," Justin said. "Through studying the elements, they learned how to borrow other magik. That's when other factions began to fear them."

"Borrow other magik. So, you can use whatever magik you want?"

"The only magiks I know and have studied are wind, fire, and water. Learning more has a downside: It makes the chaos harder to control," Justin said.

Ryan frowned. "What about healing?"

"Ah yes, that's a trick I learned from my wife. I can't conjure lightning or anything fancy, but I can heal and use some of my energy in ways others can't," he said.

Ryan sighed and curled tighter on himself. "I don't want more power. I want to be me."

"So long as you remain true to yourself, you can't lose who you are," Justin said. "It's easy to get lost in the darkness of life, but there will always be good things. If you find your light, this gets easier."

"Like what?"

"Like your brother or Kara." Justin's voice softened. "It's a setback, but you will survive, Ryan. You're stronger than you think."

He knew how strong he was. That was never an issue. A part of him wondered if he was in the situation he was in because of how strong he was. Sighing, he looked at Dawson's blue-painted headstone and hummed to himself. *One day at a time.*

Ryan didn't have much time left if Dante was right and would indeed fall under Angel's control. He had to make the most of it to ensure everything would be fine without him. He had to be there for Killian for as long as he could. He took a shaky breath and nodded. Owls hooted in the distance, and he shivered.

"Can you help me?" he asked.

"Help you with what?"

Ryan blinked and turned his head to stare at Justin. "Teach me to respect magik before it's too late," he said.

A ghost of a smile flickered across Justin's lips. He nodded and set his cup down. "I will do all that I can."

Some relief washed through him, quieting the worry and anxiety he had fought with since leaving Avery in Rochester. "Is Tory alright?" he asked.

"Of course, I'm an exceptional healer." Justin chuckled. "No permanent harm done."

At least he hadn't killed anyone... yet.

Once the Full Moon Rises

ANGEL

"It's a boy, you know?" Jessica said, letting the magik fall from around her hands. "He's strong too and growing every day." Her voice was gentle as she tried to coax Rebecca into a sitting position.

The woman didn't smile, she had forgotten how since the letter. It was only a moon after she received the news that she discovered she was with child. Jess had broken the news to her over breakfast one morning, and Rebecca hadn't gotten out of bed since.

"You'll have a piece of Aryn, Bec. This isn't the end of the world," Jess whispered.

What would you know? You're happily ever after built you a damn house. Rebecca didn't move. She let her sister change the blanket and open the blinds in the guest room she had been holed up in.

"At least eat something today. You don't want to risk something happening to the baby," Jess said with a sigh. Her voice was still soft but had grown a little firmer.

Rebecca sat up with a snarl. "Just leave me alone."

Jess frowned, her concern fading with the smile. She crossed her arms, and her hip jutted to the side like when she was angry. "We're not doing this anymore. Get up and get out of bed. We're going on a walk, you're getting new clothes, and you're eating. If you aren't out of this room-"

Justin grabbed his wife's arm, pulling her into the hall, where they had a harshly whispered conversation before Jessica stormed away. Justin returned, tying his hair back into a ponytail, and gestured to Rebecca.

"What?" she growled.

"Let me show you something," he said. "There's a place I think will help you."

Rebecca was seconds from biting his head off, but at the warm smile and extended hand, her rage subsided a little. "Are you using magik on me?" she asked.

"Never would without permission. Is that a yes?" There was a tad of amusement in his tone, but his brown eyes remained serious and calm.

Rebecca never understood how their relationship worked because her sister was so hotheaded that she often couldn't see past her emotions to have normal conversations. Justin was the opposite, although he managed to have an impressive amount of silent arrogance.

Justin took her outside, and Rebecca stared at the bright blue sky. A soft wind blew through the grass, playing in Nick's shoulder-length hair as he giggled on the front lawn.

The boy looked up as they walked out. His eyes were bright and cheery. "Morning! I made you flowers," he said, pointing to a patch of grass at her feet.

She stepped back as bright purple and blue flowers sprouted to life, making her eyes mist over. Rebecca knelt and brushed her fingers across the long, slim petals, which reminded her of the velvet cloths her dad used to bring home.

"I hope they make you feel better," Nick said, a wide grin spreading across his chubby, freckled cheeks.

Rebecca smiled back. "It does."

Justin waved him away, telling him Jess had sweet bread in the kitchen for him. He ran off, not needing any further prodding. Justin smirked and gestured for her to follow.

Rebecca stood again and sighed. She had already committed this much, so now she figured she might as well see it through. Setting a hand on her firming stomach, she walked after him.

"I know things have been hard." Angel stood before a massive crowd in front of Yorklyn Towers. "Since the horrible attack on the school, we have lost many good people." Her voice was steady despite the swirl of emotions in her mind. "My heart breaks with every mother who had to say goodbye to their child." She pressed a palm to her chest and furrowed her brow to look sympathetic.

A soft murmur ran through the crowd as sparks of energy burned to life outside the veil of chaos. Her spell was wearing thin since Ryan's curse. Her eyes flicked amongst the stern, worried faces of her citizens. There had to be a way to salvage the situation. If there weren't, everything she did would be in vain. Her heart fluttered at the thought. She wouldn't admit defeat, not yet.

"We will rebuild stronger. So strong that no one will be able to take it from us again," Angel said. Her voice carried without a microphone, as it always did, but she tried to keep it soft and understanding. The best way to lure people out was through a false sense of security, and since hurting the kids had reversed so much of her spell thanks to love, she had to be sure to step carefully. "There will be a memorial built for all the lives lost that fateful day, and I will up the guard to ensure that no other magiks can get in these walls," Angel said.

"Kill them all!" a woman screamed. Probably one who lost her snot nose, little brat.

Angel bit back a smile and allowed her face to fall. "There's been enough death, and many were orphaned. I propose a work solution where parents who lost their children can be mentors to those who lost their parents. We all need to pull together…"

"You can't replace what you've taken from us!" a man shouted.

There was an angry chorus of agreement from different families.

Angel bit her tongue and tried to keep her face impassive. It would feed the fear if she got angry now, and more would break free. "I am not trying to replace anything. I cannot replace a child that was-"

Another woman cut her off, "How would you know? You don't even have children!"

Angel took a steadying breath and clenched her hands on the podium. The snarling, angry faces staring back at her were of broken, terrified people who didn't know what was happening to them. She couldn't blame them for overactive emotions when losing a child.

"I *am* a mother, but I lost my son when he was born," she said, barely keeping herself from shouting.

A hush fell over the crowd. Angel paused, expecting some backlash or maybe an argument, but when no one spoke, she continued, "My baby boy died shortly after I gave birth. I didn't even get to say goodbye because I had fallen unconscious, so don't tell me that I don't know what you're feeling. I understand better than anyone."

There was some weeping and a stifled sob from the unhappy mothers to her left. Angel steadied her nerves and patted the podium with a nod. "I am establishing stronger ties to Rochester. Expect new shipments," she said. She got off the stand and walked toward the tower without another word.

Her heart thrummed in her ears as she tried to forget what she had brought to the forefront of her mind. It had been years since she thought of her loss, and she couldn't handle a breakdown right now.

"The Rochester envoy will be arriving soon," her General said in a low voice.

Angel nodded and pinched the bridge of her nose. She had one more thing to do, so it was time to freshen up.

The smile was back on her face as she stood in the lobby of Yorklyn Tower awaiting the envoy. She wanted this meeting to be the absolute best impression so she could weasel her way into the homestead, courtesy of Avery. Without him, this meeting wouldn't have happened, so she had to make sure to get it right. When the green jeep pulled in front of the building, Angel opened the glass doors and stepped out so no one could call her an ungracious hostess.

"Welcome!" Angel said the moment a weathered woman stepped out of a military-grade jeep. She smiled wide and held her hands out peacefully.

The older woman had a leathery face and dark eyes. Feathers and beads dangled in her snow-white hair, peppered with dark gray. She carried a long, feathered staff that was cracked and dry like her skin. She looked up briefly at Angel before murmuring to her fledgling child and waving her hand.

Angel was wise enough to know the woman was frustrated with something. Her eye twitched, but she didn't let the smile fall.

"Grandmama wants to know where nature is," the young priestess in training said. Her eyes were clear blue and as stern as her grandmother's posturing.

They wore beautiful skirts and robes hand-sewn from Rochester's finest fabrics. They wore dark reds and oranges with embroidered patterns along the hems. The priestess wore a baggy top adorned with certain crystals and gems. The same gems were on bracelets that she covered her wrists and ankles. The younger of the two wore tight shirts that exposed her middle and shorter skirts with fur lining the edges. Her outfit was more straightforward, stating her status in comparison. Neither wore shoes, and their feet were dingy from the forest floor.

"Nature doesn't survive within the walls," Angel said, gesturing to the towering steel structures. "This place was intended to save people after the war, not nature."

The priestess spoke in her guttural language and didn't bother looking at Angel. She waved her staff, and something jingled on it. The woman was quite upset about the lack of trees.

Angel huffed. Maintaining her composure with someone who wouldn't look at her was harder. Angel had to remind herself that people outside Yorklyn didn't view her as a leader. She had to prove herself to them before they would accept her.

"Grandmama isn't comfortable being away from the forest. She won't stay long," the child said. She jutted her chin out, but her trembling hands gave her away.

Angel nodded and walked them inside the tower. "I know this is different from your home, but I believe my city has a lot to offer," she said, holding her hands behind her back.

The younger girl translated everything that was said. The priestess curtly replied and waddled ahead of Angel to look at the plastic trees in the lobby.

Angel looked to the child for translation. Although she grew up outside Rochester, the language had long left her when she left it behind to take over the city.

The priestess's face was red, and she wouldn't make eye contact. "She doesn't agree."

Angel kept the smile in place despite recognizing some of the unsavory words the holy woman spoke. "I'm sure we could find some agreement. I mean, Yorklyn has many bright minds," she said.

What was the point in accepting her invitation if they didn't want anything to do with her? Trying to use a spell over them now would be too suspicious. There were too many people watching, and she couldn't risk the priestess' mind being too strong to counter her spell.

"Grandmama only came to invite you to the new moon ceremony," the young girl said.

Angel frowned. Leaving the city to trot around the woods wasn't appealing.

The old woman cackled at the look on her face. "She doesn't like idea," she said. "Told you, witch in disguise."

Angel bit her tongue to keep from saying anything harmful. Why didn't she tell Angel if the old bat understood the common tongue? This woman kept her cards close which meant she had something to hide.

"I'm no witch. I aim to protect our world from witches." Angel crossed the room, her heels clicking against the marble.

The sound echoed off the walls and glass windows of the structure. She didn't know the plan, but she must have looked intimidating because the young woman ran ahead to place herself before her elder.

Angel sighed and pinched the bridge of her nose. "What is it with you outsiders? I am only trying to extend a kindness," she said.

The young girl kept her face stern. "We've come to extend a hand to you," she said. "Will you come to see our ceremony at the end of the cycle?"

Angel pursed her lips and nodded. She watched the priestess stroke the plastic plant in disgust before moving away from it. "Yes, I would love to come," she said.

They both perked up and stared hard, no doubt trying to determine if she was lying. Angel put on her most charming smile and held out her hand. "I look forward to seeing your community," she said. "Maybe then we can build a relationship."

Oh, how she would love to shove that priestess into a lake.

"Go back to forest now," the woman said. "Done here." She waddled back to the doors, and Angel smiled and waved.

This meeting didn't go as well as she hoped. Hopefully, the next one will be better.

Avery was waiting in her room when she finished seeing the envoy off. A smile split his face when she walked in, and she frowned. He was in a torn hoodie and jeans, looking remarkably normal.

When he saw her face, he sighed. "I teleported in, so stop lookin' like someone might figure you out," he said.

"That's not what I'm concerned about. Surely you own something without holes in it?" she asked, walking over to him and wiping some dirt off his cheek.

He slapped her hands away as he rolled his eyes. "Come on, I'm nearly nineteen. Will you stop treatin' me like a child?" He kicked his feet up on her end table until she crossed her arms with a glare.

"Stop acting like one, then. What is it with kids thinking they're magically adults when their age changes?" she asked.

"Did you take the invite to the moon ceremony?" Avery asked. "Because I can get Ryan there. Easy to pick him up and bring him home."

Angel was momentarily confused until she remembered what Avery was there for. "Wait, you're getting the fire boy to the festival?" she asked.

Avery clicked his tongue with a childish grin. "You hired me to do a job,. Did you think I wouldn't deliver?" he asked.

She opened her mouth and shut it again. He had arranged a meeting with the high priestess to hand deliver the cursed boy. Angel smiled warmly and bowed her head. "Thank you," she said. "I accepted the invitation."

"Good, then I'll be seein' you in a few nights," he said, hopping out of her chair and walking to the door.

Angel watched him go and opened her mouth to say something but shut it again. Aside from what had already been said, she didn't know what to say, so she let him go with just that smile. One of them did their job; now, it was her turn.

Welcome to the Shadow Realm

KILLIAN

Killian took a breath and walked onto Avery's front lawn. They had agreed to do the shadow realm thing first thing in the morning because the absence of the night would help reduce Killian's strength in case something went wrong. He held a cup of steaming hot coffee as a peace offering because if he knew anything about Avery, he wasn't a morning person.

"You're here too damn early," Avery slurred, covering his eyes from the sun. It was much harder to understand him when he spoke common when he first woke up.

"You said first thing in the morning, and this is morning, so.... Unless you want me to go and try again later," Killian said, nodding back to Haven.

Avery blinked, bleary-eyed, and stared at the cup in Killian's hands. "What's that?"

Killian shrugged and held out the cup. "Um... coffee. I thought maybe because you were... I don't know. Do you want it?" he asked. That was odd. What was he nervous about?

Avery took the cup without giving him Helwe. "Thanks," he said. His voice was gruff and thick with sleep, and Killian cocked his head to the side curiously.

Ryan was the only person he had seen first thing in the morning, and his brother was often less than pleasant. Killian looked back toward Haven, wondering if he should give Avery a few more hours to wake up.

"Do you tend to memorize the homes of people you don't like?" Avery asked, downing the cup in three goes.

"Um, no, I just..." Killian trailed off and furrowed his brow. He memorized where Avery lived and hadn't even struggled to return. It had been three days since his last brief visit, and he still got there without a problem. "Maybe," he added.

Avery yawned and set the cup down. "Alright, tell me a little about the special place in your head where the magik is contained," he said.

Killian shrugged. "Um... it's dark. With a piano," he said. It had been months since he was in that tiny little room with the murderous creature, so he couldn't say for sure.

"That's... helpful," Avery said, nodding for him to continue.

Killian shrugged again.

Avery chuckled and clapped his hands. "Show me," he said.

Killian considered the pros and cons as he developed a list. If he didn't get help, Justin would eventually kill him. If he did, Avery would know every one of his deepest secrets because this was a space in his head that not even Ryan was allowed to traverse.

Avery chuckled and leaned against a tree. "What're you afraid of? I might see those demons and judge you. " His voice was too casual about Killian's internal crisis.

Killian sighed and ran a hand through his hair as he fortified his mental barriers to keep Ryan unaware. It had been difficult hiding this from him for the last couple of days, but he had done it.

"You wanna do this inside or out?" Avery asked.

"Doesn't matter." Killian kept his voice calm despite the internal panic.

Avery nodded and sat in the grass. "Fine, let's do it." He held out a hand again and smirked. "I'll keep my thoughts to myself," he said.

"I don't know how to do this," Killian said. He also didn't get to control it; nine times out of ten, he ended up in this realm without wanting to.

"Just imagine being there," he said. "And when you do, imagine me there too. So long as we're touchin', it should work."

Killian had a million questions. How did Avery know about this? Why had Killian never heard of it? He didn't understand how a Descendant of Water knew so much more than he did. Was this safe? Could they die? He should have waited to do it until he got answers, so instead of asking, he slipped his hand into Avery's and nodded. This was called a leap of faith or whatever. It's not like it would be the end of the world if something went wrong.

He closed his eyes and tried to clear his mind. Normally, the shadow only came out when he was upset or angry, but since he had kept his emotions in check, that hadn't been a problem.

Let me in.

The shadow roared through his head, and Killian flinched. He squeezed Avery's hand, forgetting himself, and then the world melted around them. One minute, he was on the forest floor, and the next, he was in a familiar dark room. A smiling black shadow with crimson eyes stared at him from a piano with raven keys. Red curtains lined the walls and dripped with blood.

The shadow moved, and Killian's heart whooshed through his ears. *I'm going to die. I can't do this. Bad idea. Terrible idea.*

"So, this is where you go. I see the thing about the piano. Kinda gloomy," Avery said. He nodded as he looked around as if appraising a new piece of land. He paid zero attention to the creature behind the piano.

Killian's stomach lurched. "I want to go back," he hissed through clenched teeth.

Avery shook his head. "Now, calm down. Let's see what we've got with this big bad shadow," he said. He was going to provoke it.

Killian didn't think he could handle an out-of-control shadow. It was already mad. His fingers dug into Avery's skin. "Please don't," he whispered. He hated how weak he sounded.

Avery shot him a look.

Killian shivered under his gaze and dug his nails deeper into Avery's palm. His fingers hurt from clenching, but he was afraid to let go. What if Avery left? Killian hadn't faced his shadow since Yorklyn since he denied it what it wanted after saving his brother at the cost of multiple lives.

Avery frowned and reached up, brushing his knuckles to Killian's cheek. "It's goin' to be alright. Breathe."

The shadow curled its lips over fang-like teeth.

Killian grimaced but didn't move. "I'm not ready. Let me go back, I thought I could, but-"

Red eyes flicked to Avery, and an oily tongue slipped from the shadow's mouth. *"You're a pathetic brat. Did you think bringing someone else would save you from my wrath?"* The shadow laughed and loomed over Killian, stretching as far as the room would allow before wrapping around him, clenching him in a vice.

Killian let out a gasp as the air was squeezed from his lungs. The shadow ripped him from Avery's side, and his heart plummeted. *Let go!* He squirmed against the shadow's hold as his lungs screamed for air.

"You're even more pathetic," it hissed, glaring. Those eyes burned into his soul, and his body went limp.

Avery, please! He didn't want to be killed in his head. The pressure didn't release, and a shard of ice tore through his chest like he was submerged in water. His vision began to spot black.

Avery growled and pressed his palm to the shadow's body. A black-light encased it, and the pressure around Killian lessened, allowing him to suck in some much-needed air. "Let go before I do somethin' we both regret," he said dangerously. His voice was an animalistic growl, and his eyes flashed blue.

The shadow dropped Killian, screeching in fury. A wave of terror washed over him, and Killian buried his face in his hands. *I can't do this.*

The shadow slid around the room, moving in slow circles. *"You're weak. You'll always be weak."*

Avery kneeled between Killian and the shadow. He smiled softly and said in Nivet, *"Of all the people with low self-esteem, I didn't... you're not weak."*

Killian looked at him, tears clinging to his eyelashes, and the room brightened. Candles around the edges of the circle lit up, and the shadow screeched, recoiling from the light.

Avery looked around and smirked. "Well, that's all it takes. A little firin' up?" he asked. He stood and held his hand down.

Killian stared at it. There were some abrasions around his wrist from where he had been clinging when they first arrived. Blood beaded the superficial wounds, and his lip wobbled. *I'm pathetic.*

Avery smiled down at him. *"Hey, we're alike, you and me. Bein' scared and feelin' like the world will collapse. All that matters is how you deal,"* he said. *"So, how are you goin' to deal?"*

Killian set his hand in Avery's and let him pull him up. "I'm going to learn to control it," he said, but he didn't sound as sure as he felt.

"Then let's go home." Avery grinned—one of those joyous, bright things that Killian hated. *"Don't say the word home. If you do, we'll end up on Justin's land, and he'll run a spear through my chest."*

Killian blinked in mild surprise. "That's an oddly specific thing to say," he said.

"We all have our secrets," Avery whispered, gently squeezing his hand.

The shadow roared and surged across the candles, putting them out. Avery clasped his hand and shook him. "I don't want to die here. Get us out, now!" All joy and happiness were gone as he demanded Killian release them.

Killian closed his eyes and pulled them back to Avery's yard. Everything was silent aside from the raging form in his head.

Avery's face split into a massive smile before he leaned back and covered his face. "Holy, that just happened. I've never - I got no words. Has that ever happened?"

Killian wasn't in such high spirits. He wasn't sure how Avery bounced back so fast. "Can you not talk for a minute?" he asked, trying not to sound rude.

Avery chuckled and tapped his fingers against his thigh. "I'll try to contain my excitement," he said.

It was a relaxing gesture. Killian watched Avery's fingers dance along his shorts with fascination. It was also something Ryan did when he was nervous, and Killian wondered if Avery was where that habit came from. The longer they sat in silence, the slower he could force his heart rate.

When he returned to normal, Killian sighed and fell back into the grass, a small smile flickering across his lips. "Let's not do that again," he said.

Killian sat on the bedroom floor with crossed legs and closed eyes. Ryan kicked the door shut as he walked in, his footsteps thumping across the boards in agitation as he stormed to his bed.

"You look like you've had a good day," Killian said with a smirk.

"If you call avoiding the crazy man a good day, mine's been terrific," Ryan muttered as he threw his pillow over his face.

Killian opened his eyes and leaned back on his palms with a chuckle. He was in a good mood, considering he almost died that morning. "Justin isn't so bad, he's trying to help, and you're... being you." Killian waved with a shrug.

Ryan fingered his side and looked at Killian. "I think he broke my rib when I told him he was a dick," he said.

Killian laid back and stared at the ceiling with a smirk. "I woulda done the same."

Ryan pulled the pillow away from his face and stared at the ceiling. There was a painting above his bed, and Nicholas had supposedly done it years ago, along with several others. This one was of a beautiful tropical forest with ivy and flowers. The colors were so vibrant that Killian could almost smell the sweet scent of pollen and fruit.

"Can I ask you something?" Ryan asked, keeping his eyes on the painting.

Killian dropped his gaze and studied his brother's profile. He was tanning from spending so much time in the woods and training, but he looked troubled tonight. "What?" he asked.

Ryan hesitated before finally looking over at him. "Why are you hanging out with Avery so much?" his eyes flashed with concern and worry, though Killian didn't know what he could worry about.

He went rigid. His walls hadn't been as foolproof as he had thought. "We had an unspoken agreement not to talk about anything we pulled from each other's minds," he said.

Ryan sighed and rolled onto his side. His hand fell over the side of the mattress, and he traced shapes into the soft rug with his finger. "I think we should... do something with it."

"With Avery or..." Killian trailed off. He didn't like where this conversation was going and honestly didn't want to be forced into a lie with his brother.

"No, the mind thing," Ryan said. Killian was still trying to figure out how to reply when his brother sighed in irritation and continued, "What's going on with Avery? I mean, you hated him when we were kids. Don't you remember how mean you were?"

"Can we get off the subject?" Killian asked. He couldn't help the bite in his voice, and he looked away before Ryan could read the mounting frustration in his gaze.

"I just wanna know what you're doing," Ryan said, sounding defensive. "You were the one who told me to watch it, and now you're hanging out with him."

Killian shot off the floor, trying to build the wall back in his head. It wasn't fair for him to blatantly disrespect the rule. "I don't!" he shouted, punching Ryan in the arm. "And even if I was, it's not your business."

Ryan pouted but didn't say anything more.

Killian scoffed and fled the room before he could say something he regretted. He didn't hang out with Avery all the time, and the only reason he was was to avoid hurting someone – to avoid hurting Cody.

'I didn't mean to...' Ryan's voice was cut off when Killian snapped a black wall between their minds.

Silence. For once, he wanted silence. He hurried down the metal stairwell and ignored Nicholas' prying eyes as he rushed out the front door into the crisp night air. His throat tightened as he zipped through the shadows, using his teleportation spells to propel him as far from Haven – from Ryan as possible.

He stopped when a flash of blue jolted before him, and he crashed into Avery. Killian swore out loud as they flew to the ground with curses and grunts.

"Wow, you... I mean, come on. Do you not look where you're going when you shadow walk?" Avery asked, rubbing his head. A trickle of blood slid from his temple as he pushed himself into a sitting position.

Killian's world was still spinning as he tried to catch his breath and rebuild his drained energy. "Sorry," he muttered.

Avery groaned as he stood, wiping his hands on his pants. "What's wrong?"

"Ryan." Killian didn't want to talk about it. He was content with sitting behind his black walls of silence and ignoring the world.

Avery held down a hand and smirked. "Want to go for a run?" he asked.

No, I want to be alone. Killian took Avery's hand and stood, shaking from the exertion. *I don't even have the energy for it.*

And that's how Killian began a run when the moon was at its highest. He had difficulty seeing without using his spells and tripped himself up a handful of times, but when he found his stride, he broke through the trees without problem. Killian managed to stay close behind Avery despite having previously exhausted himself. His chest swelled with pride at the thought. Nicholas' stamina training had been helping.

Killian took in the strong scent of pine and pollen as they ran through. His lungs burned, and his heart pounded against his ribcage, but he felt amazing. His energy surged around him, and he flickered in and out of sight as he ran through the shadows and whooped with glee. They stopped at the bottom of a cliff, and Killian doubled over, wiping the sweat from his face and panting. His chest was tight, and he had a hard time breathing, but his mind was clear, and he felt more like himself than he had in a long time.

Avery smirked and leaned on the rock wall, shaking his head. "You don't get out enough," he said.

Killian gathered the energy to flip him off, but he grinned as he did it. He didn't care about anything, which meant Avery couldn't say anything to upset him. Avery lit up a cigarette and sighed heavily. Smoke streamed through the air, and Killian wrinkled his nose. He thought he escaped that smell when Ryan quit.

"I have bad days, too," Avery said after a while.

Killian looked at him curiously. He didn't understand where that came from.

As if sensing his confusion, Avery continued, "I was cold to you and Ryan when we ran into each other... I took it out on you. The bad day."

Killian looked away and fiddled with his shirt sleeve. "Is this your way of apologizing?" he asked.

"No, I don't do that," Avery said with a smirk. "This is my way of tellin' you that I don't always mean how I act."

Killian nodded and refused to meet his gaze. "Yeah, well... thanks for earlier. The shadow realm thing, I... I appreciate you being there for me." Something tightened in his chest, and he felt it had nothing to do with the fact that he had just run however many miles.

Avery dropped the smoke and stamped it out, leaning forward so Killian could see the humor in his black eyes. "Friends then?" he asked, holding out his hand.

Killian smiled. "Fine, yeah, friends. What's the worst that can happen?"

A New Me

KARA

Killian was on the porch reading a book he picked up from Justin's library. Every so often, he would go through Justin's shelves of books in his room, take a few, and read them in days. They were always about war or strategy, but she caught him reading one about two people falling in love once and swore he was crying. When she approached him about it, he punched her in the arm and dared her to bring it up again.

She climbed up the porch steps and leaned on the rail. "Hey, Rochester is-"

Killian cut her off, "No." He didn't look up.

"You don't even know what-"

"The full moon festival. No, I don't want to go. Have fun," he said, cutting her off again.

Kara grumbled to herself and pushed away from the white railing. "You're no fun," she said.

Killian shot her a look that could kill the strongest of men. "You've been wickedly cruel the last few weeks, sent Ryan into a depression and yelled at everyone who looks at you wrong. Why the Helwe would I want to go to a festival with you?" he asked in a completely monotone voice.

Kara flinched as if he had physically struck her. The words stung, but he wasn't wrong, so she didn't let herself get overly defensive. "I know," she said with a long sigh. "I'm trying to be better, alright? I know I've been awful and... I'm sorry." She turned to look at him, though his expression didn't change. "I was so stuck on myself and my pity party that I didn't care what I was doing to the rest of you. I am trying to be better," she promised.

He nodded, and his eyes flicked back to his book. "You're forgiven," he said.

Kara beamed. "So, you'll-"

"No."

She sighed and went inside, less eager to have the same conversation with Ryan. If he didn't want to go, she could take Tory and Nicholas, but she would like to go with Ryan. The thought made her chew the inside of her cheek as those self-destructive thoughts tried to intervene.

I am allowed to be happy and live life, but that doesn't mean I've forgotten the pain of others. She let Justin's mantra run through her head as she climbed the stairs in the corner of the living room.

A flicker of red danced in the ceiling above her. Ryan usually didn't leave his room until it was freezing outside, so no one would bother him while he did whatever he did.

She knocked and held her breath.

Ryan opened the door, and his eyes widened in surprise. "Kara." He didn't say anything more, but he didn't sound angry. He didn't delve into an immediate lecture about her attitude, and she almost wished she would over the awkward silence.

"I'm sorry," she blurted.

"For uh... what?" he asked, looking up and down the hall like she was setting him up.

She was not setting him up, so he didn't have to look petrified. *He's probably hoping there's someone close to pull you off him when you try to kill him.* "For everything," she said. Her words spilled before she could stop them. "I've been absolute garbage, and I don't hate you, by the way. I was angry at everyone, at me. I hated myself for being happy, and then when you came back..." she trailed off. Some things didn't need to be said when she tried apologizing. Her head snapped up as she realized how she sounded. "I'm not trying to make excuses, and I want you to know I won't be that person anymore," she said.

Ryan opened his mouth, but she slapped her hand over it so she could finish. His eyebrows rose in surprise, but he didn't fight her.

"I also want to take you to the full moon festival in Rochester tomorrow night," she said. "As penance."

He chuckled and leaned on the doorframe. When she removed her hand, he nodded. "Are you asking me on a date, Ms. McKenzie?"

Her cheeks burned at the insinuation. "I would n-"

"Of course she is," Tory cut her off.

Her eye twitched in annoyance. "Where did you even come from?"

"I saw you run in and thought he was in danger," Tory said. "By the way, I'm a little offended you didn't ask me, but whatever. We're not best friends or anything." He waved his hand as he walked to his bedroom at the end of the hall.

She glared at his back. "Stop acting like you sleep in there. We all know you don't!"

The door shut behind him, but not before he glanced over his shoulder and flipped her off.

"I'll go with you," Ryan said. "But you can't try to fight me again."

She nodded and held out her hand. "I won't," she promised. The irritation from Tory's interruption vanished when Ryan's hand was in hers.

He was warm, and his hand was rough, but it always sent sparks of electricity through her body. She grinned excitedly and brushed her hair behind her ears to hide her nerves. "See you tomorrow night then," she said.

"I'm sure I'll see you before unless you plan on hibernating the rest of the day," he said with a cocky smirk.

Kara stuck out her tongue and nearly walked into the wall, trying to get into her room. "Don't say anything," she warned, slipping into her room and shutting the door. *Tomorrow might not be so bad.*

All Good Things Come to an End

RYAN

Ryan stared at Avery as the dark-haired nuisance stood with a large smile and arms held wide. He didn't know what to expect when Kara had asked him to go to the full moon festival, but it wasn't this. He blinked, trying to determine if he wanted to keep hanging out or take his chances with Justin's training back in Haven.

"Oh, come on, at least pretend you're happy to see me," Avery said, slipping into Nivet.

Ryan forced a smile and shot Kara a quick look, trying to determine if she set him up.

"I thought you would be happy to see your old friend," Kara said, confused by his lack of enthusiasm. She wrung her hands and stepped toward him nervously, her eyes shining with curiosity.

Ryan cleared his throat before she could feel too bad. "No, um… it's great!"

They were standing at the entrance of Rochester Homestead. The watchtowers overlooked the land, but no one was on duty, so they stood alone and empty. Ryan leaned on one of the log towers with a sigh as he tried to build his excitement despite Avery's presence. They were stiff and sturdy. Since his last visit home, the homestead continuously grew. The roads were slowly paved with rocks and gravel to lessen the dust clouds from stamping hooves.

Everyone around them chattered happily in Nivet and bartered with others who came in specifically for the festival. He hadn't seen people this happy in a long time, and it was endearing to know humanity could still smile.

"You could try a little harder," Avery whispered, his black eyes glinting in the mid-evening sunlight.

"You could try not to be such a dick. Did you seriously not tell her we weren't friends anymore?" Ryan didn't bother switching to common to keep Kara out of the loop. Not only was Avery messing with Killian, but now he had to watch Kara, too.

She beamed at him, her eyes glittering with absolute endearment. "You *can* speak it," she whispered.

Ryan smiled weakly. "Of course, I grew up with it," he said. Even if he hadn't used it much in Yorklyn, he hadn't let himself forget his native tongue.

"Say something else," Kara prodded.

He chuckled nervously and shot Avery the darkest glare he could. This was his fault. *"I hate you,"* he said.

Avery bowed and said, "Thank you good sir, I appreciate your company too." His snickers carried as Kara threw her arms around Ryan with a happy squeal.

At least he could still make her happy despite their rocky last few weeks.

Kara grabbed his hand and pulled him toward the growing crowd of people, blabbering about how excited she was to see a real native ritual. He winced at the wording and thought to tell her to watch her words, but he didn't think it would be too detrimental since so few people spoke common. Avery followed at a safe distance with crossed arms and a smug grin that made Ryan want to punch him in the nose.

The air was charged with joy and excitement, and some people near the center of the homestead had all sorts of meat roasting on a roaring fire. Brightly decorated candles and lanterns were set along the roadsides and outside houses for light when it began to get dark. Kara went from stall to stall, picking up wares and shoving them in his face before putting them back and moving to the next. In a few minutes, he had seen furs, leathers, and some weird rock jewelry.

Out of the corner of his eye, he watched Avery slip some coins on one of the stall counters and take a bright pink and white stone bracelet. It went straight into his pocket as he looked around as if he had done nothing.

"There's an awesome bookstore here, too, but it's not a store," Kara babbled excitedly. She talked like he had never seen the homestead, but Ryan didn't want to kill her excitement, so he let her talk. "You can read them anytime you want," she said.

He nodded with a forced smile and tried to keep an eye on Avery, pacing between the stalls and flirting with all the shopkeepers – man and woman alike. It looked like he hadn't changed.

When they stopped for food, Avery procured a few bits of smoked meat and juice fresh from pineapple and coconut water. Ryan took a swig and paused, holding the tart, tingly liquid in his mouth as Kara oozed about how excellent the meat was. She turned to show Avery something, and he spit it on the ground, grimacing at the yellowish liquid.

Avery smirked as Ryan dumped the contents of his cup into Avery's the next time Kara turned her back. *"Not a fan?"* he asked.

Ryan shook his head, his tongue still tingling. *"Gods, no, what is that?"*

"A new concoction. You want the usual sugar-flavored water?"

Ryan nodded, and Avery slipped back into the crowd, returning with a cup of water flavored with berries and orange. Ryan savored the sweet mix of water and juice, trying to get the nasty pineapple off his tastebuds.

Kara held out her hand. "I want to try," she said.

He smirked and handed his cup over, letting her take a swig. Her eyes widened, and she took another two gulps before he wrested the clay cup from her fingers.

"Get your own," he said with a smirk.

Avery shot him a sideways glance. "Take your own advice." There was no actual anger in his voice, though, so Ryan shrugged and drank the rest of his berry water.

Kara ate her meat and then Ryan's portion because despite Avery insisting he knew Ryan, he still bought a handful of jerky for all three.

Unexpected pain cut through Ryan's arm as Kara started conversing with Avery about his magik and why she couldn't read his energy. Ryan tried to focus on the conversation despite the heat surging through the healed wound, increasing his irritation and frustration.

"I'm a man of many talents. Stayin' hidden is one of them," Avery said, his eyes cutting to Ryan as he stopped walking.

Ryan rubbed his arm, trying not to dig his fingers into the skin, and people brushed by without noticing him, ignoring the way his eyes shot into their backs like daggers. The pain wrapped around his forearm and squeezed like a horrible muscle cramp, and he doubled over with a muffled groan.

Kara turned in concern as he gripped the surge of pain, trying to ignore it. "Are you alright?" she asked.

"They are all against you. None of them want you around," Angel's voice swam through his mind.

He wanted her to leave him alone. Of course, she would do this to him now because he was happy. Ryan hissed when another wave of pain coursed through him. He imagined that if he could feel the burn of a fire, this would be what it felt like.

Avery's hands pulled him off the ground and tightened on his shoulders. "Get it together, man. We got this," he said. For once, he didn't have a cocky smile on his stupid face. They both knew what was happening, and neither knew how much time he had.

Everything sounded so far, and the bright sunlight made his head throb. Ryan tried to shake it off, but Angel's presence bared down like a hunter who caught a small animal.

"Let me take you. You can use me for more strength." Angel's promises sounded so sweet.

Avery shook him again, and everything returned to normal.

Ryan snapped out of the trance and looked around. His hair stuck to his forehead from a combination of sweat and humidity. "I'm fine," he murmured, swaying on his feet. He brushed Avery off and caught Kara's eyes.

She had gone pale, and she twisted her face in concern.

So much for a fun outing. Way to go at being a spazz. Avery reached for him once more, but Ryan scowled. "Back off. I said I'm fine."

His non-friend let him go and nodded. "The ceremony is going to start. Do you want to watch?" he asked.

Kara opened her mouth to protest, but Ryan shook his head. He needed this to be something happy he could remember when the darker days came. "She brought me to have fun," he said. "We're seeing it."

"I don't have to-" Kara began, but he sent her a death-defying glare that shut her up.

He didn't come all this way to run home with his tail between his legs because of a bit of pain. Angel didn't own him yet. "It was a spasm. It's gone. I'm fine," he said, trying to keep his voice level.

As if sensing his desperation to drop it, Kara nodded. Avery kept looking over Ryan's shoulder, so he turned to see what was happening. Aside from a growing crowd, he saw nothing of interest. "What's wrong with you?" he asked.

Avery shook his head. "Come on, we need a translator." He was off through the crowd before Ryan could hope to read him.

I'm a translator. What are you looking for, Avery? Ryan couldn't voice his concerns, but something set him on edge about how Avery pushed through the crowd, not even glancing back to see if they were following. Ryan grabbed Kara's hand and followed, ignoring the panic in his chest. Before they could get next to the bonfire, he felt her. *Angel.* Ryan's heart slowed as he looked up and saw her standing next to the priestess.

She was right there, her hair pulled into a ponytail, but she looked out of place in her tight skirt and fancy white blouse. The priestess began the ritual chant, and soon, everyone joined.

Kara tightened her grasp on his hand, and Ryan assumed she saw her too—the woman who killed her brother and took her parents.

He couldn't breathe. The world stopped as Angel's eyes flicked to his, and a cruel smile slipped across her lips. If they ran, she would catch them or, worse, find Haven.

"I see you, boy." It was her smug voice that pulled Ryan out of his trance. He had to get Kara away.

Kara lunged forward, but Ryan wrapped an arm around her waist and dragged her to his side.

"What're you doing?" she snarled, her eyes burning with anger.

"You can't fight. The people will never forgive you for disrupting the ceremony," Ryan said, keeping his voice low as he tried to pull her away. They had to get close to Haven, where Justin and Nicholas could help them if a fight broke out.

"I don't care," she said, kicking him in the shin.

He scowled in pain and held her at arm's length. "I do. This is my culture," Ryan said. He beckoned for Avery to help him, and they pulled Kara through the crowd and down the main road toward the gates.

No one paid them any mind, and the sounds of excited chatter faded as they got further from the group.

Kara tried to scream, but Avery slapped his hand over her mouth and shot Ryan a panicked look. It would probably be frowned upon if anyone noticed two male teenagers dragging a female off.

Kara bit down on Avery's hand, and he yelped, ripping it away. "Let go," she shouted when they were safely outside the gates.

"Look, missy, you wanna start a war between humanity and magik?" Avery asked. A welt of blood appeared on his palm, and he pressed it against his tan trousers.

Ryan watched Kara's eyes clear, and she shook her head. "We should go before the witch realizes we're here," he said, looking at Avery.

Both knew the woman knew Ryan's presence, but he didn't want to worry Kara. Not when she was already so vulnerable.

"You want me to walk with you?" Avery asked.

"No," Ryan said. Because he didn't trust him despite Avery having helped get Kara under control.

Kara scoffed. "Let's get Justin and take her down." Her words were cold, and Ryan couldn't help but shiver.

He flicked his eyes toward the sky as they hurried through the forest. It was getting dark, and the path was unclear. He stepped over logs and roots without a problem and helped Kara when she stumbled. He knew the path by heart. He couldn't count how often he walked to the homestead in the dead of night to clear his head.

Kara huffed when her foot caught a root for the fifth time. She was about to faceplant, but Ryan steadied her. "Since when do you run from a fight?" she asked in a snappy tone.

"I'm running to save your life," Ryan said. He pulled her along and froze when a shadow fell over them.

The quickly dying light of the day took the warmth and replaced it with an icy wind. Ryan peered through the trees and saw Angel a few feet before them. He should've known there was no escape.

The red-haired woman stepped out from under some low branches and brushed pine needles off the front of her shirt as they fell. "I'll just be taking what's mine now," she said.

"Oh, your poor attitude?" Ryan asked. "Sure, see you around." They needed backup. He had speed on his side, but he couldn't leave Kara. He should have taken Avery up on his offer to escort them home because three was better than two.

"It's cute to see you're still spunky. We'll break that spirit in no time," Angel said, stepping toward them.

"Bite me," Ryan growled. His eyes flicked to Kara. He couldn't leave her alone, though. If there was anything worth it, it had to be her. Passion fueled his flames, and there was nothing he was more passionate about than the young woman for whom he stayed in Haven.

Kara squeezed his hand and tried to keep him moving. Her breath came in short gasps as Angel's energy surrounded them, locking them in a bubble of chest-crushing pressure.

"I'll leave your little girlfriend alive if you come willingly. Can't say what I'll do if you refuse." Angel's voice darkened under the lightness of the fake cheerfulness she maintained.

"Don't you dare use me like some damsel in distress," Kara said. Her voice was hot with offense as she sized Angel up. She stood her ground even with chaos licking after them like a rabid dog.

Angel laughed and pretended to wipe a tear from her eye. "Sweetie, please. The grownups are talking."

He couldn't fight Angel. The throbbing had already started. It was excruciating, and Ryan wasn't sure he could run if he wanted to, but he could buy Kara enough time to get out.

"What do you suppose we do?" Kara whispered.

Ryan's eyes darted through the foliage, and he shook his head. He let go of Kara, snapped his fingers, and summoned his twin short swords. They were heavy in his hands, heavier than usual, and he took a steady breath, knowing what awaited. He stepped before Kara, never once taking his eyes off their enemy.

"Get help," he ordered. His hands trembled, and he squeezed the hilt of his blades to steady his nerves.

"I'm not leaving," she said, sounding appalled.

"Kara, neither of us can take her. I have enough energy to get you out of here. Please, get Justin," he said. "I'm trusting you." He cast one glance at her over his shoulder, knowing Angel wouldn't dare attack yet.

Kara's eyes watered, but she bit her lip and nodded.

Ryan flew at Angel, giving the woman exactly what she wanted.

Angel cackled in glee and waved her hand, releasing her energy into the air.

He tumbled to the ground when pain seized his body. Ryan clutched his stomach, and his weapons vanished the minute he released them. What energy he managed to build was gone with a flick of her wrist.

"Pathetic, you can't reach me," Angel's voice cut through his thoughts. It was like being linked telepathically with Killian, except Angel's voice made him want to puke.

Kara shouted something, but it sounded so far away.

He didn't know if she was running, but his head swam. Green and brown blended before him, and he squeezed his eyes shut. Seconds later, he emptied his stomach with a low groan. *Killian.* There was something he could do. Ryan pushed the barrier away from his side of their bond so he could freely communicate with his brother.

"I need your help. Angel's got us pinned outside of Rochester." Ryan sent the message as quickly as he could. He didn't have much time with Angel bearing down on him like a hungry predator.

Twigs snapped as Angel crossed the forest and stopped in front of him. "You're never going to be what you want. Let me help," she said in that soft, seductive voice.

"Ryan, move!" Kara held out her hands.

So much for getting her out alive. He didn't need another warning. As Kara shouted her spell, he dove to the side, landing on his stomach and propping himself up on his arm. Thunder boomed, drops of rain fell, and lightning streaked across the dark gray sky. What little light they had left was about gone, and a bolt of violet lightning struck the earth, spraying dirt in the air.

Angel shrieked and backed up, waving her hands to brush off the energy.

Ryan shook his head as chaos surged through his veins, burning his skin. His hands clenched in the dirt, crushing leaves under his fingertips. His nails cracked from the pressure, but he barely felt the pain as adrenaline coursed through his body. He had to move.

A sheet of rain dropped from the sky, and he hissed in pain as the splashes of cold water made his body ache even further. He rolled under the shelter of a large oak and shook his shirt, trying to dislodge most of the water. *So much for using magik now.*

Kara's lightning spell crashed into the ground three times, but Angel was faster. She redirected the lightning using the tip of her ice spear and sent it crashing into a tree that instantly caught fire.

"Oh no," Ryan whispered. Outmatched was a gross understatement of what they were. He tried to get back to his feet, but the rest of his energy vanished, leaving him useless. His stomach rolled as a wave of nausea threatened to suck him down. Ryan squeezed his eyes shut and took a steadying breath. This wasn't going well.

Angel reached down and grabbed his chin, forcing him to look up. "I can make you great," she said.

An arrow whizzed through the air and cut across her skin. Tiny droplets of blood splattered the foliage. Angel let him go and turned to look at her attacker.

Ryan opened his eyes and wheezed.

Killian stood not far away, holding a bow. "Back off." It looked like his aim hadn't suffered from his lack of being able to practice with it.

Ryan smirked. *My hero,* he couldn't help the sarcastic thought from slipping down their link.

Killian bristled with anger, but he didn't look at Ryan. To be fair, it was probably best he kept his attention on the power-hungry woman trying to kill them.

Angel curled her lips in displeasure. "Another pest who doesn't know his place," she said bitterly.

"Kara, get help," Killian said. "I got Ryan."

Ryan hung his head. So, his brother wasn't as bright as he hoped. He tried to will himself to his feet again. Leaves crunched in the direction of Haven, and Ryan smiled. At least Kara's sense had returned.

Angel whirled around. "You're not going anywhere."

Ryan wouldn't allow it. He wouldn't sit back and let Angel hurt another person he cared about. Thanks to Kara, magik was out of the question, but if Ryan could stay ahead of Angel, he shouldn't have a problem. Finding the smallest reservoir of energy deep within, Ryan got up and placed himself between Kara's exit and the bloodthirsty woman. Ryan heaved deep breaths and tried to stand tall, but his body wasn't cooperating.

"She isn't your problem," Ryan hissed.

Angel scoffed. "And what is a child going to do?"

"Keep acting like you're the top dog. I'd love to be the one to knock you down a peg," Killian said, dropping the bow. He snapped his fingers and recited one of his many summoning spells.

Angel scoffed and waved her hand. "Sweetie, this is a real fight. Not something you do for a birthday party." Her voice wasn't amused, but she hid her discontent well.

A slew of daggers flew around Killian, and he plucked two from the air. "I've learned quite a few tricks since we last saw you," he said. His eyes flashed red without the ring on his finger, and Ryan prayed that anger wouldn't be turned to him.

His vision darkened, and he shook his head several times to clear it. Moss and mud had overpowering, musty scents, which mixed with the smell of rain. Another crack of lightning rang across the sky. It was hard enough to see Angel in the downpour if he hadn't been using the last of his energy.

Killian stood getting soaked on the other side of Angel. His bright red eyes were the only thing Ryan could easily see. Killian was poised like a serpent, watching and waiting for his chance to strike. Ryan tried to mirror his brother's actions to look stronger than he felt.

"You won't win, so you'd best submit before I kill everyone you love," Angel whispered through his head - a private conversation just for them.

Ryan closed his eyes and huffed in exasperation. He didn't know what to do or how to act. If he went with Angel, everyone would be okay another day. If he didn't...

"Accept it," Angel whispered. A twinge of desperation lurked in that tone.

Ryan opened his eyes in time for him to watch Angel stick a knife in Killian's side, causing his brother to scream in pain. Ryan's anger flared, and he dove for the witch out of instinct.

Angel threw Killian back; he slammed into a tree and crumpled to the ground. His eyes closed, but Ryan focused on the rise and fall of his chest. A wave of relief washed through him, and he ducked under Angel's dagger. She snapped it through the air like a whip. Her weapon was an extension of her body, and she stayed taught and tense, reminding him how outmatched he was.

Ryan slipped on some slimy leaves and fell forward. His world went in slow motion as Angel grabbed his shirt and slammed him into the ground with an ungodly amount of force.

Something cracked in his chest, and he coughed until his tongue was coated with the sickening taste of copper.

Her steel blue eyes burned into his. "You lose," she said. Angel's energy snapped at him like angry dogs.

Ryan screamed as the chaos surged through his veins and straight to his head. Darkness took him.

Wherever Ryan ended up, it was better than he thought. He opened his eyes and floated in a swirling gray mass of nothing. He was suspended in the air like flying, but invisible ties and ropes tethered him. It felt like he was lifted into the night sky without the stars. Everything was silent. He hadn't experienced true silence in ages. The expanse of black was never-ending and spread all around him. Ryan looked around and found that even though everything was black, he had no problem seeing. The only problem was the need for things to look at.

"Hello?" he called into the void hesitantly. His voice echoed around him, making him flinch. When one was suspended, they were also unable to move. He could kick his legs and wave his arms, but all he was doing was swimming in place.

Red eyes appeared in the black space before him, and his skin crawled. In those eyes, Ryan could see every terrible thing in his life - being bullied as a child, watching his mother walk away, the library fire, the multitude of executions he was helpless to stop, and then Dawson's death. The stream of visual information made him close his eyes and his heart pound. Ryan didn't dare open them again until he was sure he could handle the onslaught of terrible memories. He blinked sternly at the red gaze before, a gaze as red as blood and as chilling as ice.

"It's awoken," a deep, guttural voice hissed.

The voice scratched and clawed inside his head, making Ryan hold his hands over his ears. He bit back a terrified yelp and tried to calm his racing heart.

"It doesn't like us," another voice cackled in glee.

Dead. Be dead. Let me have died, and this is Helwe, Ryan thought to himself as he chewed on his tongue. Death was preferable to this.

"It doesn't even know what it wants," said the first voice, which sounded like dying animals.

Ryan scowled and took his hands away from his ears. He could hear the voices no matter what he did, so he had a new goal—to get them to stop talking. "I'm not an 'it'!" That wasn't the plan, but there was a current disconnect between brain and mouth.

The voices went silent. Maybe they didn't expect him to talk back. Ryan tried to move but only succeeded in flailing like a fish out of water. He took a deep breath and closed his eyes, trying to reach his brother. *"Killian, where are you?"*

When Ryan tried to access his magik, he was left with empty space. His eyes fluttered open, and he sucked in a breath. There was a different feeling in his head, one that he hadn't been aware of until now. It was empty and quiet. Whatever connection he used to have, wherever his magik was, it wasn't with him.

"Oh, this isn't good," he whispered.

If he was without his magik in some unknown realm, he really would be screwed. Ryan squeezed his eyes shut and dug deep, searching for a trace of the thing he had been familiar with since childhood. There had to be a spark of energy somewhere, but nothing happened. This place was devoid of life.

"Where am I?" he demanded.

Every sound and noise was amplified, making it hard to focus on his thoughts. If he wanted to figure this out, he would need honest answers from the only other beings he knew to be there – the thing with red eyes and the two disembodied voices.

"In your head."

"It's in its head." The voices began talking at once. They bounced back and forth off the invisible walls, shaking Ryan to the core.

"Stupid human doesn't even know what it is."

"Thinks it knows everything, doesn't it?"

The voices were distinct, yet they spoke simultaneously. Ryan didn't expect to be able to make out what the voices were saying because of that, but he understood them both. The second voice was more pleasing to listen to, but it was often overpowered by the thing that sounded like death.

"Shut up!" his voice cut through theirs. "One at a time. Who are you?" Pressure built behind his eyes, and Ryan had to take a few breaths to quell it. The only thing he could hear was the beating of his heart. He exhaled slowly and tried to focus on how the air sounded as it passed between his lips.

The voices stayed quiet for a short time. "It dares give us orders. Squish it. Squish it."

"It doesn't need to be dead to be miserable," the dark voice said. It sounded like it was amused by what was happening.

Ryan chewed his lip until it was bloody. Even if he could get a straight answer from the voices, it would take time to figure out what they meant, seeing as they didn't seem inclined to answer anything. He wasn't dead, but he wasn't in the forest either, which meant he had to be somewhere in between. Ryan didn't believe he was actually in his head. Maybe it was one of Angel's tricks to make him think he had left the forest, but he was still in a trance.

"It's confused. Let it stay confused," the voices said together.

Ryan pressed his palm to his forehead and tried to focus. "Who are you?" he tried again.

"Fire and Chaos. Truth and Lie. Death and Life."

"That doesn't make any sense," he roared. His anger was quickly rising.

"Show it, oh please, brother, show it," the high-pitched voice pleaded. "Let me show it."

The darkness parted like a curtain at a show, and Ryan blinked. He was staring at the forest around Rochester. The pines and oaks were bare and limp from the changing weather, and the sky was nearly black. Thunder and lightning still roared and streaked across the sky. The view changed, like someone was moving their head, and he could see Angel and Kara. They were staring right at him, but they didn't look confused.

Kara was screaming something. Her cheeks were red, and her eyes watered, but he couldn't hear what she said. She reached for him and then froze. Her lips trembled, and she brought a hand to her cheek. Blood slipped down her face, and she stepped back. A black blade was lifted and pointed at her chest, and his stomach fell. That was his sword. He recognized the ancient language carved into the black blade as what was on his Descendant swords.

Justin appeared before Kara and deflected the sword with his rigid wood staff. He didn't hesitate to blast wind at the sword wielder. Before Ryan knew it, he was staring at the sky. Stars twinkled in the distance, and he held his breath. *This couldn't be happening.*

"It can't figure it out," the voice said, laughing again.

"Oh, no," he whispered.

"I think it's figuring it out," the high-pitched voice said. It's so sad. I wanted to see it suffer."

"Which of you is chaos?" Ryan asked, his throat raspy and hollow.

The deeper voice chuckled. "Maybe it isn't that dumb." Chaos would sound like a cat being thrown off a building.

"You and me. We're sharing a body now," Ryan said. "But you have control?" he asked. It didn't make sense to communicate with his magik like a living being, but Justin did say weird things happened in the Descendant's world.

Chaos laughed loudly. It boomed across the space and nearly burst Ryan's ear drums. "I'm not what it thinks I am," the being said. "It calls me 'chaos,' yet it has yet to discover what 'chaos' truly is."

Ryan didn't understand. He wrinkled his nose. "You have a name?"

"No fair, you gave it too many chances," Fire screeched. "Why did you let it guess?"

The voices chattered inaudibly before falling silent. The curtain fell back over the night sky, blocking his view of what was happening in the outside world. The voices left him alone for the first time since arriving. This total silence stole his breath and shattered any walls he had in place. If Helwe was a place, Ryan found it.

Racing Against Time

KARA

Killian appeared looking furious, not that Kara was surprised because lately, he always knew when to appear if Ryan was involved. This day wasn't supposed to be about Angel, so when Kara spotted the woman at the fire with the high priestess, she lost her mind. Her anger got the best of her, and she was determined to make the red-haired harpy scream. Only when they were attacked did Kara realize how out of touch with reality she was.

Angel's energy coiled and snaked about her and the trees, never wilting or faltering as the woman's rage grew. The chaos was a den of defensive snakes, prepped and ready to strike at a moment's notice, and Kara noticed the intent was to bring Ryan down.

Killian drew a bow and shot Kara a stern look. "Kara, get help. I got Ryan," Killian said. His voice was tinged with rage, and his eyes were red, a sign he had lost control. It had been a long while since she had seen him in such a frenzied state, but given the situation, she understood.

Kara cocked her head to the side and tried to read his energy to determine if Ryan was indeed safe. The last time Killian lost control, he attacked his brother, and this situation wouldn't be fair with two-on-one. Killian did well to keep his energy shrouded, and she pursed her lips. *When did he learn to do that?* There was another person whose energy she couldn't read, and the thought was mildly worrying.

Killian shouted at her again, "Kara!"

She flinched, turned, and fled into the forest in time to see Angel throw Killian into a tree with a sickening crunch. *He has it under control. He can do this.* Kara didn't want to leave them, but they were outmatched. Kara had to get help. She had to do something before the boys could be hurt. *Don't fail them like you did Dawson. Don't fail them.* She would never let Angel take someone she loved.

Kara tore through the trees, managing her breathing so she didn't run out of energy before returning to Haven. This would have been easier if she had some sort of teleportation spell or superspeed like Ryan. *Leave it to Killian to help without alerting the others that something is wrong. It would've taken him two seconds, but no, he had to be complicated.*

Justin and Nicholas were on the front lawn when she broke through the tree line, waiting for something – maybe waiting for her.

Nicholas stared with concern as she called for them. "You alright?" he asked. His eyes flicked to the path behind her from which she had come like a savage animal.

Twigs clung to her clothes and hair, and more than a few abrasions burned as sweat slid into them. "Angel, Killian. Ryan," Kara panted, slipping a few words out between breaths. Air had never tasted so good. "In the woods. Needs help."

Justin nodded and gestured for his brother to follow. "It seems our dependents are in danger. Come with me. Kara, watch Cody." He left little room to argue, but that was a line she would cross.

"No. What if you need me?" she asked.

"Little Mouse, as much as I love the initiative, you aren't helpful," Justin said without bothering to sugarcoat it. "Your magik is too unpredictable."

Tory stepped out the front door and onto the porch. He frowned. "What happened?" he asked.

"Ryan's in trouble," she shouted. It was hard not to hyperventilate, and she watched her energy swarm across the ground in bright golds and yellows. It was like a burst of spring, except this spring was tainted with the thought of losing the twins.

Tory sighed and crossed his arms against his chest. He didn't look surprised, but he didn't look displeased either. He leaned on the porch post and looked at Nicholas. They had a silent conversation before he nodded. "I'll stay with Cody," he said.

Justin cursed and pointed at Nicholas. "I'll leave it up to you. Join me when you're ready, and try to make it quick." He vanished a second later in a flurry of leaves and flower petals.

Nicholas shook his head and waved his hands. He stepped toward Kara and jerked his thumb at the house behind him. "Stay here. This isn't going to end well with you being out for vengeance," he said,

Kara bit her lip. "What does it matter if it is about vengeance?" she asked.

"You'll make mistakes, and I don't have time for mistakes," Nicholas said shortly.

Tory stepped off the porch and walked over to join them. He looked down at Kara, cocking his head to the side and smiling softly. "Maybe let the people who can handle Angel do this," he said. "We'll get in the way and be a burden."

Kara pursed her lips and shook her head. "He needs help, Tory. I was why he was there. Killian's there too, and they... they are important to me. Please, let me help save them."

Nicholas cursed under his breath. "We don't have time. If you want to come, fine, but you better stay out of the way." He grabbed her arms, and a hole appeared about five feet wide in the ground. Nicholas crushed her to his chest and jumped in.

Kara squealed in surprise when everything went black, and the wind rushed through her ears as they traveled faster than she had before. When everything stopped moving, they were in the middle of the forest. The scent of moss and dirt vanished and was replaced with the acrid smell of smoke. She wrinkled her nose and stumbled when Nicholas pushed her away.

A long ribbon of fire snapped between them like a whip, hissing and sizzling in the air. The heat washed across Kara's skin, and she shivered. She hadn't been there for two seconds and was already being saved.

"Keep your guard up, Little Mouse. Remember everything we practiced," Justin said, ducking under Angel's spear.

Kara took a breath and steadied her nerves. She let her magik wash over her like a soothing blanket and looked around.

Ryan stood in the middle of the forest inside a fire vortex despite the pouring rain from her last use of magik. It lashed out at Justin, who was locked in combat with Angel, and she cackled in glee. Angel dodged and avoided his attacks with well-timed shields and moves a woman her age shouldn't be able to do – backflips, high jumps, and somersaults like a world-renowned athlete.

Kara wanted Justin to be able to maintain his sight, but as the purple haze of chaos began to descend, she held out her hands. If a spell would come to her, now would be the time. When she first started learning, Justin told her spells would come to her in her time of need.

She charged her energy through her arms and palms with a steady breath. *Come on,* she thought to herself. *This has to work.*

Nicholas grabbed the back of his brother's shirt and pulled him out of the way of an icicle ramming through his chest. "Pay attention to what I'm telling you," he snapped.

A surge of fire rushed between the brothers, separating them.

"Ryan, stop!" Kara shouted.

Justin held his hands up, and a sweep of wind put out the current flames, but they kept coming. "I can't hold him off. We need to count it as a loss."

"What happened?" Nicholas shouted over the crackle of fire. His face was pale, but he didn't look confused.

Killian hissed in pain and tried to stand, but he quickly crumpled to the ground and clutched his side, panting. " I think she's controlling him."

"What do we do?" Kara asked. She moved to help, but Ryan appeared in front of her. His eyes were empty and cold - there was nothing behind them. It was like he was a puppet; she knew Killian's observation wasn't far off.

"Ryan, stop!" Killian shouted.

Kara took a hesitant step back and trembled. Facing Angel was one thing, as terrifying as it was, but this was someone she knew. This was someone she dared to care for. "Ryan..."

He raised his sword, which was at his side, in a flash of silver and black.

Kara's eyes widened when her cheek burned, and something wet trickled down her face. She barely saw him move.

Killian snapped his fingers, and a dagger flew at Ryan. It sliced across his shoulder, but he didn't flinch. Ryan just flicked his wrist, and a black ball of fire went straight for Killian.

"Nick, I'd love it if you got these damn kids out of here," Justin said. His cheeks were bright red, and he narrowed his gaze, trying to pinpoint Angel. He barely managed to avoid a strike from her weapon when she charged from the right.

Nicholas huffed in irritation, and the earth trembled. Spikes of rock and metal flew up and dove for Angel at a few words from him. "I'm trying to keep you alive. I can only do so much," he muttered.

Kara's eyes widened in horror as the black flame exploded before Killian, and smoke billowed into the air. "Killian!"

As it cleared, Avery stood over the boy with stormy eyes. A black shield fell from around them as he eyed Ryan and Kara. "Need assistance?" he asked.

Nicholas scowled at his appearance but didn't say anything as he slammed his fists together, and a set of rock gauntlets appeared. They were an ugly brown, but they pulsed with energy Kara had never seen. "I'm pissed now." He punched the ground, and the earth rocked like a boat.

Angel snarled when Justin fired an arrow into her bicep. She swung the spear, and icicles shot from the tip.

Kara shouted her shield spell and a white bubble flowered around him.

Justin flinched when the ice struck her shield and shattered it like glass.

Kara clutched her chest as pain splintered across her heart. Tears stung her eyes, and she gasped for breath. When they were practicing, the others had never hit her with a spell that powerful. She knew shields were tethered, but she didn't imagine the pain would be like getting plowed by a tank. She looked up with misty eyes as Ryan held the tip of his sword to her throat with a cruel smile. Strong arms wrapped around her and lifted her off the ground.

Avery teleported back to Killian and set her beside him, ruffling her hair. "Sit tight, love. Let me see if I can diffuse the situation."

Killian threw her arm over his shoulder and stood. "Come on, let's get you home," he said.

"Trust in the light, child. We're here for you."

"Descendants of the past would never abandon their own. Take this spell. Believe in yourself."

"Fight back, little Descendant. We must never let evil win."

"Your light is the only thing saving this world. Don't. Give. Up."

Kara's body thrummed with energy she had never felt. She pressed a palm to Killian's chest to stop him before he could whisk them away. A spell was coming to her. She spoke the words on the tip of her tongue: "Mother of light, bring my enemy down: fallen light."

The sky cracked and boomed as her energy surged out and up. Justin grabbed his brother's arm and threw him to the ground before throwing a shield around them.

Purple electricity crackled and shot from the sky. It struck the ground, shaking it with the sheer force. One after another, the lightning bolts hit the ground and danced around Kara's enemy. One would have struck Ryan but he disengaged with Avery and jumped to the side.

Killian tightened his hold on Kara and watched as his twin tried to decapitate Justin for the third time. "Ryan, stop. You're not yourself!"

Angel's shrieking laughter filled the air, and the wind whipped their clothes back and forth. Dust and dirt swirled up, and Kara shielded her eyes. "He's mine now, don't you understand? Do away with these insects."

Avery summoned a giant two-bladed ax and appeared before Killian and Kara. He smirked in amusement and held up the weapon. "Defend yourself. I'll keep tabs on the girl."

"I'm not going to fight my brother," Killian said.

Avery ducked out of the way when a fire whip cracked the air.

Nicholas flicked his wrist and took two seconds to create shackles from the earth and bind Ryan.

Angel surged forward, stabbing out with her weapon to stop him, but Justin intercepted. He moved in front of Nicholas and brought a beautiful, light blue shield up. The spear rebounded, and Angel stumbled back. Kara's eyes widened in surprise when the shield didn't even crack.

"Your fight is with me," Justin said.

Nicholas grabbed Kara's shoulder. She jumped, not knowing when he moved. "Take my energy, heal up, and drain Ryan. We can't let him leave," he said. His voice was strained from exhaustion, but he was still trying.

Kara shook her head, and her lip trembled. "I can't." The only spell she managed to use wasn't even a good one. It had only bought them a few seconds, and Angel managed to dispel it.

"Believe in yourself. You are exactly what you need to be," Nicholas said.

Killian screamed in pain, and Kara's eyes flicked to him. He got a few feet away, and Ryan planted a sword in his stomach.

Kara placed her hand over Nicholas'. If there was a chance she could do something and save them, she had to take it. Her thoughts flickered to her brother and the way blood stained his lips. He wasn't even afraid at the end, but she was terrified now. Terrified of going through that again, of being unable to move on and let go. Losing anyone else wasn't an option.

Kara steeled herself and took a breath. They might stand a chance if she could pull enough energy from Nicholas to use against Ryan. "Parted powers take peace in my energy: transfer."

His magik poured into her, and the pain subsided. She could do this. She had to do this. Kara faced Ryan and held her hands out. He was locked in combat with Avery, and his attention was away from her. She never absorbed energy without touching someone, but as Avery liked to say, there was a first for everything.

"Ancestral magik guide my hands: drain."

Ryan's erratic, spiking lines of red and violet entwined energy stopped circling him. He froze as she pulled the colors toward her body.

Avery tackled him and pressed his blade to Ryan's neck. "Stop fightin'. You've lost."

Angel slammed her palm into Justin's sternum and dove past when he doubled over, coughing into his hand. Nicholas let Kara go and tried to move in front of the woman, but a blast of wind propelled Angel forward, and she flicked her wrist. "Water rise and fall: torrential downpour – ice type." Sharpened icicles rained from the sky.

Ryan jumped off the ground when the energy siphon stopped. Angel touched his shoulder, and they vanished in black smoke.

"No!" Justin screamed.

All at once, the world went silent. The icy rain stopped, the fire went out, and they could only stare.

Killian blinked at the spot where his brother stood in complete shock.

"Kill, I-" Avery started to say something but stopped when the boy turned.

Killian's eyes flashed red and angry. "Leave me alone," he grunted. As night began to fall, Killian stormed deeper into the forest.

Kara stared at her bloody, muddy hands and blinked back furious tears. She gave it her all and still hadn't made a difference.

"Let's go home," Nicholas whispered, putting a hand on her shoulder.

She nodded, and he limped after her as she headed for Haven. She looked back once and saw Justin standing in the same spot with clenched fists and white knuckles.

"He needs time," Nicholas said.

She shot Avery a look as she walked past. "Thanks for trying," she said.

He offered a weak smile. "Sorry, I couldn't do more."

She shook her head. "Go home and try not to worry." Her thoughts went to Killian, and she pursed her lips. "Keep an eye on him. He won't be okay," she added.

He saluted and hurried off.

Nicholas raised a brow. "Where did you meet him?" He was more curious than he was letting on, but she knew he wouldn't press her for more right now.

"In the forest," Kara said, not offering more.

Nicholas tried to walk like he wasn't hurt, but the pain was etched on his face, and his limp got worse the closer they got to the cabin. His hands were balled into tight fists at his side. They walked the rest of the way in silence. Tory met them at the door and fussed over his boyfriend. Nicholas recounted what happened, and Tory ran a hand through his hair. He looked at Kara like he wanted to say something but kept his mouth closed. After all, what's one supposed to say at the end of the world?

Time to Give Up

KILLIAN

Killian stormed away from the group, slipping through the shadows to get further because the last thing he wanted was for Justin to come after him. His heart pounded, and Killian struggled to ignore the panic as the link between himself and Ryan weakened.

When Ryan vanished, walls descended around his emotions and thoughts, and Killian had been cut off. It was a more painful experience than anything he had been through thus far, and it wasn't something he could make go away with a snap of his fingers.

All his life, his and his brother's emotions had made him whole. Sometimes, they built walls between their thoughts and feelings, but there was a space inside Killian that Ryan encompassed, and right now, it was blank. There was a void in half of his soul that was nothing but bitter silence, making him want to tear out his heart.

Avery appeared in front of him before Killian could make a clean escape. He dropped from the trees like a monkey and was silent as he landed despite the leaves flying around him.

Killian didn't want to deal with him, not with anyone. He jumped into the closest shadow and ran through the realm without looking back. Even if Avery could track him, Killian moved faster in this realm than Avery could in the real one. Being wrapped in the darkness was almost comforting, but not enough to make him forget the black pit inside him.

Killian jumped out of the shadows when he was on the verge of collapse. Being spent and having no desire to keep moving, Killian slumped against a tree on the forest's edge, burying his face in his hands.

"You overdid it," Avery said.

Killian looked up and groaned again. "How?" he croaked.

Avery smiled sadly and squatted. "I've dealt with a lot of flighty Descendants of Shadows. Once I can lock onto your energy, you ain't goin' nowhere," he said. His voice was gentle, but that sounded eerily like a threat.

Killian growled because that's all he had the energy for.

Avery didn't touch him, but he watched with those beady black eyes.

"Go away," Killian hissed when he found enough fire, and his stomach wasn't threatening to explode again.

Avery shook his head. "Kara asked me to look out for you, and I'm gonna."

Killian bit his lip and squeezed his eyes shut. He didn't want to cry in front of Avery. He needed to let it out, to scream and beg, but he didn't want to do that in front of the one person he couldn't stand.

Avery had seen enough of his secrets. There was no reason to keep adding to the information that could be used against him.

"Kilua..." Avery didn't get to finish his sentence before the tears started.

He sobbed like a baby. Killian sobbed in a way he didn't know was possible. He wasn't sure which was more mortifying, the sobbing or the Avery part, but it didn't help slow the tears. The idea that someone was witnessing such weakness made the tears flow harder and faster.

Avery still didn't touch him. He stayed stiff as a statue and stared at the ground, waiting for the emotional breakdown to stop.

Ryan left behind a void, like a wound that wouldn't heal. Killian didn't know how to feel without his brother's energy comforting him. Being attached to someone like that was annoying, but he didn't want it to vanish, even if he had complained non-stop about it. Right now, he would do anything to bring it back. *I'm sorry. Please, don't leave.*

Killian's chest and heart hurt as his brother's absence weighed on every part of his mind and soul. *Normal siblings don't feel like this.* His reaction was over the top and stupid; Killian knew that, but he couldn't stop. Ryan had been there his entire life and was just gone. It was like losing a piece of himself—no, not a piece, half.

Ryan's hole left room for something else—a space where all his anger and rage could build - a new home for the shadow.

Killian's eyes snapped open as the shadow hissed in his head, and the tears stopped. He caught his breath with a light gasp as he tried to regain control of the dangerous thoughts running through his mind. *Death. Kill them all. Die!*

Avery's hand whipped out a second later and caught his wrist just in time for them to be transported to the shadow realm, hand-in-hand, just like last time.

"Foolish little Descendant, you thought you could escape me!" the shadow roared, towering over them.

Killian didn't have it in him to be afraid. Any emotional response he might have had was drowned out by the self-pity running through his clouded thoughts. He stood and faced his challenger with a deep scowl. His hands balled into fists at his sides.

Avery held tight to Killian's wrist, trying to jerk him back. "We have to go," he shouted.

It took Killian a moment to realize the wind was howling. There was never wind in the shadow realm. The seasons and weather rarely affected the space in Killian's head where he met with his unwanted friend.

"I owe you for the last visit you paid me," the shadow said, slinking around the darkest areas of the room like an agitated cat. Its voice was a slimy hiss, and Killian wished it would stop.

The shadows in the room rippled and screamed a disastrous tune of despair. This noise was embedded deep in Killian's mind, making him cringe, but he stood his ground. The more his anger grew, the wilder the shadow became. Deep red spots appeared on the shadow's black body, and it roared in agitation as if being burned alive.

"Stop!" Avery screamed, tugging his arm again.

Killian couldn't think straight. He heard Avery, but his words went in one ear and out the other. It was hard to focus on anything but the rage.

The wind howled and blew like hot breath against his skin. It smelled bitter, but it was a smell he couldn't place.

The shadow grabbed Killian in an icy claw and squeezed. Last time, the pain almost made him pass out, but he barely felt it this time. Killian couldn't feel anything, and a wicked smile crossed his lips. *I can be a part of you this time.*

Avery shouted a spell, and Killian's world went black.

Killian pressed a palm to his temple and grunted. His head throbbed. This was one of the worst headaches of his life. He closed his eyes despite it being dark and dim from the low glow of the fire.

"How are you feelin'?" Avery asked. His footsteps faded in and out, and a clay bowl was put in Killian's hands. "You need to eat," he said.

He didn't want to eat. Killian rolled onto his side and tried to hand the bowl back.

Avery sighed and sat on the edge of the hay bale. "I need you to try and eat," he said again.

Killian didn't respond. He chanced, opening his eyes again, and ignored the prickly hay and smell of horse.

"You used too much energy, Killian. That headache won't go away," Avery tried again.

Killian thought for a moment and pushed himself up. Then he downed the bowl and prayed he wouldn't throw it up.

Avery refilled the bowl, but he didn't give it back immediately. He waited a few minutes and then handed it to him. "One more," he said.

Killian didn't protest this time. He drank the soup and wiped his mouth with his hand. It was dull and flavorless, but somehow, it was the best thing he had ever consumed.

Avery took the bowl and sighed again. There was a knock at the door, and he stood, gesturing for Killian to stay put. Not that he had any inclination to go anywhere, given how dark it was outside. He had probably spent hours away from the house. It was a wonder Justin or Nicholas hadn't come for him yet.

Ryan. Killian hesitated and pulled his shirt up. There were no stab wounds or lacerations from his fight. He frowned in confusion and sat up as the front door opened.

"I really don't got time right now, babe. Maybe later," Avery's voice startled him out of his thoughts.

Killian shifted on the makeshift couch and hissed when a spasm of pain snaked down his side. The last thing he remembered was being in the shadow realm and dangerously low on energy. Avery had done something, though, hadn't he?

"Do you wanna talk about it?" Avery asked, reappearing in the living room. The fire crackled softly behind him, and Killian shook his head.

The house smelled nice, like flowers and honey with a hint of cinnamon. They weren't smells Killian would associate with a hunter, let alone someone like Avery. He slid down on the hay bale and groaned deeply. "How long have I been out?" he asked.

"No more than an hour," Avery said. "I tried to keep you awake, but you kept hittin' me." Avery's fingers fiddled with a few straws of hay as he talked. His accent came on strong, and he combined words and left letters out of others.

It took Killian a minute to absorb what he said. *Ryan, where are you?* Their link hadn't changed since he had fallen asleep, and Killian's stomach tightened. *Great, just great.* What the Helwe was he going to do now?

Avery cocked his head to the side. He studied Killian until it got awkward, and then he let the back of his head hit the stone wall behind him. "Sorry, when I get worked up, I know I'm hard to understand."

Killian ran a hand down his face and looked around.

"When do you want to go home?" Avery asked.

Killian chuckled to himself. He was barely awake, and he had already overstayed his welcome. "Gimme a minute. I'll get outta your hair," he said wearily.

Avery shifted uncomfortably and scratched his cheek. "That's not why I was askin'," he mumbled.

Killian sighed and rubbed his eyes. The straw poked him in the back and side, but he didn't mind. It took the attention off the shooting pain in his head. "Did I hurt you?" he asked.

"Nah, I knocked you out before anythin' happened," Avery said. His voice was soft as if he honestly didn't care if Killian tried to hurt him so long as Killian was alive and well.

"I'm sorry," Avery said.

Killian shrugged. He didn't want to talk about it; he couldn't even remember what had happened after the shock of everything. He turned on the couch, facing the wall, and closed his eyes. "The wounds... why don't I have any injuries?"

Avery shrugged. "I think your anger and rage sent your energy into overdrive, but I don't know for sure."

Killian frowned and lay back down. He wanted to sleep forever.

Killian woke to a loud bang and thump. He bolted to his feet and looked around.

Avery appeared in the living room with a bundle of wood and an evil grin. "Well, look who came around. You been out cold for hours," he said. He dropped the wood before the hearth and wiped his hands on his trousers.

Killian stepped back and toppled over the makeshift couch. He yelped in pain when he smacked the back of his head against the stone wall.

Avery shot him a look and held out his hand. "Dude, how do you have any brain cells left?" he asked.

If one were to ask Ryan, Killian didn't have any. He hesitated before swatting Avery's helpful hand away. "Back off," he muttered as the thought of his brother's name spiraled his mood.

Avery retracted it and set some wood on the fire.

Killian struggled to his feet as he clambered back over the couch and onto solid ground. "How long have I been here?"

Heat washed across his back, and he looked over his shoulder. Avery's eyes flicked to the window to study the moon through the trees. "Few hours," he said.

Killian should get back; he knew he should, but he had no desire to. There was nothing in Haven he wanted to return to. Kara kept them from leaving just by being alive, and if they had gone sooner, maybe Ryan would've been able to fight the curse. Maybe he wouldn't have let himself be taken in by Angel's anger and spellwork if he didn't blame himself for Dawson's death. *Maybe...*

Avery held out his hand and smirked. "Come with me," he said.

Killian cocked his head to the side and frowned. "Where?" he asked.

"Trust me. Come on," Avery said.

Trust. The word almost made him scoff in humorless amusement, but he took Avery's hand despite not wanting to.

"I've got just the thing," Avery whispered, squeezing his hand.

I don't even want to know, Killian thought with a small smile. It was hard not to let Avery's energy infect him. It took a second to realize what happened. "Don't use magik on me." He ripped his hand away and forced a scowl.

Avery chuckled and grabbed his hand again, pulling him outside and did a squat before gesturing to the woods. "Try to keep up," he said, taking off two seconds later giving himself just enough time to let Killian's hand go. His footsteps crunched through the leaves and dying brush, and he howled like a wolf, vanishing in the distance.

Killian sighed and shook his head. Running at night. He wasn't sure that was a wise idea, but he followed. It was too cold to stand there doing nothing, and if he ever planned on getting home, he might as well humor the man. Killian followed Avery through the forest until his lungs burned. Unsurprisingly, the hunter had more stamina and was better at dodging roots and bushes.

Killian cursed the fourth time he tripped and landed on his face. He was doing worse than he had the last time they did this. Training with Nicholas didn't help with cardio, it was more about sustaining long spells.

Avery stood over him and slapped his knees as he laughed at Killian's recent faceplant. If they turned this into a sport, Killian would get top marks. "Almost there, come on," Avery said, smirking.

He always made sure to stay in sight, but he was always too far to catch.

Killian groaned but got back up to continue chasing the elusive deer that was Avery. He was too deep now, but he would keep up despite the emotional storm raging a defiant war in his head.

Sweat soaked his shirt, and dirt and thorns clung to his clothes, but when Avery stopped, Killian's head was finally clear. He could think without wanting to punch someone in the throat.

He wiped the back of his hand across his forehead and leaned against a rock wall, panting. His body was too tired to ache and too exhausted to focus on anything.

Avery smirked, giving him enough time to catch his breath. "We're climbin' the wall this time."

Killian shook his head and wiped the sweat from his brow. "Yeah, no," he said, still panting. He just ran a mile and a half, and now he was expected to scale a wall. *That's not going to happen, buddy.*

Avery slapped him on the back, nearly sending Killian into the dirt again. "You can do it!"

Killian stared pitifully at the wall and peered up. The top of the cliffside disappeared into the night's abyss, making it impossible to judge how high it went. "That sounds like a bad idea," he said, his voice raspy from dehydration.

"Uh-huh, kind of like facin' the shadow," Avery said, pulling a leather bag off his belt and tossing it to Killian. "Drink up because we're doin' it," he said. There wasn't room for refusal.

Killian pressed his palm to the rock and sighed. He downed half the water bag in a single gulp and waited a few minutes before drinking the rest. If he didn't want to die of dehydration, he needed to keep it in his stomach. "I've never free-climbed anything larger than a tree before," he said. *I didn't plan on starting in the middle of the night, either.*

"It's the same. Don't overthink," Avery said, attaching himself to the wall and clambering upward. "I know my ass is juicy, but come on." Avery stared down when Killian didn't move. His eyes were tiny black pinpricks, dancing with light like the stars in the abyss above.

Killian huffed and grabbed the rock, pulling himself up. *This is such a bad idea; it's not funny.* Killian focused on the next step and where to hold it. When he started getting tired, he had no clue how far off the ground he was, but he didn't dare look down. Heights had never been a strong point, and this was well past the boundary of high.

Avery was still well ahead but looked down occasionally to ensure Killian hadn't fallen to his death. Their eyes met once as the sky lightened, and Killian smiled weakly.

"Almost there," Avery said after gods knew how long.

Killian's body shook, and every muscle in his arms and legs constricted. He pressed his forehead to the earth, closed his eyes, and inhaled deeply. He smelled moss, dirt, and a flowery scent. Killian tried to pinpoint the smell to distract himself from the ache in his body.

"Keep movin'. Stoppin' will only make it worse," Avery called from above.

Killian grunted and pushed himself up on a shaking leg. He reached up as the rock crumbled from beneath his foot, and he slid a good foot down. His hands burned as the rock cut through his palms as he scrambled to find purchase on something. He gasped and dug his fingers into the rock, finally stopping his descent.

"I can't," he hissed, clinging to the wall like a terrified kitten.

"Yes, you can. You're almost there," Avery said, trying to be encouraging, but he sounded more amused than anything.

Killian looked up and shivered as the chilly wind blew across his sweat-soaked back. He was a few feet from the top, and Avery was there, staring down and waving his hands like that would make Killian move faster.

Killian bit his lip and reached up, grabbing the next rock and forcing his body to move again. *I'm too high. Way too high.* His heart thundered in his ears, and adrenaline coursed through his veins. *Almost there. Keep going.* When he was close, Avery held a hand down, and Killian grabbed it. He clung desperately as Avery helped him up the last bit of the climb and onto safe land.

Killian groaned and fell onto his stomach, burying his face in his arms with a relieved laugh. "I'm never doing that again," he whispered.

Avery shook his shoulder and pointed out. "You gotta take in the sight. It's the best part."

Killian wasn't sure he could move. He turned his head to look across the land. Trees, bushes, and rivers sprawled out across the land like some magikal painting. It was a glorious sight, and his breath caught in his throat as he admired it. The sun rose over the horizon, painting the sky a brilliant orange and pink that illuminated thin white clouds across the expanse of blue. Rivers twisted and turned across the land, breathing life into the forests and providing nutrients for the animals. Spatters of sparkling water ran below the mountainside.

Killian inhaled the fresh air and closed his eyes. *This is what life is: experiencing new things and seeing new sights.*

Avery chuckled beside him. "How do you feel?" he asked.

"Ryan, I don't know if you can hear me, but we've gotta do this once. Just the two of us," Killian said through their link. He tried to push his

emotions and some of what he was seeing through, but the other end of that link was quiet and closed off.

Killian stood, barely managing to get up, and set his head against Avery's shoulder and smiled. "Thanks," he said.

Avery went rigid under his touch. "For what?" he asked when he finally relaxed his shoulders again.

"Not leaving me alone," Killian said.

Avery wrapped a hesitant arm around his waist, and Killian's knees gave out.

At least he made it to the top.

The Next Phase

ANGEL

"Come with us to the river," Jess said, beaming. She grabbed Rebecca's hands, her eyes shining with hope. "Please, Summer misses you."

Rebecca smiled weakly and shrugged. Her fingers traced shapes into her rounded stomach through the soft fabric of her shirt. "I don't know," she said, trying not to sound too hesitant.

"Okay, Summer doesn't care about anyone but herself, but she's bringing her boys," Jess said.

Rebecca perked up and nodded after a moment of thought. "Okay, I'll go for the boys."

Jess clapped excitedly and called for Justin to meet them. She pulled Rebecca out the front door and into the fresh summer air. Rebecca breathed deeply, smiling as she savored the soft scent of pollen and honey.

Nick had created gardens of vegetables and flowers across almost every inch of Haven's lawn. He ran through the tall grass, talking to a few squirrels who followed in his wake. Chittering animals always surrounded the teenager, especially the quiet ones.

"Nicky, we're going to the river. Are you going to join us?" Jess called as they walked down wooden steps on a makeshift path Justin had created.

"Nope! I'm playing hide-and-seek with the squirrels and pigeons, but thanks," he said.

Rebecca smiled softly and let Jess lead her into the grace of the shaded forest where she could get out of the sun. "Are you sure Summer won't mind me being there?" she asked.

"Of course, and the fresh air will do you some good," Jess said cheerfully. Her voice was warm and gentle as it always was. She had been in a good mood lately, but nothing Rebecca did seemed to dampen it.

Love makes her this way. One day, Rebecca wanted to find that same joy in someone.

"Remember, Summer doesn't know about your magik. Let's keep it that way for a little longer," Jess said as they neared the river spot where she hung out with her friends.

Rebecca gulped but nodded. Her magik wasn't easily understood by many, and while Justin and Jess supported her and taught her, Summer wasn't under the same belief that chaos was a legitimate branch of magik.

"Oi, you two knock it off, or I'll give you somethin' to fight over!" Summer's voice carried through the trees, setting Rebecca on edge.

She let go of Jess' hand and hurried into the clearing where she could see the two little boys fighting by the river's edge. The water trickled by lazily, but her heart squeezed with concern as she rushed forward to yank them closer inland.

"Can you not let them play so close while you're lounging over there?" Rebecca snapped, shooting Summer a glare.

The twins cackled with glee and wrapped their tiny, pudgy arms around her legs before running into the trees, calling each other names. Toddlers were so little and fragile, but Summer made no effort to follow them and ensure they weren't in danger.

Jess smiled sympathetically at Rebecca's cross look. "Mornin' Summer. How's the day treating you?" she asked warmly.

Rebecca whistled and followed the white-haired boys before they could find themselves as a larger animal's snack. They hadn't gone far and were back to pushing and shoving.

"Hey, hey," she separated them with gentle hands and knelt despite the quaking in her knees as her weight bore down on her.

"Fat," one of the boys poked her round tummy and giggled.

"Baby," she corrected with a smile. "I'm having a baby boy like you." She poked one of the boys in the chest, making him giggle and throw his arms around her as best he could.

"Not a baby," he said, giggling more.

Rebecca smiled and kissed his forehead, making herself return to her feet. She grunted and groaned as she struggled to straighten, and the boys tried their best to help her get up.

"Up!" the boy called, holding his arms up and clenching his fingers.

Rebecca smiled and ruffled his hair, shaking her head. "I can't lift you right now, child. Come along, let's go see Mommy," she said.

The second twin hung back, his face falling still as he twisted his hands together and shook his head. His hair flopped into his emerald gaze, and Rebecca frowned, ushering the other boy on.

"Come on, Ryan," she tried again.

The boy shook his head more fiercely and stayed rooted to the spot.

She closed the distance between them and held out her hand. "We'll go together then." She smiled and wiggled her fingers.

Ryan strained against the chains holding him, screaming as the blade cut into the soft side of his arm, drawing blood.

Angel stopped as the memory surfaced. Her hand stilled as the chaos seeped through the new injuries, sending a fresh wave of agony through the boy. *What an inconvenient time to be sentimental.* She wiped the blood off her dagger and walked out the cell door, catching her breath and leaving him screaming behind her.

The cell door slammed shut, and she tucked the dagger into a hidden sheath on her thigh. Skirts were good for more than just looking nice. The fluorescent lights in the dungeons hummed and flickered, making her shut her eyes against them with a deep breath. How long ago was that, and why was she now remembering it? She set her hand against the slimy, cold rock wall to steady herself as the world spun into a mess of gray and black.

Those little boys belonged to Summer, and it felt like ages ago she had seen them toddling around, shouting at each other in their made-up language.

"Ma'am." Her General stopped before her, saluting. "There's a visitor in your chambers." His voice was gruff.

Angel pinched the bridge of her nose and took another breath. "Yes, thank you. Dismissed."

The man didn't question her order as he turned and walked back to the elevator, leaving her amongst the blood and misery of her dungeons. Ryan was finally under her control, and while he had a wild spirit, his energy could easily be shrouded and bent to her will. So, why did she suddenly have to remember the days she used to long for?

She would relish breaking him into pieces. She had to do this for the good of the world. To make things better. She approached the elevator to meet her visitor, but purple smoke exploded between her and the only exit, making her back off. Havoc materialized in front of the elevator door before she could enter. A thin smile stretched across his face. "Hello," he said, his smile never wavering.

Angel pursed her lips. "What do you want?" she asked. Her voice was curt. There had been no hide or hair of Havoc since fight.

The man chuckled and put his hands on the staff before him. "My dear, I wanted to see how you've been," he said. "Is the make-believe son still doing what's asked of him?"

Angel clenched her hands. "Avery is not up for discussion," she said.

Avery could be a little over the top and dramatic, but that was part of his charm, even if she was one of the only ones who could see through it.

"I was just wondering if you know what he's been up to. I mean, he tried to negate your efforts to take Ryan. Are you curious as to why?"

Of course, Havoc had been watching. She should have known that he would watch everything she did even if he wasn't around. Men like Havoc hated losing, and he lost her.

Angel pursed her lips. She chose not to answer. If she gave too much away, he would use it against her. Her little spat in the forest was unplanned, but it went a long way to convince the others Avery was on their side. Angel wouldn't hold it against him if it meant he could get in better with the group, considering there was one more twin she needed to get a hold of.

"He won't replace what you've lost. It's not the same as having your own," Havoc sighed.

The man didn't move, and Angel didn't dare get too close. Not with the way his energy was subdued. If she knew anything from dealing with Descendants, it was that subdued energy was only the calm before the storm.

His words did strike a chord, though.

"Do you know what to do with the boy you've captured?" Havoc asked, changing the conversation.

"I don't need your help," Angel snapped. "I told you we were done."

Havoc chuckled lowly. His eyes flashed angrily, but that smile stayed in place. It was hard to read him with that mask. "I'm allowing you to rebuild our partnership before I'm proven right."

Angel frowned. He treated her like a child, and she wasn't going to tolerate that. She was well past her childhood years. Helwe, she was well past her teenage years. "I don't wish to rebuild anything. I'm going to fulfill my plans *without* you."

Havoc's lips quirked into a snarl before he composed himself. He vanished with a wave of his hand.

Angel cooled her temper and reminded herself she had plenty of help. She was bound to be unstoppable with Avery and now Ryan, especially given Avery's strength.

She knew enough about the old religion to understand how to get Malsumis into their world. Angel had pure blood, Ryan, and now she needed to find a spot to spill his blood. A spot that was unaffected by chaos. She thought for a long while before smiling – there was one place.

The watering hole was the only untouched place she could think of. A Descendant of Water purified it a long time ago. Plus, she wanted to maintain the only bit of nature she had within the walls. A small piece of it reminded her of home despite her show on how awful nature and magik was.

Angel pushed open the steel door, which moved with a long, drawn-out creak. The sound reverberated down the narrow hall before dying somewhere near the elevator. She wiped the grime from her hands and peered into the cell's darkness.

Ryan was slumped in the corner, half asleep after their little "training" session. His clothes were stained with blood and dirt, and his hair was a wild, tangled mess. Once she had him better under control, she would have to let him shower. The newest cuts she had opened on his arms trickled blood, but most were already scabbed over. Nothing would show by morning.

Angel tapped into his energy and took a breath. He was muted this morning, so he should be reasonably easy to handle. She noticed that in the days after their sessions, he was a little more lethargic and quieter. She had yet to determine if it was from blood loss or depression – maybe it was a bit of both.

Since she had come to acquire him, he had a moment of lucidity, which made controlling him easier. She knew the time that would last was limited, and she had to make the most of it. "Ryan," Angel called to him and flicked her wrist. A stream of chaos wrapped around his chest and squeezed.

He lifted his head, and she was delighted to see nothing behind that emerald gaze.

"You are to meet me at the watering hole behind the baker's," she said. "You are to do nothing else and contact no one. Nod if you understand."

The blonde nodded.

"Good, now go." She waved her hand in dismissal.

Ryan vanished in the blink of an eye.

Through the curse she placed upon him, Angel kept a careful tether to his mind and emotions. It was no easy matter to stray into the mind of someone she had no attachment to, but Angel had been practicing. She used the citizens as practice dummies to ensure she could get what she needed from this boy.

She walked down the narrow corridor, her heart racing and a broad smile on her face. Havoc was gone, Ryan was hers, and nothing could ruin her day. Pesky memories wouldn't hold her back from the greater good; one day, they would all thank her.

Angel pressed the button for the elevator and jumped when the doors swished open, and Avery was there. Her smile fell. "What's wrong?" she asked. "I thought you were in my corridors?"

He was pale; dark bags lingered under his eyes, but he didn't look harmed. Angel calmed her heart when she was sure he hadn't been attacked.

"You have one of the twins," he said. "I have the other."

Angel's face broke into a large, relieved smile. "Oh, that's great news. Don't scare me like that. I thought something was wrong." She pushed the button for the lobby after joining him on the elevator and wiped her hands on her skirt.

Avery rubbed the back of his neck and forced a smile. "I've not been sleepin'," he said. "Sorry."

"What's going on?" Something was wrong, and asking and evaluating was the best plan so she could help.

"I'm not as good at this as you," he said, his hands tightening to balls at his sides.

She cocked her head to the side. "What do you mean?" It was hard to understand someone who didn't give context to what he was talking about. She eyed his white knuckles and longed to reach out and comfort him. She wasn't sure that would be acceptable as they were only starting to mend their relationship.

"Killian is..." Avery trailed off. His dark eyes stared past her, though she knew he wasn't looking at anything specific. "Why do you want them?" he asked after a while.

Angel hesitated. She knew if she didn't state her case right, she might lose Avery to this new feeling of doubt. Leave it to the boy to catch feelings for one of the instrumental beings in her plans. "I plan on using them to clean the slate," she said. Her voice was quiet. When the elevator stopped, and the doors opened, Angel pressed the button to close them and stop the machine. "I want to fix what was broken for our people," she said.

Avery sighed and slid to the elevator's floor. He buried his face in his hands and shook his head. "Will it hurt?" he asked.

Angel knelt and pulled him against her with the click of her tongue. "No," she said. "I won't hurt them. And when we're done, they'll be heroes. Magik and humanity will be reunited."

Avery relaxed into her touch but didn't uncover his face. He seemed to think hard about what she said. "Are they going to die?" he asked.

"No," she said.

He nodded and put his hands down. When he looked at her, he smiled. It wasn't bright and joyful, but it was enough to calm her fears. Avery always managed to bounce back. He just needed to hear the right words. Once he realized the severity of their situation, he wouldn't mind a couple of sacrifices.

"Wanna get lunch?" he asked, straining to lift his mood for her.

Angel smiled and patted his back. "I have a meeting, and then we can go. Why don't you wait in the conference room for me?" she asked, pushing the elevator button again. The doors opened, and she stepped out.

Avery gave her a thumbs-up. "Sure thing. How long is this meetin' goin' to take?" he asked.

She didn't know. Hopefully, she could contact Lord Malsumis quickly and be done within the hour. "Not long, now off you go," she said.

Avery shrugged and jammed his thumb against the elevator pad. The doors closed, and the machine whirred to life. Angel took a breath to steady her emotions. She didn't expect Ryan to beat her to the watering hole, but family was more important. She walked down a large, empty hall and into the lobby. Security guards and officers chatted around a desk in the middle of the room. They saluted as she walked by but didn't otherwise ask where she was going. Light filtered in from the windows wrapped around the steel building, and she sighed, patting her hair into place as she exited the tower.

The streets were mostly empty as it was a work day. There were a few elderly women in the streets gossiping back and forth, but Angel didn't pay them much mind aside from a wave and smile. That generation didn't like her. They could still remember the wind, trees, and flowers, and they felt like Angel's walls and city destroyed it. They were a hard demographic to get along with when she wasn't in a mood, let alone when she was in one. The gossiping stopped as she walked by, and the women stared hard. Neither was brave enough to call her out or say their minds, but their wary, wrinkled faces were masks of disapproving scowls.

Angel smiled politely and nodded them on as she walked by. There was no need to sow more seeds of discontent. Not when the city was already threatening to fall apart at the seams. This was a tricky game she was playing. She couldn't keep forcing chaos down the citizens' throats to maintain her hold. She had to be charismatic and charming to win them without risking blowing it up.

She walked past the bakery, and the sweet smell of dough and sugar briefly chased away the strong smell of pollution. Angel paused to savor the scent and closed her eyes with a deep inhale. It broke back less than painful memories.

Jessica had been in the kitchen. She loved to bake and always made sweets when Angel was under the weather. They had been in Haven for about four months, and things were supposed to improve, but Angel wasn't. She was sick and tired, and nothing made sense except the growing life in her belly. It was the only comfort she had that things would get better. Jess made sweet bread with powdered sugar and a honey lime glaze on the day everything broke. The limes were a treat from Portlandia that Justin had brought from one of his trips.

It smelt amazing. Angel remembered how her mouth watered when Jess carried a silver tray into her room, the warm bread wafting its scent everywhere...

A tantalizingly sweet and tart fruity smell made her sit up and rub her eyes.

"There you are," Jess had said with a knowing smile and bright eyes. "I was wondering how to get you out of bed." She looked at the sweet bread on the tray and sat on the edge of the bed. Jess was always careful around her, even when Rebecca told her she didn't have to be.

"What is it?" Rebecca asked. Her voice was so quiet and rough from crying.

"Sweet bread, try it." Jess held out a piece of the fluffy golden bread.

Rebecca hesitated but took it from her as soft as a momma cat lifting it's child and stuck it in her mouth. It all but dissolved on her tongue and was filled with sugar and butter. She moaned in delight and tore the bread into pieces for them to share. "This *is* good," she said.

Angel blinked the memory away and the tears that came with it. She sniffed and slipped between the bakery and a shut-down shop, trying to gather her thoughts. There were a lot of good times with her half-sister. She loved Jessica so much and obviously couldn't deny that. Perhaps it was why it still hurt, and she longed for the days when it was just them.

Angel continued to the end of the alley where a decrepit wooden gate stood. When opened, it hung off its hinges and squealed like a stuck pig, but beauty was on the other side of that ugly fence. She stood at the top of the hill and took a breath. At the bottom, a small watering hole with a rocky shore and shadowy depths sat.

Ryan stood at the edge of the water as still as a statue. It was like he didn't see what was before him. Knowing how her spell worked, there was a good chance that he didn't.

She climbed down the hill and walked to Ryan. Without hesitation, she snapped her fingers and pointed to the stream. "Get in."

He made a face but obeyed; his body tensed as the water climbed up his chest. She knew little of Descendants of Fire, but most of them had an issue with cold water. It was assumed that it was due to the higher body temperatures, but no concrete evidence had ever come from ancient studies.

Angel steadied her nerves and held her hands over the water. "God of Chaos and Darkness come to me. I offer this vessel as pure as can be. Join me here on Earth." She waited for something to happen, but there was no change.

Ryan hadn't moved. He stared at his rippling reflection in the water.

Angel pursed her lips and dropped her hand. Piecing together the incantation to call Malsumis over was one of her happiest moments. That joy began to dwindle as she realized something was wrong. She tried once more and huffed in frustration when nothing happened. "Oh, for the love of..." Angel tapped her temple and closed her eyes.

Horns in the distance and the hum of the factories making weapons and new tools for her soldiers filled the air. Smog made breathing hard, and the absence of wind caused the veil to linger above the city. That veil was nothing compared to the storm brewing in her head.

She was about to call Ryan back when the water rolled around him, the clear bed turning black. The darkness started around Ryan and seeped from him like squid ink. Her eyes widened, and soon, she stared at a clouded, distorted face under the water. However, while the water rippled, the face didn't.

Angel bowed and looked at Ryan. His eyes were black, and his head tilted to the sky. She didn't know what to do. "Do I kill him?" she whispered, not asking anyone in particular.

A deep, throaty voice came from Ryan's lips. He rumbled a low growl as he faced her. "You've done well thus far," the voice said.

A surge of chaos tore through the city, and her chest ached. There was so much power in the air. Angel's breaths came out in quick gasps as she tried to adjust. She let the magik run through her body and breathed it in and out like it was a part of her. "What do I do now?" she asked breathlessly.

"He is too pure to be my vessel. I need the other to complete the transfer into your world," Lord Malsumis said. "You told me there were twins before." A twinge of anger ran through the God's deep voice.

Angel flinched. "Yes, My Lord. He... I am still working on securing him. I thought you could manage with the stronger one," she said. It was hard to keep the tremble from her voice.

Lord Malsumis roared so loud she thought her eardrums would burst.

Angel resisted the urge to cover her ears and squeezed her eyes shut. There was no point in acting unafraid. It was apparent in the way her body shook.

"I need both. One as sacrificial and one for the vessel. This one is no good, not strong enough." Lord Malsumis' voice weakened as his image faded. "Bring both. Blood for blood, an eye for an eye. Without both, I will never see your world."

The red eyes vanished, and Ryan fell backward into the water. Just like that, her lord was gone.

Angel stayed still until she remembered her new puppet was submerged in water. She fished him out before he could drown and sat next to his body as she scanned the horizon. Both twins needed to be present for this sacrificial lamb thing. She might call it quits if she couldn't find a way to get the other brother there. If it wasn't for Avery, her entire plan would fall apart.

"Oh, my day is not going as planned," she muttered. And she still had to get Ryan back to his cell and meet Avery for lunch. She dropped her chin and sighed. It was going to be a long week.

Time to Make Good on Promises

KARA

She waited all night, hoping Killian would return to Haven after the fight with Angel. Justin and Nicholas disappeared throughout the day, and Cody had been forbidden from asking questions. She wasn't sure to what purpose, but the boy obeyed when his dad was around.

Killian didn't come home the night Ryan was taken. Or the next day. Or the day after that.

"Do you want to come see what my magik does?" Cody asked, sitting next to her on the couch.

Kara brushed her hair, letting the frizzy strands slip through her fingers like a horsetail. She needed a cut; it was well past her shoulders. Plus, when it was hot and humid, she looked like she was part lion. If she had been back home, Dawson and she would have had a spa day before stopping at the bakery.

"Do you think Killian will come back?" she asked. *Is he safe?*

Cody nodded. "I think he will." His words were simple, and he didn't try to reassure her with false hope.

She sighed and set the hairbrush aside, shaking her head and rubbing her eyes. It had been a long couple of nights of little to no sleep, and while her world had stopped, nothing else had. Justin insisted on training. Nicholas said practice made perfect and took over Ryan's role in helping her learn the sword.

"They act like nothing's happened," she said sadly. This wasn't something she should vent to a child about, but Kara couldn't help it. There was no one else she could talk to, and Cody was right there.

"It bothers Jay more than you think. He just won't let you see his sadness," Cody said, cocking his head to the side. He set a hand on her shoulder. "It's going to be alright," he added, his face solemn.

Kara smirked, ruffled his hair, and shook her head. That stern, serious look didn't fit his energy and flamboyant outlook on life. "Well, we'll just have to figure out how to get him back, won't we?" she asked.

Cody grinned and nodded as if sensing the change in her mood. "I knew you'd hatch a plan," he said.

Kara didn't have a plan because she didn't know enough about strategy, but if Killian ever returned, she could ask him for help. It was apparent they couldn't leave Ryan to Angel, no matter how difficult things had been since their arrival.

"Want to help me train?" she asked.

Cody nodded and jumped up. "That means I can use magik," he said.

Justin had a strict "no using unnecessary magik" rule with Cody. Kara thought he was worried about what could happen should the boy lose control, but she has never seen anything dangerous come from the boy's experiments.

"What kind of training?" she asked, leaving it up to the master. She didn't know what to do outside of swinging a sword and meditating.

"Oh!" Cody froze in the hall and faced her. "Archery," he said.

She cocked her head to the side and wrinkled her nose. "I dunno if I'd be any good at that," she said.

Cody bolted down the hall, and the front door slammed behind him. It looked like she was going to learn archery.

After an intense session of shooting arrows into the dirt because Kara wasn't strong enough to pull the bow back to hit the target, she sat in front of Dawson's grave for the first time in a long time.

The stone marking his burial site was a black rectangular rock with blue spray paint splashed across the front. Sometimes, the weather wore the paint down, so Ryan would come and add fresh color for her. A pang staked through her chest, and she shook the thoughts away.

After feeling like she could finally return to normal, something else had to happen. She had been cruel to Ryan, and in some ways, he had been cruel to her, but they were friends. She never wanted anything bad to happen to him, especially if Angel and her sadistic tendencies were involved.

"I wish you were still here," Kara said to the rock after finding her words. "It's not been easy." The wind blew around the stones as if greeting her back. There was rarely a day without rain. Winter was coming in full force, and she had missed most of the fall.

There was rustling in the bushes, and Kara looked up as a massive white wolf stepped into the clearing. Its snow-white fur and piercing blue eyes made her cock her head to the side to watch them flash in the sunlight. The sight of the animal filled her with a warm, loving feeling. It bubbled through her chest, and her body relaxed as she smiled. "I know you," she said, holding out her hand.

The animal didn't growl or snarl but stayed at the forest's edge. Its ears swiveled and flicked as it listened to its surroundings. The wolf held his head low, and his eyes bore into hers, but his hackles didn't raise, and he didn't bare his teeth.

"I saw you when I first got to Haven. With Avery," she said. "What are you doing here?" She dropped her hand when she realized the wolf wouldn't come. "He was going to hunt you."

A few weeks ago, Avery had mentioned something to her about the wolf hanging around. He had thought it had something to do with Kara because white wolves weren't typical.

It whined and lay down, placing its head on its paws. Nicholas had amazing abilities. For a moment, she wished she could talk to animals like him, even though he complained about it often. She wouldn't mind seeing how the little critters thought and felt.

"I feel like I'm failing." She looked back at the stone and leaned back on her palms. *Would he even accept me?* Deep in her heart, she knew Dawson would never say anything negative. He would've been so happy for her because he loved anything to do with his family. There was nothing she could do to make Dawson reject or hate her.

"There's a whole part of my life I don't know," she said. "I'm from Rochester, I can't speak my native language, and my family were Descendants." Kara spilled her guts to a wolf and a black rock.

Her parents fought in a magikal rebellion because they were Descendants. As far as she knew, her brother didn't have magik, but somehow, she did. As Justin called her, she was a special case—someone who woke late.

"What am I?" she asked. "I grew up with people filled with hate, and I didn't know I was different." Kara laughed and shook her head. "No, that's a lie. I knew. I didn't know to what extent."

Everyone around her was powerful - too powerful. Ryan could use magik without talking, Killian could summon weapons and kill without hesitation, and Tory could use someone's blood to control them, though he was told he must never enact such magik. She wanted to find where she fit in and make things right, but she couldn't figure out her part in everything.

"They lied to me my entire life," Kara said. "Mom and Dad. They protected us, but I think I'd be better prepared if they were honest. I wouldn't be scared, or maybe I would be terrified of the right things." She scoffed lightly. "I should talk about the positives in case you want to hear something good." Kara shuffled through her thoughts to try and find something worth talking about. "I'm fast thanks to running in the morning, and I can run further every day. I've even learned about gardening," she said, "I don't like the dirt, but the flowers are beautiful when you can get them to grow."

Nicholas made them work in the garden whenever they got in trouble. It wasn't the worst punishment, but as the weather got colder, it became harder to maintain the small plants, vegetables, and fruit trees.

The wolf yipped, drawing her attention. It had crawled a few feet closer on its paws, flat on its belly.

"And then there's you. You were the first animal I saw in this new world." She chuckled when the wolf's tail stopped thumping against the ground.

The wolf crawled to her side, and his wet nose nudged her hand. She reached out and brushed her fingers against his soft fur. He was warm and fluffy, nothing like she thought a wild animal would feel without regular baths or brushing.

"I train, read, and meditate. Sometimes, new things happen, and I panic because I don't have good coping skills. Everything got worse since I left home." Kara sighed and shook her head. She didn't know what she was doing. She stayed and spoke with the wolf and her brother even if she knew she was talking to herself. It still gave her a sense of relief when she finished, and she felt lighter.

As she petted the wolf, Kara lost herself in time and let her thoughts wash away. Each one was allowed to be acknowledged, and then she released them, no longer wishing to feel the pain of anger. Shadows fell across her lap, and she looked up, peering into the brightened sun. Her nose wrinkled as she tried to figure out when it got so hot. Her long-sleeved shirt stuck to her back, and she peeled herself off the ground with a grunt. Leaves, twigs, and dirt stuck to the back of her pants, but she brushed it off with a huff.

Kara looked around at the bright, green-leafed trees and beautiful flowered shrubs. Her heart skipped. This was wrong. It was the middle of winter, not summer, and unless Nicholas was playing an elaborate joke, the forest wasn't currently this green. She squeezed her hands together and reached for her wolf friend, but he vanished without a trace.

When she looked for her trail back to Haven, her eyes fell on a brick-paved path. It was well-kept and beautiful; the soft scent of pollen lingered in the air. Bees buzzed by her head, and she ducked when she looked up and saw a hive before scurrying off with mumbled curses.

Kara hurried up the path and stopped at the top of a slight incline. There was Haven, but it also wasn't Haven. She froze. Two people stood on the lawn, surrounded by furniture, clothes, and books. She stared at the man and woman as they pecked each other's lips, and the woman laughed hysterically before falling into his arms.

"That's Justin," Kara whispered, staring in shock.

He was young, but it was Justin. His eyes were a beautiful earthy brown, and she recognized his angled chin and high cheekbones even without the jagged scar. He had pale skin and freckles, and his hair was thick and wavy. It was so much like Kara's that she swore they could've been related. He wore a loose white shirt and a pair of baggy shorts. He was thin like a stick, but he was smiling. That was a smile

Kara had never seen on his face before - it was carefree and downright joyful.

A teenager ran out of the unfinished house, holding up paint. He had braided brown hair and bright brown eyes. His skin was darker than Justin's, but they had the same angled face and pointed noses. He was a short, tubby teen, yet Kara knew without a doubt who it was.

"Nicholas," she whispered.

She couldn't believe how adorable he was or that she was seeing it. Kara blinked, expecting the vision to fade, but it didn't. She was still there with Justin, Nicholas, and what she assumed was Justin's wife.

A tall black woman with gorgeous, full, dark brown hair wrapped in a pastel ribbon atop her head. It looked fluffy and soft, and Kara wanted to touch it so badly, but she didn't even think she could. The woman was slender and dressed in a flowing pale-yellow sundress that flowered around her like the petals of a blooming tulip or daffodil. She was beautiful, and joy lit up her delicate features.

Kara walked through the yard. "Justin, I'm lost in your past," she said, approaching the couple. No one looked at her. Kara's breath caught. There's no way she was invisible. She waved her hand in between them and got no reaction. "Oh, shoot," she said. As she dropped her hand, it fell through Jessica's shoulder, and Kara bit back a terrified scream.

Maybe she died, and now she was stuck in some weird limbo where she had to find clues about a messed-up past to warn the next poor sap about some dangerous future.

Jessica straightened and turned her head when Kara went through her. Their eyes met, and a small smile crept onto the woman's face. "I do believe we're being haunted," she said.

Justin rested his forehead against hers. "What's that?" he asked.

Jessica returned her attention to him. "Would you check on my sister? I want to make sure she's comfortable."

He kissed her cheek and chuckled, letting her waist go. "Of course, my love," he said. Justin walked backward a few feet and turned with a flamboyant wave of his hand. Unlike the man Kara lived with now, he was over the top and dramatic.

Jessica held out her hand and wiggled her fingers, beckoning Kara forward. "Where are you, little Descendant? I can feel you," she said. Her tone was more serious now that they were alone, but she smiled.

Kara sighed in relief. She wasn't invisible, and that was good to know. "You can see me?" she asked.

"No, but I can feel you," Jessica said. "You're quite powerful, but you sound so young. Your energy is... confused. I can sense your fear and sadness; you just suffered a terrible loss. I'm so sorry," Jessica said, reaching up. Her hand went through Kara's, and she grinned a little. "But you have so much fire."

Kara was freaked out by the hand floating through hers, but she bit back another scream and swallowed it. "Why didn't you hear me before?" she asked, trying to take her mind off it.

Jess chuckled and dropped her hand. "I wasn't focused on you before. If I expel enough energy, I can almost see you," she said.

"Can you help me get home? I don't know how I got here. This is the past, isn't it?" Kara asked. It had to be because Justin's wife wasn't alive, but this was her.

"We energy magiks have some interesting abilities. Yours must just be awakening," Jessica said. She smiled again and dropped her hand. "You tapped into a memory of the past."

"Great, but how do I go back?" Kara asked.

"You think of your home. Tell your magik to return you," she said.

Kara nodded and hesitated. If she stayed, she could learn more about Justin and Nicholas. "How can you talk to me?" she asked.

Jessica smiled, apparently glad Kara had decided to stay. "We are both Descendants of Energy, so we draw on magik from the same source," she said, her voice light and sweet.

"Will our interactions alter this time? Could I tell you things that would ruin your future?" Kara asked. She didn't know if she could save Justin's wife, but if she could, things would be easier for Justin's family in the present day.

"No, you didn't time travel, my dear. This is a memory. You aren't communicating with the real me," the woman said as if this was obvious.

Kara huffed and crossed her arms. She didn't understand. "How can I communicate with someone I didn't know and didn't know me? I wasn't here for this," she said.

"Memories leave an imprint all over the world. You can find them in ancient ruins, old houses, and the comfort of a once beloved home that stands silent in heartbreak," Jessica said.

"Can I see you again?" Kara asked.

"Not in this memory. It's only around as long as the energy can sustain it," Jessica said. "I imagine that since you tapped into it, it will become one with the universe as all things do."

Kara looked at the beautiful log house and bright green grass. This was paradise. She could see why they called it Haven. "He misses you."

Jessica nodded. "As he should. I'm the best thing that's ever happened to him." Her words were spoken gently but with amusement.

"I think Cody does, too," Kara whispered. She didn't know why she bothered if this wasn't even the real Jessica, but she had to let her know. Let her know she was loved and not forgotten.

Jessica held her hand up once more. "Tell Justin this for me: he must always walk the lightest path even though it's the hardest," she said.

Kara cocked her head to the side and held her palm against Jess'. She kept their hands from going through each other, and it almost looked like they were touching. "Why?" She could feel a warm surge of their entwining energies that calmed her heart and anxieties.

"Use it when he needs it the most. It's a special spell I made for him, so he'll understand," Jessica said.

Kara nodded and closed her eyes. It was time to go home. When she reopened them, she sat with her wolf friend before Dawson and Jessica's headstones. Nothing had changed aside from the air getting a little colder. Finally, she was growing, which felt pretty good.

Days, Weeks, Months... Years?

Ryan opened his eyes, stuck in his mind's swirling black and gray abyss. He had an empty head, and for all the jokes he managed to come up with, there was no one to tell them to. He tried talking to the crazy voices of his "life and death" friends, but they didn't currently like him because of his attitude. *Attitude. Like they aren't a part of the problem.*

The void was increasingly exhausting, but awakening only to deal with Angel was worse. Those memories came and went, mostly in his half-asleep state, though he didn't need to sleep. In this world, Ryan didn't get hungry or tired. He just existed. Hopefully, his body was managing just fine.

There was a tug on his magik because that was something he could feel deep inside when his body used it, but he never knew for what purpose. Contacting Killian had been widely unsuccessful, and while Ryan still tried to maintain their bond, he couldn't even find his way to that place in his mind. He spent his time meditating and reviewing everything he had done wrong because he knew things would be different when he got out of this. Analyzing his weaknesses and staying ahead of them was the only way he would survive.

He named the disembodied voices Fyre and Chaol because he had to call them something, and Fyre responded to the name. Chaol was hit or miss, but at times, it too would deign to announce its presence.

Ryan closed his eyes and attempted to reconnect to his energy and magik with a furrowed brow. The red and orange flames of passion built around him, flickering like candles nearing the end of their existence. The energy vanished before he could call upon them, leaving him frustrated and grimacing.

"This is ridiculous," he muttered, fanning the flames of his weak will to life.

This time, when he reached for the spark, it sat in the palm of his ethereal hand, allowing him a glimpse of normality. Fire surged through his veins, and Ryan closed his hand around the spark before it could vanish. With a deep breath, he let the pull of magik flow through him and jolted upright back into the real world.

It was cold and smelly - that was the first thing Ryan noticed as he awoke. He wrinkled his nose and stared around the dim, stone cell. Green slime and ooze dripped from the rocks, pattering on the uneven ground. As far as accommodations went, Angel could've done better, but he wouldn't complain as far as complacency would go.

"Ryan!" Killian's voice, emotions, and memories slammed into him the moment he was conscious.

He was flooded with images of Avery – every single one of them was Avery. Ryan squeezed his temples and groaned low, trying not to pass out from the emotional warfare. He wasn't sure Killian was aware they were back in connection, but the messages came in bits and pieces like they had all been stopped at a wall and then surged through when Ryan allowed them to.

"Stop, shut up." Ryan managed to send a message through all the noise, and in less than two seconds, it stopped. He sighed in relief and

blinked back tears, thanks to his now-pounding head. *"How long has it been?"* he asked.

Killian took his sweet time replying, which irritated Ryan even though he knew his brother was trying not to overload him. *"Almost three weeks."*

Ryan hissed and doubled over when his stomach clenched, and a wave of nausea tore through him. *Three weeks with Angel.* And yet, there was a blank hole in his memory where everything should be. *The last thing I need is the witch messing with my head.* Ryan took a breath and tried to think past the thundering pain, but that made it worse.

On top of the massive migraine, the skin around his wrists burned and itched. He dragged a finger along the smooth red lines and huffed. Dried blood crusted around his fingers and on his arms, but there was no trace of scarring or a recent injury. Ryan swallowed and pushed himself to his feet. His throat was as rough as sandpaper, and he resisted coughing, trying not to alert the witch wherever she was hiding.

A large steel door was in front of him, allowing the tiniest bit of light through the barred window. It wasn't large enough to climb through. If he was going to escape, he had to play it smart. Ryan took stock of everything around him, but aside from green goo and water dripping somewhere in the distance, he didn't have much to work with.

"Ryan?" Killian's voice wavered. It wasn't hard to tell he was upset, probably worried. *"I've been having dreams,"* he said.

Ryan wrinkled his nose again. He brushed a hand through his greasy hair and grimaced. He needed a shower. Had she not let him shower in three weeks? The musty stench of sweat and dirt-riddled clothes was close enough to an answer.

"Dreams?" Ryan asked, trying to pinpoint everything in the cell before he got sucked back into his head.

"Bad things. I wake up screaming and can taste blood. What is she doing?" Killian asked.

Torture. The thought sent a spike of pain through his temple and made him lose his train of thought. By the time he remembered he was talking to Killian, the thought was long gone, and he couldn't remember what the problem was. *"What are your dreams about?"* he asked, deciding it was best not to answer.

Killian was silent for a long time. *"What's wrong with you? I just told you,"* he said when a few seconds passed.

Ryan pressed his hands to the steel door, almost not hearing the second voice in his head. *"Mmm, specifics,"* he said.

"She cuts you, and you're always screaming," Killian replied with little hesitation.

Ryan wished he could say something more comforting but couldn't think of anything. Mainly because Killian's dreams were sometimes just dreams, and he couldn't recall any physical pain since arriving in this Helwe hole.

The steel sizzled under his hands, and Ryan shoved the rest of his energy through his palms. A lock clicked, and the door swung open, making as much noise as possible.

"Ryan?" Killian nagged him as he hurried down the hall, trying to keep his softened senses open.

Everything moved in slow motion and spun like he was trapped in one of those nightmares where he was being chased. The stone walls weren't helping him find a way out because they all looked the same, and he couldn't even see straight, thanks to the flickering fluorescent lights. *Is there even an exit?* There had to be because he was there, so there had to be a door.

"Are you there?" Killian was like a gnat in his ear, but no matter how often Ryan swatted his presence away, the brat kept returning.

A flicker of familiar energy zapped through Ryan's mind about halfway down his third hall, and he froze. It smelt like honey and lavender and was warm. Ryan stared at a solid black door to his left. The hall was narrow, and aside from his door, this was the only other one visible.

"Ryan!"

Ryan swatted the air by his ear, forgetting momentarily that Killian wasn't there. *"Shut up, I'm fine. It's a dumb dream,"* he said to get his brother off his back.

"What's happened to you?" Killian asked. He was getting worked up, and the frustration seeped through their bond.

If Ryan had the energy, he would block his brother, but that wasn't an option. *"I don't know. I'm kind of busy,"* he said. It was hard not to cut his voice short.

"What could you possibly be busy with?" Killian demanded. Now, there was no hiding the frustration. It swept through their bond in a hot wave of electricity, and Ryan bit his tongue to keep from shouting out loud.

He reached out and pushed the black door open, trying to keep his focus. It slid back without any resistance, and his hand trembled. He told himself it was the lack of food. Within the cell sat a lone, blonde-haired woman. His heart thrummed in his ears, and Ryan stepped back, shocked. He didn't recognize her until she looked up. Her emerald gaze was unfocused and dull.

"Mom?"

Not only was she alive, but she was still in Angel's cells. Justin was right. He told them she was fine, but Ryan hadn't believe him.

A hand grabbed his shoulder and tightened, making him jump. Angel threw him out of the room with more strength than a woman her size should have.

Ryan gasped when he hit the back wall and slid to the floor. The air whooshed from his lungs, and he clutched his chest.

"You just don't know when to quit," Angel said, exiting the room. The door shut behind her with a slam that echoed down the hall.

Ryan shook the shock off and scrambled to his feet, but she already had a weapon drawn. The knife sliced across his right forearm thanks to his mind still moving slowly. He tried to duck out of the way of the second attack, but the knife ended up in his thigh the second time.

Angel grabbed the front of his shirt and pushed him into the wall, keeping him from sliding to the floor. "I'm getting sick of you," she said.

Ryan bit his tongue, trying to keep the tears at bay. "Aren't we just getting started?" he forced the words between his teeth. His mom was right there. He couldn't believe how close she was and how he couldn't do anything for her.

The flames of his energy fanned to life at the promise of his anger.

"Why didn't she look at me when I walked in?" Ryan asked.

Angel smirked and gestured to the door behind her. "That pathetic shell? Oh, she doesn't talk much these days."

Ryan glared, and his energy flashed around him. Heat surged down the narrow corridor, and he grabbed Angel's wrist. Flames burst to life around his hands. The smell of searing flesh burned through his nostrils, and she screamed in pained agony. The sound was ear-splitting, and he winced in sympathy unable to feel victorious even when torturing someone like her.

Angel snapped her hand back and cradled it against her chest, sobbing in pain.

He forgot how destructive fire could be to others. Ryan was almost too shocked to move. Almost. He tore away from the wall and ran down the wall. With his magik and energy reconnected, he should be able to get somewhere.

Avery appeared in front of him, looking physically ill.

Ryan stopped. He blinked, processed, and blinked again. "Oh, you've got to be kid..." his world went black.

He woke up in the expanse of darkness. Ryan cursed, screamed, and yelled, but it didn't improve his mood. Being suspended in the air made throwing a temper tantrum difficult, and he had the strongest desire to punch something.

"Avery, of course it was Avery!" he shouted.

There was snickering in the distance, and Ryan perked up. Chaol and Fyre were returning to add to his depressing, messed up little life.

"It almost made it," Fyre said in its high-pitched, squealy voice.

"Attachments make it weak," Chaol added.

Ryan pinched the bridge of his nose, finally understanding how Justin felt about managing them. Someday, he would need to apologize to that man for everything he and Killian did.

"It wants out so bad, but it stops at the sight of a woman." Fyre was judging him. It didn't say it aloud, but its tone made it clear that it didn't approve of Ryan's actions.

Don't explain yourself. Don't do it, he thought, struggling to maintain his temper. The voices swirled around him and laughed. It didn't matter if he voiced things; they could always hear him.

"They'll never come for it. It's useless," Chaol said with a sniff of disdain.

Ryan opened his mouth to argue and stopped. He clenched his hands and looked at his feet, finding nowhere else to look. He wanted to argue and say they were wrong, but Killian said he had been with Angel for three weeks. If anyone were going to come, they already would've. No, it looked like he was in this mess until he figured out how to break the curse.

Killian appeared in front of him. He materialized out of the shadows, and Ryan bit his cheek.

"Why would we come for you?" he sneered.

Chaol laughed again. "Even your family doesn't want you."

Ryan wasn't dumb enough to fall for that trick. It was apparent his brother wasn't there, and his subconscious was projecting his insecurities to make his mind more compliant. Still, Ryan couldn't help the sting of Killian's words. Any being wearing his brother's face would hurt because as much as Ryan wanted to believe Killian would never think such things, he couldn't be sure.

There would always be doubt in his mind. Killian's life would be easier without him. Killian wouldn't have to watch out for Ryan's anger or despair. When things got hard, he wouldn't have anyone to blame but himself. Ryan tried not to dwell on the less-than-ideal thoughts. That wasn't his brother, so whatever it said didn't matter.

"There was also that time he blocked you completely. Now, where did he learn to do that?" Chaol asked with a hum. The longer they talked, the more human it seemed.

Ryan didn't bother answering and stared at the Killian copy. It was nice seeing another body, even if it wasn't real.

The fake Killian laughed coldly and vanished. His body evaporated into a bunch of little lights that could've been considered beautiful in a dim setting if his life wasn't a crap show.

Killian was hanging out with Avery, and Avery was working with Angel. Now, they had a real problem.

"It's worthless. No one will save it," Chaol said as the voice faded to silence.

Ryan closed his eyes and took a steady breath. He didn't need anyone to come. He got himself into this mess so he would get himself out. The first thing he would do after he escaped was kick Avery's ass, and Ryan was finally able to relax with that thought.

The Ultimate Punishment

KILLIAN

He didn't go back to Haven for days. Nicholas eventually tracked him down and dragged him back at the insistence that Killian was overreacting and needed to grow up. He snuck out that night and hadn't returned since, mainly staying with his grandmother in Rochester and hanging out with every bad influence he could find because it numbed the pain and silenced the darkness.

It started with smoking and then turned to drinking. The drink was gross and bitter, but it also shut his mind down and kept him from feeling too much of anything. *It's bad for you. You shouldn't be doing this, so stop.* But his thoughts didn't matter. With every late night, he had an equally long morning that left him nauseated and unable to eat.

Avery tried to help and keep things calm in his mind, but Killian didn't want that either. He didn't like how comfortable Avery was getting around him when he wanted to wallow in self-pity. After the shit year he had, he was entitled to something, wasn't he? To keep the nightmares from destroying him, Killian learned to use mental shields and keep them in place most of the time. Occasionally, he dropped them in case Ryan reached out. They had only talked once in weeks, and it was a disappointing conversation.

"Hey, you want some?"

Tonight, he found a busty blonde and her four male admirers. She was one of the sexually free women in Rochester, and because of that, she often had a gaggle of men around her.

Killian shook his head, leaned against the wooden gate of Rochester, and sighed. His world spun comfortably, and his mind was numb enough that he couldn't recall how he spent his day. Tonight, nothing had to exist but him and this feeling. His tongue and lips were numb, and when he moved his head too fast, the world turned into a muddled mess of green and black.

It was a quiet night, and not even the animals made noise, which usually meant something bad was coming. Killian might have heard the crunching leaves or his drunken allies getting up and running off if he was in his right mindset.

"Come on, we need to get you home," Avery said in a voice that filtered through the clearing. A familiar pair of black boots stopped in front of him.

Killian looked up lazily, a slow smile crossing his lips as he studied the dark anger swirling through Avery's deep eyes. *"Mornin',"* he said in the sloppiest Nivet he could manage.

Avery knelt and shook his head, brushing a strand of sweat-soaked hair from Killian's face. *"You were supposed to stop doing this,"* he said softly. There was a hint of a warning there, but again, Killian wasn't in his right mind, so he didn't pay attention to it.

When Nicholas appeared behind Avery with a stern face and crossed arms, Killian knew he was about to meet his maker. "So, this is where you've been hiding," he said. While that phrase could've been playful in any other pretense, his voice was ice.

There was no talking himself out of this situation. "Oh shit," Killian murmured. He shoved Avery's hand away when he held it out to help him up. "Screw off, you told on me?"

Avery's eyes dropped, and he shrugged.

Nicholas stepped around him and yanked Killian up by his shirt collar, nearly choking him in the process. "You're lucky he complied, or I woulda beat the snot outta both of you. You're coming home, now get moving," he said.

Killian's knees about buckled when Nicholas let him go, but he pressed a hand to the wood walls around the homestead and groaned. "I can't walk."

"You'll manage," Nicholas growled. Avery moved to help, but Nicholas swatted him away. "Your job is done," he snapped.

Avery chewed his lip and took a step back with a nod.

"You backstabbing, dick," Killian growled.

Avery frowned. "I'm not going to apologize. You've been avoiding me and them, and you do this every night. Don't think I haven't heard about it. This isn't healthy, and you've got to find a new path before this one destroys you."

Killian snarled in reply and stumbled toward the homestead.

Nicholas caught the back of his shirt and shook his head. "No, you're going back to Haven. No more Rochester," he said.

Killian managed a bitter laugh. "Are you grounding me?" he asked.

"Until further notice." It would have been a hilarious joke if Nicholas was joking.

Killian could tell how serious the man was, even in his numbed stupor. "You can't be for real."

"Act like a child, get treated like one. Let's go," Nicholas said again.

Killian scoffed and took another step but hit the ground with a muffled yelp. He tasted dirt and grass, the most unpleasant combination of tastes on his tongue. Justin's oat mush was a thousand times better.

Nicholas sighed and ran a hand down his face, jerking Killian off the ground again. He teleported them home, which was a nightmare because the minute the world spun as they traversed the deep underground, Killian's stomach somersaulted. The second the world stopped, he threw up. It took his eyes forever to adjust, but he quickly realized he was back on Haven's lawn. The hiccups started about the same time the tears stopped. He didn't know if that was a plus.

"You're smarter than this. You've lost something big here, but Ryan's still alive. There's still something we can do, but what do you hope to accomplish by acting like this?" Nicholas asked.

Killian pulled away, snarling in rage. He didn't get it, and he never would. Having a sibling was one thing, but having an identical brother, someone who was a piece of his heart and soul, was completely different. They shared thoughts, feelings, and blood. The tears started again before he could catch them.

"You don't get it," he hissed, wanting to hurt someone as badly as he was. His chest hurt, and his body physically ached like he had been beaten within an inch of his life.

Everything was empty and silent, and he didn't know how to cope - he *couldn't*.

"You don't think I get it?" Nicholas asked, his voice rising in anger.

Killian's head snapped up, and he had to stop himself from throwing up again when the world nearly turned upside down. "How could you? My brother is half of me. Have you ever felt Justin's pain or read his thoughts? Did you ever have to stitch up his wounds or fight his bullies? Oh, I know your parents must have left you with nothing, so he was all you ever had and made you who you are. Don't you get it? Ryan is my other half, the best half of me, and without him... I'm nothing." Killian glared despite the tears streaming down his cheeks and the feeling of a fist running through his chest.

He spoke fast and loud; by the end, all he wanted to do was laugh hysterically and climb into bed. This was all a horrible nightmare because it couldn't be the real world.

Nicholas was quiet for a long while. Shock flashed across his face, and Killian could tell by his clenched jaw and balled fists that he wanted to keep yelling, but he controlled himself. He sighed, ran a hand down his face, and paced. He muttered to himself, but Killian couldn't understand what he said. When he came to some conclusion of how to deal with this, Nicholas cursed... loudly. His voice echoed into the darkness and bounced off the trees.

"This isn't how you deal with things. When you need help, you ask for it," he said after his voice stopped traveling.

"I don't want your help," Killian said. His anger surged, and he wished he could do more than sit in a heap on the ground.

"Yeah, well, I don't want to watch you spiral," Nicholas huffed and collapsed beside him. "It's a part of your life you will never get back, and who knows how many bridges you'll burn." His voice was softer now.

Killian scowled. He didn't care.

"You won't care right now; I get it, trust me, but later, you will. It will hurt worse, but if you let me help, we can stop it before it gets to that point," Nicholas said.

Killian grumbled to himself and dropped his chin to his chest. He wasn't alright. He knew he wasn't, but Nicholas couldn't magically fix his feelings. "I don't need your help," he whispered. His voice wasn't as defiant as before.

"I don't care what you want," Nicholas said. "You're getting it. And if you end up hating me, fine. One day, you'll see I was right."

Killian woke with a start and jolted upright. He was tucked neatly into his bed in Haven. The sun blazed through the windows, and he shielded his eyes with a hiss of pain. His head throbbed, and his mouth felt like he licked tree bark all night, and his stomach growled. He didn't know if it was hunger or anger from the crap he put in his body. "I might die today," he whispered, rolling over and throwing the blankets over his head.

"Good."

Killian nearly jumped out of bed at the sound of Avery's voice. He sat back up and turned to face Ryan's bed. Avery sat cross-legged on the mattress with a look of disdain and frustration. He picked at the blanket with one hand and held a half-eaten apple in the other. "You're in Haven," Killian said, pointing at him. He blinked repeatedly to make sure he wasn't hallucinating.

"Nicholas thought I could be useful, so I've been granted temporary access. If I mess with anyone or look in Cody's direction, Justin will castrate me," Avery said. His back was straight, and he didn't stop fidgeting with the blanket.

"Then why are you here?" Killian asked.

Avery shrugged. "I told you last night that I was worried."

Killian scowled and flopped back down on the bed. "Leave me alone," he said.

There was the crunch of an apple and some lip-smacking. It was loud, and Killian didn't doubt Avery did it intentionally. After two or three more crunches, his head snapped up so he could glare again. "What. Do you. Want?" he asked.

Avery gave him a cheeky smile. "Someone woke up on the wrong side of the bed."

Killian growled in response. He wasn't in the mood, and his head was pounding.

"Nicholas told me to make today as painful as possible," Avery said.

Killian scoffed. "I have a breakdown and get punished. That sounds like a good way to raise a kid."

"You're not bein' punished for the breakdown. You're bein' punished for stayin' out all hours, drinkin' yourself into a state so bad that you can't defend yourself." At the look of murder on Killian's face, Avery cleared his throat. "Those are Nicholas' words," he added.

Killian didn't care whose words they were.

Avery read the look on his face and grinned wider. "You're pissed. Wanna spar?" he asked, practically bouncing on the bed.

"Get out of my room before I kill you," Killian said, laying his head back down and throwing the blanket over it.

"Oh, *darling*, if you think you're man enough to take me, bring it." Avery drawing out the word sweetie was enough to set Killian on fire. It was worse than being told to calm down.

Killian didn't think he could hold the contents of his stomach in a fight, but that didn't stop him from flying across the room and slamming into Avery. They fell back off the bed and landed on Avery's front lawn. The teleportation disoriented Killian, and he froze for a second too long.

Avery rammed his elbow into Killian's jaw and switched their positions so that Killian was on his back with a sharp rock jamming in between his shoulders.

He struggled uselessly against the Descendant of Water as Avery pinned him.

"You're a Descendant of Shadow who refuses to use the shadows. Give me the slip," Avery said.

This was turning into a training session. "I'm not sparring with you, damn it," Killian snarled. He thrashed like a fish out of water, and leaves crunched under him.

Avery caught his jaw in a bruising grip, and Killian stilled. His heart thundered in his ears as Avery's dark eyes bore into his. "I didn't ask what you wanted, did I?"

Killian's heart stuttered, and he frowned, unable to place that feeling.

"Now, why don't you be a good boy and do as you're told," Avery growled, his voice low.

Killian shivered but melted into the shadows. Anything to get that feeling as far from him as possible. His instincts took over as a fighter, and he traveled through the shadow realm, trying to avoid Avery's prying eyes. He was a Descendant of Shadow, but Ryan could always move faster. There was never a point in using his camouflage spell. Killian reappeared behind Avery but didn't touch him.

Avery chuckled and swiped his legs under Killian's, sending him to the ground again. "You had an openin', and you hesitated," he said. His voice was light again. It was like he forgot he had sent Killian into an existential crisis two seconds ago.

He was so shocked he forgot to be mad.

Avery stood over him for a second before offering a hand. "Get your head in the game," he said. "I told Nicholas I would punish you. Don't make me a liar."

Killian grabbed his hand and let Avery pull him back to his feet.

They ran the same drill for nearly an hour. Killian was sore and bruised by the time Avery decided to call it quits. The Descendant of Water smirked and plopped down in the grass beside the sweaty, sticky Killian. He felt gross.

"Stop fearin' what's gonna happen if you let loose," Avery said.

Killian didn't want to let loose. He had already removed the ring, what else did this man want from him? "I'm not afraid," he said after a while.

Avery leaned back on his palms and stared at the sky. "You're steeped in fear. That's all you are."

Killian didn't argue. It was a pointless battle to have with someone who read his emotions better than his twin.

"You know..." Avery trailed off.

Killian turned his head and smirked. It wasn't often the other was at a loss for words. "What do I know?" he asked.

"That you're an idiot," Avery finished. He didn't make eye contact and shoved his hand in his front pocket to take out his cigarettes.

Killian wrinkled his nose and turned his face away.

Avery tightened his grip on the pack and hung his head. "You don't like the smell," he said. It wasn't a question but confirmation of something he already knew.

"Doesn't matter what I like, does it?" Killian asked.

Avery chucked the pack away and fell onto his back.

Killian fidgeted with the dirt then his shirt and even pulled a couple of strands of his hair as he tried to figure out what to say. He didn't like small talk and never felt compelled to partake.

"You're stressin' me out. Say what's in your head," Avery ordered. His voice was tight and tense, as if he didn't know what to do either.

Maybe Killian was overstaying his welcome. He jumped to his feet and saluted like a moron. "See ya, I'll tell Nicholas you tortured me good," he said.

Avery caught his ankle before he could run, nearly tripping him. "That's not what I meant, damn. Sit," he said.

Killian hesitated. He was torn between obeying and telling him to screw off. In the end, he ended up sitting.

"Look, I just... if you ever need somethin', don't hesitate to ask, 'kay?" Avery asked. He let Killian's ankle go and brought his hand up like he was wiping something from his mouth. "I just don't want somethin' bad to happen to you out here. It's a shit place, and I'd... it'd be bad if it did. So, yeah. Just call, I'll be there."

Killian's face burned, and his stomach fluttered. He was sure these weren't normal friendship feelings.

Avery chanced a look at him in the unending silence.

Killian went rigid and turned his face away before Avery could see the heated redness rushing across his cheeks. This was a new feeling, and he didn't know what to do with it.

"No, stop! Please, stop," Ryan screamed. Tears streamed down his face, and he fought the chains holding him to the wall. His voice was so full of terror and pain that Killian felt it, too.

Killian's chest tightened, and he reached out to make Angel stop beause she didn't seem to hear him. Her blade made quick work across Ryan's arm, and blood splattered the wall and floor. His brother was suffering, begging the woman to stop, and she wouldn't.

"Ryan!" Killian jolted upright as the vision faded and left his head pounding.

Avery set a hand on his shoulder, jolting him back to reality.

Killian stared at the pale sky and panted, trying to force the images away.

"You alright?" Avery asked, not removing his hand.

Killian sat dazed momentarily before nodding and running a hand down his face. "You let me fall asleep," he said.

Avery shrugged. "You looked like you needed it, but you gotta go back to Haven before dark," he said. At Killian's cross look, Avery held up his hands. "Not my rule. It's Nicholas'."

That's right, he was grounded. Killian fell onto his back and took a deep breath with a low groan. "I feel like crap," he whispered.

Avery lay next to him wordlessly. They stared at the sky side-by-side silently, but it wasn't uncomfortable.

Their hands brushed, and Killian had an overwhelming desire to grab the dark-haired nuisances' hand, but he didn't think it would be accepted. *Why would you want to touch him anyway?* Killian's hand moved independently and slipped into Avery's, sitting still against his palm. Avery's fingers were calloused but warm, and he could feel the dry patches of skin around the back of his hand.

Avery's hand closed around his, and he stroked the back of Killian's hand with a small sigh.

"I remember a thunderstorm when we were kids. Ryan told me you were a trout man," Killian said.

Avery chuckled and shook his head. "Mhm, I remember. It was quite interestin' getting' a teddy bear hucked at my head in the dead of night," he said.

"I wanted to protect him. I thought I could," Killian murmured. Maybe he had never really protected Ryan. Not from their mother or grandmother or the kids who made fun of him. "Am I a bad brother?" he asked.

Avery was quiet beside him.

Killian sighed and closed his eyes, squeezing Avery's hand and praying he could stay anchored through this storm. Every day was something new, and he didn't know how much more he could take.

"It'll be alright," Avery whispered.

Waterproof

ANGEL

"Are you sure you don't want to come to the cliffside with us and watch the meteor shower?" Jess asked once more.

Rebecca smiled and shrugged. "No. Enjoy your date night without your sister cock-blocking," she said.

Jess smiled and wrung her hands together nervously. She nodded to Rebecca's pregnant belly. "He's growing well. He'll be strong. Can I... can I touch?" she asked.

Rebecca nodded and stuck out her stomach, setting her hands on his lower back for support. "Oh, go for it. You're always rubbing my belly anyway."

Jess's smooth hands cradled the unborn babe, and she giggled happily as she whispered words to him. "Any day now, little one. We're all so excited."

It was the last thing she had from him – from Aryn.

"Have you named him yet?" Jess asked.

Rebecca shook her head. "No, not yet." She was torn between the name Aryn wanted for a son and the name she had wanted from her childhood.

Justin appeared in the living room, dusting leaves and flower petals from his hair. "Yo, we gotta go. The sun's setting soon, and I wanna claim our spot," he said.

Rebecca chuckled as Jess straightened and beamed at her husband. "Yeah, go, go. I can manage a night alone. Who knows, I might enjoy it," she said brightly.

"We'll be home later," Jess said, kissing the top of her head and grabbing Justin's hand. "See you soon."

Rebecca smiled until they vanished in a flurry of magik and wind. She sighed and ran a hand over her stomach, shaking her head. "Your auntie is never going to let you go, you know?" she said to the baby.

If she had her way, she would never let him go either.

Angel opened the door to Ryan's cell and stepped in. Since his escape attempt, she had done a rather fine job containing him – not to toot her own horn, of course. "We are going to work on a new project today," she said. "I think you'll find it fun."

Ryan grimaced. "You can't keep me here forever," he said. "I know I'll change in time." His words were weak, but there was still a spark of fire in them.

Angel smirked and unhooked the chains from the wall, taking them in her hands. "You know about the change? I figured Justin would've told you," she said. The stench of blood was pungent, and she was careful not to breathe too deeply.

He cursed under his breath, barely having the energy to say her name.

Angel smirked in response and led him down the hall with a couple of yanks on the chains until they got to her underground lab. It had shiny instruments and tiled walls and was buried so deep inside the earth that no one could hear the screams. It was where she took her *special* subjects and the ones who most often this was the last place they saw. She kept an eye on Ryan as they walked, and though he stumbled a couple of times, she didn't trust he wouldn't take off the second her attention was elsewhere.

Aside from the void of emotion behind his emerald gaze, Ryan was filthy. His clothes were stained with dirt, blood, and sweat. He smelled foul, meaning she would need to allow him to bathe soon. His hair was stringy and greasy, and patchy stubble had appeared on his face. His clothes hung off him like old bags - he would need to be fed, too.

The narrow hall opened into a cavernous room filled with shiny machines and rows of transparent glass cells. It was all bullet-proof-grade material imbued with her scientist's creations that repelled magik. Many Descendants had spent time in those rooms, and not one had left alive. One cracked the glass ages ago in a last minute escape attempt, but he hadn't survived. The stone floor turned to tile, and they crossed the cavern to one of the larger rooms in the back.

She slid open a thick glass door and gestured inside. "Go on," she said.

Ryan complied without a sound. When the door shut behind him, Angel pressed her thumb against a green pad on the outside. It flashed white, and a lock clicked into place, sealing the room. She beamed and clapped her hands like a child. It was exciting when her plans worked. She waited a long time for this to pay off, and now she could finally make it happen. She turned and bounced up some metal steps, feeling years younger, and stopped before a large console. The device was full of flashing lights and beeped occasionally.

She tapped a microphone and turned it on, staring at Ryan's petulant glare through the glass. "It's good to see you're awake," she said.

Ryan still didn't talk. Fire encased his hands, but he didn't move.

"I wouldn't bother, dear. This glass is magik resistant," Angel said, waving her hand. She spoke into the microphone. A little green light flashed under the stick to tell her it was transmitting. "What's the biggest problem with Descendants of Fire?" she asked.

Ryan flipped her off, and his lips moved, but she couldn't hear him.

"Let me save us all some time. Water. When a Descendant of Fire gets wet, they can't use magik," she said.

Ryan froze. Every muscle in his body tightened, and his eyes widened a fraction of an inch. Someone not paying attention wouldn't have noticed the minuscule detail change in his face, compressing it into a picture of fear.

Angel chuckled and tapped her fingers on the metal console. "I'm going to teach you how to overcome that weakness," she said. She pressed a black button near the top. With an unholy grating sound, a panel slid open in Ryan's cell, specifically the ceiling.

Ryan jumped out of the way and looked up, his eyes wide and alert. He crouched like he was about to spring out, but Angel chuckled and hit a small red button. Water began pouring into the water-tight room and pooling on the floor.

Angel tapped an invisible watch on her wrist. "You better figure out how to channel your fire," she said.

Ryan ducked away from the onslaught of pouring water and threw his shoulder against the door. His energy reverberated throughout the room, building up before dispersing. He was fighting himself. If there was any way to break a person, life or death situations were the way to go.

"You're not gonna be escaping from there," she said, trying not to enjoy herself too much.

He glared. It was almost no fun taunting him without a reaction. The water pooled around his ankles in less than a minute.

She tsked and flicked her finger back and forth like the pendulum of a clock. "Running out of time."

Ryan cursed under his breath and pressed his back to the door.

She couldn't see what he was doing, and while she would have loved to see his process, it wasn't necessary. There was a long silence before a spark lit up the cell and fizzled out.

Ryan hissed in pain, and after another minute, the water was around his waist. His lips moved silently as he held his hands before him with closed eyes. His energy built in his palms and around his hands, but it kept going out as the water climbed inch after inch. It looked like he was going through every spell he knew. *Interesting. He knows saying them out loud strengthens the magik, so why doesn't he do it more often?*

Angel was impressed. It took her a long time to figure out that she was cheating herself out of power by not speaking the spells. When the water was up to his shoulders, and he still hadn't produced more than a spark, she sighed. Perhaps it was too soon. She could try to enrage him, but his anger was hard to stoke thanks to the chaos.

"Perhaps I should go get your brother. He might be a good motivator," Angel cooed.

Ryan didn't let the water distract him from his work. The water went up his neck, and while he could tread water, eventually, the water would have nowhere to go.

She gave it another minute, and he had to break his stance to tread water, but his lips didn't stop moving.

Angel sighed, and her finger hovered over the button to empty the room. She didn't want to lose the boy so soon after acquiring him, but she also had to push him to his limits. As she debated letting him out, an explosion rocked the building. The water was gone in ten seconds, and she blinked in shock.

Ryan sat against the far wall, clutching his chest and breathing deeply as he coughed up water. Droplets rolled down his face and dripped from his hair as she leaned forward to take in the sight.

A crater the size of her office occupied nearly all the space in the cell's floor.

Angel smiled and opened the door. He would be fed and showered tonight, and then she had another task. She knew he would be ready if he could pass this last test. Once she had total control and no risk of slipping up, she would have Avery bring Killian.

"Return to your cell," Angel said, letting the chaos take over the boy's mind again.

Ryan didn't have the energy to fight. One minute, he was in the room; the next, he was back where he belonged. Angel rubbed her hands together and stared at the mess. *Yet another thing to get fixed.*

Angel left a tray of food in Ryan's cell as he slept. She also left a change of clean clothes and a razor to shave if he so wished. The shower would have to come later since she didn't trust him just yet. She returned to the elevator to finish her day and stopped outside Summer's cell.

Since Ryan discovered his mom was there, he didn't fight as hard. If Angel had known to keep him around, it would have been to mention his mother; she would've done it long ago.

Angel entered the small cell, and the woman's green eyes flicked to meet hers. "Your son is exhausting. No wonder you left," she said with a mock sigh.

Summer giggled a little hysterically. "Went out for a hunt, and Mommy disappeared."

"Right. Now, let's give you a little lucidity so I can pick that mushy brain," Angel said, flicking her wrist.

The chaos loosened around the Descendant of Wind, and she slumped to the floor with a low groan. Chaos could numb and ease the world's sorrows, so one could do anything without worrying about pain or emotion while under its influence. It was a skill that could be useful or deadly under the right circumstances.

Summer was likely feeling the full weight of her deprived body now that she was free of the dark energy that warped her mind. "What the-"

"Good, I missed our little chats." Angel smirked. "I'll grant you freedom in exchange for something."

Summer lifted her head, and her body trembled with the effort. "You'll not get anything from me."

Angel trailed her fingers down the jagged stone wall. She didn't dare get too close in case Summer decided to lash out. "Oh, but what's a little information for freedom?"

Summer laughed bitterly. "Freedom in what, death?"

"I don't have much use for you. I could just kill you, but leaving you alive would be much more humiliating, don't you agree?" Angel asked innocently.

Summer growled and pulled at the chains, keeping her tethered. They rattled and shook in her anger but didn't budge. "Where are my kids?" she demanded.

Angel walked closer, her skirt swishing around her, brushing cool air across her legs. "Where's mine?" she asked, her voice just as cold.

Summer bared her teeth like a wild animal, and even as she was emaciated and filthy, there was fire in her eyes. The same fire that sat in her son's. It infuriated Angel to no end. Here was this Gods awful woman who

"I have no idea what you're talking about," Summer whispered.

Angel came to gloat. She wanted to gloat and rub Summer's nose in her superiority to prove to the wicked witch that Angel was just as strong and capable. Now, it was turning into bad dreams, memories she would rather forget, and a strong desire to slit the woman's throat.

"You stole my son. An eye for an eye, my love. He's already under my control, which means he'll be like me any day now. Just. Like.

Me." Angel couldn't help but hear the venom dripping from her voice.

Summer screamed, and wind filled the cell, whipping Angel's hair in her face. Angel held up her arms as dust and dirt whipped through the air, making her eyes water. She opened her mouth to shut her down, but Summer was faster.

She spoke her transformation spell, and a blinding light filled the space.

Angel cursed herself for allowing the woman such freedom but didn't have the time to react aside from throwing herself out of the way of a bladed weapon. This small, frail woman who should've been sucked dry was standing as a full-fledged Descendant.

Summer held dual chakrams, and a red and violet mask rested across her cheekbones. Her disguise was different from when they were younger. She wore thick leather armor along her arms, legs, and torso. Her Descendant's mark was splayed across her chest. A beautiful work of art that spanned from one clavicle to the next and filled with color. Bright blue, yellow, and pink sprinkled through a design that could only be described as abstract. Tiny dandelion seeds blew in the colorful wind across her chest. Summer slammed the chakrams down in unison, severed the chains' connection with the stone floor and emitted bright sparks into the air.

Angel called her spear to her hand and surged forward, thrusting it at the woman's chest.

Summer ducked under the weapon and brought a chakram up, slicing across Angel's wrist. Blood spurted from the wound, and pain spasmed down her arm, forcing her to drop the spear, shouting out in pain. Summer whirled around and aimed a high kick, but Angel backed off and held up her good arm, protecting the rest of her body from the blunt force trauma Summer was determined to rend.

Well, I suppose freedom isn't for everyone," she said, holding her useless arm at her side, listening to the blood 'pit-pat' against the stone floor.

Summer flashed an arrogant smile. "Please, the only one not getting out of here is you," she said.

It was so arrogantly like Ryan's that Angel couldn't doubt they were related if she wanted to. Ryan's power made sense now that Angel could see Summer in all her intensity and hatred. Magik resided in the bloodline, and if Summer could build her energy this fast after ten years in captivity, it would be a wonder if Ryan didn't do the same.

Angel's magik coiled around her, posing to strike, but Summer grinned. She vanished in the blink of an eye, leaving a snarky laugh behind.

"Damn it," Angel cursed. Her day most certainly couldn't get worse.

Oh, but it could. When she returned to her quarters, she found a teary-eyed Avery with a watery nose.

Angel cradled her injured arm and tried not to turn her anger and frustration on him as she shut the door behind her. "What?" she asked.

He jumped to his feet and grabbed her injury, waving his hand over it, and murmuring an apology. The skin stitched back together, and the pain disappeared.

Avery winced and clutched his wrist, sitting back on her bed with a sigh. "What happened?" he asked.

"Nothing," she said, keeping her voice level even if the ice was prominent. "I had a mishap in the dungeon."

Avery's head snapped up. "Ryan?" he asked.

"No," she said with a huff and sat beside him. "Why are you here?"

He was quiet for a while, sitting and fiddling with his fingers like he was about to break the worst news imaginable.

"You caught feelings for the boy," Angel said, not needing a further explanation. Angel caught her breath in desperation at the thought of everything falling apart. Of course, he would fall for the one person he shouldn't when he could have anyone else. She forced her face to remain neutral as she gathered her thoughts. When she was sure she could talk without yelling or being angry, she said, "Feelings aren't bad; they aren't a weakness, but these feelings might hurt the plan."

Guilt crossed his face, and he looked away. "I don't know how I feel..." his voice was so quiet she almost couldn't hear him.

Angel placed a hand on his shoulder and hugged him to her chest. "I know you like him, and it's alright," she said. "I shouldn't have asked so much from you."

He was too strong to control, and now he was catching feelings. That was a dangerous combination, and she shouldn't risk it, but she viewed Avery as her child, and she couldn't help wanting to give him motherly advice.

"You're not mad?" he asked.

Angel sighed and ran her fingers through his hair. "No, I'm not mad."

He was still young and had much to learn, but if she kept him sympathetic to their cause, she could neutralize any fallout between them.

Angel did everything she could for him and made many mistakes, but that didn't mean she didn't care. It just meant she had to keep trying to be better for him. To create a world where people could see them both as normal, breathing humans instead of something to be exterminated.

"Is Ryan okay?" Avery asked.

Angel pulled away and chewed her lip. "He's unharmed," she said, not wanting to let Avery know more than necessary until this Killian situation was cleared up.

Killian could turn Avery away from her, and she would be in big trouble if these feelings were left to grow, leaving her powerless to stop him.

Avery took a shuddering breath and shook his head. "You said he'll be fine, and I believe you." It sounded more like he was reassuring himself.

Angel didn't open her mouth to make it easier for him; she just smiled and nodded.

"I'm sorry I messed things up," he said.

Angel frowned. She didn't want him to think his feelings were terrible. Emotions were vital to existence, but she didn't want Avery to believe he shouldn't feel anything. One of them was already like that, and she wouldn't wish her life on anyone.

"Did I ever tell you about the time I fell in love?" she asked.

Avery shook his head.

"There was a man a long time ago. He was from Portlandia, and we didn't share a language. Even when I could speak Nivet, we didn't communicate well," she said. She smiled wistfully at the happiest memories of her life. "I used to draw at the river. It was one of my favorite hobbies, and he would join me. We would sit, laugh, and make pictures in the clouds, all without saying a word. I drew pictures for him, and he drew them back, but he wasn't good. His drawings were horrible, but they were fun," Angel said.

She had been so young when they met. He was a roguishly handsome young man who traveled for work. He traded goods with the other homesteads, and most of what he got was given to the orphans and people who took them in.

They started teaching each other the language by pointing things out and saying them. Over time, she learned his name, Aryn, and he learned hers, but he could never say it which is when he began calling her his little angel.

Avery licked his lips and looked away as she finished her story. His foot tapped against the floor, and he shook his head after a long while. "What happened to him?" he asked.

"He was killed," Angel said with a small smile.

Avery buried his face in his hands and laughed hysterically. "And this is supposed to make me want to feel things?" he asked.

"Feeling love was one of the most extraordinary instances in my life," Angel said. "We just have to be careful of who we love." She reached over and put her hands over his to ease his trembling. "Love is beautiful and terrifying, but if you love loosely, you will end up hurt," she said.

Avery smirked and shook his head. "Thanks," he said. "For tellin' me. I think it kind of helps."

She didn't know if he was lying, but hearing that something she had done made a little difference. Maybe... just maybe, he could be enough.

Learning to Move On Together

KARA

K ara sat in Cody's dungeon with him as he tinkered with a tiny device that was barely visible in his palm. He sat at his work-table with a magnifying glass in one hand and a small screwdriver in the other. She traced some black stains on the metal tabletop, felt the grooves of the metal sheet he had procured from some unknown benefactor, and sighed.

"If you're going to pout, get out," Cody barely breathed when he spoke as he focused desperately on the thing in his hand.

Kara sighed again. This time, louder and more obnoxious.

Cody deadpanned and lifted his gaze to look at her.

She smiled and leaned over the table. Sometimes, she terrorized Dawson in the same way. Her favorite time to bother him was when he did homework. The faces he used to make as he stared at his assignments were the cutest, and she used to copy them to make him laugh. If anyone asked Dawson, he would call it mocking, but she liked to refer to it as loving admiration.

"What do you want?" he asked.

Kara shrugged. "How's Cheri?"

His cheeks turned red, and he returned to his project. "None of your business."

"Is someone getting defensive?" Kara asked, raising her eyebrows.

He shook his head with a grunt.

"Since Killian fixed your school problem, I don't see much of you anymore. Maybe I miss you," Kara said. She flicked a metal shaving at Cody's hand.

He fought a smile as he looked at her again. His hands stilled, and he set the magnifying glass down, giving her his undivided attention.

"What are you working on?" she asked.

Cody set the tiny pieces on a white cloth and turned around in his wheelie chair. He slid open a rusty drawer on an old metal box half his height and took out a small black box. After he turned back around, he held it out. "This," he said.

Kara took the box and ran her fingers across the soft felt. When she opened it, a tiny oval— no larger than her pinky nail—was inside. "What is it?" she asked.

"It's supposed to be a communication device. I haven't worked out all the kinks yet, but I figured when you guys go to save, Ryan, I'll have them ready," Cody said. He set his elbows on the table and leaned forward with a wide smile.

Kara didn't want to risk removing the communication device from the box, so she returned it. With her luck, she would drop or break it.

Cody chuckled as if reading her mind and dumped it into his hand. "Look," he said. "You can't lose it. I'm a Descendant of Technology, remember?"

"I still don't know what that means," Kara said. "You don't use your magik around me... ever."

The boy kept quiet well. She wondered if that was his preference or his dad's.

Cody shrugged. "I haven't had much reason to use my magik. It's not the most useful thing to have in the middle of nowhere. I could demonstrate," he said.

Kara took the communicator from his palm and brought it to her face. It was a little piece of machinery with little gears and bits of metal. "I can't believe how complex this is," she said.

He smirked when she handed it back. "It's a gift," he said. Cody set the device back in its box and tossed it into the drawer from which he had taken it. He didn't even turn around; he just threw it over his shoulder and nodded when he heard a 'thunk.'

"I can see how careful you are," Kara muttered.

"It's a prototype that doesn't work as well as I would like," Cody said. "Once I work out the formula, the new prototype will be better," he said.

Kara never understood the boy's words, but he liked talking about those things, and because he liked it, she would pretend it was fascinating.

Cody stood and stretched with a yawn. "Do you want to go on a walk?"

Because the house was too empty and quiet, Kara shrugged but didn't stand. She didn't want to go on a walk and be reminded of everything. "Do you believe in time travel?" she asked.

Cody frowned and studied her, making sure she wasn't playing some sort of joke. "Time travel?"

Kara went back to tracing the spots on the rough tabletop. "You know, going into the past." She had yet to discuss her new ability with anyone, fearing it having been a fever dream. She was sure Justin could shed some light on it, but a voice in her head said 'no.'

"I know what time travel is, or at least the concept. Why do you ask?" he asked, raising his bushy red eyebrows.

Kara shrugged. She moved her hand too quickly and knocked the screwdriver to the floor. "Whoops," she murmured.

Cody scooped it up and tossed it into the metal box with his lousy prototype. "Do you want to time travel?" he asked.

"No, I..."

The house rumbled dangerously, and bits of rock and dirt shook loose from the ceiling. Kara frowned and looked up as a massive swirl of energy unfolded overhead. It was black and violet, exactly like Ryan's energy when he left with Angel.

"That's not good," Cody muttered. He returned to tinkering as if this were an everyday occurrence. "Best to stay here."

Kara squinted at the ceiling as the colors evaporated. "What's going on up there?"

"Jay's in a mood. Sometimes, he gets like this and trashes the house." Cody still didn't sound concerned.

That sounded like a good reason to be worried, especially with a man as well-controlled as Justin. Kara stood and walked over to the stairs leading to the hidden door in the hall wall. "I'm just going to make sure he's fine," she said.

Cody shot her a look. "Be careful, okay?"

"Are you not coming?" she asked.

Cody frowned and waved his hand. "He's mean. If you go, Uncle Nicky will probably kick you out anyway, so no big deal."

Kara took that as a no. She had dealt with mean people her entire life, and she doubted a man in his thirties would take pleasure in ridiculing a child he had taken such care to train. She started up the stairs without another word.

The closer she got to the house, the more pressure built on her chest. It weighed her down like irons or weights. She huffed in exasperation and stepped through the wall. Cody had disguised his lab so unwanted guests would be deterred. It was all a fancy illusion that few people could see through.

The energy in the house was so thick she had to blink a couple of times and remind herself it was part of her magik. She could choose to see the house as it usually was. Her breaths came in short gasps as she waded through the house like it was a swamp.

Kara stepped into the living room, peering around for Justin or Nicholas. Everything swirled and things moved slowly. Kara rubbed her chest and coughed, hoping it would relieve the pressure. Dark purple and violet energy swarmed the living room, coating everything in a tar-like substance. Her heart thundered in her ears, and she stepped forward only to fall to a knee.

Justin appeared in the center of the living room. An electric blue haze filled the milky white of his eyes, and smog covered his body. It wasn't his usual energy - this was something darker, more terrifying. It reminded Kara of the time she spent in Yorklyn with Angel.

Justin's eyes landed on her; his face was contorted with rage. It wasn't the face of the man she had come to know.

"Kara, sweetie, are you alright?" Nicholas knelt in front of her, blocking her view of his brother. "I need you to get outside." His voice was muted against the pounding thump of her heart.

"What's happened?" she asked.

"We're dealing with some... things. It's no big deal," Nicholas said. A light brown shell surrounded them, and Kara wondered when he put a shield up and why she hadn't recognized it.

She found breathing much easier without Justin's energy bearing down. Kara studied the man's muddled energy and tried to understand why this was happening. His usual silver and sky-blue energy was buried under the black lines around him. There was a single spike of red around his heart – no, through it. A stake of pain embedded so deep that she didn't know if anyone could get it free. Kara understood that pain. The pain of losing someone and not being able to let go, and she wondered if her heart also looked like that.

She pressed the spot above her heart and closed her eyes. "You're not alone," she whispered. How many countless nights did she spend worrying about her parents or brother? Were they safe? Was her brother happy? That red stake hurt so bad that Kara wished she knew how to pull it free. Her eyes snapped open, and she stood. She *did*. "I can help," she said firmly. She was going to because she needed to. This was not about understanding someone else's pain but because this was the first step in understanding hers. This is how people healed – together.

"Kara, not now," Nicholas warned.

"I need to," she said. She might lose her mind if she lost another person she cared about. Kara was sick of wallowing and going from hot to cold. This wasn't the time to question herself, but it was finally time to act. She would be that person if Justin needed someone, even if it meant getting roughed up.

Nicholas shook his head, but she wasn't listening. He wasn't allowed to talk her out of this because he didn't understand. He could shut his brother down without ever dealing with the problem, and she wouldn't allow it. They had to heal – had to move on. *Let this work.*

"We have you, Little Descendant."

"You're never alone."

The voices of the past swirled through her head, giving her the confidence to stand tall.

Justin's energy attacked Nicholas' shield like a viper, and brilliant white lights sparked through the air every time the two collided. It was hauntingly beautiful.

"Let your barrier down," Kara said, not taking her eyes off Justin.

His electric blue eyes shone as he fought to tear through his brother's defenses.

Kara said a prayer to her ancestors – *please, hear this and help me. I cannot do it alone, nor do I want to.*

Nicholas grabbed her arms and held her tight. "Kara, please!"

A spell appeared on the tip of her tongue, and instead of fighting Nicholas, she spoke, "Energy abide by my word: dispel." It wasn't the spell Killian helped her with or gave her advice on – no, this was *her* spell.

"Make the magik your own," Justin had said that what felt like years ago.

The heavy energy of Justin's magik dissipated. Nicholas' shield vanished, and the viper-like energy turned into a thin thread. She had seconds before Justin recalled his power. Kara wrenched out of Nicholas' hands and ran toward the blind man, giving all her strength to him. She threw her arms around Justin's waist and held him, squeezing until her arms ached. Her energy reverberated through her body and flowed around them, wrapping like a ribbon.

"You're not alone. You have to stay on the path of light even if it's the hardest," Kara said.

There was an explosion of smothering magik before it vanished. Kara dropped to her knees, her hold on Justin failing as her energy fell, broken apart like pieces of paper in his energy's wake.

"Kara!" Nicholas' voice sounded far away, but she lifted her head.

Justin had gone rigid, his back straight and firm as the blue in his eyes flickered out. His hand went to her head and nestled into the frizzy black locks as a weak smile spread across his pale lips. "Where did you hear those words?" he asked.

"A Descendant of Energy told me," she whispered. "She said she's the best thing that ever happened to you, but you can't let it stop you from living."

Something wet hit her cheek, and Kara flinched until she realized what it was. Tears streaked down Justin's lined face, and he never looked older. He knelt and wrapped his arms around her, crushing her to his chest. "Thank you, Little Mouse," he said.

Kara sniffled and buried her face in his shoulder. "Don't leave like everyone else, Justin. Please, don't leave."

He chuckled a broken laugh and held the back of her head. "Never."

She could make a difference. Kara could save people, and the next step was saving herself.

"Do you want to talk about what happened earlier?" Justin asked, knocking on the door jamb.

She looked up with a small smile, happy he was finally leaving his room. "If you want to," she said.

He nodded and entered, finding his way to her bed and sitting at the foot like her dad used to do when she was down. "I would like to know how you came to talk to my wife," he said.

"Only if you tell me what that magik was," Kara countered, trying not to sound too sly.

He smiled and nodded again. "Very well, you share your secrets, and I'll share mine."

It didn't seem like a bad deal, but Kara was sure she would regret it. She wondered where to start and if she should listen to the voices screaming at her to keep it quiet. She trusted Justin, and he was kind to her, so why would it be a problem for him to find something like this out? "I interacted with a memory of the past," she said before she could talk herself out of it.

Justin's hand splayed flat on the blue comforter she slept with. "How?" he asked.

"I don't know, it just kind of... happened." There was no real explanation, and she hadn't managed to do it since. "I was sitting at the grave site, and when I got home, you and she were standing in the front yard. It used to look different," she said, choosing her words carefully.

"What was I doing?" he asked.

"You went inside; she sent you there for something and talked to me," Kara said.

Justin's face was unreadable, but he cocked his head to the side as he listened. His fingers picked at the blanket's seam as he thought. "I don't recall anything like that happening," he said.

"She told me it wasn't happening and that it was just a memory stored with old energy," Kara said.

He hummed thoughtfully before shaking his head with a sigh. "Magik is a world of uncertainty and confusion, is it not?"

She smiled weakly. "Sometimes people's energy lingers, and maybe I can tap into it."

He opened his mouth to say something but shut it again without a sound. He tapped his fingers before standing and running a hand through his hair. "The magik I employed earlier was that of Chaos," he said.

Kara frowned. Her eyes swept across his pale, thin face as she searched for a joke or lie. It was hard to tell sometimes, but there was nothing but certainty. "Wait, what?"

"I am a Descendant of Chaos, Kara. Much like Angel, except my powers are used for what I believe to be good." His voice was deadly serious with a hint of apathy. It was like he was announcing his run for mayor instead of a life-changing fact.

"Who else knows?" she demanded. "Why didn't you tell us?"

"My brother and son, of course. Ryan before he was taken, and I'm assuming Tory because he's dating my brother," Justin said. His face was eerily cold, like it was chiseled from stone. She bit her lip and tried not to be hurt by the news. "Does it change what you think of me?" he asked.

Kara's eyes widened as she realized the implications of what he told her. She jumped up and slammed her hand on her bedside table, nearly knocking the candle she lit when the dark was too much. "Are you serious?"

A brief look of surprise crossed his face before he steeled his features again.

"You thought I would change toward you because of your magik? That's the stupidest thing you've ever said," Kara snapped.

His energy danced around him in muted blues and silvers without a trace of chaos. She had seen chaos around Ryan and Angel, and now she knew what to look for to find others like them.

"Chaos has been a thorn in your side," Justin said.

"And so was my little brother, but I loved him just the same. Just like I'll continue to lo- appreciate you," she mumbled the last part.

Justin smiled warmly and nodded, ignoring her almost slip-up. "Well then, thank you for being more mature than I was willing to admit." He walked out of her room with a bow of his head, his hands trailing the walls.

Kara wanted to call after him and tell him she loved him, but she didn't know how to say it to someone who wasn't her dad. Honestly, if she couldn't have her dad, Justin wasn't the worst substitute.

Bending Under the Never-Ending Pressure

KILLIAN

J ustin was just as keen on punishing Killian for his behavior as Nicholas was. The man had bound his magik and told him that he would return every night without fail if he wanted to stay in Haven. Killian would've ignored it had Justin not looked seconds from killing him.

He pulled his shirt over his head and wrung out the water. His latest punishment was wading through the river, clearing it of any debris. Without access to his magik, it took much longer than he wanted it to. Plus, it was the middle of winter, so he was freezing.

"Well, isn't that a beautiful sight?" Avery's voice made him jump and then scowl.

Killian didn't even look up as he shook out the shirt. His cheeks flushed, and he stopped his thoughts before they could run off. "Don't talk to me. You have no clue how unbelievably pissed I am," he said. He waded out of the river and put his shirt back on. With his pants riding low on his hips from the water, his Descendant mark was mostly visible. It started on his hip and spread up toward his rib cage.

It was a black-cloaked figure that looked almost like a ghost, with circles and triangles around it and something akin to paint splatter in the background. Killian huffed in frustration and looked at Avery when he didn't say anything and just watched. "What are you doing here?" he asked.

"What's goin' on with all of this?" Avery asked, raising his eyebrow.

Killian shrugged and held out his arms. "You *told* on me, and now I'm being murdered, so thanks."

Avery didn't miss a beat and went on with the conversation, "What's the punishment?"

Killian gestured to the river. "Cleaning out the river," he said apathetically. *In the middle of winter. I think he wants me to get hypothermia.*

"That's not the look I've come to love so much," Avery said. He knocked his finger under Killian's chin and smirked.

He scowled and slapped his hand away. "Did you come for a reason other than to torment me?"

"You're just mad they got you doin' manual labor," Avery said, pulling his tunic off and tossing it aside. "So, I thought I'd help."

Killian stared. He didn't mean to, but a shirtless Avery wasn't bad. Avery was tone: a sculpted piece of work from years of running the forest and hunting. It made Killian's heart flutter and gave his stomach a weird, nauseating sensation. He frowned at the unfamiliar feeling. It was a mix of doing his favorite thing and failing his least favorite class.

"Sorry?" he asked. His throat was dry and scratchy even though he had been staying hydrated.

Avery whistled, drawing Killian's eyes away from his abs with an amused smile. "Yo', my face is up here. Come on, let's get to work," he said.

Killian shook himself out of it and hurried back to the river. He didn't even have it in him to be angry. "I'll be slower," he said. "No magik."

Avery jumped into the river and splashed Killian on the bank. "You got no magik but plenty of spunk."

Killian sat by the water's edge and stared. He trod water in place, the water barely rippling around him. "You're not a Descendant of Water anymore, are you?" he asked.

Avery clicked his tongue, and a small wave splashed from the river and fully drenched Killian. "I dunno, I'm pretty much the same," he said.

"Tory doesn't lose control like you, and his eyes don't flash colors."

Avery shrugged. "So, my magik's evolved. No biggie," he said with a smirk.

"You don't use spells," Killian pointed out.

"Nah, haven't had to do that in a while—probably at least a year," Avery said.

Killian wrung out the hem of his shirt again before slipping it on with a few choice words. When he was done, he stuck his feet in the water. "Justin says it's rare."

"Is it?" Avery asked.

"You tell me." It would be a good day if he could get more out of Avery than usual.

The young man shrugged and floated on his back. He laced his fingers and placed them behind his head. *I've met many Descendants who don't speak spells to life."*

Killian scowled at Nivet. "Why do you keep doing that?" he asked.

Avery raised a brow in question.

"Slipping between languages. It makes my head hurt."

"It's easier. This is my first language, and there are still some things I can't say in the one you insist on usin'," Avery shrugged. The water rippled around him every time he talked or breathed.

Killian found his eyes on Avery's stomach again and found it increasingly difficult to remove them. "Like what?" he asked absently.

Avery smiled again and beckoned to him, straightening out to tread water. *"I'll answer questions when you start to cooperate."*

Killian thought long and hard. After a few minutes of contemplation, he slid into the water and swam out.

"Close your eyes and feel the water," Avery said.

Killian rolled his eyes but did as he was told for argument's sake.

"Everything has energy."

"Right, but I've been blocked from my energy," Killian huffed. He opened his eyes and blinked at Avery.

"Why do you think we're trainin'?" Avery asked with a sly smile. *"Don't you wanna test your abilities against Justin's?"*

"Wait, are you going to teach me how to use magik when I'm blocked?" he asked, drawing his attention back to the Descendant of Water. This was something he would enjoy.

Avery shrugged and righted himself in the water. *"Only if you're willin'."*

Killian grinned and nodded. "*That's* something I want to learn."

Killian woke up the following day and teleported straight to Avery's. If anyone noticed Killian's absence, they didn't say anything.

Avery was on his porch with a cup of coffee and a wicked grin. "It's good to see you all bright-eyed," he said.

"Shut up, what's today?" Killian asked. The training sessions with Avery taught him much and helped with his anger. As the days went on, Killian wanted to scream as long as he kept his mind occupied.

"Show me your Descendant guise. I wanna know what we're workin' with," Avery said. Killian waved a hand over his hip, but Avery caught his wrist. "Without sayin' the spell."

Killian wasn't sure he understood what was being asked. He didn't do magik like Ryan and Avery. "What?" he asked.

Avery shrugged and sipped his coffee. "Transform without sayin' the spell," he repeated slower.

"I've never done that," Killian said.

"There's a first for everythin'." Killian glared but didn't argue.

Killian tossed a berry in his mouth and chewed. It was tart—not inedible, but it could have been better. A few days later, he sat on the hunter's lawn, waiting for him to get home. However, Killian didn't get a break because Justin insisted on having to do some mental shielding exercises, just in case. Though, he wouldn't say for what.

Avery collapsed next to him and leaned back on his palms, closing his eyes. "How was lunch?" he asked.

Killian shrugged. "I didn't get one thanks to the pissed-off Descendant of Wind I currently live with."

Avery smirked. Turning his head to the side, he watched Killian rifle through a bush for more not-so-good berries. "Don't have plans for more today," he said.

"I know. I didn't want to do anything." Killian offered one of the blueberries and grinned. "We could hang out. Unless you have other plans?"

Avery took the fruit and threw it, making a face as if he were offended by the offering. "You're disgustin'. These are for rabbits and squirrels."

Killian popped another one in his mouth. "And foxes, opossums, raccoon— "

Avery slapped a hand over his mouth, cutting him off. "Shut up," he said, trying to contain his laugh.

Killian chuckled, discarded the rest of the fruit, and leaned back to relax. The sun was setting, leaving a brilliant orange and yellow streak through the sky. He watched the clouds pass and mix with the dying light of the blue sky. "Do you have other plans?" he asked again.

Avery shook his head and tugged a strand of Killian's blonde hair.

His eyes widened in shock, and a flicker of pain split his heart. It was an action so familiar that Killian didn't want to think about it. He grimaced and pulled away, brushing his hair behind his ears. It was about time to cut it.

Avery frowned and dropped his hand. "Sorry," he said. There was a question in his voice and eyes, but Killian didn't want to answer.

"Nope, not a problem. Anyway, about those plans." Killian wanted to move on. He knew if they lingered, unwelcome feelings would ruin his day.

"I miss him too, you know? But he's not dead. We can get him back," Avery said.

Killian nodded, and his throat tightened. "Yep." They needed to be better prepared, so he was fighting to improve himself because if he got stronger, he could bring Ryan home.

Avery scooted a little closer so their shoulders brushed. "I don't have plans. Wanna come in and eat real food? I think I've got some deer left."

Killian looked up and clutched his chest mockingly. "The way to every man's heart. Meat."

Avery smirked. "This is the most excited I've ever seen you," he said.

Killian would be excited about anything that would distract them from his brother. He shrugged in reply and waited for Avery to lead the way as he got to his feet.

Avery slipped his hand into Killian's without missing a beat and entwined their fingers. The touch made Killian's heart jump and something coiled low in his stomach. He frowned, staring at them.

Avery tugged his hand with a light grin. "What're you starin' at?" he asked.

It's a move. He uses it on everyone, which is why so many people find him attractive. Is he attractive? Killian studied Avery's smooth skin and long eyelashes. His bright black eyes were full of humor but also questions. He was conventionally attractive.

"Hey, what's goin' on? You're studyin' me like I'm a book." Avery's voice was still light, as if he was trying to joke, but there was underlying concern pressing in his tone, and his fingers tightened with nerves.

Killian blinked, and the moment passed. "Yeah," he said. "Sorry, I'm fine. Let's go." He ignored that he hadn't pulled his hand out of Avery's.

"Dude, seriously, you gotta tell me what you're eating," Tory said, poking Killian's bicep.

Killian smirked and downed another bowl of porridge. "I eat the same thing you do. Just been doing some hunting," he said nonchalantly.

"I need to start," Tory said, looking at his muscles.

Kara laughed and poked his bicep. "You can't even pull back on a bow. Be real," she said with a snort.

He pulled his arm away from her and frowned. "I wield a great sword. I think I can use a bow," Tory said.

Killian shrugged and shuffled some of the food around on his plate. "It's not the same kind of strength."

They began eating breakfast together at Kara's insistence. Some bonding-something or another.

"What do you know?" Tory muttered, pushing his porridge around.

Killian frowned. They didn't know what he did with most of his free time. "Ask Cody how well I shoot a bow," he said.

Tory sighed and set his fork down. "I'm being attacked."

Nick walked into the dining room and froze when he saw Tory. It only lasted a second before he returned to normal, but Killian caught it. The way his eyes widened, and his throat trembled.

"Hey, Nick." Killian could solve this. "Tell Tory he's too weak to shoot a bow."

Tory paled and focused intently on his breakfast. "Shut up," he muttered.

Nick walked over to the table and shoved his hands in his pockets. "Tory, shooting a bow? Yeah, I don't see that happening," he said. "Takes a different arm strength."

Tory's cheeks went red, and he side-eyed Killian venomously.

Killian smirked.

Justin walked into the dining room and looked around. "I have a new technique I wish for you all to learn," he said. "Kara, do you have a transformation spell yet?"

Kara didn't have the one spell every Descendant woke with: her disguise spell. Justin was insistent she get it to see if it helped further her training.

Kara looked up from her eggs and bacon. She swallowed a mouthful of food and cleared her throat. "It's a work in progress," she said.

"Liar."

Kara flicked a piece of egg at him. "Shut. It."

"That's the first spell every Descendant learns, and yet Kara's first cooks everyone within twenty yards of her," Killian said with a wicked smile.

"I'll *fry* you," she muttered.

Justin rubbed his eyes in quiet exhaustion. "We're not starting this. Nick, run Kara through meditation drills with Cody. I'll take Tory."

"I don't want to meditate anymore," Kara said, sulking.

Justin shook his head. "Until you get that spell, you can't learn this. Concentrate your efforts on that," he said not missing a beat.

A twinge of pain spasmed down Killian's arm, and he winced. Over the weeks, it had become more common. A part of him wondered if Ryan was trying to reach out to him, but when he searched for the familiar tie between them, it wasn't there.

Killian gulped down the rest of his food and clicked his tongue. "I've gotta do something, be back later," he said before anyone could call him for training.

Killian grabbed a mug of coffee off the table and turned around. Waving his hand over the ground, he spoke his teleportation spell and stepped through. Killian arrived on Avery's stoop and knocked. There was shuffling from within the home, and a feminine voice cursed. When the front door opened, a woman stepped out, slipping on a shirt.

Killian's heart stuttered, and he looked away. He hated it when Avery had company but didn't know why. It made his chest ache like he had lost something but couldn't for the life of him remember what.

Avery turned as a red-haired woman approached. *"Leavin' so soon?"* he asked, giving her one of those charming smiles.

Killian cocked his head to the side as the woman pecked Avery on the lips and brushed some hair out of his face. Her cheeks were pink, and her eyes crinkled in delight when they spoke.

"I've got work," she said with a grin.

"See you tonight then?" Avery asked, brushing his thumb across her bottom lip.

Her blush deepened as she looked at Killian as if the public display of affection was something she didn't want him to watch. He wondered what it felt like to be touched by someone you wanted to be touched by and kissed.

His heart fluttered, and he looked away, brushing his fingers against his chest. Could he feel that way about someone? He didn't even know if it was possible. No one had ever been close enough for him to consider experimenting.

She smiled despite the flickering uncertainty behind her brown eyes. "Have a good day," she said, switching to common.

"Let the blessed morning be yours." Killian deliberately greeted her with the traditional words of Rochester in her native tongue. He didn't break eye contact as she hurried past him, mumbling an apology.

Avery rubbed the back of his neck. "I guess I won't be seein' her tonight," he muttered. "Why you gotta do that?"

Killian glared and waved a hand. "I didn't do anything. Is she your girlfriend?" he asked.

"Yeah, for a night or two. Well, a night. Because someone can't control the..." Avery gestured to his face. "The murderous intent."

Killian was frustrated. He didn't like Avery romantically; he didn't think he did. Killian cocked his head to the side again and took a step forward. "What do you feel when you kiss someone?" he asked. He internally flinched. Why did things leave his mouth without his consent?

Avery frowned. His brow furrowed as he tried to figure out where this was going. "What do you mean?"

"Is it like fire and ice?" Killian asked.

Avery blinked as the frown smoothed out. Something seemed to dawn on him, but Killian didn't know what. "Fire and ice," he mused softly. "Who told you that?"

"Kara," Killian said.

"I guess it depends on who you're with." Avery shoved his hands in his pockets. He looked uncomfortable to be having this conversation.

According to Kara, fire and passion went together, or at least it was that way. Killian didn't understand where the ice came from.

He frowned and gestured in the direction the other girl left. "Was it fiery with her?"

Avery's jaw twitched. It was almost like he wanted to smile but couldn't. "Spicey," he said.

Killian scowled and waved a hand. "Forget it," he muttered. If Avery wasn't going to take this seriously, he wasn't going to ask.

Avery caught his arm before he could leave. "I'm not screwin' with you," he said. His voice was curious and amused. "Spicey. It's - I dunno how to explain it. Kind of like angry and aggressive." Avery tried to find the words that suited what he had with the woman.

Killian calmed himself when Avery didn't let his arm go. "Angry and aggressive," he whispered, mostly to himself.

Avery's dark eyes and rough hands flashed through his mind. *"Now be a good boy and do as you're told."* He had said those exact words.

That was when the weird feeling started, or at least when Killian noticed it. Was that what spicey was? That seemed aggressive. He didn't have any reference to what spicey felt like, but he had liked how that felt... didn't he?

"Hey, where'd you go?" Avery snapped his fingers in Killian's face. "Are you feelin' okay?" There was no hiding the worry in his voice this time.

Killian blinked and looked up, pulling himself back to reality. Had Avery meant it that way? Or was he just doing what Nick said and torturing him? "I'm fine," he said. He couldn't precisely tell Avery what was going through his head without sounding insane. He shook the thoughts away and forced a smile. "Sorry," he said. "I don't know what came over me."

Avery's eyes were hungry and dark. Even if his voice conveyed worry, the rest of him didn't. His body was rigid as if he were afraid to do something. "It's fine. I never took you to be interested in romance."

He wasn't. Killian had no desire to see do those things, but he might be willing to try if it was Avery. The shocking thought that he ripped his arm out of Avery's hold and backed up. "I've got to go."

"Wait, what? Where are you..." Avery's sentence was cut off as Killian vanished into a nearby shadow.

Killian had to go home as much as he didn't want to. He appeared on Haven's lawn because even though Avery had been granted access, he rarely used it. Killian's heart hammered in his chest, and he wondered if Justin had any books explaining these feelings.

Or maybe Kara. She went to the bookstore in Rochester and brought home all sorts of things to read. He wondered if any of her books had his symptoms and explained them, but this wasn't a conversation he could have with a girl. Especially a girl he had felt all of Ryan's feelings for.

Killian hurried inside and sighed. He had talked to Tory before but brushed most of what the Descendant of Water said away. Now, he had to revisit that. Killian ventured through the living room and looked for the brunette. Tory wasn't downstairs, so Killian knocked on the young man's bedroom door.

Tory opened it and frowned before stepping aside to let him in. "You're not whisking me away, are you? I'm trying to unpack this junk," he said.

Killian shook his head. "No, I need to talk to someone... a guy."

Tory closed the door when he stepped inside. "Sure thing. What about?"

"Something's wrong with me," Killian said, not bothering to beat around the bush.

Tory chuckled and went to one of the boxes against the back wall. His room was mostly empty except for a bed, dresser, closet door, and small window across from his bed. There was a pile of boxes in the corner with clothes, knickknacks, and some weird toys Killian didn't recognize.

"What do you think is wrong with you and why?" Tory asked.

Killian sat on his bed and fell onto his back. He stared at the ceiling and blinked. This room was different from the others. It was devoid of paintings. Nick had yet to paint any walls, bed posts, or doors. Every room had some Nick signature, so it was odd this was clean. Killian propped himself on his elbow to inspect the rest of the room in case he missed it when he walked in.

"It was Jess' room for a while," Tory said, reading his mind. "He wanted to paint it when she was alive but could never find a good mural. After she passed, he couldn't bring himself to defile it."

Killian frowned. "How did you..."

"Get stuck in it? I think it's part of the reason Justin hates me, but I doubt that's why you're here," Tory said, moving on in the conversation.

"Justin doesn't hate you," Killian said.

Tory chuckled and shook his head, removing some clothes from a box. "Stop stalling and tell me why you're here."

Killian sighed and laid back down. ""Alright, fine; I think I have a crush on someone," he said.

"I mean... okay?" Tory folded his clothes and stuffed them in a drawer. "And that's bad?"

"What's the point in folding them if you're going to..." Tory cut him off with a solid glare. "I've been getting these weird symptoms: nausea, tachycardia, dizziness, and weird chest pressure. I think it might be heart palpitations," he listed some things he recalled every time he encountered Avery.

Tory puzzled over the words. "I don't know... are you not human? I mean, what the Helwe is tacky-cardy," he muttered.

Killian pushed himself back up. "I feel sick, and my heart beats too fast."

"That was easy, wasn't it? Killian, so what? You're having feelings! I prefer it to the murderous look you're always giving people. Or the complete lack of care for the world in general," Tory said, trying to keep the frustration from his voice.

Killian opened his mouth to argue and shut it. He did have a general lack of care for most people. In his defense, it wasn't entirely his fault. The rest of the world had been cruel since he was very young.

"Are we done?" Tory asked. He put his hands on his hips and stared. He reminded Killian of one of the mean girls in the halls at school from an age he could barely remember.

"You weren't helpful." Killian pushed himself up. "But I guess so."

Tory chuckled and gathered some more clothes from his boxes. "The most I can say is stop overthinking. Do what you feel is right. It's instinct."

An instinct Killian didn't have. He understood enough of what Tory was saying, though. "What if I never kissed anyone before?" he asked.

"I'm not the person for this conversation. Have a good night," Tory said, ending the talk.

Good to know. Killian stopped at the door and looked back. "You seem agitated. Do you need to talk?" he asked.

"Get out of my room," Tory said.

Killian nodded and stepped out.

Kara was stretching for her morning exercises when Killian found her. Her eyes flicked to him as he approached, and a small smile crossed her face. "You look grumpy," she said.

He shrugged noncommittally and huffed. "You wanna learn to shoot a bow? Justin says you've been asking."

Kara brightened and popped off the ground like a kid's toy. "Yes," she said. "Do you think you can convince Avery to teach me?"

"No, I'm going to," Killian said. They didn't need Avery for something like that.

Confusion crossed her face before he grabbed her wrist and dragged her over to the training grounds. She initially protested but ultimately decided to follow without giving him problems.

"You *are* grumpy," she said.

Everyone kept saying that when he wasn't in a horrible mood. Killian frowned and cocked his head to the side. He should work on his bedside manners. He forced a smile and summoned a bow for them to use equipped with a never-ending quiver of arrows.

"Stop, that's creepier." Kara deadpanned.

He thanked her and dropped the smile, holding the weapon out. "Try it," he said. "I may need to tweak the weight."

Kara took the bow and held it in front of her. It was a sleek black oak longbow with a silver string. "Like this?" she asked.

He corrected her posture. "Don't hold it sideways. It's not a crossbow."

Kara nodded and let him help her. He moved her foot back, pushed her elbow up, and turned her chin so she was looking ahead. "This is uncomfortable," she muttered.

"You can breathe," he said, looking over her form.

She was rigid like a statue, and he shook her shoulders. Kara snarled and snapped her teeth like a piranha. "Stop."

"Loosen up. You don't need to be made of stone. I'm not going to do anything to you," Killian said.

Kara's shoulders dropped, and she took a breath to let the rest of her body follow suit. When she looked more comfortable, Killian stood behind her. "Alright, now..."

He walked her through the steps, pulling back on the string and keeping her sight straight. Killian summoned a second bow and showed her different angles to shoot and how to know how high or low the arrow would go.

Kara copied his every move and listened intently; her eyes shone with an excitement he had never seen in her. She let the string twang off her fingertips and shouted in pain when it flicked off the opposite forearm and cut into her skin. Kara dropped the bow as blood steadily dripped from her arm and into the grass.

"Whoops." Killian let the weapons dissipate and took a look at the wound. It wasn't horribly deep, but it would bleed for a bit. "Sorry, I forgot the arm guard," he said.

"There's supposed to be an arm guard?" she snapped. Pain clouded her eyes, and she scrunched her nose with a wince.

He rubbed the back of his neck and shrugged. "I didn't think about it."

"Avery would've been a better teacher." Kara always found a way to cut without using weapons.

"He's not here. I am. So let me help," Killian insisted. "We'll get Justin to heal you and..."

Kara scoffed and stormed toward the house, holding her bleeding arm. "What's it matter who teaches me? You never want to help me with this stuff."

Killian teleported in front of her and blocked her access to the house. "I'll teach you to teleport then," he said.

Kara sighed and hung her head. "What's wrong with you?" she asked.

"I can't fight Angel alone. "My brother has been gone. I need to get back to the city with people who can back me up, and I know I'm not the best fighter, but please... let me help." Because that was easier then telling her about Avery and his weird feelings.

Kara pursed her lips and nodded. "You can help me on one condition."

"What?" he asked.

"Nicholas teaches you to use a sword," she said.

Killian kicked the grass and grunted. "Fine, I'll learn. It's best to have more than one way to fight anyway."

"Good."

Killian grumbled the word back and let her go back inside. He hated swords.

Nick stared at a rapier and then looked at Killian. "What am I supposed to be teaching you?" he asked.

"Swords," Killian said.

"Why?"

They were standing on the front lawn. Nick was barefoot and bleary-eyed but agreed to the extra training session.

Killian swallowed thickly. "Because we're a team," he said, trying to sound cheery.

Nick set the rapier on the ground and wiped his hands on tan shorts. "I don't like this version of you. Can we go back to the whiny teenager who sulks?" Nick asked. "I don't have the energy."

"I don't sulk," Killian growled. "And I need to learn this." Because his brother was adept at kicking his butt, so Killian wanted one thing he could hold his own on

Nick nodded. "You make it sound like you are planning something," he said.

Killian held up his short sword in response.

Nick sighed. "You are, aren't you."

Killian smirked. This Angel thing wasn't over. He had a purpose until that woman was good and dead.

Nick nodded and scooped the rapier back up. "Fine, let's do it."

Avery stared down at him as Killian lay in the middle of Rochester, letting the dirt settle into his clothes. "What happened?" he asked, holding out his hand.

Killian took it with a smirk. "I'm learning to use a sword," he said. There was pride in his voice even though his duel wasn't good.

Avery nodded and gestured at the blood smeared on his face and arms. "Uh-huh, and this is yours?" He knew it was.

Killian didn't know why he had to point out the faults. "Yes, yes, but... I didn't die."

Avery sighed and looked around. The crowd had already dispersed, and most people just walked around them. "How long have you been on the ground?" he asked.

Killian shrugged. "I was waiting for the world to stop spinning."

Avery grabbed his hand and walked him to the leather stand. "Let's see what I've got."

Killian leaned on the counter while Avery hopped it and dug in the back for medical supplies.

"Who's teachin' you to use a sword?" he asked.

"Nick, but he didn't show me enough." Killian watched Avery dig through some bags and tan pouches, his eyes wandering ever so slightly to the young man's butt.

"When did the trainin' start?" Avery asked. His voice was worried, but he tried not to let it show.

Killian shrugged. "Yesterday."

Avery nodded and mumbled something under his breath. He returned to the counter with some bandages, green paste, and alcohol. When Killian reached for it, Avery slapped his hand away. "Not for drinkin'," he said.

Killian made a face. "No crap, give it to me, so I can clean some of these."

Avery reluctantly let the bottle be wrenched from his hand. "Why are we doin' this?" he asked.

"So, Ryan can't beat me," Killian said.

They didn't talk for a long while. Killian drenched some of the lacerations in the alcohol and hissed as they burned. It wasn't the worst pain, and he knew he was being overdramatic to avoid further conversation. . Avery slid the paste across the deeper cuts, and the burn vanished in seconds.

"Are we goin' to talk about what's goin' on in your head?" Avery asked.

Killian had nothing going on in his head. He felt great. "Would you kiss me?" he asked.

Avery laughed before realizing Killian wasn't joking. He cocked his head to the side and stared like Killian had grown an extra set of teeth. "I'm sorry, what?"

"For an experiment," Killian said.

Avery stared long and hard. His eyes flicked across Killian's face in pure disbelief. He must have thought Killian had a concussion or was already drunk. Neither of those things was true, but Killian didn't correct his train of thought.

"How much blood have you lost?" Avery asked, sitting on the counter and setting the medical supplies aside. "How long were you sitting in the dirt, bleedin'?" He changed how he asked the question before Killian could give a snarky response.

Killian moved until he was standing between Avery's legs. They were eye-to-eye, and it was easier to study him. "A quick kiss," he said.

Avery had sex with anything that moved, so why did the mere thought of a kiss with him make his shoulders jump to his ears? Avery's eyes narrowed, but he didn't move. "Dude, what's goin' on in your head?" he asked.

Killian leaned in. He felt emboldened, almost like he had been drinking. He smirked and set his hands on Avery's thighs for support. "Is that a no?"

Avery was tense beneath him. He barely breathed, but his face didn't change. He brushed a lock of hair behind Killian's ear and sighed. "Are you serious?"

"Deadly."

"Is this some messed up part of trainin' I don't know about yet?" Avery asked.

Killian made a face mixed with annoyance and disgust. "No, why would it be? I'm just curious why all those girls keep returning to your house," he said.

"It would take more than a kiss to show you that, but I'll indulge you if you think it's going to... do what exactly? Fulfill a secret desire to kiss someone you despise?" Avery asked. He was still prying for information, trying to figure out where Killian's head was.

He wanted to figure out why these feelings kept bothering him. Killian was past the point of ignoring what his body was telling him.

Avery shrugged and slid off the counter. Killian backed up to give him room to stand. They weren't even anymore, which meant Avery had control. He caught Killian's chin in his fingers and turned his head up.

Killian's heart stuttered, and he chewed his lip. It was that feeling again—the pleasant one.

Avery leaned down and gently connected their lips. It was over in seconds. He didn't use his tongue or bite his lip; it was a simple joining before Avery broke it and let Killian go.

It was enough to make Killian's skin tingle in the best way. He opened his eyes, wondering when he closed them, and stared into Avery's smirking face. "Is that enough for your research?" he asked. His voice was cocky for some reason like he had just gotten something he wanted without Killian knowing.

Killian frowned and pulled himself back to Earth. He jerked away from Avery's touch and shrugged. "Yeah," he said.

"Good." Avery patted his cheek and walked past him.

Killian watched him go with a sinking feeling in his gut. He had done something wrong, and now things would be weird. "Great," he muttered. *Back to square one.*

What's Worse Than Death?

RYAN

Ryan focused on his energy and pursed his lips. He hadn't been in control of himself since Avery screwed him. Angel gave him a brief moment of lucidity, however long ago, when she tried to drown him. The only upside was he didn't have to fear water, though it still burned like a son of a gun when he got wet.

He sat in his dark mind and listened to Chaol and Fyre fight. The calmer he was, the worse they went after each other. He hadn't been talkative since the conversation with fake Killian. Ryan was stuck on the fact that the others might not want him to return. Sure, he hadn't been nice before he left, but he tried at the end. Apologies were due, that was for sure, but he couldn't very well apologize if he was left here to rot.

"I don't own magik. Magik doesn't own me," Ryan whispered, trying to practice Justin's meditation.

Ryan wanted to talk to his brother. His real brother, not the one constantly berating him in his head. He was in the middle of gathering energy when he was ripped from the starless sky. He sat in the cell again, this time staring up at Angel.

She was in a piss poor mood. Her steel blue eyes shone angrily, and she reminded him of a porcupine with her red frizzy hair sticking out like pins around her head. "I've got a job for you," she said. There was darkness in her gaze. Something upset her, and he was going to pay for it. "Go into the city, burn half the residential district, and return."

He tried to scowl and get angry, but he couldn't. Whenever he tried to concoct a lucid train of thought, he was blocked by a wall of chaos. It was one of her tricks he hadn't learned to overcome... yet.

"Don't bother trying to wake yourself up," Angel said. She waved her hand and walked out of the cell. "Follow."

Ryan didn't want to, but when he tried to resist, a spike of pain shot through his temple. The door was open when they passed the cell his mom was in. The shock was enough to jolt him into lucidity when he saw the door open wide and no one inside. "Where's my mom?" he asked.

Angel whirled around and backhanded him.

Ryan was so shocked he didn't know how to respond. It seemed like such an innocent move for a woman like Angel. A woman who liked to kill and maim had just backhanded him like he was an annoying fly.

Angel pursed her lips and crossed her arms. She gestured to the elevator and looked away. "Go terrorize some people, and let's say, at the very least, five die."

His heart leaped to his throat at the thought of turning into a murderer. These were people he, not long ago, defended and tried to stop her stupid executions. She was supposed to sacrifice him, not make him someone others fear. Ryan forced himself to stand still despite the pain tearing through his head. Her order ran through his thoughts like a broken record, making it hard to think about anything else.

"I don't know what you're waiting for; off you go," she said, stepping aside, allowing him to leave.

Ryan moved. It took less than two minutes to get to the residential district, most of which was spent in the elevator, gripping the rails and trying to force his mind back to his control. He stood before a group of cookie-cutter white housing, staring at the lifeless yards of gravel and stone. People in those homes had no clue what was about to happen.

He lifted his trembling hand, biting his tongue hard enough to taste blood, but it happened just the same. He closed his eyes as he snapped, unable to watch. The heat from the fire was the first thing he felt, and the stench of burning wood. Houses went up in flames, and he stood in the middle, directing the balls of fire toward every house on the street. People screamed and ran, holding kids and shouting for help. When they noticed him, they pointed and yelled, terrified he was there to end their lives.

Stay away, please stay away. His eyes strayed to those holding children, and his body shook harder as he fought Angel's control. *Please, don't let me hurt a kid.*

A few of the men shouted as they realized he was the reason their houses were blazing wildfires that nothing could tame. "Get him!"

Ryan summoned one of his swords and waited for the men to attack. It was heavy in his hand, and his knuckles hurt from clutching. He couldn't do this. He had to stop. Men rushed at him from every angle, but he stood his ground.

Angel's words echoed in his head. *"Kill!"*

The first man threw a punch, but Ryan blocked it and stuck the sword in his attacker's stomach. The man fell back, gasping and holding the wound. Blood poured from the injury, and he fell to the ground, forcing the others to hesitate. The fog of chaos kept Ryan's emotions at bay as the others began attacking in groups.

Ryan stepped out of the way and ducked under knives and fists. There was no challenge, no fight as the men stood around confused, unsure how he was moving so quickly. One of the men grabbed him, and fire burst to life against his skin, climbing up the man's arms, making him scream in agony. The sound rooted him to the ground. A stabbing pain shot through Ryan's temple as he disobeyed and stared in horror at what he had done. A knife stuck into his thigh, deep into the bone, sticking when it struck. The pain was immense and immediate, and he dropped to his good knee, panting.

"Kill five," her words were loud and impossible to tune out.

He gripped the handle of the knife in his leg and ripped it out, crying out as the knife cut through his flesh. The pain, combined with the absolute horror of his actions, spurred a wave of energy to wrap around him, dispelling the chaos almost instantly. Ryan looked out from the invisible shell at the crying women and children as smoke clogged the street and burned across the sky. The crackling flames were a melancholy symphony seared into his brain like a brand he would never escape.

Crimson painted the pavement, and Ryan's hands shook. No, he was done. *No more.*

The citizens ran and called for help as wives torn from their husbands rushed to the bodies, begging them not to die. Blood soaked his pants, but Ryan pushed himself to his feet and vanished before the guard could shoot him, though, at this point, that death would be swift and fair.

Ryan didn't stop until he was back in the cell, pressured by Angel's commands and wrath from his momentary lapse of obedience. His eyes burned, and he slid to the slimy floor, pressing his back against the wall. His stomach twisted and churned. Ryan always prided himself on being a voice for those who didn't have one, which is why he got in so much trouble. He defended them when they couldn't, and today, he took three lives. Three innocents were gone by his hand, and his chest tightened at the thought.

She would keep making him destroy people and use him in nefarious ways. There was no breaking free.

The fake Killian appeared in front of him.

Ryan didn't budge. It wasn't going to make it any better listening to his subconscious tell him how much he sucked.

"Mom was right about you. You're a monster," Fake Killian said.

Something in his mind chipped and cracked like glass. Small lines spiderwebbed across the surface of his mental state as Ryan tried to hold himself together. He closed his eyes and focused on his energy. "Magik doesn't belong to me. Respect magik and it respects you," he whispered, intent on drowning out the hallucination.

Fake Killian laughed. "Please, don't bother with that crap. You know there's only one way out of this."

Something clinked on the stone ground, and Ryan's eyes snapped open. He blinked at a flash of silver reflecting the fluorescent lights outside his cell. A razor. Ryan lay curled against the wall for a long time, staring at the blade. There was one sure way out of this Helwe, which wouldn't take much. Angel's words rang through his head on a loop.

Ryan couldn't stop the memories from childhood. As he obsessed about every horrible word and action of the woman keeping him captive, his mind was drawn to another. Another time in his life when he felt just as trapped:

His mother had stared at him with cold green eyes. Her words had been affectionate, but her body language was anything but. "You're Mommy's special boy. Stay with Mommy, Ryan." She always said the same thing. She never let him out to play or trusted him to make the right decisions.

Ryan didn't want her love, and he cried every time she refused to let him out.

The memory shifted, and he became a little older.

"Finish your dinner. It's almost time for the healing ritual." Mom's fingers always brushed the mark on his arm. She had to see if it changed. Her eyes had always been filled with fear when she looked at him. Aside from keeping him locked up, she had never wanted anything to do with him for as long as he could remember.

The first time he ran away, he was about the same age. Despite his protests and pleading, one of the Rochester villagers found him and dragged him home. Ryan would have given anything to never go back.

"Good boys don't act like that," Mom said in a cold, terrifying voice.

He cried even before they were alone. Tears coated his cheeks, and he blubbered despite being nearly ten. He had never measured up. All he had ever wanted was her approval, but she had never given it.

"Mommy loves you. I'll always love you." She said these words after every ritual or punishment. She always used them when he was tired, broken, and unable to cry anymore.

She didn't love him, though, not really. It wasn't the right kind of love, not the love of a mother.

The glass shattered with a thunderous crack.

When Everything Goes Wrong

KILLIAN

Killian smirked as Cody tried to describe what Cheri did at school that day and fell out of his chair. He was in good spirits these days. Since Killian handled the school problem, Cody rarely frowned, and the bruising stopped, which meant he was well on his way to making friends.

Nick finally stopped punishing him for his late-night parties. Killian wasn't about to bring his lousy behavior back to light. It had been a rough change, from his mess of a life to finally accepting what was happening. It didn't reduce his resolve to help his brother, but now there was a clear thought in his head. He couldn't do things alone, and if he was going to help Ryan, he had to be strong enough to do it.

The burning began after Killian took a bite of the veggie stir fry. It was a mild irritation across his wrist and easy to ignore, so he didn't focus on it as Cody finished his story.

"How's your crush?" Tory asked, looking at Killian. Since their talk, he had been asking more personal questions, trying to figure out the identity of this person Killian had brought up.

In hindsight, going to Tory had been a poor decision, but he was desperate, and Kara was too nosy. Tory was no better, so Killian would have to stop this.

Kara perked up. "Killian has a crush?" she asked. "Who?"

"No, I don't," Killian muttered. The burning intensified, and he brushed his fingers across a welt on his wrists. It itched like crazy, like poison ivy, but he hadn't spent any time in the forest because he promised to help Kara train.

"Who's the crush?" she asked, looking at Tory. She knew she wouldn't get information from him.

Tory smirked and yelped. There was a thud under the table, and his hazel blue eyes cut angrily to his boyfriend.

Nick's demeanor didn't change as he slurped up his food.

"I must've been mistaken," Tory muttered, flicking a carrot piece with his fork.

The message must have been received, but now Kara stared at Killian like he had three heads.

"It's nothing," Killian ground out. Something pulled at the back of his mind, and he pushed his hands under the table to rub them together as the burning intensified. His fingers sought out the thick red welts that now sat on both wrists, and he could barely move his fingers thanks to the spasming muscles through his palms.

Kara caught the flash of pain across his face. "Are you alright?"

Killian's heart thudded, and his chest was so tight he almost couldn't breathe. "I'm fine," he said. He wasn't sure if he was yelling or whispering over the sound of his beating heart.

Sweat dripped down the back of his shirt, making his skin tacky, and he tried to reach through his mental shields to reach his brother. He couldn't find Ryan in the vast black sea that took up most of their bond.

She cocked her head to the side, face scrunched in concern. "Are you sure?"

Killian smiled and nodded, looking down at the growing marks. Blood whooshed through his veins, pulsing through his ears, and making the room spin. He blinked to steady himself, and the welts split open, revealing bone and muscle. Blood pooled at his feet, and he shoved away from the table with a panicked shout.

The talking and laughter stopped as everyone stared.

Killian blinked, and it was gone. There were no injuries, welts, or pain. He shook so hard that his vision blurred. "Ryan's in trouble," he said.

Nick studied his face and scratched his jaw with clenched teeth. "How do you know?" he asked.

Killian couldn't explain it, but he could always tell when Ryan was in a bind. It just never happened to be a danger to himself before. This wasn't an emotion he was used to dealing with, so he didn't even know what he could do, but he had to try. "I have to find him."

Kara stood and reached across the table, but Killian jerked away. He wasn't going to be lulled into a false sense of security. He leveled Nick with a firm stare. "My brother needs me, Nick. Please," he said. His voice was soft, and he used the man's nickname only his family used. Killian meant it as a term of respect and endearment, but he wasn't sure it came across that way as Nick's eyes widened, and he blinked quickly like something was in his eye.

Nick cleared his throat when he recovered and said softly, "We don't know where he is. It would likely be a trap even if you could find him."

Killian's head ached, and he pressed his palms against the table as waves of memories washed over him. They were all Ryan's. Times when their mother berated him, checking his mark for changes, and threatening to separate the twins because Killian was acting out.

Killian squeezed his eyes shut, trying to sort through it. He had to find Ryan while they were connected. He didn't know how long it would last.

"Help me find you. For the love of Gods, please," Killian begged, forcing his thoughts down their link. He retreated to the place he and Ryan shared —the place of their bond. The ethereal bit of rope between them was frayed on Ryan's end. It split into multiple pieces and frizzed in the middle, threatening to snap. Where the magik met in the middle was a storm of blackened emotions.

"Killian," Kara started to talk.

He cut her off with a wave and forced himself back into the zone. Killian stared at the two ends of the rope and grabbed his end. His energy flowed down it, calming and reassuring. If he was going to find Ryan, he had to get through the storm first. The energy in the middle zipped around and cut across his arms and face like shards of glass.

"Ryan, please!" Killian shouted out, begging his brother to respond.

Screams echoed through the air, and Killian flinched. These weren't screams of physical pain but an emotional one. A pain buried so deep it had probably never seen the light of day. Killian let go of his end of the rope and walked toward the ball of emotion. While it was usually a beautiful mix of their energies, this one was primarily Ryan-dominated. More images were forced through his head, more of Ryan's memories.

Being bullied in school when they were little, hanging out with Avery at the river when he could sneak away from Mom, spending his days reading, writing, and doing math to appease their mother, resorting to using all his energy and training himself, so his magik would stay in control.

Killian forced the memories back and pressed his hand to the orb. It was freezing and burned as ice crackled along the surface, but he didn't let go. *"Let me find you,"* he whispered. *"I need to find you."*

The orb shivered under his touch and swallowed his hand. Killian didn't hesitate to step forward into the burning light.

"Killian!" Kara's scream was the last thing he heard before he was swallowed by darkness.

He looked around. Killian was in a dim, dingy cell that reeked of blood and urine. Kara, Nick, and Cody were all gone. He let his eyes adjust to the darkness and wrinkled his nose before his eyes adjusted, he stumbled to the back of the cell and peered into the dimness.

Ryan was slumped against the ground, blood pooling around his arms. He reached for his brother, but Killian's hands went right through him. His heart stopped, and he stared at the fading color in Ryan's face. "Wake up. Come on, Ryan, wake up," he shouted.

It wasn't fair. He couldn't be expected to watch his twin die. Killian jumped to his feet and looked around. There was nothing but old clothes, chains, and a razor. It was tucked in between Ryan's limp fingers. His skin had a horrible, gray pallor. If Killian didn't do something soon, he would lose him.

Killian reached for the door but went through that, too. He was invisible and not there, meaning he was probably unconscious in Haven. *I can't help if I can't touch anything!* "Ryan!" Killian ran back to his brother's side desperately. He held his energy around him like a blanket, praying it would do something. If he made a big enough commotion, Angel would have to come.

She wanted him alive so she would save him, right?

Killian closed his eyes and built upon the stack of energy. He kept collecting the loose strands of magik and adding them to the ball swirling around him.

Angel could tell when anything went wrong in her city. She had to be able to feel Killian. She couldn't ignore this – ignore him. Tears slipped down Killian's cheeks as he strained to keep the bond with Ryan intact. The thread twisted and bristled as small pieces of twine snapped between them.

Don't leave. You can't leave me. For the love of... fight for me!

The ball of energy nearly filled the room when the door swung open. Angel stormed inside and scowled down at Ryan's unconscious body. "So dramatic. This is what happens when I try to be nice," she growled, tapping her foot against the floor.

She flicked her wrist, and Killian's energy vanished. He panted and stared hard at Ryan as the flesh on his wrists came together enough to stop bleeding. Angel pressed a button on a black electronic watch. "Will you come down here and take the boy to the infirmary? He's done something stupid," she said. There was no sound on the other side, but she was content because she dropped her hand and let the button go. Her eyes flicked around the room and landed on Killian, but she looked through him, and he didn't know whether to feel relief or fury. "What was that?" she asked herself. Her lips pursed in confusion, but she didn't dwell long.

Killian was ripped out of the cell and returned to Haven before he could make sure Angel didn't kill Ryan herself. He stared at the hanging light in the living room and listened to a crackling fire.

Kara was crying over him, and Justin held his hands over his body. A dim light shimmered in the air as he tried to assess the situation. Killian pushed the man's hands back and sat up, rubbing his eyes.

"Oh my god!" Kara threw her arms around him, bawling. "I thought you died!"

Killian winced at the bone-crushing hug. His mind was foggy, and he looked around, trying to figure out what happened. It took a long moment for everything to come back.

"Let him go," Nick said, pulling her back. "We need to make sure he's not in shock."

Shock was a good word, and it would explain the prolonged thought process.

"What happened?" Justin asked.

Cody was nowhere to be seen. He wasn't at the table or behind them, which meant he had probably gone to his room or lab.

Killian blinked and tried to stand, but Justin set a firm hand on his shoulder. "No," he said. "I'm assessing your injuries."

He was worrying too much. Killian wasn't physically injured. He wanted to say that, but when he tried to push himself up, pain shot through his wrists. Killian winced and fell backward, holding his hands up. Thin lacerations covered each wrist. One on each side. "Ryan," he whispered.

Justin perked up. "What about Ryan?" he asked.

Killian closed his eyes and shook his head. How could he fail so monumentally as a brother that Ryan wanted to die? The sound of worrying and crying was replaced with owls hooting. A brisk wind washed across his skin, startling his eyes open. He was in the middle of Rochester Homestead. Killian turned his head to investigate the smell of burning cedar.

His grandmother's hut sat in front of him, with a candle in the sitting room window. She was sitting on her stoop, smoking a pipe, and staring. *"Hello there,"* she said, smiling. She spoke in Nivet, and it was such a comforting sound that Killian couldn't help but follow her lead.

He brushed the tears away and sat up. *"I don't know why I'm here,"* he said.

The homestead was silent at night. Everyone was in their homes, preparing for tomorrow's day. The hunters were already asleep, and the gatherers were packing the catch for today. Some might be making preserves or jellies. Killian loved it when his grandma let him help with her canning.

"You're heartbroken," she said, beckoning him over. *"It's okay; I heard you coming."*

Killian didn't know how, considering he didn't even know he was coming. *"Ryan's in trouble. I know you don't care, but he's in trouble, and I can't do anything."* He didn't move.

"Boys will be boys," she said. *"What kind of trouble is he in that you won't come to see your grandma anymore?"*

It frustrated him how happy she was. She didn't care about his brother; he knew that so why was he angry about it?

"He slit his wrists, and all I could do was watch him bleed," he snarled. *"What good is being telepathic if I can't be there when he needs me?"*

His grandma's face was leathery and old, aging even faster than the last time he saw her. Her thin, wispy hair fell in waves around her round face, and her smile faded. She shook her head and sighed. *"You never figured it out,"* she said with a slow sigh.

Killian didn't understand, and he was getting frustrated. The last thing he wanted to do was argue over something he couldn't understand.

"The magik that runs through your veins is more than enough to help your brother," she said with a chuckle.

Killian blinked at her, and she held out her arms once more. He sighed and got to his feet, walking over to let her hug him. He didn't understand, but he was sore, tired, and unsure his brother would make it through the night.

Grandma made Killian his favorite dinner: noodle soup with chicken and dough. It was always delicious, but Killian wasn't feeling it. He sloshed the soup around and stared glumly. The murky stew might tell him something important if he stared long enough.

"Your brother is strong. You needn't worry about him," Grandma said, clicking her tongue. She took out her pipe and lit the tobacco leaves, inhaling. Little puffs of smoke blew from the corners of her mouth as she sucked on it.

Killian looked up from the cloudy soup and shrugged. *"I'm not hungry."*

There was a knock on the door, and his grandma waved her hand. A rippled shadow on the floor opened the door so she didn't have to move.

Nick peered in, trying not to look uncomfortable. "Am I disrupting anything?"

Killian scowled. "I'm not going back."

"I know. I wanted to make sure you were alright," Nick said, stepping inside at the wave of welcome from Killian's grandmother. "I know this isn't easy, but..."

Killian jumped to his feet, forgetting about the bowl in his lap. It dropped to the floor, spilling the chicken soup in the dirt.

His grandmother yipped her discontent and threw her sandal at the back of his head.

He winced when the heel struck the base of his neck. Killian rubbed the sore spot and scowled.

"Listen to the man who doesn't want to mess up my house," she snarled.

Killian suddenly remembered where he got his temper and lack of patience from.

Nick smiled weakly. *"I am sorry to intrude, Ms. Wilson. I'll be on my way in a few minutes,"* he promised.

"It's not you that I'm mad at. You keep talking," Grandma demanded, pointing at Nick.

Nick nodded and waved his hand over the soiled spot on the floor. The dirt shuffled at his command and pushed the mud below the dry. In seconds, it was gone. "Look, Ryan will feel some things right now, but he can overcome them. You've got to maintain a cool head because you feed off each other's emotions."

Killian crossed his arms against his chest. He didn't dare open his mouth with his grandma staring like she was.

"We're going to find a way to help him, but until Justin and I can do that, we need to make sure you're ready," Nick said.

Killian frowned and sat back on his grandmother's bale of hay. This didn't help his current situation. Ryan was in trouble and hurting now, but none of this mattered if he didn't survive the night.

"You don't need to come back to Haven immediately, but try to let us know you're alright," Nick said.

It wasn't the first time he had been to his grandmother's. He often went to see how she was and spent time with her. He was slightly surprised his shock-induced self hadn't gone to Avery's. Lately, when he was having a crisis, Killian sought Avery first.

When Killian refused to respond, Nicholas spoke with his grandma in hushed tones. They spoke Nivet, but it wasn't like he didn't understand them. The longer Nicholas and Grandma talked, the angrier Killian became until he stormed from the hut, growling under his breath.

Killian stepped out of his grandmother's house and through a portal on her front stoop. He came out on Avery's lawn but stopped when he saw an old, scruffy man with a limp on the porch.

The man wore a ratty brown tunic with graying hair and a pudge nose. His eyes were as dark as Avery's and rimmed red like he had been crying... or drinking.

He slammed his fist against the wood the third time, and Avery threw it open with a snarl. *"You got any idea what time it is?"* His face was screwed up in such rage it was almost terrifying.

Killian had never seen Avery look ready to kill, but that's all he could see behind those dark eyes. Murder.

The man wasn't put off by Avery's anger. *"Why's the shop not open? Screwing the boy from last night?"* the man slurred when he spoke.

"It's only midnight. Are you drinkin' again?" Avery asked, baring his teeth. His accent was thickest in the morning, which Killian found quite by accident.

"What I do with my free time ain't any of your business, you ungrateful brat. I shoulda never had you," his dad said. It was difficult to understand most of what he said through the slurs.

Avery pinched the bridge of his nose before tensing. His eyes flicked to Killian, and the pale blue ring appeared. Now, he was mad. *"Go home, Dad,"* Avery said. He stepped off the porch and shut the front door. *"I'll let you know when the shop is open."*

There was a glint of light as the man withdrew a knife, and Killian moved. He didn't mean to. It was instinct. Killian slipped through the shadows and caught the man's wrist. He disarmed him without a word and tossed the knife aside, keeping his body between Avery and the man.

"Who the Helwe are you?" Avery's dad grunted.

He was already angry, and if he didn't blow off some steam, he might kill someone. He hoped the venom would steer the man away from starting anything. *"Leave."*

"Ah great, another worthless fa-"

Avery pushed Killian aside and punched his dad in the face. The man fell onto his butt, looking around like he was in a trance. *"Get off my property. Now."* His voice was ice.

Killian wasn't sure it was that simple, but the man pushed himself to his feet and stumbled back into the woods. Avery muttered to himself, but it wasn't anything Killian could understand.

"I'm sorry," Killian said. This wasn't the time to drop his problems on Avery, but he didn't want to go to anyone else.

Avery shook out his hand and winced. "I tucked my thumb. Never tuck the thumb." It took him a moment to register what Killian said. "Wait, what? Why are you apologizin'?"

"I need help," Killian whispered. He dropped his gaze. "I don't want to burden you, but..."

Avery shook his head and waved his hands. "Hey, no biggie. Tell me what you need. Is everythin' alright?"

It was anything but. Killian chewed his bottom lip until Avery caught his chin and forced him to look up.

He pulled Killian's lip from between his teeth and smiled gently. "Talk to me," he whispered.

Killian's eyes watered, and he blinked the tears back. He wasn't going to cry. "Ryan tried to kill himself," he said.

Avery looked Killian up and down before crushing him against his chest. He squeezed Killian and buried his face in his neck.

Killian froze. He didn't know what his body was doing, but this was new. All of it. His stomach flipped like it would fly right out of his mouth.

Avery's breath was hot against his skin, making him feel electric. "I'm sorry," he whispered.

Killian wasn't sure what he was apologizing for. For a moment, he couldn't remember what they were talking about. When he did, he wriggled out of Avery's touch.

"There's nothin' I can say to make you feel better," Avery said. "Is he alright?"

Everyone kept asking that. How could Ryan be okay if he just tried to end his life? Killian growled in frustration and shoved Avery. "No! Would you be alright? How would you feel if you felt like no one would come for you? No one would be by your side when you woke up from that nightmare." His voice rose of its own accord.

Avery grabbed his wrists when Killian pushed him again. His hold was firm, but it didn't hurt. "Stop," he said. "I can't help if you push me away."

"I don't want help," Killian shouted, twisting in Avery's grasp. "I want my brother. I want to leave this god's forsaken place behind. I want my mom. I don't want everyone to keep telling me it's fine. Nothing is fine!" His voice echoed off the trees and throughout the forest. Killian couldn't help himself. He broke, his knees buckled, and he sobbed.

Avery went to the ground with him and rubbed circles into the back of his hands. "I'm sorry, Kilua," he whispered. If he apologized one more time, Killian might take him out.

Not Part of the Plan

ANGEL

The rain started after Jess and Justin left for their amazing meteor shower date. The dark sky boomed and screamed its discontent, dumping buckets of water upon them.

Rebecca lit candles and placed them around the living room, taking calming breaths as her heart jumped with every boom of thunder. It wasn't the storm that scared her as much as the dark. She rubbed her stomach and hummed softly. "It's okay," she whispered. "We'll be okay."

Rain pelted the roof with the fierceness of a stampeding wolf pack. Her eyes fluttered closed, and a spasm of pain ran through her but could easily be smoothed when she rubbed in small circles.

Rebecca looked out the living room window and sat on the ledge, frowning. She hoped Jess still got to see the shower. They had been talking about it for ages. Thunder cracked, and lightning streaked across the sky, lighting up the angry roll of clouds that moved fast as the wind whipped them by.

Another spasm of pain overtook her, and Rebecca hissed, doubling over. "Oh, child, you're causing problems before you're even here," she groaned. She rubbed her lower back, hoping to ease the pain, but it didn't help this time. Water gushed down her leg when she stood, and Rebecca paled.

She cried out when another contraction hit her. It felt like she was being split in two. She dropped to her hands and knees and practiced her breathing. It was supposed to help, according to her sister, who had never carried or borne a child. There was a knock on the front door, but Rebecca didn't move – she couldn't. She breathed in and out, counting to ten each time. The contractions came and went. Rebecca screamed in pain, and sweat broke out across her chest and back.

"I cannot deal with this now," she whispered, balling her hands into fists, trying to push herself to her feet. "For the love of the gods, not now, child."

"Oh my, it looks like the baby's coming," someone said in a soft, lilting voice.

Rebecca looked up as tears trickled down her cheeks both in joy and pain.

Summer stood in the living room entryway. Her hair was chin-length and flared out like a wild child. Her beautiful green eyes roamed across Rebecca's stomach hungrily.

"Please, get my sister. They're at the peak, watching the shower. I can't do this without her," Rebecca said, her voice shaking.

Summer smiled and helped her stand. "Sweetie, she sent me to help, don't worry. It's going to be alright."

Rebecca tried to protest, but another wave of pain tore through her. She was being ripped apart. If this is how she died, at least she was doing something noble. No one told her how painful this was.

Summer rubbed circles into her lower back and ushered her down the hall into her room. "Deep breaths, imagine doing this with twins," she said with a laugh.

Rebecca didn't want to think about it. If she could get one out of the way, that would be terrific. She lay on her bed and pressed her back into the mattress, groaning. "Oh, I need Jess. Why isn't Jess coming?" she almost shouted.

"This baby is coming. I'm going to help, but you need to push hard," Summer said.

Rebecca fisted the bed sheets, and sweat poured down her forehead. Her clothes were soaked, and she screamed as she obeyed Summer's orders. Her body was not cut out for this. She couldn't bring a child into this world.

"Come on, push, Rebecca, push," Summer said, trying to encourage her.

Her face burned, and she screamed again. She didn't know how long it took, but the thunder accompanied her screams, and the wind howled outside. There was a horrible tearing feeling and then a single cry. Rebecca bit her lip and cried out as Summer held up a beautiful baby boy with dark red hair and chubby pink toes and fingers. Rebecca sobbed happily, holding out her arms to take him.

Summer shook her head and wrapped the baby in a white cloth. "Descendants of Chaos, don't have children. It's an abomination, just like Mommy."

The air in the room went still, and Rebecca gasped. It was like everything had been sucked out, leaving nothing behind but a sense of dread and absolute terror. "No, don't do this Summer, please. Give me my baby, please," she begged, trying to move. Her body was slow and heavy, and something wet flooded the sheets. *Blood. I'm bleeding... a lot.* She was going to die, bringing this child into the world that Summer would likely kill.

"No, please!" she screamed as Summer turned to leave the room. "Don't hurt my little boy." The baby stopped crying, and Rebecca blacked out.

Angel sighed and ran a hand down her face. She was going to need a full-time babysitter for this child. Her doctors worked around the clock to give a proper transfusion to ensure his survival. Ryan hadn't woken since she found him in his cell, but his color was returning.

There was a knock at the infirmary door, and Angel looked up. She got off her chair and crossed the room. The infirmary hadn't been used since she eradicated illness. There were too few injuries to even have a running hospital. Plus, if the soldiers were after someone, it was to kill. For that reason, the room was more of a storage. Today, it had been cleared a little to make room for an IV pole, medication, and a suture tray.

She was able to stop the bleeding with magik, but the wounds were unstable. To fully heal them would cost a price she wasn't willing to pay. Angel opened the door and sighed as Avery smirked at her. "I don't have the time," she said, pinching the bridge of her nose.

Avery frowned and peeked around her shoulder. "What's goin' on?" he asked.

She stepped aside and let him in. When he moved, she shut the door and returned to her chair. "Ryan did something stupid last night," she said.

Avery paled, but his face didn't change otherwise. He followed her further in and cocked his head to the side when he saw Ryan. "What did he do?"

"Slit his wrists. It was my fault for thinking he would be responsible with something sharp," Angel said. Her voice was toneless. She was going on a whole night of no sleep.

Avery didn't move. His muscles were tense, and he flexed his fingers a few times.

Angel watched him with curious eyes. "Are you still spending time with his brother?" she asked.

Her voice pulled him out of whatever trance he was in. He walked around the makeshift sterile bed and sat next to her on a bunch of boxes. "Yeah, sometimes," Avery said. His voice sounded far away.

Angel groaned and slumped in the seat. "This is exhausting. Why can't he behave like you did?" she asked.

Avery fidgeted and shook his head. "I'm a little more laid back. You think he's bad, you should see Killian."

Angel didn't know much about the brother. She already had her fill if he was anything like Ryan. A thought dawned on her, and she perked up. "Hey, you're the same age. Why don't you work with Ryan? Show him the ropes. Let him know I'm not awful," she said.

Avery forced a smile. It didn't reach his normally glittering eyes, but he nodded. "That sounds fun."

"If it's too much, you don't have to. I just thought that if there was someone he could build a relationship with, he might come around," Angel said.

Avery nodded. "No, I get it. I'd be happy to help wherever I can."

Angel smiled. She knew she could count on him. He was way more reliable than Havoc, and she knew he wouldn't betray her. "You're a good kid," she said.

He chuckled and yawned. "Well, I guess I'll hang out until he wakes up. Why don't you get some rest?" he asked.

It wasn't a horrible idea. Angel nodded and stood, stretching her back. It cracked and popped, releasing some of the tension. She let out a content groan and walked out of the room, yawning again. Some sleep would do her good, and then she could figure out what to do with Ryan. She was going to have to keep him in closer quarters. He might've died if it wasn't for the weird surge of energy through her dungeons.

With Avery's help, she was sure to break through to Ryan. He would see she wasn't horrible to work with and maybe even not have to be forced to do things.

Angel snorted in amusement and walked down the hall to the elevator. Right, and she might be the Queen of the universe one day. When she returned to her private room, Angel went straight to bed. She was exhausted, and all she wanted was sleep.

Step Up or Back Down

Kara sat on the coffee table in the living room with closed eyes, meditating. Sitting on the floor was hard because she could only focus on Nicholas' energy, and sitting outside had the same effect, with the added benefit of feeling Justin. If she stayed off Nicholas' domain and away from Justin, she could almost make herself sit still for a few minutes.

Since the dinner where Killian fainted, Kara had pestered her mentors for answers when the blonde didn't come home. After losing Ryan to Angel, she worried Killian might leave and never return.

"Hey, can we talk for a minute," Avery's voice made her scream.

Since Nicholas and Justin allowed him access across the barriers, he spent every waking moment terrorizing her when he knew she was alone. Avery teleported in and out of Haven, though he never crossed either of the house owner's paths which told her he was constantly watching. He wouldn't even talk to Tory or Cody. It was only her and Killian.

"Good morning, and how are you?" she asked using her best Nivet. She was excited to get a reaction, but he waved his hand, and her heart fell in disappointment. Kara clutched her chest. "That's cold," she said.

Avery knelt before the table and grabbed her hands. "Say you'll come with me, so I don't have to spill my guts here," he said. Something wild and terrifying lingered behind his dark eyes.

Kara frowned and nodded. "Okay, where are we going?" she asked. While he had proven to be a stout ally, she wasn't entirely all about wanting to go alone with him.

His energy was hard to read – sometimes. Since they spent more time together, she was getting better at seeing him for who he was. He could act like a jerk, but he had a bright, unrelenting energy which gave her reason to trust him.

He didn't answer, just teleported them to his stall in Rochester. The lingering smell of animal carcasses and fresh leather was not fun. She had to brace herself to keep from gagging.

"What's wrong?" Kara asked.

Avery sat on the stall counter and shook his head. He kicked his feet limply. "I'm a bad person," he said.

Kara frowned. She didn't know what to say to that.

"I know where Ryan is, and I don't know how to tell Killian," he said, looking up at her. His eyes shone with tears, but they didn't fall. "He needs help."

Kara fidgeted. She could ask many things to make him clarify, but she didn't want to. She was in the middle of an abandoned shack with him in the middle of the night - pissing him off was not on her to-do list. Even if she was *mostly* sure he wouldn't hurt her.

"Look, I know how it sounds, but... you have to believe me. *I didn't know what would happen,*" Avery started in the language she understood, but his words quickly fell into Nivet.

She had been reviewing Justin's notes but wasn't qualified to start translating between the languages. Kara blinked wildly and tried to catch any word that would make the conversation make sense.

"Stop lookin' at me like that," Avery said.

"Alright, I didn't get most of what you just said. Can we try that again?" she asked.

Avery took a breath and closed his eyes. "If I tell you where to get Ryan, will you go for him?"

She chewed her bottom lip until it hurt. Every fiber of her being told her to ask how he knew. It would be an easy question, but she knew that Avery would give her an answer for which she couldn't forgive him. Closing her eyes, she breathed past the writhing nausea and nodded. "Where?" she asked. Kara would leave it because Avery had done so much for her, and she couldn't risk something tearing them all apart again.

"Yorklyn Tower. Angel has an underground cell where she keeps prisoners," Avery said. He chose his words slowly, and his eyes were still misty.

"Okay, I will make sure Killian gets the message. I'm sure he will have no problem retrieving his brother," she said.

Avery cleared his throat and smiled in relief. It was a wobbly smile, but at least he tried. "Thank you," he whispered. "And don't... don't tell Killian I told you."

Kara froze. A couple nights ago, Tory asked how Killian's new crush was before the blonde disappeared. He didn't mean Avery, did he? She never got the whole story and had forgotten to ask when things calmed down. "Why does it matter?" she asked.

It was Avery's turn to shift. A desperate plea crossed his face, but he didn't voice it.

"You've been the one training him. "Is he at your place?" she asked.

"No, he doesn't stay with me. He's at his grandmothers down the road," Avery whispered.

Kara leaned over to look past him. She could go see him and sort this all out. It was worrying how terrified Killian had been.

Avery shook his head and snapped his fingers to grab her attention. "You can't go," he said. "He would know it was me."

She frowned but knew he was right. Keeping secrets was stupid. They should all have a normal conversation like adults. "Avery..." she started to talk when he jerked his head up so fast, she was surprised he didn't get whiplash.

He leaped over the counter and beckoned for her to get down.

Kara sat and tried to hide in the shadows of the stall despite not understanding.

"Killian, what're you doin' out here?" he asked, his voice suddenly jubilant.

Killian's voice was gruff, like he had been sleeping. "Don't do that crap with me."

"Do what?" Avery asked.

Kara felt stupid. She was hiding from someone she knew because Avery was too chicken to tell Killian what was going on. If she could teleport, she would take her butt back home.

"Act happy when you're not. Why are you here?" Killian sat on the stall counter with a grunt. His heels kicked the wood behind him. "It's too late to be doing house calls."

"I'm not," Avery's voice dropped.

Kara blinked in surprise. She didn't think Avery was himself around anyone, especially someone like Killian. It was possible she didn't know them as well as she thought, but hearing the change in him at Killian's request was shocking.

"Then why are you out here?" Killian asked again.

Avery sighed. It was hard to see what was happening, but Kara could hear the dirt shuffling as he paced. "Nothin', I don't know. Can't sleep, I guess," he said.

Killian kicked his feet a little more before stopping. "I keep having nightmares."

Avery hummed in acknowledgment, but he didn't say anything.

Kara felt rude. She was eavesdropping on a conversation she didn't want to. She would have liked Killian to talk to her about these things, but this isn't how she wanted him to do it.

"Your quiet tonight," Killian whispered. His voice fell. It was hard hearing him, and Kara knew they could finish the rest in private if she covered her ears.

"I'm havin' a rough night," Avery said. "It's a bad day, Kilua..."

Kara didn't want to hear anymore. She put her hands over her ears and closed her eyes, singing a song. She didn't realize Killian was this head over heels for someone. She didn't know Killian was capable of romantic interests, let alone in men. That may be why he didn't have an interest in the city. He didn't want to feel out of place more than he was. She sang songs, went through spells, and worked out quadratic formulas in her head without knowing if the answers were correct. It was still nice and dark when Avery put a hand on her shoulder, so she had no clue how much time had passed.

Kara jumped and blinked at him, frowning.

"Sorry," he said.

"I didn't know you guys were romantically involved," she hissed, standing and brushing the dirt off her clothes.

Avery stared at her like she had lost her mind. "I'm sorry, what?" he asked.

"I didn't need to be privy to that lovely conversation you two were having. Look, if Killian wants to keep it a secret, let him. Don't drag me into this," Kara snapped.

"Whoa, whoa, whoa. Killian and I are not romantically involved. He would castrate me if he ever heard you sayin' that," Avery said, lowering his voice as if Killian would appear at his name.

"Don't lie to me," Kara said, holding out her hand in defiance. "Take me home."

Avery grabbed her shoulders and stared her in the eye. "We're *not* together. I don't do relationships. I'm helpin' him, that's all."

Kara studied his face but couldn't detect a lie. His features didn't shift or twitch like they usually did when he was keeping something from her. That made their conversation even worse. "Gross. Take me home," she said again. If they were going to live in denial let them, but she never wanted to be involved in something between hose two morons again.

Avery opened his mouth to ask, but she shook her head and pointed in the general direction of Haven. He took her home and dropped her off on the porch without a word.

Kara stormed inside and mentally cursed him out. She hated boys.

Killian walked through the front door while she was eating an apple a few days after her adventure with Avery. She watched him with dark eyes as he stoked a fire in the hearth and rubbed his hands together. His hair dripped with frozen water that wasn't quite snow. "Stop staring at me," he muttered.

Kara made a face at his back. "Good to see you're alive," she said. Her voice was almost as cold as it was outside.

"Sorry," he said. He wasn't.

She knew he was only saying it to shut her up. "So, what did you see with Ryan? I've only ever seen him act like this, not you," she said, trying to get more information.

Killian shrugged. "Nothing." His voice was tight, and he still didn't turn around to face her.

Kara pursed her lips and threw the apple at his head.

Killian ducked before it could make contact, and the apple flew into the fire with a thud. "You trying to kill me?" he asked, looking at her.

"We're going after him," she said.

He blinked and scratched his cheek. "What?" Dark bags hung under his eyes, and he yawned.

"Ryan," she said. "I want to go after him." If getting Ryan back was what it took to bring Killian back to life, she would take Avery's advice.

"Kara, I'm tired. I need to sleep," Killian muttered, waving his hand. "Leave me alone."

She shook her head. "No, he needs help. You're a mess and can barely manage. Can we just... will you let me help you?"

Killian narrowed his eyes.

It wasn't as terrifying when he looked seconds from passing out. Plus, she was getting used to his moods.

"I don't need help. I'd like to sleep," he ground out, barely containing his rage.

"I do mind!" Kara jumped to her feet and sent her book and blanket to the floor.

Killian scowled.

"I'm worried about him too, you know? You're not the only one who cares," Kara said, fighting to keep her voice level. "I lost mine, and I can't bear to lose more, so please..."

Killian squeezed his eyes shut and took some deep breaths. It took a long time before he opened his eyes again and stared at her. The anger and frustration were gone, but he didn't look more willing.

"And where do you suggest we look?" he asked.

"Angel lives in the tower. He must be there somewhere," Kara said. It was an automatic response, but she knew she couldn't tell on Avery despite the strongest desire to spill everything. If Killian refused to talk to anyone but him, she wouldn't take his only willing means of support. Nicholas barely got the boy to open up to anyone.

Killian nodded and rubbed the back of his neck. "It's probably a bad idea, but fine. We can go check it out," he said.

"Don't sound like I'm putting you out." Kara frowned.

Killian shook his head and stood, walking over to the side couch. It faced the stairwell, about half the size of the main one. He collapsed on it and curled into a ball, closing his eyes.

"Let me sleep a few hours, and we can go," he whispered.

Kara smiled to herself and sat back down, collecting her book and blanket. It wasn't the most productive conversation, but they were finally doing something together aside from eating breakfast or destroying weaponry.

Tory cleared his throat.

She looked up, and her smile faded. "How can I sense everyone but you and Justin?" she asked.

He stood in the front hall, looking into the main room. "You used to be able to sense me, but I put a stop to it," Tory said, walking into the living room.

Kara sighed and leaned back against the couch as he sat. "Are you going to tell on us?" she asked.

Tory made a face like he sucked on a lemon. "Please, like I would do that. So long as you're not trying to kill each other, I don't care what you do," he said.

"Then what's the face for?" she asked.

"I want to come," Tory said. His voice was dead serious, but she couldn't tell if he was.

She waited for him to say, 'joking' or 'sike,' but the words never came. "Why?" she asked. Tory and Ryan had never gotten along before, so it didn't make sense for him to want to tag along.

"Because I think Ryan should be home," Tory said.

Kara pursed her lips and draped her arm across the back of the sofa. Tory hadn't done anything with her outside of training in ages. It would be interesting to see him work.

"Our chances are better with more than two of us," Kara said. There wasn't an obvious downfall; Tory could get Ryan wet, rendering him unable to use magik.

"I won't tell Nick," Tory said. "I swear."

Kara nodded. If they could convince Killian, everything would be fine.

"You should get some sleep," Tory said.

She looked at Killian, who somehow fell asleep in ten seconds flat. "Yeah, I suppose I should."

Tory flicked her forehead with a weak smile. "I won't let him leave without you, don't worry."

Kara sighed and nodded again. It would be wise to have the appropriate energy to enter the city. She pulled the blanket to her chin and huffed, falling onto her back. *Avery better not be wrong about this.* If she went on a wild goose chase and ended up getting someone hurt, she would kill him.

Kara jolted awake when someone shook her. Her energy was called to her palms before she realized who it was.

"Whoa, don't fry me," Killian whispered. "And don't be too loud."

Kara blinked the sleep away and let her energy die. "What's wrong?" she asked.

Killian chuckled and shook his head, sitting on the coffee table. "I think I have enough energy to plan a breakout. Are you still in?"

Kara rubbed her eyes and nodded. "Tory, too," she said, yawning.

Killian quirked a brow in confusion. "I'm sorry, what?" he asked.

I said the same thing. She was too tired to smile, though. "Yes, he wants to help."

Killian sighed but nodded. It looked like he didn't have enough energy to argue, or maybe he saw the pros as well. "Go get him then," Killian whispered.

Kara scrambled off the couch and tiptoed up the stairwell. Her heart jumped in excitement. She had never snuck out before, and to be fair, her parents worked all the time, so she never had to sneak out.

"Stop acting like you're breaking the rules," Killian snapped.

Kara stuck her tongue out and leaned over the railing. "Why are you still whispering if we're not breaking the rules?"

He opened his mouth and shut it again, shooting her a withering glare.

She smirked and continued up the stairwell. "Technically, you're grounded."

He growled behind her as she vanished around the corner with a snicker. They were sneaking out and breaking the rules, and the best part was that if they brought Ryan back, Justin couldn't even be mad. Kara hurried to the end of the hall and tapped on Tory's door. He snored from within, and she smirked. He didn't stay awake either. She turned the handle and pushed the door open, freezing when Nicholas' head popped up from behind Tory.

"What's wrong?" Nicholas asked blearily.

Kara wracked her brain, thinking of a way to get Tory alone. "I had a bad dream," she said.

Nicholas blinked himself awake and elbowed Tory before rolling over. "Your escape artist is here," he mumbled. "Don't die," he added as an afterthought before falling back asleep.

Kara frowned.

Tory sat up and ran a hand through his hair, yawning. "Oh man, I musta fallen asleep," he said.

"You *told* him?" Kara asked as loud as she could while still whispering.

"Hey, we're leaving. I'm not gonna not tell anyone we're leaving. That's a dumb idea," Tory murmured, getting to his feet and throwing a black hoodie on.

Kara scowled. "I shouldn't have told you."

"You didn't, I found out via spying. Now, come on before Killian leaves us," he said.

Kara growled in frustration as Tory closed his bedroom door behind him. "Now Nicholas knows," she said, giving chase.

"Yeah, good. So, if we don't return, someone knows where to look for us," Tory said. He sounded frustrated, and his voice was still thick with sleep.

Kara glared. She wanted this to be a secret mission they did together. "You didn't have to tell," she said.

"Do you know how childish you sound right now?" Tory asked.

Kara stuck out her tongue to prove his point. It didn't matter so long as Nicholas didn't insist on coming, and it wasn't like he was stopping them. She grabbed the back of Tory's shirt, and he almost fell down the stairs.

He caught himself on the banister with a snarl and whirled around. "What's wrong now?"

"Why's he letting us go? Justin would never allow this," she said.

"Justin doesn't know, and Nick only agrees because I'm going. If you refused to take me, you could bet he'd be on your ass," Tory said, shaking her off.

Kara scoffed. They stepped into the living room arguing, and Killian shook his head, running a hand down his face. Kara stopped snapping to look at him. "He told Nicholas," she said.

Killian sighed and pinched the bridge of his nose. "That's not an awful idea so long as he doesn't stop us from going."

"Thank you," Tory muttered. "Even Killian agrees, and he never agrees with anything, so can we get this over with?" he asked.

"You're no better fighter than Killian is," Kara protested.

Tory rubbed his eyes. "Yeah, well, we're both better than you. At least if I come, Killian doesn't have to worry about playing body-guard," he said.

She bit her tongue. That was a low blow, and he knew it.

Killian held out his hands, one for each of them. "We get Ryan, we come back." He was obviously done with their argument.

Kara placed her hand in his and took a deep breath. "We get Ryan," she repeated, trying not to scowl at her supposed best friend. Tory didn't bother saying anything. He just took Killian's hand and grunted in affirmation. Killian summoned a portal, and the three of them exchanged looks. At least they were finally doing something as a group. Justin should be proud. They stepped through the portal together, and Kara's world went black.

Kara's vision stopped swimming when the light returned. It was dim and quiet. Kara used to find it comforting, but now it was eerie and terrifying, knowing the night wasn't truly silent. A few lamp posts lit up familiar walkways and white houses clumped together. They looked the exact same, with gravel yards and concrete roads. Nothing exciting, boring even.

Killian looked around and cursed under his breath. "I don't under-stand. I've never missed." He looked around the darkened street and paced.

A lot of the houses had been burned or singed. Kara looked around in horror, and her eyes fell on a house at the end of the street. A boarded-up home with yellow tape and dark windows. "Mine," she whispered.

Killian groaned and whirled around on her. "You hijacked my spell."

"I didn't mean to," she said. "I didn't want to see this place." Her throat tightened with the thought.

"You might've screwed this up." Killian's voice continued raising as his anger grew.

Kara almost slapped him. She couldn't help raising her voice. "You're not the only one who wants to help your brother."

Killian threw his hands in the air. "I don't know why I bothered."

Tory stepped between them and looked around. "Stop. You don't want to alert anyone we're here," he said. "Unless they got lax on the rules since I left," he added under his breath.

Kara clenched her hands and opened her mouth when a flash of red burned through her mind. She clutched her head as pain tore through her temple. It was the worst headache she had ever had.

Tory grabbed her shoulders and looked her over. "What's wrong?" he asked.

Killian's breath caught.

A second later, Ryan stood in front of them. He held two short swords—one black and the other crimson. Both had gold swirls etched along the blade's dull side, and Kara blinked. Ryan's emerald gaze was empty, devoid of all life.

Kara watched a black snake wrap around Ryan's torso. Violet spikes were staked through the red and orange energy around his heart. Killian stepped forward, a flash of relief crossing his face. Kara grabbed his arm. She shook her head and blinked through the burning pain behind her eyes. "It's not his energy." Her hand trembled as she struggled to maintain her composure.

Killian scoffed. "I think I can manage," he said.

Tory stared strangely and shook his head. "No, something's wrong. I'm with Kara."

Killian didn't listen. He walked past them, focusing on his brother. "Ryan, you scared the Helwe out of me."

Tory grabbed his arm and jerked him back two seconds before Ryan summoned a sword and swiped at his brother. They all froze.

Kara's heart raced in her ears, and she stepped closer to Tory. He was the oldest, meaning he should know what to do. Considering the fight in the forest when Angel first took Ryan, she should've expected things would go poorly. She had been so excited about sneaking out and breaking her first rule that she forgot they were in the middle of something big.

"What do we do?" she asked.

Killian hesitated before responding, "Um, we talk sense into him? I don't understand how he can hold the swords. He slit his wrists," Killian whispered.

"What do you mean he slit his wrists?" Kara asked. This was the first time she was hearing of this. "When did this happen?"

Killian waved a hand to quiet her. "Not important right now," he said.

She thought it was important. Like Killian said, if Ryan did something like that, he shouldn't be able to hold his sword, let alone fight.

Tory opened the bag of water he kept on his person during training. He waved his hand over it, whispering his total control spell. A ribbon of water flowed from the back and danced in a circle around him. "Well, it doesn't look like he's in much pain," he said.

Kara traced Ryan's energy through the air and tried to find a way to break through. The chaos kept a tight shield around his heart and mind, making conversing difficult. Kara didn't know how she knew that.

Tory stayed in front of her and surveyed the scene. His arm was held out protectively. He kept his body tight and tense in case he had to spring into action. So far, Ryan only moved if he was approached. After Killian backed off, he went still. "Okay, so what do we do?" Tory asked. He was letting Killian lead because it was his brother.

Kara pursed her lips and turned her attention away from him. Chaos shrouded the city, making it difficult to see through the fog. It was a wonder she had not noticed this before. The horrible headaches made a lot more sense, though.

"He's only reacting when you get close..." she trailed off when Killian stepped forward again. No one was listening.

Killian held out his hands, talking to Ryan in a low voice. He hadn't finished his sentence when Ryan slashed his swords across Killian's chest. Killian backed up, brought his arms in front of himself, and yelped when the swords caught across his forearm. Blood splattered the concrete, and Kara swallowed thickly. The strong scent of iron made her gag a little.

"Keep it together," Tory muttered.

"Stop approaching him; he's reacting to you," she hissed, grabbing Tory's bicep.

He pulled away and pointed at Killian. "Do you want me to back him up?"

Killian had already summoned a weapon and was locked in combat with his brother. Their swords clashed and rang into the night, making Kara flinch. This wasn't going to end well.

She let Tory go and said a silent prayer.

Tory kept his water close at hand and exchanged looks with Killian. "Pin him?" he asked.

Killian nodded. "Slow him down enough to get him to Haven. We can go from there," he said.

Kara watched Ryan's energy shift. It became bolder and brighter, and she knew he would move in for the kill. She held out a hand and closed her eyes. "Mother Light, hold us in your arms: shield." Her spell went into effect as Ryan threw a fireball at Killian and Tory.

It crashed against the walls of her white shield, and she clutched her chest, thankful the adrenaline rush kept most of the pain at bay.

It wasn't nearly as strong as the one that wiped her out in the forest, but it was close.

Tory turned and flashed her a thumbs up, and she flipped him off. The least he could do was pay attention.

Gravel crunched underfoot, signifying that Killian was on the move again. Kara kept her eyes on Ryan and his energy, shielding Killian only when she thought Ryan's hit would take him down. Killian was slow and clumsy with a sword. He could parry his brother's attacks, but whenever he managed one of his own, he left a side open and got hit.

Tory splashed a handful of water in Ryan's face the third time he tried to bomb one of them. That didn't help. Fire consumed Ryan's body, and he slammed his palm into Tory's sternum.

Kara groaned in sympathetic pain and ran towards him as he fell. She wasn't about to heal that kind of injury, but she wanted to make sure he wasn't going to die. She leaned over Tory as Killian took the space between him and Ryan. "How are you feeling?" she asked, waving her hand over his chest. "Show me what I need to know: diagnostics." Red energy pulsed around Tory's chest and heart, which meant no breaks. If it were a pulsing blue light, they would have a problem.

"If he would just talk to me," Killian said, yelping in pain when Ryan's sword cut across his shoulder. "Why won't he talk?"

Kara looked up from her work. "He isn't himself," she said. It was like Ryan wasn't there. She knew he had to be, but his eyes were blank like a doll.

"Why's he here if he isn't going to talk?" Killian snapped.

Tory sat up when Kara ended her spell. He wheezed and rubbed his chest in slow circles. "I think he broke something," he said.

She shook her head and pointed at Killian. "Energy transfer." When about a fourth of her energy left her body, Kara dropped her hand and panted. If anyone needed to train in stamina, all they had to do was go out with one of the boys. "Nothing's broken," she said.

Tory stood slowly and froze when Ryan appeared in front of him. The blonde pressed his sword to Tory's neck and smirked. It was the first emotion she had seen him emit. Kara pushed Tory to the side without thinking. The sword nicked his chin, but he escaped unscathed.

Ryan blinked in surprise and turned to face her when a chain wrapped around his wrist.

They all looked back, and Killian jerked his weapon, ripping the sword from Ryan's hand. His eyes rimmed red, and he snarled in anger. "I'm done with this. You're going to come home if I have to drag you kicking and screaming."

Blood dripped from Ryan's wrist and splattered on the ground.

The world slowed, and Kara clutched her stomach with a grunt. This was not the time to be sick. Killian and Ryan's fight continued around her, and Tory waved a hand in front of her face. His lips moved, but she couldn't hear a sound.

A flash of fire lit up the chain on Killian's chain scythe, and he dropped it, his face screwing up in pain.

Kara's eyes dropped to Ryan's wrist, where the blood flowed steadily. There was no sound of clashing metal, but the sharp tang of copper made bile rise in her throat.

Tory ran behind Ryan and grabbed his arms, pinning them to his sides. The water surrounding him acted like rope and snapped around Ryan's wrists and arms. Ryan's energy burst to life, and the water flew apart, splashing Killian and Tory.

Kara had to do something.

Ryan threw his head back, catching Tory's nose. The second he was released, Ryan moved away from the Descendant of Water and appeared behind Killian. He was too fast and strong. Her breath was all she could hear as she tried to move past the blood. The longer they fought, the more accumulated. She hadn't quite gotten past this part in training.

Killian summoned daggers and ducked under Ryan's swords. He was trying to talk to him and make Ryan stop, but as Kara said before, he didn't want to talk. There was no one to talk to.

Tory froze the ground, and Ryan slipped, dropping to his knees. As he slid past Killian, Ryan turned the blade outward and cut across his brother's thigh. More blood splattered the ground. Kara closed her eyes and breathed. She had to steady her emotions if she was going to help. *Blood isn't the end of the world. I can do this.*

When she opened her eyes again, the sound returned. Tory and Killian shouted back and forth to each other as their plans fell one by one. They didn't work well together.

"He's targeting me, you moron. Be smart," Killian said, his face red and angry. He pressed a shaking hand to his bleeding thigh. His face was pale, and his movements slow.

Tory, on the other hand, had a couple of nicks and scratches but was mostly unscathed. Killian was right. Ryan *was* targeting him. There had to be a way to use that to their advantage.

Kara focused her energy and wrapped it around her like a blanket. The chaos around her retreated as if it could not touch her magik. She directed her thoughts to Ryan. She didn't know much about fighting but knew enough to know this wasn't going well.

Killian was a bloody mess, and he was doubled over. He panted heavily, refusing to release his hold on a sword he didn't know how to use.

Tory was in front of him, his calculating gaze flicking across the landscape. He flicked his wrist and pointed to a dark street that led into the city. "I have a plan," he said.

Kara ran to Killian and set her hands on his back. She chanted her healing spell and tried to control her energy flow so she wouldn't hurt him. Their magik didn't often cooperate.

"He won't follow you," Killian said. He spat a mouthful of blood on the ground.

Tory flashed them a confident smile. "Trust me, hold him off for a few more minutes."

Kara nodded. She bit her lip and finished healing what wounds she could before the pain became too much. Her leg, back, and arms were throbbing when she was done. Blood trickled down her chin as she tried not to let on how badly she hurt.

Killian stood and nodded his thanks. If he noticed the pain she was in, he didn't say anything. He held up his weapon again and faced Ryan. Tory had taken off on one of his ice trails when Kara and Killian agreed to hold Ryan. It shouldn't be complicated so long as Killian didn't move.

"Go to Haven," Killian whispered. "Get Justin and Nicholas, I think we made a mistake."

Kara looked around and pressed her hands to her chest. Her vision blurred, and she was seconds from passing out. "I don't think I can," she said.

Ryan charged, but Killian held his ground. He pulled the sword up, and the two weapons clashed. Killian redirected Ryan's attack, and the point came awfully close to Kara's face. If she had the reflexes to move, she would've. That was out of the cards until the pain vanished. Ryan circled like a vulture, but Killian stayed put. The brothers eyed each other as they contemplated their next moves. Killian pushed his heel back, closer to Kara. His back was to her, and he didn't turn his head, but she knew he was aware of her every move.

"You can fight, Ryan," Killian said, trying to buy time. "This isn't the end of the road, not for you." Killian kept his voice low.

"How cute is this?" Angel's voice made them jump.

Kara looked up weakly, and a few stray tears ran down her cheeks. She was able to move a little, but her arms were still killing her. The price of magik was much worse than she ever thought.

Angel stood across the way. Ryan was at her side, and Tory held in front of her. She had a dagger under his chin, digging into his throat. A bead of blood bubbled to the surface against his olive skin.

"Damn it," Killian muttered.

Angel laughed and fluffed her fiery red hair. "And here I thought I would have to fight to get you to me," she said.

Kara frowned, barely tracking the conversation through muffled voices and blurred vision.

"All you've got to do is keep my brother from coming home," Killian said. He stood his ground. "I'll come to you every time."

A sadistic smile flashed across Angel's face, and she gestured to Tory with her free hand. "Want your little friend back? I have a stipulation," she said.

"What's that?" Killian growled.

"You stay," Angel said, almost sneering.

Kara wondered how much self-control the witch took to keep from screaming and yelling. When Killian moved forward, she grabbed the back of his shirt. "Don't," Kara said. "Can't you feel the air?"

Killian scowled and ripped his shirt free. "Go to Avery," his voice was low enough so only the two could hear. "Tell him what happened and that I need help."

If Kara was going to get anyone, it would be Justin. She doubted Avery could take Angel alone. Plus, Avery didn't want to be involved in Killian's quest for his brother, and Kara didn't want to make him choose. "I'm not leaving," she said. It was the easiest way to tell him it wouldn't happen.

Angel cleared her throat and called out to them, "Whispering is uncalled for, my dears. Do we have a deal or not?" she asked.

Tory tapped his fingers to his thigh and kept his eyes on the ground. He had a plan. She recognized that look from their time in high school.

"Fine," Killian said. "We have a deal."

"Good, then walk toward me, and I'll let him walk to the girl," Angel said. She knew what she was doing. Thankfully, she was too arrogant to pay attention to her hostage.

Killian took a step forward, and Kara let him go. He didn't question her sudden lack of defiance. Angel let Tory go, and he took a step forward. A flash of ice zipped across the ground, and Tory jumped on it, summoning a giant sword. As he whirled around to strike Angel, Ryan moved before her, holding his arms wide.

"Watch out for my brother!" Killian shouted.

"Wait, don't..." Kara tried to stop him before he could ruin things, but Killian was already moving. He charged forward and shoulder-checked the brunette, sending him flying to the ground.

Tory slammed his elbow into the concrete with a sickening crack, and he screamed in pain, cradling his arm. His sword flew in the air and vanished in a blue light before it could hit the ground. "Seriously?" he shouted, tears streaking his cheeks.

Angel grabbed the back of Killian's neck when she realized Tory was down for the count. "It's been fun! See you next time," she said with a feral laugh. The three vanished in purple light, and Kara sank to her knees.

Justin was going to kill them.

Tory pushed himself up with a grunt and shot her a look that said the same thing. They both knew they were dead. "Nick's not gonna cover," he said.

"I don't want him to. We have to get Killian," she said.

"Right, well, I think broke my arm."

They had no choice but to get Justin. She groaned and hung her head—unless she did get Avery. If they did that, no one would be any the wiser, especially if they brought at least Killian back.

"No more ideas, we're going to Nick and getting Justin," Tory said. He was the responsible one.

She shook her head and stood. "One more idea. If it doesn't work then we go back," she said. All she could hope was that Avery was still at his stand.

Tory hesitated before letting her help him up. "This is a horrible idea," he said.

Kara smiled and then frowned. "How do we get back without Killian?" They were both silent. *Oh, Helwe....*

Glass Walls Always Break

RYAN

"Ryan, wake up." Killian's voice flickered through his head

Ryan grunted in his sleep and wished for the mirage to leave him alone. He was exhausted and didn't know if he could open his eyes even if he wanted to. "Ryan, don't make me splash water on you." The threat was so real and so Killian that Ryan couldn't stop himself from reacting.

He bolted upright, forgetting how badly he hurt. His arm reminded him, seconds later, when it collapsed under his weight, and he fell onto his stomach on a cot. A slew of curse words slipped through his lips before he righted himself. He wasn't in the cell anymore, and boy, he hurt.

Ryan looked around with bleary eyes and felt pain throb through his arms and wrists.

Killian sat next to the cot. His arms and legs were chained to a steel bar screwed into the floor. A dull look stretched across his face, but Ryan saw it. The flicker of anger was so intense that it would've burned if Ryan could touch it. "What're you doing here?" Ryan asked, his voice raspy and throat sore. He didn't know how long it had been since he had water or food. His eyes flicked across the room. It was small and filled with boxes, but Angel had tossed a cot and some medical supplies in it.

His last lucid memory was slitting his wrists, and he assumed that's where Killian's look of anger came from. "How long has it been?" Ryan whispered.

Killian blinked. "Since when? The suicide attempt or total?" he asked.

It was Ryan's turn to shrug. He didn't have a sense of anything these days. "Well, you cut your wrists a couple of nights ago, or do you not remember that?" His voice was so cold that Ryan was afraid to say something witty. "In total, you've been gone about a month."

"Gods." Ryan pressed his hands to his face and took a few breaths. An entire month. He had been with Angel a whole month and was no better than before. "It didn't- I didn't know it had been that long," he said.

"You've cut off all forms of communication," Killian said. "And if you say it was to protect me, I'll break your nose." His fists clenched as if he were about to make good on his promise.

Ryan didn't have words to describe his terror at this revelation. "I don't have a choice. When I'm not myself, I go to this place where I can't use magik," he said. He couldn't help the exhaustion in his voice.

Killian's jaw tightened but didn't say anything. The sound of splintering glass rang out, and Ryan took a breath. He couldn't go down that road again.

Killian grabbed Ryan's hand and squeezed. He set his forehead against the cot, and his shoulders shook. It didn't take a genius or a mental connection to tell him Killian was crying, and Ryan's heart squeezed. "I'm sorry," he said, but he didn't know how to fix it.

Killian shook his head. His sobs were silent but strong enough to keep him from talking. He was covered in cuts and dried blood, and Ryan eyed them carefully. Most of them were defensive wounds and by all rights he shouldn't be standing.

"You shouldn't be here," Ryan said slowly.

Killian turned his face so he could make eye contact despite not lifting his head. "We were going to rescue you," he said, his voice nasally.

Ryan frowned. "And Angel did all that?" he asked. Killian's silence made his blood run cold. He squeezed Ryan's hand tighter, and his eyes flicked away.

Ryan tried to pull back, but Killian wouldn't let him go. "It's fine. I'm fine," he said.

This was beyond the measly fights in Haven. Ryan had drawn blood, and a lot of it—enough for Killian's shirt to be soaked through in some spots.

"This is anything but fine," Ryan snapped, pulling free. "How can you let me do that? Didn't you fight back?"

"Of course, I fought back!" Killian was shouting now, matching his brother's anger and tone.

Guilt gnawed in Ryan's stomach, but he couldn't make himself apologize. "You should just forget it. I'm not getting out of here, and the sooner you move on, the better," Ryan muttered. If he couldn't make it better, he would make things worse. He's pretty sure Killian called that self-sabotage.

"That better be a joke. I did not just get stabbed and punched for you to act like a selfish prat." Killian's anger was palpable, but at least he wasn't crying anymore. Blood crusted around Killian's nose, and he was putting most of his weight on his left side. He had two black eyes and a nice split lip.

"What's the damage?" Ryan asked, lowering his voice. Shame prickled along his skin and made sweat break out down his back. Even if he wasn't in control, he let it happen. "Broken nose, maybe a few ribs. Some cuts and lacerations. Nothing that hasn't happened before," Killian said. He didn't go into much detail, and Ryan couldn't help but think it was because Killian didn't want to set him off.

"You need to leave. Teleport out of here and don't come back," Ryan said.

Killian shook his head but didn't say a word.

Ryan's frustration grew, and a spike of pain shot down his arm. He had yet to take account of his damage. After a moment, he checked his injuries and deemed them inadequate. The worst was a gash in his forearm, which looked like a dagger went through. He cataloged any numbness in his fingers or loss of feeling and shrugged it off. He was fine in the most basic sense of the word. There were also a series of cuts around his wrist, but those didn't hurt.

"You haven't learned anything," Killian said after a while.

Pain flashed behind Ryan's eyes, and he tried to sort through his thoughts. "I don't know what I'm supposed to learn," he admitted. He was waiting for this supposed change that refused to happen. Ryan knew he was unstable, and he knew he was an accident waiting to happen. Killian was sitting next to him, bloody and bruised because Ryan wasn't strong enough to protect him.

There wasn't a shining knight in white armor coming. If Ryan had any hope of surviving, he would have to be his own. "Who was a part of this botched rescue plan?" he asked, trying to take his mind off his own thoughts.

Killian sighed and sat on the edge of the cot, trying to get comfortable. "Tory, Kara, and I," he said. He sounded glum as if he were waiting for Ryan to make fun of him.

It took a lot not to comment. Ryan smirked and nudged his shoulder against Killian's. Their bond opened between them so they could share silent conversations and different memories.

Ryan's stomach twisted at the stuff about Avery. That was still happening. Killian was still seeing Avery and getting assistance from him, and while it was a horrendous thought, Killian was happy.

"Hey, what's wrong?" Killian asked, sensing his anger and hurt through the bond.

"Was Avery a part of this rescue?" Ryan asked, trying to sound neutral, and to keep his darker thoughts to himself. *Killian is happy, and he deserves something.* But would Avery lead him to danger in the end?

Killian stiffened beside him. Apparently, he shared things he didn't want to. "No, he... I've been... it's been weird," he said.

Weird. Ryan could see weird, but all he saw was a crush. Killian finally developed a crush, and it had to be on a traitorous moron.

"Why's it been weird?" he asked, knowing he would regret it. Ryan trusted Avery once, too, and this is what he got. *Don't let Killian make the same mistake.* But then again...

Killian chewed his lip before looking up. He tucked his hands under his thighs and fought a paper-thin smile. "I get these feelings," he said.

Feelings. Ryan held his tongue as his own feelings conflicted with what he wanted to say.

"He makes my stomach feel queasy and fluttery. Kind of like I'm flying," Killian said.

Ryan nodded and swallowed. His throat was too parched, and his mouth too dry. "I think you've got a crush. Which... I mean, I don't understand," he said.

Killian punched him in the arm, making them both wince. "It's not a crush. He's just... nice."

Only because he wants something. Ryan struggled not to tell Killian how bad Avery was. Honestly, these feelings were new, Killian had never expressed an interest in anyone, so, naturally, he chose a walking red flag.

"Was I not nice enough to you as a kid?" Ryan asked, forcing a weak smile to let Killian know he was joking... mostly.

His brother chuckled and shook his head. "I know, it's weird. I hated him, and then he hated me, and now... we found a good middle where no one hates each other."

A memory zipped down their link, and Ryan flinched. Avery's dark, smoldering eyes and a racing heart. *Good boy.* Ryan shoved the image away as forcefully as possible, and shook his head, growling, "Yeah, I'm sure you like him."

Killian gestured to the chains around his feet and ankles and nodded. "Now, it's time to get out of here," he said.

Ryan snapped his fingers, and the chains broke with a tiny explosive pop. He was getting better at doing that.

Kara and Tory risked their lives to retrieve him, and Ryan was determined to make it worth something. Perhaps they cared more than he thought, and on a slightly unrelated note, maybe he was *worth* more than he thought. The thought was startling but didn't make Ryan freeze or flinch. He was right with the thoughts. A ghost of a smile flickered across his lips, and he went to the door, pressing his ear to it. Angel never left him alone long, and now that he had company, she was sure to be back soon.

"Let's figure this out before we can't," he said when he heard nothing on the other side. "I don't want her to catch us planning anything."

Ryan didn't know why Angel wanted both, but his every instinct knew it was for something terrible. "Oh, I saw Mom," Ryan said as an afterthought. "She's not here anymore, so we can resume our search once we escape," he said. Planning for the future was a good start at bringing hope back to the dead.

Killian smiled and nodded. He didn't need to voice his thoughts as a surge of warmth found its way to Ryan's heart.

He could get better and prove Angel wrong. Helwe, he could prove his mother wrong, too. Ryan wasn't going to be the monster everyone thought he was. If the others were willing to risk their lives to come for him, then he could make an effort, too.

"What's the plan?" Killian asked.

Ryan didn't have a plan. That wasn't new for him, though. He rarely planned his attacks from beginning to the end. It all worked out without incident nine times out of ten.

"What's the plan?" Killian asked again.

"I guess we bust the door down and see how far we get," Ryan said, biting back irritation as he opened the door.

Killian grumbled under his breath, "That's bad even for you."

"Do you have a better idea?" Ryan asked. He held up a hand to shut Killian up. "You know what, even if you thought you did, I don't wanna hear it. You brought Kara and Tory to a city to save my ass and then end up getting kidnapped. Your point is invalid."

Killian shrugged. "My plan isn't here yet," he said.

Ryan didn't like the sound of that. "What do you mean?" he asked hesitantly, turning to face his brother.

"I told Kara to get Avery. She's going to make sure we get out," Killian said, almost beaming.

Ryan kept a straight face. His brother was going to get them killed. It was good to know Killian didn't have many survival skills or common sense. "Mhm." Any hopes for the future he might have had went right out the window. *You're an idiot. I love you, but you're an idiot.*

"Why don't you look happy? I just told you we're getting out of here." Killian frowned. He stepped forward as the door flew open behind them.

Avery waved for them to follow as he looked up and down the hall. "Come on," he said. "We don't have a lot of time."

No, we didn't. Ryan grabbed Killian's hand and squeezed. He had to tell him that Avery was working with Angel, especially if Killian was going to rush in with this dick head.

Avery read his mind and shook his head. "I'll make it right, but there's no time. Please," he said. "We want the same thing." His eyes landed on Killian, standing awkwardly behind Ryan.

Killian cocked his head to the side and tugged Ryan's hand until he got his attention. "What's wrong?" he asked.

Ryan shook his head. "Killian gets out," he said.

"We all do," Killian corrected. He looked between them in confusion, trying to read the silent conversation.

At least, that was something they could agree on. Ryan bit his tongue and let his brother's hand go. This isn't how he wanted to be split up yet again. If it wasn't Angel, it would be Avery. *Stop throwing these curveballs at me... for once.* He begged whatever God or Goddess was listening.

The three ran down the hall toward the elevator. Ryan blinked at the green pad beside the machine, which emitted a light glow.

"We need her fingerprint," Ryan said.

Killian cursed under his breath. "There has to be stairs. This wasn't here when we were here last time," he said.

Maybe she upped her security because of us.

Avery clicked his tongue and stared hard at the green light. Ryan knew if he set his finger on it, the elevator would start up. It would also alert Angel that Avery was helping them, or maybe he was leading them into a trap.

"Teleport," Ryan hissed at his brother. "Can't you teleport us out?" It was a long shot.

Killian couldn't teleport out of the city before because of the wards, but now that he was stronger there had to be something he could do.

"Not all of us. Most of my energy went into defending myself. Avery?" Killian asked, looking at the traitor with shining, excited eyes.

.

Ryan wanted to beg him to leave but didn't let himself. His brother wouldn't leave him there, so he had to find a second option until they were caught, or Avery stepped in.

"Hey," Killian smacked him upside the head, pulling the young man from his thoughts.

Avery was also deep in thought. "What?" he asked.

"Teleporting us out?"

Avery paled and shrugged. "I need a moment. I just teleported Kara and Tory back to Haven and then all the way here. Let's keep searchin'," he said.

Ryan took the lead because he didn't trust Avery. They ran further down the marble-floor hall, which had pictures of Angel's conquest on the walls. Their footsteps sounded louder due to the eminent panic attack coming. He pushed a door open and peeked inside. It was an empty conference room, and he shut the door, moving on. There had to be something to get them out. The following three rooms were more conference rooms, and one was a bathroom. He huffed and shot Avery an annoyed glance.

"I don't know. Why are you lookin' at me?" Avery asked. He kept his voice to a whisper, but Ryan didn't know why.

They were well enough away from Angel's rooms to not be a bother. The only way they would get caught now was when she went into that room and found out they weren't there. Ryan didn't know how long they had, but it couldn't be long.

"I'm going to scout ahead. I think I can go faster," Killian said when the following rooms were also empty conference rooms. That's all that was in this place, it seemed.

Ryan growled in frustration as Killian took off further down the hall, using the shadows to move quickly.

Avery froze when they were left alone.

"If Killian doesn't leave here, you're dead," Ryan said. He kept his voice low to keep his brother from accidentally hearing. "I don't care how much Angel likes you, let anything happen to him and I'll tear you apart."

Avery nodded and pursed his lips. "I know. You think I'm doin' this for the Helwe of it?"

"This could be a trap, I don't know. Point is I won't let you screw my brother over," Ryan snarled.

Avery ran a hand through his hair and looked away. "This wasn't my intention, I mean... it was, but I didn't know what she was gonna do, I swear."

"Right, because she's a model citizen," Ryan growled.

Avery huffed and turned away. "She's the closest thing I have to a mom, alright?"

Ryan didn't want to believe him. "I told you to leave my brother out of your games. When I get out of this, you're gonna wish she killed you," he promised.

Killian returned panting with pink cheeks. "There's nothing. I don't know how to get out of here without her fingerprint."

There was a cackle behind them, and Ryan whirled around. His head throbbed before he saw her.

"Now, this won't do. Ryan, you're going back to your room like a good boy," Angel said, snapping her fingers.

Chaos washed over him like a waterfall, and he was paralyzed by her orders. He wasn't going to leave Killian with her. He couldn't.

"You two are such problem children. It looks like I'll need to keep you in separate cages," she said, walking over to him. She grabbed his bicep, and his arm burned.

He cried out in pain but couldn't move.

"Let him go!" Killian shouted, lunging for her.

A portal appeared before him, and he jumped into it. His face was a mixture of shock and anger as soon as he realized what happened.

Angel shrieked, and Ryan dropped to the floor when she let him go. His head swam, and before he knew it, he was back in the starless sky with Chaol and Fyre.

No Rest for the Wicked

KILLIAN

One minute, he was lunging at Angel; the next, he was on Haven's front lawn. Killian landed on his knees and looked around, shocked. It was night; the owls were hooting, and the cicadas were whirring. He was still trying to figure out what happened when Kara and Tory appeared beside him.

"Apparently, he found them," Kara said, looking around. She beamed when she saw Killian. "You're alright!" She threw her arms around him, but he snarled angrily, making her back off like a wounded animal.

Tory scrunched his nose in distaste as Nicholas and Justin ran out of the house. "And I'm pretty sure we're about to die," he said.

Kara instinctively tucked herself behind Tory.

Killian wasn't a Descendant of Energy, but he could feel Justin's palpable rage tearing through the clearing.

"Care to explain where all of you've been?" Justin asked.

Killian was still in shock. He had been with his brother. Ryan was going to be all right and was even talking about escaping. He couldn't just leave him there, not like that. "Avery screwed me," he whispered.

"Avery teleported us back," Kara said, cocking her head to the side. "What do you mean?"

Justin clapped his hands, stopping the argument in its tracks. "I don't care! I woke up to empty beds, no notes, and Nick told me he let you go to the city... alone," Justin said. His voice got louder with each infraction he listed.

"We wanted to save Ryan," Kara whispered.

Justin stormed off the porch and confronted them. His face was red, and his lips pulled into a deep frown. "You ran willingly into a city controlled by a powerful Descendant of Chaos, who takes pleasure in killing people. *Alone.* You went into this city *alone*. Whose idea was this?" he demanded.

Kara opened her mouth, but Killian spoke over her. He would get in trouble anyway, so he might as well get it over with. "Mine. I talked Kara into it by telling her Ryan tried to kill himself. Tory overheard. They both came to protect me," he said.

Ryan shut off their bond once more, so Killian's thoughts were miserably silent. He had no clue what Angel was doing to him, or if he would survive the next few nights and his throat tightened. *Don't you dare cry again.*

"Do you know how irresponsible that was? You could have been killed, and no one would've known," Justin snarled.

"No one else was doing anything, and Ryan tried to kill himself!" Killian shouted.

Justin jammed a finger in Tory's chest. "I expected more from you. These children may not have the sense not to run into danger's arms, but you're an adult. You know better," he said.

Tory looked to Nick for help. "We were careful. There was a small fight, but nothing happened," he said. "I went to make sure everyone stayed safe."

"Yeah, we retreated the moment we realized we were over our heads," Kara added, trying to lessen the man's anger.

Justin took a breath and pinched the bridge of his nose. "I can't with you right now. Rooms. I'll deal with this in the morning."

Killian should've counted himself lucky he wasn't murdered immediately. They filed into the house under Justin's watchful, unseeing eyes. Killian was tempted to go to Avery's and beat the Helwe out of him, but it wasn't a wise decision to take off when Justin was on the brink of a murder spree.

Killian helped Kara more with the bow and sought Avery out several times over a week. He was never at home, or his stall, and Killian was beginning to worry since he hadn't seen the young man since the night with Ryan.

Kara shouted joyfully and jumped around when she hit a bull's eye. Her gloating game was strong, and he forced his thoughts back to the present as she practiced. "I. Am. Awesome!" she shouted, grabbing his shoulders and shaking him.

Killian chuckled and shook his head. "It was one bull's eye. See you if you can do it again," he said.

She had come a long way, but there was still further to go. He couldn't risk bringing her to the city again until she was able to stand the sight of blood. "Don't rain on my parade," she said, jabbing him in the chest with the end of the weapon.

He winced and rubbed the spot as it throbbed. "Watch it," he murmured. "That's a precious artifact."

Kara giggled and waved her hand. Thunder boomed in the distance, and water dropped from the sky.

Killian fled for the house with a curse, but Kara squealed and tackled him. They landed in a heap on the wet grass, and he groaned. "No! Get off me," Killian whined, shielding his head as best he could.

"Go puddle jumping with me!" Kara demanded, squeezing him for dear life. "Oh, please go puddle jumping with me." He could barely hear her over the sound of rain and wind.

His mind was obviously miles away if he hadn't seen the storm rolling in. A cold wind blew across the lawn, and Kara shrieked again. This was a squeal of excitement, and she jumped off him to dance. Her hair was plastered to her face, and she moved around wildly, laughing and holding her stomach.

Yorklyn didn't have weather like this. Kara didn't seem to like the little showers that happened all day most days, but she loved thunderstorms. It brightened her mood and made her act like a kid in a candy store.

Killian scrambled off the ground, slipping once, and ran inside before she could realize he was moving. He slammed the door behind him and shivered, dripping water all over.

Nick got up from the couch to check the noise. "What's going on?" he asked when he saw Killian stripping off his shoes, socks, and shirt.

"Random downpour," he mumbled. "The girl's still out there being psycho." He jerked his thumb at the door.

Nick smirked and shook his head. "Send Tory out with her. They'll have loads of fun."

Killian shook his head and gathered his wet clothes. "No, I'm going to my room." The heat from the fire flashed across his bare chest and stomach, chasing the chill as he walked by.

"Tory! Get out there with your best friend. The other one won't go out anymore," Nick called as Killian shut his bedroom door.

The other one. When did I become a best friend to anyone?

The sky was a horrible gray and black with streaks of lightning every so often. This was one of the worst storms yet. Killian grabbed a towel from the washroom connected to his bedroom and stubbed his toe on Ryan's bed. He yelped in pain and slammed his palm against the wall, trying to contain the sudden anger. His mood reflected that of the sky.

"Are you busy?" Avery's voice sent a sliver of relief through him.

Killian whirled around and rubbed the moistness out of his eyes. "No," he said. "Where've you been?"

Avery put a finger to his lips and held out his hand.

Killian gestured to the window angrily, still holding the towel he would use to dry his hair. "Not out there. I'm done with... that."

Avery smiled—he was always smiling, even when he wasn't happy. This was one of those times. The smile didn't reach his dark eyes. His shoulders were hunched, and his hair was a mess. It stuck out every which way and frizzed in the thick humidity swimming through the air. There were bruises, healing cuts, and some dried blood on his hands and around his neck and wrists.

Killian cocked his head to the side. His foul mood cleared when he realized something bad had happened. His pulse spiked as his mind went to his brother. "What's wrong?" he asked.

"Not here," Avery said. "Please."

Killian nodded and hurriedly put a shirt on. He grabbed an old one from Ryan's bed and took Avery's hand. They teleported back to Avery's house, and the first thing he noticed was how cold it was. There wasn't a roaring fire in the hearth, no chopped wood, and the house was freezing.

"Good lord, man. Where have you been?" Killian asked again, running his hands up and down his arms for warmth.

If Avery couldn't take care of himself, Killian would have to do it. He ran outside and grabbed some of the wood from under the cover Avery kept it under. It wasn't necessarily firewood, but they didn't have many options. The worst case is it would smoke to Helwe. Killian hurried back inside and threw it in the hearth, looking back at

Avery. He was still standing in the middle of the living room, staring blankly.

"Sit." Killian grabbed his wrist and tugged him onto the hay sofa. He had never seen Avery look so lost. If not even he could keep it together what hope did Killian have?

He searched the house for blankets and came across Avery's room. The bed was as untamed as Ryan's, and he had clothes everywhere. Killian shook his head and slipped the comforter off before throwing it on Avery as he walked back into the living room. It took him longer than he would've liked to get a fire crackling in his heart, but the warmth it offered was immediate. Killian rubbed his freezing hands together and looked up at the statuesque Avery.

"What's going on?" he asked, trying once more and hoping he could get a response.

Avery looked at him with big sad eyes. "I tried to fix what I broke," he whispered, his voice cracking with pain.

Killian didn't understand. He took a steady breath and climbed up onto the couch next to Avery. "What did you break?" he asked.

"I can't tell you."

Killian nodded and reached out to offer a comforting touch but hesitated. He didn't know how to do that. He flicked Avery's wet hair instead. "Do you have towels?" he asked.

Avery cleared his throat, trying to clear the hoarseness from his voice. "In the bedroom."

Killian went back to the room and searched through Avery's mounds of mess. When he found one that was relatively clean, Killian returned to the living room and tossed it over Avery's head. He dried his hair as best he could and relaxed in the warmth as the hut slowly warmed. Avery wasn't going to talk, but Killian could do the little things.

"When's the last time you ate?" he asked.

Avery shrugged and leaned his head back. "I don't deserve it," he said.

"Okay, well, you're still overly dramatic. I'm taking that as a good sign," Killian muttered. He sat back on the couch when Avery's hair was as dry as it would get. He tossed the towel to the side and leaned against the man, trying to offer his own form of comfort.

They sat in silence and listened to the fire pop in the stone hearth, filling the home with a warm, sappy smell. Killian wrinkled his nose when it got a little smoky, but he waved it off with his hand. He didn't know how to get people to talk, or if he should even get Avery to talk.

Avery shifted beside him and pulled the blanket over Killian as well, extending his arm to encircle his shoulders. *Cuddling*. That's what this was. Killian tilted his head up, looking at Avery from an upside-down position with a small smirk. His dark dilated eyes flicked across Killian's face, trying to read something as they burned through him.

There was a long moment of hesitation before Avery finally leaned down.

Killian's heart jumped at the thought of getting a real kiss, but they didn't kiss. Avery pressed their foreheads together, and a calloused thumb brushed Killian's cheek. "Please don't," Avery whispered, "I can't do this with you."

A weird pain rippled through Killian's chest, but he wasn't going to think too much about it. Killian misread the situation, and that was fine because he was Avery's friend. They honestly shouldn't do anything while Ryan suffered at Angel's hands anyway.

"You cuddled me," he said, his voice raw and cold. "I don't know what the deal is with you, but can you... can you stop screwing with me?" Killian right himself feeling stupid and played.

"Kilua..." Avery started to say something and stopped himself.

He didn't need to make it harder. Killian calmed his thoughts and took a steady, silent breath. "It's fine," he whispered. "Tell me what happened." He might as well get something out of coming here. It's not like the rejection was unexpected. Avery hadn't been the same since that peck on the lips in Rochester. It didn't make it hurt any less.

There was a knock on the front door. They both jumped.

Avery cursed and untangled himself from the blanket, forcing himself to his feet. He limped to the front door.

Nick stood on the other side.

"How did you know where I lived?" Avery asked.

Nick glared. "I make it my business to know where my brother's attempted murderers stay," he said. "I need to talk to Killian."

Attempted murderer? Killian frowned. He didn't know Avery was on any sort of terms with the Breanin brothers aside from being untrustworthy. He stood as Avery let Nick in.

"Is everything alright?" Killian asked, knowing Nick wouldn't search him out unless there was a problem. His cheeks were still red from the inevitable rejection.

"No, it's your grandmother," Nick said. "I got a call from some of the ravens she feeds... she's gonna be gone soon." His voice softened as he finished his sentence.

Killian paled and didn't think twice. He was inside Avery's house one minute and at his grandmother's the next. The downpour still wreaked havoc on his clothes and hair, but he ran to the door of his grandmother's hut and wrenched it open. She was sickly and pale, puffing away on her pipe with weathered old hands.

"Oh, that busybody; I told him not to bother you," his grandmother said, her voice weak but snappy.

Killian couldn't help the tears. It was family and, as far as he knew, the last of it. Ryan said their mother vanished from Angel's cells but had no clue where she went.

"Don't be ridiculous. If something's happened, of course, I want to be here," Killian said, rushing to her side. He sat on the floor beside her hay bale and grabbed her free hand.

She was so thin, and her hands shook in his hold. A fire had been started in the hearth, and Killian wondered if it was Nick who started it. She hadn't been this poor of health a week ago, so why was this happening? "It doesn't matter, boy. Unless you can control death, my time has come," Grandma said, coughing violently as she set her pipe aside. "Let me tell you one last thing before the ravens take me home."

Killian nodded and wiped the tears off his cheeks. She wasn't an emotional woman and wouldn't like it if she saw them, especially knowing they were for her.

"You have power in you. Both of you do. That's why your momma was so scared," Grandma said. Her voice was raspy, and she coughed again.

Killian rubbed her hand. "You can tell me later," he said.

She squeezed his hand as hard as she could and shook her head. When the coughing fit subsided, she panted. "There is no later. I need to say this before I go. Your bloodline goes back many generations," she said.

Killian didn't care about his bloodline, considering most of them had been dead for years. He still smiled and nodded to let her know he was listening.

"A bloodline filled with magik passes down to each generation stronger than before. Ryan's never spoken a spell to life, has he?" his grandmother asked. She already knew the answer. For most of his life, she was the one training him.

"No, Ryan has always been very talented," he said.

"It's not talent. That's what I'm trying to tell you. Your brother, as strong as he is, you hold the same power in your hands."

"How much magik is in our line?" he asked, mostly to appease her.

"Many generations. Your mother chose a great mate. The problem was, she didn't want two kids." His grandmother stared into space.

Killian looked away. He didn't remember a lot about his childhood – not the way Ryan did. "My mom had us intentionally because we would be strong?" he asked. Maybe if he kept talking, she wouldn't leave. It was a foolish thought but one he couldn't let go of.

"You were the better option because you could be molded. Ryan would never bend to her will. She underestimated your strength."

It was hard to argue with a dying woman about power and strength. "I'm not my brother, Grandma. Ryan will always be stronger," he said weakly.

"You are identical twins. His power is yours. The only difference between you is that he's *embraced* what he is."

Killian looked at the ground. He had never truly accepted his magik. His life had been spent running from it. "Okay, Grandma. Try to rest now," he said, keeping his voice soft and warm.

She cursed a few times and poked his forehead. For someone on her deathbed, she was wound up. "Don't talk down to me, boy. You forget who you're dealing with!" The shadows on the floor and walls rippled in her anger.

Killian bit his tongue, trying not to aggravate the woman in her final hours. "You don't care much for him anyway, Grandma. Why does it matter?" he growled, trying to contain his frustration.

The old woman's eyes sparkled. Her leathery face was drawn with age, but he could see the glint of amusement behind her cloudy eyes. "I would have taken you both and run if I were kind. I loved you and couldn't bear to lose you. Of course, your mother couldn't have known that; she would've run off with you."

"Then why? In Rochester, you were cold," Killian whispered. Now, it was getting hard to control his voice and emotions.

She admitted that she did everything for them but then easily chased Ryan off. Grandma knocked him on the head lightly with her knuckles. "Ryan doesn't respond to coddling."

"You hurt him," Killian said.

The woman laughed. "The boy needs to be stronger if he's going to survive what's ahead. Who do you think will have to subdue him? Can Justin? Or even that earth boy?" Her voice got weaker the more she talked.

Of course, Justin and Nick could stop Ryan. The idea was to get stronger so he could defend Kara and help fight back the soldiers if that's what it took. Killian had no intention of fighting his brother.

"They will not hold him. Be wary of those who say they can," Grandma's voice got softer and weaker as she calmed. "Be wary of the witch who manipulates with loving words, be wary of the dictator who rules with blood and fear, but most of all, be wary of the brother in disguise."

Her hand slipped from his and went limp.

"Grandma!" Killian shook her, but she was silent.

Her eyes stared at nothing, glassy and lifeless.

The Worst Betrayal

ANGEL

The boy blinked at her with wide dark eyes that matched his fluffy black hair. He held out a flower, smiling as they crossed paths that once. Rebecca didn't know what made her do it, but he was sweet and innocent, and she wanted him. She bent and took the flower with gentle fingers, passing a surge of energy through them when their hands brushed.

He jerked back with a startled yelp, waving his hand thanks to the mini shock he suffered.

Rebecca smiled and ruffled his hair before moving on. In a few years, she would come back for him, and he would be ready to train with her. Especially with the way the world would outcast him for having such terrible magik. Soon, he would be like her, and maybe she could adopt him when the world around him fell apart. *Avery*.

"Do you have any idea what you've done?" she asked, grabbing the front of his shirt the moment Killian vanished.

Ryan dropped to a knee, crying out in pain as her energy thrummed through them both. "Stop!"

She barely heard his pleading voice as she shook the one, she wished would listen. "This could undo everything, Avery!"

He didn't flinch and his gaze darkened, eyes burning with anger like charred coals. "You lied to me," he said. "You swore he wouldn't get hurt."

She scoffed and shoved him away before she could be tempted to hurt him. "This is for the good of our people! Our world needs to know that chaos isn't something to fear but to embrace it," she snarled. "Now, we're back to square one, and he's even weaker than before."

Avery bristled and clenched his hands at his sides. "You made him that way. He needs to eat, sleep, and train, but all you've been doing is torturing him."

Angel scowled and shook her head. Not in a million years would she imagine the son she raised would turn his back on her over a boy.

"Angel, please!" Ryan screamed as the chaos tore through his body and mind.

Avery pushed past her and knelt beside him, pressing his hand against the blonde's back. "Breathe," he whispered.

The chaos dissipated, and Ryan whimpered, dropping his chin to his chest. Fresh tear tracks marred his cheeks, but he carefully kept the pain from showing.

Angel growled and summoned her spear. She pressed the point to Avery's neck, but he didn't flinch. "You have no idea what you've done," she hissed. Her eyes blurred with tears. Everything was about to be taken, and she didn't know what to do with that overwhelming feeling of anger.

Avery wasn't afraid, and he didn't fight. His face had a resolute firmness that let her know he knew exactly what he had done.

"I would've given everything for you," she whispered as the anger melted into a terrifying hole of sadness.

Avery shook his head. "No, you wouldn't. You won't give this mess up, and you're continuing to hurt people," he said. "No one will accept chaos if you're always hurting them with it."

Angel scoffed and flicked her wrist. Chains bound him to the floor, and his eyes widened in terror for a second. She would never hurt him, not like that, and a twang of pain thrummed through her heart at the look on his face. "I can't have you messing this up. You've done enough," she said, shaking her head. "Since when do you care what I do in the city?" she asked, desperate to make him understand.

"Since you want to hurt Killian," Avery shouted. He struggled with his bonds before huffing. "You can't keep me here," he snarled. "We both know I'm leagues above you in power."

Angel smiled sadly and snapped her fingers. A black leather whip appeared in her hand, and she shook her head. "This isn't about keeping you here."

Avery flinched when she snapped the whip. He steeled himself but didn't otherwise move.

"And when we're done, we'll pick up the pieces and try again," she whispered. "Ryan, I'd like you to leave."

The Descendant of Fire didn't move. He stared at Avery, pleading with his eyes.

"I gave you an order," Angel snapped.

Ryan vanished.

Spots of blood stained her skirt, and Angel picked at them. They were long dry by now, and she looked away from them with a sullen frown. She couldn't let everything she worked for be ruined because of a rebellious teenager. Angel sighed and buried her face in her hands. It was too long of a day for all of this to be happening.

"I told you he wasn't on your side," Havoc said behind her. For once, his false righteousness was gone, and he was almost a man.

Angel didn't want him to see her weakness. She knew he would come to gloat the moment Avery caught feelings for Killian. If Avery kept helping Ryan out of every bind, the boy would learn to control the chaos faster, and she couldn't allow that until her plans were done. The moment he changed; she would lose all control.

Angel had kept barriers in the parts of his memory with the special lessons she had been giving him. A sort of way to keep the memories repressed until the change took over. After that, she wouldn't need to worry about him killing her right away because every awful thing about his life would bombard him at once and incapacitate him long enough for her to escape.

It was a genius plan, but the walls were already beginning to bend. It was barely two months, and Ryan was slipping from her control. There was no more time to waste. She had to reunite the twins before it was too late. Avery just moved the timeline up.

Angel stood and faced Havoc. She pursed her lips in distaste and resisted the urge to kick him from her quarters. "This is just a quirk in the plan," she said.

"After what you just did, he won't return with open arms," Havoc whispered.

Angel smoothed her skirt. "He escaped, so barely anything happened," she said with a sniff.

Avery overpowered her without so much as trying, and while it had been expected, it didn't make it any easier to swallow.

"He won't come back, and if he does, it won't be with the brother," Havoc said.

Angel shook her head. For Killian to accompany Avery in battle, Avery had to come clean. She knew he was a selfish being because he was most like her. Avery would never tell Killian what he was or had done because he cared too much about losing that boy.

Havoc read her mind, and his lips curled into a smile. "I can help you draw him in, and I swear not to touch a hair on your son's head," he said a little too sarcastically for Angel's tastes.

She shook her head. She didn't need Havoc's help to draw him out. Angel just needed to ensure Ryan did what he was supposed to. "If you can keep them in the watering hole until Ryan draws blood, we'll have what we need," she said. She didn't like letting Havoc return without a fight, but she couldn't do this alone, and Avery had proven he was undependable.

"Getting and keeping them won't be a problem, but how do you intend to make the boys harm each other?" Havoc asked.

Angel would need to put a lot of work into this. It was one thing for Ryan to attack Killian; that part wasn't a problem, but he would only accept if he were wiser about what was happening. Especially if he knew it would cost him his brother's life.

"I have to make it believable," Angel said. She couldn't just throw them in the water and let them go for it; there would be too many suspicions.

A thought crossed her mind, and she smiled to herself. "I have the perfect plan," she whispered. "Swear on your life you will not harm Avery," Angel said. She wouldn't make any other deals until she was sure the person she cared about would be safe.

Havoc nodded, though his eye twitched. "I won't harm a hair on his head. I swear it," he said.

Angel took a breath and filled him in. She wasn't overly powerful, but what she lacked in strength, she made up for in her brains. Knowledge was a powerful weapon and never failed her before.

Their plan was ready, and the stage was set. Havoc hung around long enough to praise her on her excellent work, but it sent goose-bumps down her back. She hated that man and couldn't wait to shut him up for good. If she didn't need his ability to cage and contain, she would say screw it and kill him now.

Angel changed into her night clothes and ignored the lingering screams in her head. Her heart faltered as she realized she may have pushed Avery too far this time.

Havoc was right. The young man wasn't going to return. Avery was going to hate her until the day he died.

She knew that was true in her heart, but Angel didn't want to admit that out loud. The only person in this world she wanted to protect couldn't hate her. She sat on her bed, and her fingers drifted across the surface of the pink plush comforter. It was hard not knowing what decisions to make when anger was staring her in the face. Dried blood was still crusted under her nails and fingers, but she didn't move to clean them. There was always blood on her hands; no matter how hard she scrubbed; it was always there.

Angel might've botched this one, but she could always fix it. Once Lord Malsumis was done with the vessel, she could return the twin Avery was so fond of. Once everything was fixed, maybe he would forgive her once she returned his toy. After all, family was more important than a simple crush or lust. He would understand once the world was safe for everyone, especially their people. As much as Angel wanted to believe it, she knew that, too, was untrue.

A New, Transformative Hope

KARA

Kara still hadn't figured out her transformation spell. Since their epic failure in saving Ryan, she had doubled down on trying to better her magik. The problem wasn't that she was weak; her strength had grown since she started training. Over the last two months, she was stronger, faster, and had more stamina. Her issue was blood. The sight of it made her head spin and her stomach roll, and even if she managed to overcome it temporarily during Killian's fight, it would lead to problems if she didn't beat it.

Kara sat in the small building book stop in Rochester and absently flipped the pages of the fantasy novel she was reading as people walked by idly chatting about their days and wares. The book was about a boy and a plant that grew so tall that he could climb into the clouds, where he was met with riches and a giant. The story was more of a lesson than an adventure, but she enjoyed it, nonetheless, and she found herself wondering how Dawson would react to the poor giant being killed because of a boy's recklessness.

"Fight the power," he would have said, attributing the thieving boy to Angel.

"So, this is where you've been hiding," Tory said, stopping before her.

She stared at his black shoes for a moment, covered in dirt and grime from the garden before looking up. Killian stayed true to his word and helped her figure out how to teleport, and since then, she stayed away from home as much as possible. At least, when there was a lot on her mind. She still had breakfast with Tory and Killian in the morning because she enjoyed that part of their routine. However, staying cooped up in Haven was hard. In the three months they had been there, Justin hadn't left the property for more then ten minutes, and she didn't know how.

He cleared his throat when he realized she wasn't going to react. "I've come to offer my assistance," he said. "About the transforming thing."

She cocked her head. "Justin said it has to come from within, meaning within *me*."

"Right, but I can steer you in the right direction," he said. "Considering I know how to do it." Tory sat across from her cross-legged in the dirt like when they were children on the playground and leaned forward to peer at her book. "That's a good one," he said.

Kids ran in all directions, reading books and looking at pictures. While it was loud, Kara found it calming to be around such normality. Small wooden shelves with books sat upon them like little portals waiting to be delved into. She had read most of them and had even read a couple of picture books to the little ones which helped her better grasp Rochester's language. They loved it when she read; it hurt her heart but reminded her of when Dawson asked for the same thing.

"It sounds better in your voice," he had said once, making her smile. Dawson used to love it when she read him the books they had no business owning that he got from The Smuggler.

Kara closed the book, finding herself in a mood. She shrugged. "I guess you could try," she said. Kara knew the others would back

Killian up if he decided to go to the city again, and even thought Justin ripped them all new ones for sneaking out, she caught him shooting a bow in the training grounds.

For a blind man, he rarely missed the center circle. Watching was impressive, but he turned her down when she asked for assistance. It happened for days before Killian decided he would work with her again. Her eyes flicked to the scab on her forearm where the bowstring had cut her, even though he still hadn't given her the proper protective equipment.

"Come, let's go to the river," Tory said with a smile. He didn't seem to notice the darkening mood, and if he did, he didn't comment on it.

Kara tried to remain motivated and cheerful, but she still had hard days. No matter how much she tried to will them away, they stuck to her like glue. Justin told her that was normal and that she shouldn't worry because everyone had bad days.

"Kara, are you okay?" Tory asked, finally noticing something was off.

She blinked her thoughts away as they walked through the homestead. She was wearing the bone bracelet he had bought her months ago. It was cool against her skin and gave her something to anchor herself. "Yeah, I'm fine. Today is a little difficult," she said, forcing a smile.

He frowned and stopped her. They were still in the busy part of the homestead, so people walked around them and huffed as they took up a portion of the road. "Do you want to try another day?" he asked.

"No, it'll be good," she said.

A horse whinnied in the distance, and she pulled Tory to the side to avoid being trampled. Kara didn't feel like practicing or training, but if she couldn't use this spell, Justin wouldn't let her help. He insisted on her having that disguise to return to the city for whatever reason.

He seemed to forget that she had gone to the city once without the disguise.

"It's the principle," he had said.

A horse and carriage hurried by with a man in the driver's seat. His beady eyes flicked to Kara and Tory as he shouted at his horse, pushing it faster. Someone was in a hurry to get nowhere fast. If he weren't careful, the people would catch up with him and give him a piece of their minds for being reckless, especially on a narrow street.

Dust and debris whipped into the air, and she coughed, waving her hand in front of her face. "Come on, let's get out of here," she muttered.

They left the homestead, and Tory took her to the river. Cody had been spending a lot of time here as well with Cheri. He told Kara all the stories of the kids getting together to swim, play, and skip rocks. Kara kicked a rock and looked out across the water. The river was slow and steady today, so the weather shouldn't get nasty. She was ready for something else after the last few cold and rainy days.

"Attune to my energy and watch the transformation," Tory said. He grabbed her hands and took a slow breath. "It'll help you see what your energy should do."

Kara closed her eyes. Strands of blue twine danced behind her eyelids and evened out as Tory's breathing did. It was getting easier to pinpoint energy and make her own match. Her twisted gold and purple energy entwined with his before evening out into a thin line of mixed color.

"Okay," she whispered.

"Descendant of Water; let the skies part and rain fall upon me: transform," Tory whispered his spell to not break her concentration.

Kara paid close attention as his energy wrapped him in a soft, warm shell. He vanished in a dazzling blue light before returning to his place before her.

He was clothed in a blue half-robe with chainmail underneath. A giant sword was strapped to his back, and a bottle dangled from the belt on his hips. A beautiful blue and teal mask rested across his cheekbones, and the half-robe had a hood he could pull up to further conceal his identity.

Kara marveled at the outfit and ran her fingers along the soft blue cloth. It was too real to be an illusion. *Magik is incredible.*

"I don't think I've ever seen you like this," she said.

"Then you haven't been paying attention. I've been using this for weeks, trying to learn my weapon. Or whatever Justin said about it." Tory smirked.

She knew it was him, but his eyes were light blue, and his hair was closer to blonde than brown. Everything about him changed, and that made him so different. "I don't understand how this happens," she said.

Tory shrugged. "You get used to it. Do the same thing."

"I still don't know the spell," Kara said.

"Stop trying to find it. Just do it," Tory said.

Kara rolled her eyes. That was the stupidest advice she ever got. "How do you-"

"No, don't think, just do it," he cut her off.

Kara sighed and closed her eyes. *Just do it. Anything. Say something. The first thing that pops into your head.* Her energy didn't change, and nothing came to mind. She opened an eye and peeked at Tory.

He nodded and kept waving his hands back and forth as if he were doing something helpful. "Just. Do. It," he whispered. If she had an evil voice telling her to do stupid things, it would be his.

She huffed in exasperation and closed her eyes again. If anything, Tory was making it worse. By trying not to think, she was thinking about not thinking. *Come on, great ancestors. You told me before I wasn't alone.* The last thing Kara wanted was to be seen talking to someone who may or may not be there and who adequately refused to listen to her plea. *I know all magik comes in good time, but this is the right time—the only time.* Kara didn't want to hurt people, but she didn't want to watch her people get hurt either.

Justin fought with his daily struggle of losing his wife and Ryan was off, stuck in a darkness so great that not even his twin could reach him. Killian battled with his daily insecurities and was snarky and mean, but he fought it every single day. It was her turn now, and she could do it.

You helped save me from the darkness. I won't let it take you now, not without a fight! Kara squeezed her eyes shut and held up her hands as energy built through her body, swelling into her chest, and filling her with an energy she had only felt once before. The day she killed all those students and soldiers - the day she watched Dawson die. *I need to be stronger.*

"Descendant of Energy, feel my energy and change my form: transform."

The disguise spell brought about a painful, surreal experience. Kara's world exploded in light and color as everything else melted away. She stood in a white spotlight as red, blue, orange, and green converged around her in a brilliant show. Kara reached out to touch the colors, and her skin shimmered. Warmth tingled and spread as she was dressed in a long white robe with a hood embroidered with strange symbols along the hem of the outfit.

Her head pounded, making her feel heavy and sluggish, but she was too taken in by everything else to notice the pain. A heavy brown and white staff with a pink gem at the top landed in her hands. It glowed as yellow and purple energy swarmed into it, filling her with vibrant and bold energy. Her hair twisted and curled before pinning itself atop her head. Everything was amazing and terrifying all at once.

The world went quiet, and Kara opened her eyes at the disconnect. It was the same feeling when she met Jessica in the past. It wasn't quite right, though nothing physically changed around her. Kara was still standing in a white spotlight, surrounded by the whispers of the ancient Descendants. There was a twinge in her chest, like something had changed, and then Jess was in front of her.

Jess grinned at her. "It's you again," she said, reaching out.

Kara pressed her palm to Jess's, still unsure how this worked. "I found my spell," she said. Their hands connected this time, and she gasped.

Jess' energy thrummed through her and danced in the air around them. She had a beautiful gold energy that burst to life in large flowery patterns much like the ones Nicholas grew in his garden. Everything about her radiated love and joy. "How does it feel?" she asked.

"I'm not as happy as I thought," Kara said.

Jess frowned and reached out, brushing the back of her hand down Kara's cheek. It was such a motherly move that Kara almost cried. "You're thinking too hard," she said.

Kara sniffed and fought the tears. She hadn't felt such a tender touch since her parents vanished. "I miss everything, and it feels so hard. I don't know how to do it," she said, scrubbing her hands down her face.

Jess enveloped Kara in a warm hug and hummed into her hair. "Oh, my dear, you are never alone. We will always be with you, even if you don't see us," she said. "And you've got Justin and Nicholas, and your friends will always know where to find you when you need them."

Kara peeked over the woman's shoulder at rows and rows of men and women. They were all different colors, sizes, and shapes. People from every part of the world bore the same magik as her. Her eyes landed on a woman who looked much like her mom, and a smile flickered across her face. "I can see them," she whispered.

Jess nodded and pulled away, holding Kara at arm's length. "You are light. Your magik can keep the darkest shadows from consuming the land but remember that a balance should always remain. If one gets too strong, the other could lead to great destruction."

"How did you find your spell?" Kara asked.

"It came to me one day when I was a child. It was the beginning of my magik. I accidentally killed a pig with a lightning bolt," the woman smiled as she spoke. Her words were full of sorrow but also a kind of joy that Kara sometimes experienced when something went right.

"I killed people with mine." Kara hugged herself. "And now I must find a way to make it right."

Jess held out her hand, and the people behind her vanished. "Walk with me. Let's see what you learn," she said. All around them, trees waved in the wind and flickered to life like one of Cody's holograms.

Kara took her hand and let Jess guide her through the trees. "How did you and Justin meet?" she asked.

"We met when we were kids. His dad left his mom and lived in the middle of the woods. He was our neighbor, and I remember thinking how cute he was with his dark eyes and black hair. It was always so scruffy looking," Jess said. "I think we were thirteen, and I introduced him to all my friends; the girls loved him."

Kara smiled. "He was charming." She couldn't imagine Justin being someone women fawned all over.

"Very. I remember a time when Sam and Summer fought over him. They thought he was the bee's knees. And, of course, Nick was in love with Sam. He was much younger, but Justin always let him tag along."

Kara made a face. "Wait, you knew my mom?" she asked. "Samantha?" The thought of Nicholas being in love with her mother was a tad odd, considering the man was dating her best friend.

Jess beamed at her. "You're Samantha's daughter? Well, that's why my energy calls so strongly to you. I spent a lot of time with her and Summer when we were teenagers. Of course, they were a little older," she said as she laughed.

"We all spent time practicing magik and playing games in the forest. Eventually, Summer and Justin had a rivalry. They were always competing. We all spent time doing our own things," she said.

Jess took her to the river and pointed to Rochester. It was nothing but tents and small huts. There were lots of campfires, and people were dancing around and joking with each other. "Rebecca and I used to go there to watch the ceremonies. Now, she's known as someone else." Her voice lowered in sadness.

"Angel," Kara whispered.

"Yeah, I used to think she would come home when she was done grieving, but she never did. I think she will get worse before she gets better," Jess said softly.

"Grieving?"

"Rebecca lost her child in childbirth. Summer said he was stillborn. My sister was gone before Justin and I returned from our date." Jess shook her head. "I should've stayed home."

Kara chewed her lip. "Angel lost a child?"

"She did, and she had been so excited. I like to think that if she didn't lose him, she would still be with us," Jess said. "And now I fear for your future."

Kara smiled sadly. "I'm sorry about your sister." She was but a child herself, so she didn't understand what it was like to lose a kid, but her mother always said that was the worst pain in the world.

Jess brushed a hand through her hair. "I'm sorry about your pain, too."

Kara couldn't say Angel was a stand-up individual because of her loss. A lot of people lost things, and they didn't turn into murdering psychopaths, but it was a way to relate to her as a human. Angel seemed cold and heartless, but she was only that way because of a terrible loss.

The forest vanished, and Kara was back in the spotlight. She blinked her tears away and smiled. "She's human too. I think I forgot that amid all the darkness," she said.

Jess nodded and brushed her fingers through Kara's hair. "She's hurting. We tried to make it right, but she wouldn't listen. I fear she's lost to us, but you may be able to help those she's hurt."

Kara didn't know, but she wanted to try. "I will try to right the wrongs," she promised.

"I am sorry to put this on such young shoulders, but there isn't much else I can do," Jess said softly.

Kara forced a smile and nodded. "We will do it, and I won't be alone. None of us will stop until we've stopped Angel," she said.

Jess kissed her forehead, and the light vanished.

Kara opened her eyes and blinked at Tory. Her disguise had vanished, and she was standing next to him, trembling and crying.

"Are you okay?" Tory asked. He set a hand on her shoulder. "You spaced out, and the spell went away."

She touched her heart and shook her head. It wasn't gone. She could feel it sitting and waiting for when she needed it. "I think I feel better."

Tory smiled and held out his hand. "Time to go home?"

"Yes." Kara nodded in agreement. "Time to go home."

Fyre and Chaol

RYAN

Ryan was learning to communicate with the voices competing in his head. They each had their own way of talking, and the more he learned, the easier it was to deal with them.

"It's boring us," Fyre said.

Ryan smirked and waved his hand through the silver mist. "You're not the only one," he muttered. He didn't know how long it had been since he last lost control.

Angel hadn't come to him in quite a while either. There were no special lessons, no pain, and no yelling. He felt like he was in the middle of something much larger, but he didn't know what. Being cut off from the rest of the world was quite exhausting.

"Do something. Scream," Chaol said.

"Nah," Ryan murmured. "Why don't *you* do something?"

"Mistress has no need of us. We're resting for war," Fyre said, cutting its brother off. "Its war is coming; its friends will burn." Some days, Fyre sounded more feminine; others, it was deep and broody.

Ryan tried attributing male or female to the voices, but they shifted so much that he didn't know if it mattered. There was no need to attribute these factors to disembodied voices, but he found it made interacting with them easier. He hummed and snapped his fingers. A flickering black flame appeared over his finger and thumb. Channeling his energy in the mist was getting easier. Once, it was all-encompassing and suffocated him, but now it was like an old friend. His mind was still heavy, and his body wouldn't move, but at least he wasn't miserable.

Since his conversation with Killian, it was getting easier to block out the bad voices and the cruel things they said. Sometimes, he forgot himself and felt like drowning all over, but those days were lessening.

"It's not concerned for war?" Fyre asked, cackling.

Ryan raised a brow. "Should I be?" he asked. The worst that would come of it was his death. He knew Killian would never kill him, but one of the others might consider it. "Plus, you lie all the time. How do I know there's a real war?" he asked.

He was sitting there making casual conversation with himself.

"Its friends will burn," Fyre said, its voice getting higher pitched the more frustrated it became.

Since Ryan stopped responding, the voices got more agitated and upset with him. It was easy to throw them off these days. "Ah, see, that's where we disagree," he said. "I highly doubt I'll survive. If Angel saves me, then we're back where we started." He wouldn't stand a chance against all of them. He didn't care how strong he was. There's no way he could manage more than two Descendants alone.

The voices were quiet. They quickly got bored when he couldn't be intimidated or frightened. After so many days of the same threat, it got pointless.

"Does anyone happen to have a game on hand?" Ryan asked. He was pushing his luck, but he couldn't help smiling as he talked.

"It's losing its mind," Chaol said.

"Already happened. The least you could do is entertain me," Ryan said. He stretched out as best he could and put his hands in a makeshift pillow behind his head. "Don't you guys have physical forms? Bodies or anything?"

"It's asking stupid questions," Fyre said.

Ryan huffed and clapped his hands. Fire burst forth and illuminated the area, pushing back the silver mist. As soon as the fire vanished, the mist returned. "My mind is an empty, barren place." He smirked as if making his point.

"How can we have bodies? We are just its mind."

Ryan furrowed his brow. "Could I give you bodies? We've been talking all this time, and I don't know who I'm talking to."

"Itself," Chaol hissed.

"Right, but there are two distinct voices aside from my own," Ryan said. "How's that possible?" He couldn't be blamed for trying to get information. "And when I turn into a Descendant of Chaos, will Fyre be gone?"

The voices were silent. He thought he said something wrong until Fyre finally spoke. "What name is that?" it asked.

Ryan blinked. He assumed they could read his mind, so it was interesting to know they didn't have access to it. "Well, I had to call you something. I thought I would call you Fyre. Kind of stupid to name parts of myself, but I'm lonely." There was no hint of sarcasm in his voice this time.

"If you respect magik, your magik will respect you," Justin had said.

Ryan perked up at the memory. If he showed it respect, it would be willing to help him, wouldn't it? "I also named your brother. Chaol. What do you think?" he asked.

The voices were quiet again.

"It gave us names," Fyre said. It hummed thoughtfully, and the very air around Ryan shimmered.

The black space got hot, and a beautiful fox appeared on the ground before him. Ryan's breath caught as vibrant red and orange energy pulsed from the creature, and his arm burned. He winced and grabbed the spot, realizing it was where his mark of power was. He peeked under his palm when the burning ceased and hissed in shock. The ball of fire was bright red and orange and layered against his skin, burning against the violet and black specks that threatened to snuff it out once before. The flames spread around his bicep like a chain.

That couldn't be all it took. Just respecting and being at peace was all it took to grow. Ryan looked back at the fox, and it yipped, sharing his joy. There was a small flame on the fox's forehead. Watchful yellow eyes shone with the power of Ryan's fire, and he narrowed his eyes.

"Fyre?" he asked.

The fox yipped again. He didn't understand. Ryan was set on solid ground, and he wobbled unsteadily. It had been a long time since he used his legs. He opened his mouth to ask what had happened when he had been ripped from space and returned to the real world. He caught his breath with a gasp as cold water soaked into his shirt and pants.

Avery stood over him with a bucket and a pained expression. "Oh, that worked, good."

Ryan snarled in reply and leaped off the floor. His hands were around Avery's throat in seconds. Avery slammed his palm into Ryan's sternum and doubled him over before he could get a good grip. Pain splintered across his chest and wasn't lessened when Avery brought his knee up into Ryan's stomach.

"Sorry, I'm sorry," Avery said, holding his hands out when Ryan stopped attacking. "I don't wanna fight. Can we talk?" he asked.

Ryan gasped, trying to get air back in his lungs. "Screw off," he hissed.

"I know you have every reason to hate me, but please, just give me a minute," Avery said. His voice was quiet but desperate.

Ryan cursed and punched the ground, clutching his chest. He hurt, everything hurt. "Gods, what the Helwe," he hissed, pushing himself up to inspect his arms. Deep red marks littered his forearms and wrists. He couldn't recall being sent on jobs that would cause this.

Avery knelt but kept a reasonable distance back to avoid being hit. "Angel didn't tell me what the plan was. I didn't know. She said she would help and that we could fix the world."

"You mean Descendants of Chaos?" Ryan asked, puzzling over the recent wounds.

Avery hesitated. His eyes widened in slight shock, and he exhaled sharply. "What do you..."

"Dante, or whatever his name was, he went through the motions and said what he was supposed to," Ryan said, looking up.

Avery bit his lip. It trembled when he realized Ryan put it together.

"You told me what you knew via a stranger because you didn't have the balls to tell me what you had become," Ryan said, trying to contain his anger.

Avery's breath increased, and he tried to regain control of the situation. "Dante is a friend. He wasn't a stranger and offered to help."

Ryan laughed coldly. "You've been playing me from day one. And the mark on the back of your neck? Did your little friend Dante help you with that?"

"No, I didn't lie about that," Avery whispered, shaking his head. "I was punished for that kid's death."

"So, say it," Ryan snarled. He still kept his arm pressed against the sharp pain in his sternum.

Avery's eyes flickered to the floor and misted over. "Yeah, you figured it out. I'm a Descendant of Chaos," he said. His voice was dead. "I was usin' the magik in the cave, and I was the one who told Dante what to say." His eyes hardened as he took control of himself.

Ryan punched him in the nose at the arrogance.

Avery hissed and tilted his head back, trying to staunch the blood flow. "Why make me say it if all you're gonna do is hit me?" he asked. The sarcasm and venom were back.

"You *lied* to me, and you *lied* to my brother. You're lucky that's all I'm gonna do to you," Ryan said, barely containing himself. *Killian likes you and as much as I want to break your neck, I won't for him.*

"Then why bother? Don't wear a leash because you're afraid of a fight," Avery snapped. He took a step and grabbed Ryan's shirt. "Let's do it if we're goin' to!"

Ryan bristled with rage. "Because my brother likes you," his voice was dangerously low. "I refuse to hurt you because Killian's decided he likes you."

That took all the bite out of Avery. He let Ryan go and looked away, shoving his hands in his pockets. "I know," he whispered. "And I'm goin' to hurt him."

Ryan clenched his hands and took a step away. He was going to pounce again. "What do you want?" he asked. Ryan had yet to try to look at where he was. His eyes moved around Avery carefully, but he refused to take his full attention off him.

"I didn't want this, Ryan. Angel... she was a mom to me. The homestead didn't want me, my dad sure as Helwe didn't, and after you left. I was alone," Avery said.

Ryan scoffed. "Save the sob story. Both our lives suck, I get it." It was hard feeling sympathy for someone who helped keep him locked up.

"That's not why I'm tellin' you this," Avery said, his voice sharpening again. "Let me fix this."

Ryan narrowed his eyes, crossed his arms against his chest, and shook his head. "Why bother? What do you get out of it?" he asked.

Avery frowned and touched the wall beside him. The room was dark, nearly pitch black, but Ryan's eyes were well-adjusted. He flicked a switch, and a fluorescent light hummed to life, almost blinding him. Ryan's eyes watered and burned as he blinked rapidly, trying to let them adjust.

Avery was in front of him when Ryan opened his eyes next. He grabbed his wrists and pulled them out so Ryan could look. "Because if I don't do somethin', she's goin' to kill you," he said. "And maybe Killian."

The damage was worse in the light. Ryan's heart pumped in his ears, and his mouth went dry. "You helped her keep me here," he snapped. His eyes traced the burn marks, knife wounds, and some sort of weird pinpricks that reminded him of fangs.

"She normally doesn't wake you up so fast, so you never remember what she does," Avery said. He knelt when Ryan sank back to the floor. "She told me she wouldn't hurt you."

Ryan wanted to be angry, but he couldn't. His mind struggled to comprehend this danger when he couldn't recall it happening. "How long ago was this?"

Avery shrugged. "I wasn't here. Not long enough for the marks to be gone."

Ryan shivered and closed his eyes. When one thing seemed to go right, he went three steps back. "I'm screwed," he said.

Avery shook his head and put a finger to his lips. His voice became the slightest of whispers. "They're comin' back. Maintain your hold on your lucidity. Pretend when she's around. Keep the chaos around you like a blanket, and she won't know the difference," he said.

"I don't know how to do that. The chaos doesn't do as I say. It won't listen to me," Ryan snapped. He was going to be sick.

Avery smiled weakly. "That's what *I'm* for, if you allow it."

He stared for a long while before nodding. What else did he have to lose?

The Drunken Sap

KARA

Kara looked at the map Cody pulled up on the computer. It overlooked the city. She figured if Angel was planning to do something with Ryan, it would have to be at one of the places they were hiding. Cody had been told he wasn't allowed to interact with the city's mainframe in any way. Kara guessed Justin was worried about someone tracking them. Which seemed a little insane. No one had ever come across Haven's barriers, and she didn't think that would start now.

Killian plopped across from her and set his chin on his hand. He hadn't left Haven since his grandmother's death. There were bags under his eyes, and they were rimmed red. "What're you doing?" he asked.

Kara looked up. Her hands stilled against the paper, and she studied him closely. His temper had been worse than Ryan's, so she watched herself. "Looking for what Angel might be planning."

"With a map?" he asked.

Kara nodded. "How're you feeling?"

Killian shrugged. "I kissed Avery, and now he's avoiding me," he said, his voice was wobbly as he tried to keep himself from crying.

She blinked and blinked again. There wasn't anything simple she could say to that. Avery told her they didn't have a romantic relationship, and now Killian told her they kissed. It sounded like things were going well in Rochester.

"Actually, I *made* Avery kiss me, and now he's avoiding me," Killian corrected, still staring at the map. "Oh, and he cuddled me the night my grandma died and told me he didn't want me. It's been great."

Kara hummed a high-pitched whine and tried to find the right words for that. "Can you really make Avery do anything?"

Killian shrugged.

She looked at the map again, pushing her fingers under her thighs. She didn't want to get into this conversation after the guy lost his grandmother.

"I was inconsiderate because I was curious," Killian said. "And my grandmother told me a prophecy. I think it was a prophecy. I don't know what it was."

Kara looked back up. He wasn't making eye contact but kept looking at her in his peripherals. He was waiting for an answer, and she didn't have one. "I mean... it's Avery. Is he ever considerate?" she asked. "What did your grandma say?" Maybe that was a topic she could handle.

Killian scrunched his brow and whispered the words before saying aloud, "Be wary of the witch who manipulates with loving words, be wary of the dictator who rules with blood and fear, but most of all, be wary of the brother in disguise."

"Well, some of that makes sense," she said. "Like the dictator, that's Angel. No one has to be warned to fear her. The witch is an odd one. I don't know any witches."

Killian rubbed his eyes. "Or the brother in disguise. How can anyone disguise themselves as Ryan? I look exactly like him," he muttered.

"Maybe you're the brother in disguise?" she asked.

He shot her a look, and she retracted the statement and apologized. Kara wasn't good with riddles and prophecies were just overexaggerated riddles. "Um... I'm going to find anything else to do," she said, standing and hurrying away from the table. She didn't know how to comfort people in their times of need.

A thought dawned on her, and she looked at Killian's back from the hall. When she first got to Haven, her world fell apart, and the most unexpected help came. It wasn't Ryan who made her feel like she was going to survive; it was Killian. The least she could do was return the favor.

"Bad things happen," she said. Killian's back straightened. "Without them, we can't appreciate the good things. Someone wise once told me that, but I could be wrong." Kara shrugged and hurried into the living room before Killian could throw something. He didn't look angry, but she wouldn't push her luck.

His voice chased her to the couch, "I believe your response was, I'm going to watch the city burn!"

Kara giggled and hopped onto the couch. Those had been her exact words. When everything was falling around her, she had no desire to help people or the world. Now, she better understood how to manage those emotions and where she was headed. Kara wanted to help people, especially *her* people.

Killian appeared in the entryway and leaned on the wall. A flicker of a smile was on his face, and he held out a bow. "Wanna practice some more?" he asked.

Kara's eyes flicked to the front window with the little ledge. She liked to read books there sometimes. It was drizzling and gray. "It's wet," she said,

He shrugged. "I feel like dancing in the rain today. Call it a whim," he said.

Kara jumped up and took the bow, grinning wide. There was something they could always look forward to- each other.

Avery's energy danced through the flames, winding back and forth gracefully. He stared into the fire without glancing up when Kara stumbled through the brush. Her hair was full of leaves and sticks, and she huffed in frustration as her shoe got stuck in a pile of tar-like mud.

"For the love of..." Kara ripped her foot free and shook it as the clay clung and clumped. "Gross."

Killian mentioned how Avery had avoided him since they kissed, and she had to get to the bottom of this. Not only was he sulking about his grandmother, but he was home too often for her to get some much needed alone time. His energy was like a dark cloud that refused to abate.

"Hey." She stopped in front of Avery and crossed her arms.

He looked up but didn't speak. There was a half-empty bottle of amber liquid at his side.

"You and Killian are a match made in Faierie," she muttered, shaking her head.

Avery smirked and leaned back on his palms. At least he was coming alive. Even if he was doing it under the influence of something else. "Faerie, now where'd you hear that name?" he asked, slurring.

"I read it in a book. Isn't that what a lot of people call the afterlife?" Kara asked, sitting across from him. Her eyes burned into his glazed ones.

"I dunno. Some of us don't believe in it," Avery mumbled. He rubbed his eyes, stirring the dirt and flicking some leaves into the fire.

Kara cocked her head to the side. "What do you believe?"

"I dunno. Maybe I don't believe in anythin'. When we die, that's the end," he said.

Kara nodded and wrinkled her nose. She didn't like that train of thought. If there was nothing after death, what was the point of living? Maybe Avery lived as free as he did because he didn't think anything was next. "I came to talk about Killian," she said. Might as well get to the point while he was capable of talking.

Avery's face was a cross between adoration and anger. "I don't want to talk about that," he said.

She ignored him. "He said you kissed him. Or he made you kiss him, and now you're avoiding him, so do you want to talk about that?"

Avery swiped the half-empty bottle and chugged the rest of it. "I just told you I don't," he said.

"I don't care. It wasn't a question. Tell me what happened," she demanded. Kara wasn't about beating around the bush, so she didn't want to deal with this. If she didn't, Killian would drive her to lose her mind.

Avery shrugged and tossed the bottle into a tree. It shattered against the wood and rained glass to the ground.

"Really?" she asked.

He was being overdramatic, so that meant he was mostly alright. His emotions and attitude were poor, but he would perk up—Avery always did. He shrugged again.

Kara resisted the urge to electrocute him. It might stop his heart in this state, and that wasn't her plan. "Can you try to grow up? I'm trying to have a mature conversation," she said.

Avery spat something in Nivet, and she knew it wasn't pleasant from how his eyes scrunched and his cheeks reddened.

She scowled and pushed herself to her feet. "You know what, be a whiny brat. I can't believe it; I thought I could help you. Doesn't it suck to help everyone else and let yourself be forgotten? No, well, continue on then, friend. Screw off," she said. Her voice echoed into the forest, and she turned away.

This wasn't a shining moment in her life, but Kara couldn't help it. At one point, she had been like that, albeit she hadn't drunk her feelings away. It was hard when you felt like life was going nowhere, but so many people taught her to make that conscious decision to improve herself.

Avery appeared before her, his energy fanning around them like a vice. There was a bright blue ring around his eyes, much like the one around Justin's the day he lost control.

Her heart stuttered, and she furrowed her brow. This energy was familiar. She couldn't breathe past the pressure on her chest, and she pressed her palm to her heart. It was chaotic and unorganized. Her eyes widened in realization. "You're like... Angel," she whispered.

Avery smirked and sauntered toward her. "Oh really?" he asked. "I guess I never noticed."

She stepped back and held up her hands. "Stay back," she said. Kara didn't want to hurt him, but she didn't like what his energy was doing. It scared her.

Avery's smile turned predatory, but he didn't listen. He took another step, forcing her to retreat further. "What's wrong, scared?" he taunted.

Dawson flashed through her head, and she squeezed her eyes shut. Blood trickled from his lips as he smiled endlessly, hoping she would be the one to turn the world around.

A sob escaped her lips, and she pressed her fingers to her mouth. Her eyes snapped open, and her anger raged. "Stop it!" her scream echoed, and Avery stopped in his tracks. A powerful wave of energy washed over him like one in the unpredictable sea, and his energy sputtered and died.

His eyes widened. The blue ring around his eyes sputtered out, leaving him in shock. "How'd you do that?" he asked.

Kara screamed in frustration and shot at him like a cannonball from a cannon. How dare he use Dawson against her? Electricity burned across her skin, and her hair flew around her in the wind, creating hot and cold air.

Avery ducked out of the way, but one of the bolts on her arms jumped from her skin to his, and he jolted in pain, wincing. His arm went limp, and his fingers twitched sporadically. "Wait, wait." He seemed to sober up after that.

"You do not ever use my brother like that. Do you understand?" Kara asked as her cheeks burned with anger. She dove for him again.

Avery teleported out of the way and held up his hands. "Kara, stop! I swear, I won't do it again. I'm sorry," he said.

Her eyes misted over as angry tears built up. "No one wants to use their words, fine. Who cares, I don't. If you don't wanna talk, don't talk, but you better stop avoiding Killian. He just lost his grandmother, and Ryan's gone. He needs his friends, you moron!" Kara spat her final words and stormed into the forest. She didn't want to see Avery's stupid face anymore. If neither Killian nor him were going to take this seriously, she didn't care. Let them make their lives miserable.

Happy Birthday

RYAN

Ryan had free reign of the floor Angel stuck him on. He explored his new home the last few days, but there were no windows or doors. Food appeared in his room every morning, noon, and night, and he had access to the shower and bathroom. Ryan used as many of Avery's lessons as he could remember, but some spots in his memory made it hard to recall some of them.

He leaned on the wall and tapped his fingers against his thigh, trying to call Fyre. Since he had developed his mark, Fyre became a fox. They didn't speak like Chaol, but Ryan could always feel them. Since Avery stopped visiting, he had too much free time and did everything he could to keep himself busy.

Fyre's form swam through his head, and it yipped happily, running around.

Ryan wished he could call them to the physical realm for company, but he was sure Angel would feel it. The less attention he brought to himself, the better. Plus, he wasn't sure he was capable of creating living, breathing life.

Avery said that as long as Ryan kept himself cloaked in chaos, she couldn't tell the difference. So far, that had worked in his favor. At least, he thought it did, considering he couldn't remember much of the past week. There were some angry lacerations across his back he couldn't recall getting, but for the most part, those had finally healed. It took days, but they didn't hurt or reopen when he moved.

Ryan opened the emotional bond between himself and his brother. He rarely reached out for fear of Angel tracking him, but he was bored. The more lucidity he gained, the harder it was to stay put. Ryan began meditating, doing physical exercises, and saying equations in his head to keep his mind sharp. All the while, he kept the chaos from taking over but also kept it close enough to maintain a sense of control.

"Happy birthday, Kill?" He reached out via their link and focused on controlling his emotions. Killian's side of the bond was filled with grief and an overall sense of doubt.

His brother replied almost immediately in a weak voice, *"I'm here."*

Ryan frowned and slid to the floor, trying to keep the conversation open. *"What's wrong?"* It was unusual for them to be apart on such a special day. Since they were little kids, they had elaborate celebrations where they got lost in their world.

"Grandma's gone. She passed a couple of days ago," Killian said.

Ryan wished he felt more about that than he did. The hag dying wasn't overwhelmingly sad. He sighed and rubbed his eyes so much for a simple celebration.

"I found out a lot of stuff that's... well, some stuff about our magik and lineage," Killian said.

Ryan cocked his head to the side and hummed. Keeping their link open quickly drained him, and he felt Chaol flutter through his mind. He blocked the faceless being to avoid problems with his brother. *"What kind of stuff?"* he asked.

Killian's emotions ricocheted down the bond, and then he shared the night of their grandmother's death—the conversation and everything she said. The memory flashed through his head like he had been there. He didn't realize that Killian always thought Ryan was better at everything. The news was a little disheartening because it was only because of Killian that Ryan was as strong as he was.

He sighed, letting the headache that threatened to build behind his eyes dissipate. When he could think for himself again, he responded, *"That was a lot of information."*

Killian chuckled unpleasantly. *"Avery won't talk to me."*

Ryan couldn't place the rage that built in his stomach at the young man's name. That had been happening a lot lately, which was part of the reason he was happy Avery had stopped visiting. He didn't want to risk running into him until he figured out what was wrong with him. *"Why?"* he asked, almost forgetting he was in the middle of a conversation.

"I don't want to tell you," Killian said.

Ryan got a flash of memories that didn't belong to him. Avery was bloody and bruised, Avery kissing him, Avery being there for every down, and some training things. Things that were laced with emotions Killian didn't understand and Ryan didn't want to explain. He was torn between wanting to tell Killian he knew and pretending he never saw it.

"Why him?" he asked. His brain decided for him. *"Of all the people in the world, you had to go for him?"*

Killian was silent for a long time. It was long enough that Ryan wondered if he decided to shut down their link again. *"I didn't choose him."*

Ryan sighed and hit his head against the wall. He knew that. It wasn't like anyone romantically had a say in what they loved or wanted. It was cruel to ask Killian to do that.

"Are you mad because it's a man?" Killian asked. His voice was so quiet that Ryan had difficulty making out the words.

Ryan chuckled and hoped his laughter would not diminish the bond. *"No, I don't care that you like a man. Did I have a problem with Tory or Nicholas?"*

"Are you mad because it's your best friend?" Killian asked.

Ryan sighed. Avery was a two-timing moron that helped Angel take him captive. The last thing he wanted was for his brother to be involved with someone who could betray him. Then again, when it came to Killian, Avery kept him safe. He made sure his brother escaped when Angel took him, and he was teaching Killian to control himself and his magik.

"Ryan?"

He shook himself out of his thoughts. *"No, I'm not mad,"* he said. It was hard coming up with a solid reason that Killian would buy. Ryan could spoil it for him and tell Killian everything, but who would he have?

Killian rarely opened up to anyone. He didn't want to take that away if Avery was someone his brother opened up to. It wasn't like Avery had proved himself dangerous around his brother yet.

"Are you sure?"

Ryan forced a smile and tried to send warm thoughts down their link. He had to be comforting and reassuring. That way, Killian wouldn't suspect anything weird. *"I think it's great,"* he said.

Killian chuckled, and the words reverberated through Ryan's head. *"Happy birthday. I wish you were here."*

Ryan smirked despite himself. It was nice having a casual conversation despite the severity of their situation. *"I do, too, for what it's worth."*

"You seem to be doing alright. I had a weird dream about you and Avery the other night," he said after a while.

Ryan frowned. That didn't sound ominous. *"What kind of dream?"*

Killian sent him a series of images.

Avery stood before Ryan, covered in his blood, holding a black leather whip. Before he could delve into the images, a surge of pain tore through Ryan's head, and he pressed his palm to it with a gasp. It was such a sudden pain that he couldn't stop it from traveling between their link.

"Holy crap, what was that for?" Killian snarled.

"I don't know," Ryan said. He tried to figure out where the sudden headache came from, but it was gone. The minute Killian stopped sharing his dream, the pain vanished. He frowned and thought of the strange wounds on his back.

"Is everything alright?" Killian asked. He must have sensed Ryan's change in emotion because he sounded worried.

Ryan nodded, forgetting they weren't actually in person. The chaos pulsed around him, sending him a warning. His head snapped up, and Angel's high-pitched laugh crept through the halls.

"I've got to go," he said, shutting their connection off before Killian could argue. Ryan leveled his energy and put on a blank face as he stood.

Angel found him not two seconds later. She waved her finger and tsked. "I know what Avery taught you, but I've found a way to make that problem disappear."

Ryan didn't move. His heart pounded, but he had to pretend like he was still under her control. This could be a test, and he didn't have the time to re-establish her obliviousness.

Angel flicked her wrist, and chaos filled the room.

Ryan hissed in pain and dropped to his hands and knees before he could stop himself. A tense pressure dropped against his chest, feeling like it was about to break every bone. He didn't realize she was that powerful.

A man in a gray suit stepped out from behind her, holding a black cane. His eyes were as silver as his suit, and a mask covered any other defining features he might have. Power radiated from him that was even stronger than Angel's.

Ryan focused on breathing as he tried to build a wall between them.

Angel smirked and crossed her arms. "You've turned Avery against me, kept your brother from me, and even bothered to think you could control the chaos." Her words were colder than ice, and her eyes just as sharp.

Ryan looked up, trembling as he kept building the wall. It loosened the pressure enough to make breathing possible.

"I've discovered the best way to control someone like you is to let you think you're in control. So, while I rearrange your memories a little, why don't you enjoy the time Havoc will have with you," Angel said.

Ryan grit his teeth but didn't bother arguing. They were going to do what they wanted anyway, so the quicker they got it over with, the better. *Havoc.* That was a name he would have to remember. If Ryan could get a hold of himself long enough to let Killian know, he could warn them. It could be one of those good things he does. Even if it didn't get him anywhere, he could at least feel useful despite the horrible things Angel made him do.

Hers and the newcomer's energy swirled together, forcing his walls away and the breath from his lungs. This was not turning out to be a good birthday.

Out of Time

KILLIAN

We are out of time. That's all Killian could think when he woke up screaming. The pain burned through him, inside and out, and anytime he tried to find Ryan in the haze, it got worse. It was like being burned alive, and there was nothing he could do to ease the pain.

Justin nearly knocked the door off its hinges as he busted in, probably expecting a murder scene. Still, all he saw was Killian thrashing around in bed, trying to get relief. He did a quick scan of the energy and paled.

Killian grabbed his head as it pounded like someone was taking a hammer to his skull. "Make it stop," he begged, tears streaming down his cheeks.

Justin held his hand over him and closed his eyes. Something twisted around Killian, dousing him in an icy grip, and he was reminded of his shadow. The thing that kept him from being what he was supposed to be or whatever. The pain stopped, and he shot out of bed, checking himself.

"It was a mental link," Justin said softly. "There was no physical connection."

Killian panted and looked wildly around the room. "What was that?" he asked.

"I don't know," Justin said. "I don't have the same insight into your brother that you do."

Killian scrambled out of bed and snapped his fingers, summoning a portal. "I have to go see Avery.

Justin grabbed his arm before he could vanish. "I need to monitor you..."

Killian ripped out of his hold. "No! I have to see Avery now. Then, I'm going to get my brother. You can come if you want, but don't you dare stop me."

Justin let him go and sighed. "Very well, we'll figure it out when you return."

Killian stepped through his portal and appeared in Avery's living room. "Hey! We need to talk," Killian shouted. He hesitated to go into the bedroom in case Avery wasn't alone.

There was a thud, a curse, another thud, and then a yell of pain before Avery managed to enter the living room. He rubbed his shin and blinked in the bright morning light. "What the Helwe is wrong with you?" he asked, his voice a whine. He was shirtless and wearing a pair of holey shorts.

Killian forced himself to look past it and keep talking. "Ryan's in trouble. You've gotta come."

Avery flinched like Killian just struck him. "What?" he asked.

"I woke up like someone was flaying me. There's not much time, but if you help, we can bring him back." Killian knew he was talking fast, but he was sure Avery would get the gist.

Avery paled. "I'm sorry, could you run that by me again?" he asked.

Killian growled in frustration. "What is wrong with you?" he snapped. "You've been acting weird since the kiss, and I don't have time to fix that part of our friendship yet."

Avery scratched his chest absently. "Shit, Kill... I can't help you with this."

That wasn't what Killian thought would happen. He frowned in confusion and tried to form a coherent reply. "Wait, what?"

"I can't go. This is somethin' you're gonna be doin' without me," Avery mumbled. His voice got even softer.

Killian shook his head. "Why wouldn't you come?" His heart raced, and something told him this wouldn't end well.

"Killian, trust me. You don't want me to answer that," he said.

"No, I kind of want you to answer that." Killian was ninety percent sure this was going to end in murder - Avery's.

Avery frowned and shook his head but didn't say anything.

Killian stepped back and exhaled with a bitter laugh. "Oh, Helwe, you've been involved since the beginning." It wasn't a question because as good as Avery was at reading him, Killian was getting good at returning the favor

Avery remained silent, becoming white as a sheet, which was as close to a response as Killian needed. His hands were clenched at his sides, and his face was calm despite his dark and stormy eyes. He was a mess of panic and fear, and Killian didn't want to continue.

"You've not been on our side..." This realization hurt—more than hurt, it tore him open.

Killian had never experienced a betrayal before. It was quite possibly the most emotionally painful experience of his life, and he finally remembered why he didn't bother with things like crushes, affection, or love. His throat tightened, and he took another step back. "That's why Ryan didn't want me near you. He was warning me without ratting you out because he's a decent person," Killian whispered.

Avery shoved his hands in his pockets and stared hard at the ground like he was waiting for it to open and swallow them. He didn't say anything to defend himself.

Killian wanted to be angry, but he couldn't feel anything. He was numb, like the nights he spent partying with people who didn't know his name. This numbness was empty, though, and he waited for the anger to set in, but it never did. He wondered if it was normal for someone not to be angry when they found out the person they cared about played them.

"I'm leaving," he said. Since it was apparent Avery wouldn't say or do anything, Killian felt it was best to leave as fast as possible before he could get his anger to react. He tried to calm his energy long enough to summon a portal, but a storm raged within, rendering his magik useless.

Killian turned and opened the front door, trying not to run out. The sound of rain pelting the ground was almost enough to make him stay. Of course, it would be raining. That fit the mood perfectly. It didn't make sense. How could he not have listened to his instincts? Ryan had been hurt and angry when he saw Killian's memories with Avery and hadn't said anything.

"Why him?" Ryan's voice rang in his ear. How long had his brother known about this – from the beginning?

The door slammed behind him, and Killian fled across the front yard into the bare trees. It took seconds for his hair and clothes to be thoroughly soaked. The wind howled by as he tore through the forest, forgoing magik for one of the most important lessons Avery might've taught him – nothing could bother him if he kept his body and mind busy.

The sky was black, and lightning flashed through the clouds, lighting it like splintered glass. Killian ignored the pulsing shadow in his head as it raged. He could let it take over and wake up the next day with blood on his hands or bruises, but then he wouldn't have learned anything. Killian hissed in pain as his side ached, but he pushed himself further. *Pain is a good thing.* He stopped when his teeth wouldn't stop chattering, and his lungs hurt so bad he could barely breathe. The rain hadn't let up, and he shivered violently.

Killian was so far in the woods that he was ninety percent sure he could drown in this rain, and no one would ever find him.

Dropping to his knees, he sucked in the air and planted his hands on the ground. Mud squelched between his fingers, and something warm rolled off his cheeks. He didn't know if tears or sweat were mixing with the water running rivulets down his face and neck.

"I expected you to hit me, yell, somethin' that didn't include chasin' you through a friggin' hurricane," Avery said.

Killian laughed bitterly and dropped to his elbows. His forehead was inches from the dirt. He closed his eyes and sucked in breaths that wreaked of moss and earth. It didn't matter to him so long as he was breathing.

"Can you at least go back to Haven?" Avery asked. I can't leave you out here." His voice was emotionless, with no inflection of joy or the usual charm Killian was used to hearing.

The wind screamed in his ears, and he trembled again. *Freezing.* He was freezing.

The ground squelched as Avery walked closer. His boots splashed through puddles, throwing muddy water into the air. He knelt but didn't reach out.

Killian breathed out slowly, feeling the shadow fighting for control. He wasn't giving this one up. He stayed crouched on the ground, the mud thickening between his fingers as the raindrops stopped. His brother was in danger—real danger—and he was wallowing over a stupid crush. This was dumb, and he needed to grow the Helwe up because there was one person he could always count on, and that person needed him more than anyone else. Killian pushed himself back to his knees and sat back on his heels. Rain fell around them, but a shell covered them like an umbrella.

Avery blinked, stoic and calm.

"Why?" he asked. He felt entitled to some answers after being jerked around for months by a moron who felt nothing for him.

Avery shrugged. "Because she asked. Angel... she was all I had," he said.

Killian studied Avery's face and laughed even though it was not funny. After all, what else was there to say? "Go away," he whispered.

"I can't until you go home. You'll freeze out here, please, go back to..."

Killian screamed in frustration. He wanted Avery to refrain from giving advice or acting like he gave a crap. He wasn't allowed to care after lying, after helping that witch hold his brother. "I don't want to hate you, please! Just leave..." Killian trailed off and bit back his sobs. "You won, don't you get it? You proved to me that I can have feelings for someone, so yay me! I get to have feelings and then feel them being ripped apart as the one person, the only person I chose to trust, stabbed me in the back." He couldn't stop talking even though every fiber of his being wished he would. Once Killian started, the tension left his body in waves. The more he talked, the better he felt and the easier it was to breathe, which also caused him to become angry. He clenched his hands, baring his teeth like a wild animal, and pushed himself to his feet.

"I literally could have let the world burn. I *hated* you. You were an arrogant, obnoxious moron, and I wanted nothing to do with you, but then, low and behold, I *needed* you. Of course, I needed your help because you had information I didn't. So, I begged you to help me. I suppose that should've been my first hint." Killian shook the water from his hair, wishing Avery would tell him he was wrong and that he was confusing things.

It would make it so much easier to hate him, but despite it all, Killian couldn't dredge up a sliver of the hatred he used to feel because he knew Avery now. He knew how he smiled even when he was sad, how cold his house got when Avery fell into a slump, how hard it was to get out of bed in the morning and take care of himself, thinking everyone hated him sometimes. He was… familiar.

Avery didn't move.

Killian snorted in bitter amusement and waved a hand. He didn't have to do this to himself and didn't have to do it in front of him.

"You done?" Avery asked.

Killian shrugged and ran a hand through his sopping-wet hair and wrung out his shirt. "I'm done," he said.

"I didn't want to hurt you," Avery said. "I know you don't care about my excuses, but I really didn't want to hurt you."

Killian scowled. "Well, you did. Has this been going on from the beginning? The entire reason you were hanging out with me was…" he didn't want to know. "Don't answer that."

Avery listened and didn't answer. He shook his head and exhaled, closing his eyes. "I tried to teach Ryan how to break free, and Angel caught us. She… I had to… the night I came to your room, I hurt Ryan bad. He never remembers; she uses these blocks. He heals, and it's like it never happened."

Killian blinked a couple of times, trying to understand what Avery said. It took him a long time to realize that Avery was making it up the only way he knew how. He was giving Killian the information he needed to help his brother.

"He won't remember what she does, but your dreams are true. Everythin' you've seen, she's done. There's a floor that only she can access in the tower, and it's where he's stayin', but she's plannin' somethin' big. About to make a move to lure you to the city," Avery's voice was soft. His eyes didn't leave Killian as he spoke. "If he leads you to the waterin' hole, leave it for another day. That's where the bad thing's gonna happen."

Killian made a note of everything. "How do I know this is-"

Avery cut him off, his eyes sharp and cold. "I would *never* lure you into a trap. She could never do anything to make me," he said.

Killian stepped back, staring hard at the young man. "You won't stop us?"

"No. Nor will I tell her you're comin'," Avery said.

Killian nodded hesitantly. "Is my brother alright?"

Avery nodded again.

Killian summoned a portal. His mind was finally clear enough to be useful again. "Thank you," he said.

"Don't die," Avery whispered with that trademark grin.

Killian vanished.

Formulating a Plan

KARA

Kara sat at the table with Tory and Killian, trying to make sense of what they were about to do. They planned to return to get Ryan, but everything was jumbled. Killian's energy was wild, and Tory hadn't said anything since they decided to go. She still wasn't sure she wanted to. If she faced that city again and Angel... her thoughts trailed off. It wouldn't be good for anyone if she couldn't keep her fear under control.

Nicholas and Justin were talking in Justin's room, and Cody wasn't allowed to be involved. Since Killian announced their return to the city, the redhead vanished into his lab and hadn't re-emerged.

"He's not going to let us go," Kara said after a while.

They sat at the kitchen table in the dining room as light rain covered the outside. Droplets sprinkled on the window, making slow streaks down the pane. The boys' steady breathing and Kara's tapping foot were the only sounds.

"I'm going," Killian said.

That didn't work well last time, and Kara would've pointed it out, but it wasn't wise. Not with the way Killian's emerald gaze cut through her. He was worried, and since his most recent dream, she felt there was no talking him out of this.

Nicholas and Justin entered the dining room together. Nicholas crossed his arms, and Justin looked more exhausted than Kara had ever seen. "What's the plan?" Justin asked, turning his head toward Killian. "You want to go, so give me a reason to agree."

Killian scowled. He looked up and drummed his fingers against the solid oak table. "We all know Angel's a threat, but that's because of her army. I propose a handful of us manage the army, take away her power, and one of you comes with me to take down Ryan," Killian said, sounding too confident.

Kara didn't think splitting up was the best solution. She looked at Justin, praying he would disagree. She was disheartened when surprise crossed his face. Before Ryan was taken, Killian had taken to reading strategy of war books he got from Justin's library.

"And you think everyone can do this?" Justin asked. "Because if one of you is weak, the entire team is at risk."

Killian's eyes flicked to Kara. Her heart sank, and she slid down in the seat, wishing she could vanish.

"And what do you propose we do about Angel after this army is neutralized?" Nicholas asked.

Tory ran a hand through his hair and rested his elbows against the table. He looked jittery and nervous. "We were hoping you and Justin would come. If you did, you could take Kara and keep Angel busy. I'll take the army and manage them while Killian goes after Ryan," he said.

Nicholas shook his head, and anger flashed behind his usually soft brown gaze. "That's a Helwe no," he said.

Tory bit his cheek and glared at the space in front of him. After the glare receded, he looked up and took a breath. "I'm not saying I will take out an entire army, but I can keep them busy."

"That's a horrible idea," Kara said before anyone could agree. "At the very least, Justin should go with you, and I can stay with Nicholas. Killian would still be alone, but he can manage his brother." Splitting up and leaving one completely open was worse than splitting up in units.

Tory opened his mouth to argue, and Nicholas shook his head again. "It's not an option, so drop it," he snapped.

Justin sat at the table and folded his hands atop it. He looked deadly serious as he opened and shut his mouth several times. When he finally talked, he was quiet. "Going through with this is a declaration of war. Do any of you understand what it means to be involved in that?" he asked.

Kara clenched her jaw. She didn't know what it meant but could imagine how it would go. The thought of all the blood was enough to curdle her stomach.

"Well, you could always come with me," Tory said once he realized Nicholas was unbending.

Nicholas glared and paced in agitation. His footsteps pounded through the room as he clapped his hands and spoke, "And what about my brother? He'd be left with Angel."

What am I? Chopped liver? She tried not to be offended. As she opened her mouth, Justin waved his hand and shut them all up. "I think I could manage Angel for a short while," he said. "It's not like I'm a child, plus I'll have Little Mouse with me, and she's getting better with her shields and healing abilities."

She tried not to swell with pride at Justin's words. Although she wasn't the strongest in their group, she fiercely desired to protect those she loved. These had been her people over the last few months; she would die for them if she had to.

Nicholas groaned and buried his face in his hands. It took Kara a moment to realize Justin wasn't against this plan. Nicholas was.

"Nick..." Tory trailed off once he realized this wasn't a conversation that should be had in front of everyone.

Kara looked between the men and sighed. If this were the plan, they could use more help. "What about Avery?" she asked.

Killian and Nicholas' heads snapped up at his name. "What about him?" Killian growled.

"We could ask for help. There are too few of us to make much of an impact," Kara said. She didn't take her eyes off Killian.

They were fighting again; otherwise, he wouldn't look seconds from killing her.

Nicholas growled. "No." He was all about shooting down their ideas today.

She frowned and looked between them. "We need help. You're outmatched, and she has strength plus numbers. I sucked at math, but even I know those are crap odds."

"He won't help, so drop it," Killian said, his voice bitter. "And if you don't believe me, go ask him yourself," Killian said. He couldn't make things more difficult if he tried.

Kara wasn't sure what happened, but they had few options. "Since when?" she asked, trying not to cuss him out.

Justin clicked his tongue before a fight could break out. "We have what we have," he said, though there was a note of relief in his voice.

"I can fight with Justin," Kara said. "That way, Tory isn't alone." It made the most sense. "I can keep him alive." She was capable. Her spells were stronger, and if all she focused on was keeping him safe, she should be able to do it.

Nicholas paled. He didn't say anything, but she could see the desperation behind his eyes. He obviously didn't see her improvements as much as she did.

If Justin sensed anything, he didn't comment. They already had their argument about what would happen, and it looked like Nicholas lost. Kara almost felt bad for him, but she was glad to have Justin on their side and was willing to fight. Tension filled the room, and Kara had to build an invisible wall around herself to keep her magik in check. This wasn't the time to lose control and piss everyone off. The bloodshed should be saved for the battlefield.

Killian leaned back in his chair, making it squeak. "What if we forget the army and take them out at the end?"

They could not out-maneuver an entire army. They would have to neutralize some soldiers to get to Angel. She would have protection, plus the General would be there. Kara's heart skipped at the thought. The man who killed her brother was Angel's right hand. She could get the justice for Dawson he deserved and bring an end to one of the vilest men on the planet.

"If you think you can ignore an entire army, you're less prepared for this than I thought," Justin said, not pulling his punches. He sat rigidly.

Killian growled in frustration. "This is stupid! I don't care what we do, I'm going."

Nicholas grabbed his arm before the boy could vacate the room. His eyes burned with anger and fear. "I watched a rebellion fall," he said. "They used to plan all their attacks in this room. Everyone fell to Angel or her army, and all I got to do was watch." His voice was so eerily calm that Kara was sure he was two seconds from snapping.

Even Killian had the sense to keep his mouth shut and listen.

"If you think you're any stronger than the people who fought her before, you're a moron. We had twenty of us before, and only five survived. What makes you think a bunch of kids have any better odds?" Nicholas asked.

"We don't," Kara whispered. They all looked at her. "Our odds suck, but we have each other. It won't come down to pure strength or the power of the military, but it'll come down to who's willing to sacrifice more," Kara said, trying to keep her voice level. "I know motivation alone won't allow us to win, but you've been teaching us how magik is passion and reflects the user's will."

It wasn't much for a speech leading them into battle, but it was enough to calm Nicholas down before he could say anything else. He let Killian go, and his shoulders lowered as he sighed. "Jay and I will do all we can to keep you safe, but he's not fighting alone. Tory, manage the military until I can get to you. Once Killian has Ryan, Angel doesn't matter."

Kara shot Killian a look. "You can do this, right?" she asked.

He gave her a cocky grin. "Of course, I'm a Wilson."

She had no clue what that meant, but she hoped he knew what he was doing.

One Last Request

KILLIAN

Killian stared at the night sky and tried to remember the days when his life wasn't in danger. They finally settled on a plan that worked for everyone, but Nick was still upset. Killian couldn't imagine going up against Angel more than once. He tried to empathize like a decent human, but that wasn't in his repertoire of emotions, especially not hours before he was scheduled to take on a city.

Twigs snapped in the distance, and Avery's energy flashed through the trees. Killian closed his eyes to the blue and white and took a breath. His first instinct was to search him out because he liked being around Avery, even if it was now something he shouldn't want. Animals scurried, trying to escape the late-night hunter as he disturbed their dwellings.

Killian was tempted to return to Haven, knowing Avery wouldn't cross the boundaries without an emergent reason. He turned his head and blinked at the moon shimmering off the river. Running from his problems wouldn't solve anything. He could either learn to forgive what happened and try to rebuild, or he could let Avery go and everything they might've had.

The crunching of boots against leaves and twigs got louder, but Killian didn't move. He sat against his tree with a soft blanket around his shoulders. The footsteps stopped, and Avery's energy vanished as if he were trying to conceal himself. Killian smirked. Avery hadn't been checking his surroundings if Killian managed to take him by surprise while he was out hunting.

"Why are you out so late?" Avery asked, appearing under the tree Killian sat in.

He shrugged and clutched the blanket tighter. "I want to go back to the shadow realm. You think you're up for a visit?" he asked.

"Me?" Avery pointed at himself in confusion. He looked around and checked behind him as if he had a shadow he didn't know about.

"Yeah, you. Unfortunately, I don't have many people to turn to. If I'm facing Ryan tomorrow, I need to chat with my... other half," he said. Killian didn't know where that came from but supposed it wasn't a lie.

His shadow had been raging since Avery's betrayal. If he was to maintain a semblance of control, he needed to gain what he could over the being who wanted nothing but blood.

"What kind of trap is this?" Avery asked.

Killian shrugged, containing the sneer or bite from showing too much. It was like before when he had to play nice to get Avery's help. "It's not. You don't have to come; I just thought having backup wasn't a horrible idea," he said. "Not all of us try to screw others over."

Avery didn't move. His eyes flicked around the meadow, and he tried to find the hiding assassin he had conjured in his head.

Killian waited a few minutes before nodding. He obviously had his answer. Whatever Killian was going to do, Avery wasn't going to help. It didn't matter what he needed help with so long as it involved saving his brother. He tried not to let the sting of rejection flutter through him. It wouldn't be the first time Avery turned him away. "Forget it," he said.

Avery took a few hesitant steps. "I've taught you everythin' you need to know about self-control. You don't need my help," he said, his voice gentle but wary.

"Yeah, well, that was before you made me feel like the lowest person in the world, so I dunno how much those lessons matter," Killian murmured. He stood, wobbling on the branch as he wrapped the blanket tighter around his shoulders—the chilly night air bit at his face.

Avery's face hardened. "That's low. You know I didn't-"

Killian cut him off. He was too tired for an argument. "Forget it," he said. "I'm going home." He didn't particularly want to see his shadow, but he couldn't ignore it. If he didn't find some way to quell the rage, he would end up hurting Ryan or killing someone.

Imagine the dynamic duo they could be. Angel would love to have both of them uncontrolled at her side.

Avery grabbed the blanket and held him in place. "You're really goin' into the realm?" he asked.

Killian bit back a snarl. "No, I'm going to see my mother on a deserted island."

Avery sighed and ran a hand down his face. "Don't go alone. Give me ten seconds, and I'll be back," he muttered.

The pressure on Killian's back let up, and he took a deep breath. It wasn't too late to back out. Killian could easily say he changed his mind and leave Avery in the dust, but that felt wrong. It took longer than ten seconds but less than a minute. When Avery returned, he was in a comfortable-looking jacket and had discarded his weapons. He held out his hand. "My energy is out of sorts right now. Try not to focus much on it," he said,

The last time they were in Killian's headspace, his shadow tried to kill them both. He wasn't looking forward to whatever awaited them this time—especially given how poor his mood had become.

Killian felt fine, but he had become despondent of most other things. It was like the depression and anxiety canceled each other out, and he got stuck with the numbness of apathy. A feeling that didn't help anything just made him want to sleep all the time.

Killian grabbed Avery's hand and hated how his heart fluttered at the touch. Everything was set on turning against him these last few days. He wasn't sure how much more of that he could take. He pulled them into the shadow realm so he could stop touching Avery. The second they were in the dim, cavernous room with his shadow, Killian let Avery go as if he could feel his emotions through the touch.

Avery stayed silent this time as the shadow squared off against them.

The massive creature slid around the room in a frenzy and stopped before them, its red eyes turning to slits on its flat face. *"You're back,"* it hissed, breathing rancid breath.

Killian used to be afraid of that thing. Now, all he could do was laugh. That didn't sit well with either the shadow or his traitorous friend. Both sets of eyes snapped to him in surprise, like he had just lost his mind, and he might have. He didn't know anymore. All he wanted was a day he didn't have to worry about his damn life being in danger.

Avery's eyes widened, and breathing quickened, but he said nothing.

The shadow reared back and screeched, its horrible voice filling the space and bouncing off walls that Killian wasn't sure existed. It was a glob of black that resembled a snowman made of mud more than anything else. Killian couldn't believe he used to fear this thing. *"You dare mock me!"* the creature said, its voice carrying.

Killian was here once when he was furious with Avery over something. He couldn't remember why they were fighting, but Killian had done something to the shadow, and Avery knocked him out to stop him. This was his realm, not the shadow's. His grandmother had been trying to tell him before she died about how powerful he was, and he didn't listen.

"I'll do you one better," Killian said, not worrying about Avery past this point. He was sure the other would keep him from getting killed, but wouldn't otherwise intervene. His brother needed him, so he had no choice but to survive. He took a step toward the monster and held out his hand. *"How about we play a game?"* he asked.

It was a wonder what apathy did to a person. Before, if the shadow had even shot him a look of anger, Killian would have turned into a puddle on the floor. Now, he could care less. Nothing was inside him to break anymore; he only wanted to find the one person he knew wouldn't hurt him.

The shadow stopped roaring and screeching like a child throwing a tantrum and cocked its head to the side. Killian snapped his fingers, and the creature morphed. It screamed something horrid, like he had just taken a knife to it, and then it stopped. The giant slithering blob turned into a snake—a more fitting shape for what it had become. The snake flicked out its tongue and hissed angrily at being forced out of its natural form.

Killian smirked. "No, this doesn't fit either. I think we need something a little more... compliant." He snapped again, and the wailing continued. It became a dog, then a fish, and then a bird. One of Killian's favorites was when it turned into a warthog, but with tusks like that, he figured he should find something safer.

After ten more transformations, a black kitten mewled angrily from the floor. Threads of despair and hopelessness hung around the small creature as it finally submitted. The little ball of darkness was fluffy and soft, making Killian grin. It was a big, nasty shadow, but he quite liked it when it looked like this.

"Don't stare at me so pleased, peasant," the shadow hissed.

Killian chuckled, grabbed the kitten by the scruff of its neck, and picked it up. It thrashed in his hold, but he shook his head, turning to Avery. *"And just like that, my shadow problems are gone,"* he said.

Avery forced a smile. He hadn't moved since they got there, and he was paler than usual. *"You chose a cat, huh?"* he asked.

Killian shrugged and tucked the kitten against his chest, stroking its fur. It was silky and poofy, and he was sure he would start sneezing any second, but for now, it was lovely. He immensely enjoyed having something akin to a pet. He closed his eyes and let his energy fan through the room, not knowing what he was doing but knowing he had to do it. The room shifted and distorted, changing to fit his needs. All he asked for was a place where he could be safe with his thoughts.

It was silent. Killian opened his eyes and looked around with a small smile. His shadow realm was gone, replaced by a warm, cozy room. There was a crackling fire in a stone hearth and soft white carpets like the fur rug in Haven. Books were stacked throughout the corners of the room. A long white table rested in the middle, surrounded by chairs, papers, and tools. A plush chair was in front of the fire, and the piano rested quietly out of the way. Nothing but a reminder of what he once was.

Avery clicked his tongue, impressed. It was the most emotion he had shown. "How did you know how to do that?"

"I didn't," Killian said. He let the kitten go, and it bounded off, chasing the tail of a ball of yarn hidden behind one of the stacks of books. It wasn't real; most of it was an illusion, but he could find comfort here. "I let my magik lead me," he said,

Avery held out his hand. "You've got this under control. You can send me home," he said.

Killian nodded and stared at it. His throat tightened, and he wondered what would happen if he sent Avery back. Would they ever talk again? Would this end their friendship? *It shouldn't matter. He betrayed you and hurt Ryan. Let. Him. Go.* His eyes misted over, and he blinked quickly as he cleared his throat. *Communicate. You have to talk...*

"Are you going to go away now?" he asked in not quite a whisper but barely loud enough to be considered a talking voice.

Avery frowned, and his brow furrowed. "What do you mean?"

Killian hesitated. He didn't know how to ask without sounding desperate, so he crossed his arms to keep himself from fidgeting. "If I let you leave, will you stop... will I see you again?" he asked.

Avery blinked but stayed silent, staring at Killian like he was an absolute moron.

Killian smirked coldly and shook his head. "Never mind," he said. "That was dumb." He stepped forward to take Avery's hand and let him go home, but the other dropped his palm. He didn't stop staring, and Killian stared back until his chest hurt.

"Why would you want to see me again?" Avery asked. "Do you have no sense?" His voice rose, and his cheeks flushed.

Killian glared. He couldn't be expected to forget everything that happened between them. Whether he liked it or not, Avery was part of his life. Killian didn't choose who to accept and what people became his. He couldn't be blamed for allowing Avery to see him in every state, including his vulnerability.

"It's not like I asked for this, alright?" he asked. This wasn't the best conversation in a realm where his shadow could decide to break his control.

"You will if you keep lookin' for me!" Avery laughed and ran a hand through his hair. "For god's sake. What does it take? How about I tell you I'm a Descendant of Chaos? Will that make it any better? How messed up do you have to be to want to continue seein' the person who lied to you?"

Thanks to Ryan, Killian recognized the patterns of self-destruction. It wasn't like he wasn't used to seeing someone implode right before his eyes. He wasn't overly offended by the cold words or glowering eyes, but he did take minor offense to being treated like an idiot. "You think I don't know what you are?" Killian asked his voice icy cold. "Treat me with more respect than that; I knew you weren't a Descendant of Water. It's not like you did a good job hiding that."

Surprise flashed across Avery's face. He tried to hide it, but Killian could read him well enough now that he noticed the slight widening of the eyes and the muscle twitches in his face. "You're bluffin'," he said, narrowing his eyes.

"I'm bluffing. Yeah, I am. I had no clue that while you could teleport and Tory couldn't, you were still a Descendant of Water. Or how you could see me through the shadows or teach me how to get to this place." Killian held out his arms and gestured around. "Please, I might not be as brilliant as Ryan, but I'm not stupid," he snarled. With every reason he listed, his voice got a little louder.

Avery squirmed uncomfortably, and when he realized his self-destruct button wasn't working, he went for the next best thing - a full-on attack. As Avery reached for a knife, Killian released his hold on the shadow realm, and they appeared on Avery's front lawn.

He ducked under the flying dagger and raised his arms just in time to block Avery's thick boot. He exhaled in relief and shook his hand, trying to right himself, considering how fast Avery was. Killian doubled over as one of Avery's punches slipped his defenses and slammed below his sternum. He didn't have time to dwell on the pain and teleported out of hitting range to recover. Only, it didn't last. Because Avery was there, waiting. Killian cursed mentally and bit his tongue when Avery's elbow caught him in the face. Blood trickled down his chin, and pain stung his nose and split lip.

"You hesitated," Avery had said during one of their sessions. "There's no room for hesitation."

Killian swiped the blood from his chin and summoned a dagger. He exhaled slowly, channeling his energy around him, keeping a close eye on Avery. Since breaking his nose, Avery hadn't moved again. His chest heaved with breath as he panted, his face screwed up in anger. His eyes flickered with the blue ring, but he struggled to keep it away.

Killian threw the dagger, and when Avery moved to avoid it, he melted back into the shadows. He summoned another within the shadows and called his energy to it, duplicating it. This one, he slipped in the back of his pants. He jumped out of the darkness in front of Avery and slashed down.

Avery caught his wrist and squeezed it until pain radiated to his elbow. He dropped the weapon, and it thudded to the ground. Avery didn't even struggle as he shoved Killian's back into a tree and pinned him, holding his hand above his head with a deep scowl.

Killian smirked and slipped the second knife from his hiding spot and pressed it against the other's throat, barely catching the flicker of a smile on the corner of Avery's lips. They stood, staring at each other, still and steady as they panted. His heart hammered in his chest, and Avery surged forward, connecting their lips despite the blade cutting into his skin.

Killian froze. His heart stuttered, and his eyes widened as a bolt of electricity danced down his spine. He was sweaty and bloody, but Avery didn't seem to care as he swiped his tongue across Killian's lower lip, pressing closer. Avery's blood dripped onto Killian's hand, and he still didn't know how to move or respond, but his body did.

It was a deep, passionate kiss that tasted like blood and ash, but Killian wouldn't want it any other way. He dropped the dagger, finally able to make his fingers loosen, and grabbed the front of Avery's shirt instead. A long time ago, someone told him kissing was like fire and ice. It was a conversation Killian could barely remember, but he understood it now. Avery was nothing but hard muscle and cold hands as he devoured Killian. This wasn't loving and warm, but his kisses and touches burned, especially where Avery's hand pinned him.

"Be a good boy," Avery's words from what felt like ages ago rang through his head. Avery wasn't soft, sweet, and caring. He didn't know how to be, but that was fine.

Killian wasn't soft and sweet either.

"Where've you been?" Nick asked the moment Killian walked through the door.

He looked up bleary-eyed and still in shock. He didn't know where he had been. All he knew was that he probably wanted to keep kissing Avery, but the bastard fled the second he could. "Um... out," he said. "I wanted to watch the stars." His fingers traveled to his wrist, where he could still feel Avery's fingers burning into his skin.

Nick eyed him carefully. "You need to be asleep. How will you fight Ryan if you're half asleep?" he asked.

Killian forced a smile. He didn't plan on fighting Ryan for long. "I didn't mean to lose track of time. I'm going to bed now."

Nick said nothing as Killian climbed the stairs and disappeared into his room. His heart was still pounding, and he felt incredibly tingly. A lot needed to be discussed, but for now, he would pretend it never happened. Once he got Ryan back, he would deal with Avery.

The next morning came too fast. Killian was still sore from his late-night spar, but he tried not to let it show as he trudged downstairs. Justin and Nick promised to take them into the city to enact their plan, and Killian could feel the energy twisting through the air.

Everyone was nervous about this. No one knew how this would work out or even be worth it.

What if someone died, and he couldn't even bring Ryan home? He leaned on the stair rail for support and took a deep breath. Kara or Tory could be killed in this ridiculous pursuit of his, and he could still fail.

"Killian?" Kara's soft voice startled him out of his thoughts.

He looked up, trying to look less petrified than he was. "I'm sorry. I thought you were down there," he said, gesturing to the living room.

She smiled, took a few steps down, and put a hand on his back. "Don't be nervous," she said.

That wasn't true, but he forced a smile anyway. They were doing this because he asked. If they died, it would be his fault. It wasn't like he didn't already have blood on his hands, but if he were the reason *she* died. Killian flinched.

"I know," he said. If he didn't lose his cool, maybe no one else would. "We're just getting Ryan and then leaving."

Kara smiled back, and they descended into the living room together.

Killian tried not to stress as he looked at Justin and Nick's stoic faces. He almost offered to back out, but Ryan needed them. If anything else were on the line, he wouldn't worry. It wasn't like this was about a stranger or someone he disliked. It was Ryan, and he knew if their positions were switched, Ryan would come for him until he was dead.

Justin nodded and looked at them. "Are we ready?" he asked.

No. Killian forced himself to hum in agreement, hoping he didn't throw up with the act. Everyone else was just as down and out about it. Tory was the only one who managed to give a word of affirmation.

Cody rushed into the living room, panting. Dark circles hung under his eyes, and he held out small black boxes. "I finished them," he said. "To keep in contact. I can pull up city maps and track the soldier's movements." He held the boxes out with a triumphant grin.

Kara beamed and looked over the cubes. "That's amazing! It's like a cellphone," she said.

Cody's cheeks went pink, and he shrugged shyly. "I mean, not really. You can only talk to me because I haven't figured out the final component."

Killian took the box with his mark of power painted on top and smirked. "Good job," he whispered. He imagined Cody without his dad or uncle, and his heart squeezed again. If he was the reason Justin or Nick died, would Cody still smile at him like that? Or would it turn to resentment because of what happened?

Killian swallowed thickly and tried not to focus on it. "How do we use them?" he asked.

Cody passed out the boxes and showed them how to attach them to their inner ears. He left out the part about the tiny shock as the communicator's claws dug into the sensitive skin and attuned to the holder's energy.

Tory yelped in pain and surprise when he pressed the tiny dot to his tragus, and it shocked him. "Thanks for the warning," he said, narrowing his eyes.

Cody hunched his shoulders apologetically. "Sorry."

Kara ruffled his hair and smirked. "Don't let him be grumpy. He's just stressed," she said.

They all were, and Killian was surprised she was handling it as well as she was.

"You can talk to me directly," Cody said, explaining the process. "I can tell you when someone is in danger. I've developed software to keep me updated on your body and the stress put on it."

Justin blinked in surprise as he felt along the edges of the box put in his hands. "I'm impressed," he said. His voice was soft.

Cody beamed at the praise but didn't say anything. It was endearing how nonchalant he tried to be about it despite being excited to have earned his dad's praise.

"There's only one thing about keeping track of your body functions," Cody said, fidgeting. "You've got to stay in your Descendant's disguises. It allows my system to track your energy consumption and magikal trace."

Justin chuckled and nodded. "As if I would let anyone fight a war without their most trusted sources of defense. There is no question whether we would be civilians or Descendants."

That was news to Killian. He hadn't planned on using his disguise, but then he supposed it wasn't a horrible idea. It offered more protection and kept a crowd from pinpointing him.

"We're changing?" Kara asked, voicing his confusion.

Justin chuckled and nodded. "If you don't, I'm not letting you go. If this plan works and we manage to break Angel's control, you don't want people to know who you are."

She still looked confused but didn't ask.

Killian wanted to know what Justin was anticipating happening after this.

"Are we ready?" Nick asked. I want to get this over with." His face looked a bit green, and his voice wobbled. For someone who had seen war, he seemed the most nervous.

Justin sighed and nodded. "Very well. Suit up, little Descendants. Let's see what Angel has in store today."

Killian's stomach turned, and he suddenly felt how Nick looked. They could do this. *We have to.*

I Am Afraid

KARA

Cody passed around the devices, and Justin pulled him aside. She prayed he wasn't saying his goodbyes. She looked around at Tory and Nick, who huddled close and whispered amongst each other. Killian stood off the side, his eyes dark and lost in his thoughts. They hadn't even gotten to the fighting yet, and everyone was on edge.

She perked up at the thought of family and bounced on her toes. "I'll be right back," she said, bolting out of the room. Kara fled down the hall and out the front door toward the graves. She had to say her farewells, just in case.

Kara panted and dropped in front of Dawson's headstone, closing her eyes. She pressed her palm to the rock and controlled her breathing. "I'm terrified. I could lose everything, and I'm scared." Her voice was no more than a hushed breath. Her heart throbbed with emotion, and she bit back a few tears. This wasn't the time for emotional weakness. "I don't know if we'll succeed, and I have no clue what awaits me. You know I've never been a fighter," she said. Her throat tightened, and she had to take a minute to gather herself. "Watch over your sister. Watch over me as I failed to do for you," she finished.

A howl in the distance made her look up, and she grinned when the white wolf stepped into the clearing. Its clear blue eyes settled on her, and its tail flicked in agitation.

Kara held out her hand and wiggled her fingers in a beckoning emotion. "I know we can do this," she said. "And I'm not going to let fear stop me."

She wasn't going to let her past control her anymore. What had been done was done. Kara's breathing evened when the wolf pressed its head into her palm. She stroked his fur and ran her hand down its neck and back. It draped its head over her shoulder and sagged against her as if giving her a comforting hug. Kara wrapped her arms around it and breathed in the smell of sap, pine, and winter—a cold, soothing smell that warmed her despite being sharp on her nose.

"I let you go, Dawson. Rest in peace," she whispered.

The wolf yipped in her ear and wiggled out of her hug. It bounded around, yipping and yapping, and then it was gone. Vanished into the trees, leaving a trail of ethereal blue smoke and a low howl.

Kara wiped the tears from her face and smiled. Healing was messy, uncertain, and harsh at times, but it also left her with a new determination – to protect the new family she had built. Kara stood and brushed her pants off, returning to the house. It was just as quiet and tense as it was when she left.

Justin cocked his head to the side when she came into view. "How do you feel?" he asked, as if knowing what she had done.

Kara nodded. "Better. I think I'm ready."

Justin grinned. "Good, then I think it's time we go."

They all donned their disguises, and Kara waited to move until the pain associated with the change vanished. She couldn't figure out why a spell like that caused pain, but she asked Justin once. He said it was a sudden burst of power that her body had to adjust to and assured her it would lessen with time.

Kara recognized Tory's greatsword, blue half-robe, and Killian's white and violet embroidered hooded shirt and dark trousers. Once she knew where to look, she could spot the various daggers and knives hidden on his body. It took her a moment to realize she had never seen Justin or Nicholas in their disguises.

Nicholas was wearing a brown and green suit of armor that clanked when he moved. No weapon or sword was at his side, just the plated metal armor. She imagined it was heavier and noisier than any other disguises, and she couldn't fathom why that would be a good disguise for anyone.

As if reading her mind, Nicholas chuckled and adjusted one of his bracers. "I control metal," he said. She cocked her head to the side. "If I'm wearing it, I can turn it into anything I want," he added, answering the other unspoken question.

Kara pursed her lips in understanding. "Unlimited ammunition." She couldn't hide her admiration.

He nodded. "Might be heavy, clunky, and hot, but I can keep myself well protected."

She frowned. "Are you wearing something under it? Or..." She didn't know how to ask if he used the armor and how naked he was beneath.

Nicholas laughed out loud, finally breaking the tension. "I'm not naked!"

Justin's outfit was simple. A black trench coat and a bow slung across his back. His underclothes were a simple T-shirt and jeans, something modern and comfortable. It didn't look like he even had chainmail.

"How is yours so modern?" Killian asked, gesturing to his arsenal of weapons and armor.

Justin chuckled under his breath. "Comes with experience. You'll learn to adjust with time," he said.

Kara frowned. *Adjust with time?*

He crossed his arms with a slow smirk. "Are we ready to go?" he asked.

Tension filled the room again, and Kara had to breathe past it. With simultaneous nods, Justin flicked his wrist, and the wind billowed around them. It was time.

Justin teleported them to the middle of the city. Everything happened so fast after that Kara couldn't keep track of what was ahead and behind.

Soldiers stood at all sides, aiming their weapons, and prepared to wipe them off the face of the map. They were in front of the school, miles from the tower, but she could see it bearing down over the city—menacing and dark. Once, she saw it as a beacon of hope, so when did it change?

Kara's body stopped responding to her. Everywhere she looked, she saw convulsing, screaming bodies of her classmates and soldiers she murdered almost a year ago. Everything rushed back at once, reminding her of everything she shoved far from her mind to survive. The pain, the agony, the suffering. She didn't want to feel it. She couldn't.

Justin moved faster than she could process. The first gun rounds went off, and a circle of wind, much like a tornado, surrounded them. The bullets were blown off course or stopped as soon as they hit Justin's defenses. The clack-clack-clacking of the machine guns blocked out the sounds of everything else.

Kara's throat constricted, and she stepped back. Her heart hammered, and everything moved in slow motion. There was wind, noise, and misery all around her, but she couldn't hear it over the sound of her heart.

Justin and Nick shouted at each other or maybe at the others, but she couldn't make out what was being said. Tory and Killian were with them for one minute, then they were gone.

Kara shook so badly that her legs would no longer support her. She dropped to her knees, barely registering the rocks and black pavement cutting through the robe. She pressed her palms into the ground, begging her lungs to take a breath. They refused, and the world spun into a mass of color. Something so nauseatingly disastrous that she gagged, trying to keep the bile in her stomach.

Nick was at her side in an instant. He was talking, but she could only see his lips moving. His face was a mix of worry and anxiety. His hand rested on her shoulder, squeezing so tight it might have hurt if she could feel anything.

Kara coughed and spat yellow bile onto the pavement. Her throat and stomach burned as she tried to stop the screaming in her head. Sweat coated her forehead and made her hair stick to the back of her neck. It was hard to breathe, so hard. Sulfur and gunpowder filled the air, choking her.

Justin was over her, waving his brother away as he kneeled. His hands cupped her face, but they weren't soft or warm—just weights against the side of her face, pulling her further into that darkness.

I can't do this. I can't do war. It took her a moment to realize that it wasn't the chaos paralyzing her but fear itself—the fear of the unknown, the fear of pain, and the fear of losing more than what she already had. The world spun, and everyone vanished. She was back in the middle of her bedroom, sitting on the floor like a helpless child.

Dawson jumped on her bed and told a school story. He was so excited, but she couldn't make out the words. The boy was no older than ten, and she wracked her brain for the memory. She couldn't remember what they had been doing at that moment.

Kara reached for him, tears streaming down her face. "Dawson!" she screamed, begging him to look.

The boy kept jumping, flipping, and cackling like a mad child.

"Dawson, please. Look, I'm right here. Look at me," she shouted. Kara shoved herself off the ground but found herself rooted to the spot. "Don't leave me. Look at me." She pounded her fists on the ground.

Then he did. His eyes bore right into hers, and he waved so childishly. "Kara." The way her name sounded as it left his mouth was so innocent, so pure.

Thunder boomed in the distance, and she kneeled in the woods, staring at the blue-eyed wolf. The wolf raised its head and howled at the full moon.

Kara trembled and blinked at the creature. It flicked its tail and met her gaze, its eyes so sky blue she could lose herself.

Dawson's voice resounded in her head: *I'll never leave you. Nothing bad will ever happen because you're my sister.*

The world exploded in burning and screaming. Kara squeezed her eyes shut and slammed her hands over her ears.

Soft hands clutched her wrists and pulled them down, making her look up with wide-wild eyes.

Jess knelt, gazing deeply into her eyes and smiling gently. "Hello, Kara," she whispered.

The city was ravaged behind her. The heavy scent of blood and metal permeated the air, and bile rose in the back of Kara's throat again. It was bitter and didn't help to keep her stomach from dropping.

"It's okay," Jess whispered; her voice cracked. There was a gash above her right eye, and blood leaked down her cheek. Her long lashes were coated with soot and ash. "I've got you."

Kara's lip trembled, and she shook her head. She didn't want to be here—not here, of all places. "I can't fight." Her throat burned with the words. "It hurts so much."

Jess nodded and wrapped her arms around Kara, pulling her to her chest. "You're alright, Little Mouse. I've got you," she said again.

Kara sobbed. She wasn't strong enough. Without magik, she was nothing; with it, she only caused pain. What was the point in having magik if only to make people suffer?

"Change is scary, but we're strong enough to overcome it," Jess said, petting the back of her head. "*You* can overcome this."

"I'm scared," Kara said. "I'm terrified."

"We all are, but you aren't alone. There is something stronger than fear," Jess said, pulling away. She held Kara at arm's length and smiled despite their destruction.

"What could be stronger?" Kara asked, tears streaming.

"Your heart is full of love. Never forget what you're fighting for. That's what makes it different," Jess said.

Kara shook her head and grabbed Jess' hands, pulling them into her lap. "I can't do this. I'm not ready."

Jess brushed her thumb across Kara's cheek and smiled. Her energy was warm and inviting, and Kara wanted to melt into it and never leave. "Trust in love," she whispered.

"I don't even know what it is," Kara cried, squeezing Jess' hand. She felt like an unbelievable baby after agreeing to do this and wanting to back out so quickly.

"It's sitting at someone's side when they do the wrong thing and pushing them in the right direction. It's letting go when you know you can't keep holding on. It's pushing them to be better than what they think they are because you know what is inside," Jess said. She squeezed Kara's hands back, and a tear strayed down her cheek.

Kara gasped, and Justin appeared behind Jess. His dark brown eyes were emotionless, and he raised a sword.

Jess didn't move, and she squeezed Kara's hands tighter. Another tear strayed down her cheek when she next spoke, "Love is knowing you're going to die and doing nothing because it will save them."

The sword came down.

The world swam as she screamed Jess' name, knowing she could do nothing to stop it.

Ryan stood before her, laughing and waving his hands, beckoning to a sky full of stars. "I'll take the darkness for you," he said.

She asked him for help and attacked when he tried. Kara reached out, begging him to take her hand, praying he would see her.

"You've got the right stuff," he said, laughing brightly. "And when you're ready, I'm right here..." his voice faded with the night, and Kara looked up.

Justin watched her carefully, his eyes boring into hers. When the sound returned, she looked around at the chaos. His wall was still in place, and the soldiers shouted back and forth. "Take her back to Haven," Justin said.

Kara shook her head and pushed herself to her feet. She bent and grabbed her fallen staff and took a steadying breath. "No," she said. "I'm not going back while everything happens around me."

Jess knew what would happen if she left Haven that day during the war, and she did it anyway. She knew her sacrifice would save her husband and child, and Kara wouldn't hide in fear. She couldn't cower in terror as others died around her. Not when so many had already perished.

Nick looked hesitant to disobey his brother's orders, but he cocked his head to the side. "Can you do this?" he asked.

"I have to." It was the only acceptable answer. Kara wasn't here because she wanted to be but because she had to.

No one chose war. She would be there because it was her job to protect them. Her stupid, senseless boys that didn't know up from down sometimes. She thought of all the morning breakfasts, training with Killian, reading with Tory until she fell asleep. This was her family, and she wasn't about to lose them again.

Justin looked torn, but he nodded. "If you're sure," he said.

Kara wasn't, but there was a crack of thunder before she could respond.

Justin stood and whirled around as the gunfire ceased. "Rebecca! Long time no see," he said.

Angel's energy flourished around them like violet and purple snakes. "Whatever do you want? I was told some rats were running around," she said.

Kara stood her ground and took another few breaths. This was it. The moment when she proved she was worth something, with or without magik.

Justin pulled his bow off his back. "Nick, I'll need you to be my eyes," he said.

Nick clapped his hands and steeled his features. "Like the good ol' days. Kara, keep those shields up," he said.

Kara whimpered and held her staff out, trying to appear confident. She looked toward where Killian and Tory had been. This hadn't been part of the plan. Tory and Nicholas were supposed to fight the soldiers, but now they had Angel and her army.

Justin set a hand on her head. "I believe in you," his words were whispered, something only for her.

Angel let out a frustrated shout, and a wave of energy flew at them. "This ends now!" she screamed.

Kara narrowed her gaze. For once, she agreed.

Justin sent Angel's energy back at her with a few whispered words in Nivet.

Kara hadn't considered using another language to say spells; this was the first time she had seen Justin speak a spell to life. She stayed in the background, trying to keep her eyes on Nicholas and Justin as they danced an intricate dance around her. It was one they knew well despite not having done it in years.

Hang on, Ryan, we're coming.

Brother vs Brother

Killian was disoriented when Justin teleported him. He hadn't expected a trap, but knowing Avery was in league with Angel, he shouldn't have been surprised. Killian wiped his thoughts away and focused.

"Ah Helwe, why are we together?" Tory's voice startled him.

He jumped and whirled around to face him. "What are you doing here?"

"I don't know." Tory looked toward the school with a frown. "It doesn't matter. Let's get Ryan, and then I'll find the others," he said, making up his mind.

Killian wasn't sure he needed help, but he wasn't opposed to the idea when a massive explosion caused a building to his left to collapse in a fiery mess of brick, steel, and glass.

Tory pointed at a shadowy figure emerging from the smoke of the rubble. "How much you wanna bet that's your brother?"

The figure walking toward them wasn't the brother he knew. This one was cold, devoid of emotion. Their link was blocked, and this being wanted blood and death. *Screw me.* "Run," he said, taking off before Tory could react.

"Wait, what? Why are we running?"

Killian ran without a response. There's no way he was sticking around to let Ryan use him as a punching bag again. They needed a plan and a friggin' good one at that. *He's going to kill us and then probably laugh about it over dinner later.*

"What's the plan?" Tory shouted, hot on his heels.

"Don't get hit." Killian turned a sharp corner and jumped into a shadow cast by the wall. Tory shouted something to his left, but Killian couldn't quite make it out over the roar of another crumbling building.

Ryan rounded the corner as a red blur, and Killian jumped out of the shadow behind him. He threw two daggers and reached for his chain scythe, but his brother whirled around and slammed the hilt of his sword into Killian's stomach as if reading his moves before he made them.

Killian grabbed his middle, gasping for breath. A water ball smacked Ryan in the back of the head, and he turned, baring his teeth like a wild animal.

"Keep moving, stop trying to ambush, you suck!" Tory shouted before taking off again.

Killian grunted in reply and ducked under Ryan's blade swipe. At least his brother was set on him, so that made distracting him easy enough.

"What do you suggest we do?" Killian snapped, summoning a sword and deflecting one of Ryan's blows.

Tory wracked his brain and smiled, "I know a place." He grabbed Killian's bicep, whipped around another corner, and headed deeper into the district.

"Where are we going?" Killian asked.

A blast of fire whizzed overhead, and Killian jumped, trying to avoid getting hit and smashing into Tory's back, taking them both to the ground. They slammed into the concrete, grunting and groaning.

"You could have said duck," Tory yelled. "Duck would have worked so much better."

"Roll!" Killian rolled one way, and Tory went the other. Ryan landed in between them and his sword stuck into the concrete. "Keep going," Killian hissed, jumping to his feet.

Tory was already halfway down the block. "We can't keep this up. He's too fast," Tory shouted.

"What do you want me to do? Turn around and take him head-on?" Killian asked.

Tory huffed and turned. He tossed the water bottle on the ground on his hip and waved his hand over it. "Water, heed your master's call: freeze."

A sheet of white ice covered the top of the sidewalk, and Killian smirked. "Nice."

It melted two seconds later.

Tory nodded. "Ice, Descendant of Fire. That was a little bit of an oversight, but now that it's out there, we can avoid it."

"Weren't you the one saying we can't run forever?" Killian asked as they resumed running.

Tory pursed his lips and pulled him around a corner. "Change of plan."

Killian opened his mouth to ask what the original plan was when another flaming ball of fire tore past them. "We'll take him together," he said, praying they could figure it out. Killian grumbled to himself and followed Tory to the burned-out worship building. "Oh, you've got to be kidding. This place is going to fall on top of us."

"If it does, run. It might crush him."

"I don't want to crush my brother," Killian said frustratedly.

"Shut up and get in there." Tory shoved him inside, and they looked around.

Shattered windows, boarded-up holes in the floor, and a caved-in roof. Yeah, Killian wanted to leave. Immediately. Ryan stopped in the doorway before he could make an exit.

"Hey Ryan, good to see you," Killian said, forcing a smile. "Wanna let me through? We'll keep running." He didn't know realistically how long they could keep the game up, but it was better than being killed under rotten wood and broken glass.

Ryan thrust one of the swords forward, and Killian jumped back. It cut across the back of his arm, but his adrenaline was running too hot to feel it. "You're done running," Ryan said, his voice darker than anything Killian had ever heard.

"You don't wanna fight," Killian said, trying to buy them time.

Tory drew his own weapon and moved carefully around them. At least one of them was ready to fight.

Ryan charged, and Killian vanished into one of the shadows. Tory brought his weapon up and deflected Ryan's blow, making it look easy. Sparks shot off their swords, and Tory used the ice to slide out of the way when fire blasted from Ryan's palm. He barely managed to avoid it.

The light tore through the shadows, taking away any advantage Killian might've had. Killian let the shadow inside envelop him in its strength and narrowed his eyes. He was strong enough to do this, but that didn't mean he wanted to. "Come with us," he said. Killian would do anything to avoid a confrontation like this.

Ryan vanished in a blur of red, and Killian cursed under his breath. He summoned a set of daggers and held them up, sensing Ryan's moves before he made them. They did this enough times for him to know what his brother's first moves would be.

Killian was a Descendant of Shadow. He took Avery's advice to heart and closed his eyes. His home was in the darkness. What scared normal people didn't affect him. Ryan's energy tore through the air and headed straight for him. *I am the darkness.* Killian opened his eyes, and energy tore from his body. The shadows in the room trembled as the one within roared angrily. *I have years of magik in my blood. Let the generations of the past guide my hand.* Killian raised his weapons, and Ryan clashed against him with such force that it pushed him across the ground. "Mother darkness rise and fall, capture my enemies in your claws: strike of darkness."

I will not be brought down by the one person I strove to protect—by the one who protected me. A purple beam shot from Killian's shadow on the ground and struck Ryan in the side. Blood flew, and a part of the roof caved in as the beam tore through one of the burned-out rafters.

When they were children, Ryan had been bullied relentlessly. Killian always fought for Ryan and always would, but first, he had to remind Ryan how to fight for himself. No white knight was coming to rescue them. They had to do this themselves. Ryan stopped moving and pressed a hand to the fresh wound, confusion clouding his features. The emotion passed almost as quickly as it came, allowing Tory to move in. He threw his arms around Ryan and locked him in a headlock.

Killian surged forward, his hands shaking as he fought to help, pin Ryan to the ground. Black fire crawled up Ryan's arms and chest, and Killian hissed in pain, jerking away. Tory called forth a stream of water to try to extinguish the flames, but his water passed through as if Ryan's magik was invulnerable. Tory growled and pushed away when the fire hit his arm, licking his wrist. His water surrounded him in a raging ribbon of anger and energy.

My brother can call magik to life without a single word. His blood is my blood. I can, too. Killian didn't let up. He drove the sword forward and stabbed Ryan in the leg before his brother propelled himself back with a blast of fire from his palms. *There is no room for hesitation.* Killian shouted his shield spell before fully processing what was happening, "Mother darkness, grant me your protection: barrier."

The fire passed by without harming him, and Ryan came next, diving through the flames like a phoenix, bearing down with both swords. Killian pressed his hand to the bloody cut on his arm. "Weapon summoning." He called forth two violet daggers and held them before him like an X.

The sword ran through the top of the X the minute he let the shield down, and Killian pushed it up and away from his body. Ryan stumbled, and Killian turned, elbowing him in the stomach. When his brother doubled over, he slammed the palm of his hand into Ryan's nose with a sickening crunch. Blood spurted from the broken nose, and Ryan grabbed the front of Killian's shirt.

Tory created a clone of water and sent it after Ryan before he could rearrange Killian's face. The clone sent its sword flying at Ryan, and he was forced to let Killian go, to turn and swat the great sword out of the air like it was a bug.

Tory froze the floor, and Killian fell when his foot hit it wrong. "Crap, my bad, sorry."

Killian rubbed the back of his head with a wince and yelped when Ryan stabbed his sword into his shoulder.

"Can we not freeze the things I'm walking on?" Killian asked, throwing his body into a backward somersault and ripping the sword free.

"How's he getting through the chainmail?" Tory asked.

"I don't know!" It wasn't at the forefront of Killian's mind. He was more pissed that Ryan was besting both without breaking a sweat.

The floor unfroze, and Killian stood, parrying another of his brother's blows. It took a few more minutes, but eventually, Killian and Tory fell into sync. Tory chose to fight between his clone and himself. At any given time, Ryan didn't know who he was fighting, and it was nice to know Tory was more capable of avoiding the big hits.

"Torrents of water fall to the ground, tsunami." Tory switched places with the clone and waved his hand. The drops of water froze, and he sent them spiraling towards Ryan. Ryan lifted his swords and cut the ice before they could reach him. Ice fell in tiny shards at his feet. "Water rise: complete control," Tory shouted, jumping away from one of Ryan's blades.

The ice melted and twisted around Ryan like a chain. *Another opening.* Killian surged forward and threw another dagger hidden in one of the sheaths on his wrists. It cut across Ryan's cheek, drawing a thin line of blood.

Ryan didn't slow down.

Killian stepped to the side too late, and Ryan's fist slammed into his sternum. "Shit." Killian coughed up blood and spat it on the ground, drawing in shaky breaths as his lungs screamed for air.

Ryan pushed him clear across the building, the furthest from the door. Even if they wanted to run at this point, there was no exit. Killian raised his sword to deflect another blow, but Ryan changed course at the last minute. The blade tore through his shirt. That's where it should have ended, but it didn't. It cut across his chest like the mail wasn't even there. He hissed in pain and backed off, dropping his weapons. He watched Ryan's energy snake and twist around him. It took Killian too long to figure out how his brother made it through the chain mail.

"Energy," he whispered. Justin attacked in similar ways, using his energy as a weapon.

Pain wracked Killian's body and limited his movements. He could do this, but he needed to calm his mind. A sudden breeze caught his attention, and he ducked as a dagger whizzed overhead. Ryan could feel his struggle. He was going to take every chance he could to take Killian out.

"Come to me weapons of night: summoning." He would use the last of his energy in one last attack. Killian grabbed two of the six floating daggers and dropped the sword. He never liked long blades, anyway.

Ryan stared curiously as Killian took an offensive stance. His feet set closer together, and he leaned forward, waiting for his opportunity to strike. Ryan's breath hitched, and he took a single step back. *Now.*

Killian flew forward, throwing one of the daggers and grabbing another from the air. He slashed out when Ryan ducked to avoid the projectile. There was no way Ryan could dodge. The blades cut through the fabric on his chest, and Killian let a burst of energy fly from his weapons in a horizontal slash. While his blade stopped at the chain mail, the energy didn't.

Ryan stepped back in shock as blood spurted from the wound on his chest. His eyes widened in surprise, and Killian smirked, dropping to a knee. He figured it out – the secret to Ryan's attacks. Too bad he didn't do that ten minutes ago.

Fear flashed across Ryan's face, and he stepped back.

Killian cussed loudly just as his brother fled the scene. "No!" he forced himself off the ground and took off after him.

Ryan's ethereal energy trail was dim, but Killian could keep it. He could see it through the city's twisting streets, and he wasn't going to let Ryan escape. Tory shouted after him, but Killian barely heard. He flickered in and out of shadows, keeping his eyes on Ryan's trail. The sounds of battle passed, but he kept his attention ahead.

Killian stopped at the edge of the watering hole. Ryan used to take him here to train because it was the purest place in the city. It was the only place Angel's chaos didn't touch, and while he didn't have a name for it before, now he understood why they enjoyed sitting by the water.

It was calming. The pressure of the city left his thoughts, and as soon as he was out of the chaos, he could breathe. Ryan stood in the middle of the water. It came up to his chest, but he didn't flinch. The water flowed red around him, and he had dropped his Descendant's disguise.

Killian hesitated. Avery had warned him of the water, hadn't he? As much as Killian wanted to listen, he didn't. Avery betrayed him and did it again when he told Angel they were coming. It was probably another lie. He took a few steps forward and stopped at the water's edge. "Come home with me," he said.

Ryan didn't respond. He stared blankly at Killian, letting the water rise and fall around him. He took a step forward, and cold water flooded his boot. An ear-piercing crack thundered through the air, and a wall fell around the water. Killian lurched forward, splashing as he dove in to avoid the electrical black edge of a wall.

He stared angrily at a man clothed in a silver suit and mask as he appeared above them, clutching a metal rod. His face was a mix of indignation and pure amusement. Storm clouds blew over the city, and thunder roared. The wind whipped Killian's clothes and ruffled Ryan's hair, but his brother didn't move.

"The water is where the bad thing will happen," Avery had said.

"This is where your journey ends! The moment you draw your brother's blood, you'll be a slave to Lord Malsumis," the man called, shouting over the howling wind.

Killian didn't know what any of that meant. He clenched his jaw and forced his energy to level out. "I won't be a pawn!"

"Or, you can always let him draw your blood, and he can become the pawn," the man said, smiling cruelly.

The moment one of them attacked the other, this game was over. Killian stared in horror. He was forced to choose whether he or Ryan lived under someone else's control. He clenched his hands at his sides and held his breath. *Me.* It had to be him. He couldn't ask Ryan to suffer anymore.

"Oh, I love that look—the one of contempt and realization." The man practically swooned at Killian's abject horror.

Ryan didn't move. It was like he wasn't there.

Killian shivered in the freezing water and lightning cracked. "I draw his blood, and this Malsumis does what?" he asked, trying to sound confident.

The man grinned wickedly. His skin stretched too far across his thin face like a mask. "Lord Malsumis uses your body to bring the world anew," he said.

Killian would become the evil one. Considering his actions in the city, he supposed it wouldn't be the worst thing in the world. "I've already drawn his blood," he growled.

The man shook his head. "In the water. The blood must spill into the water. You have ten seconds to comply, or I'll choose for you," he said.

Killian chewed his tongue. It wouldn't be a hard choice if he weren't sure Ryan would be freed. There wasn't much time to review his options, so he hesitated and pulled a dagger from his boot. His brother wouldn't forgive him for sacrificing himself. Ryan would lose it if he ever found out what happened.

"Time's up." The man had barely finished speaking when Ryan moved.

He held his sword and charged for Killian, raising the weapon above his head.

Killian gripped the dagger and dove underwater, trying to stay out of Ryan's range. The blade cut through the water and missed him by a hair. Killian surfaced behind his brother and dropped the dagger when a flash of fire boiled the water. He screamed in pain and struggled to get out of range.

Ryan's hand whipped out and caught Killian by the wrist. He kept him from retreating too far, and Killian hissed, unable to find a good position to escape the heat. It scalded and blistered his skin, so he barely registered when Ryan brought his sword up and then down,

"Stop!" Avery's voice stopped everything.

The boiling water went lukewarm, and Killian nearly went limp from relief. Tears streaked his cheeks, but he stubbornly refused to cry out loud.

Ryan turned to stare.

Avery broke through the man's wall and stood before them, staring Ryan down. "You're better than this. Ryan, you have to stop," Avery said. His voice broke when he spoke, and he didn't dare move toward them. "I taught you how to do this, how to break free," he whispered.

Killian winced and tried to control his breathing. The only way out was to make Ryan bleed. If he did, he could free him from Angel and be the only one anyone had to manage. He was untrained and had yet to reach his full potential. He would be easy to contain.

"I know what to do," Killian whispered, bringing his dagger up. It was the only thing to do. Avery moved to stop him, but Ryan was faster.

Killian had barely moved when Ryan stuck his sword through Killian's arm. The pain was immediate. It seared down his arm, making him scream. He blacked out for a moment. The pain was so intense that he could have thrown up.

Avery grabbed the back of Ryan's shirt and ripped him away, and the sword came with it.

Killian's hand went numb, and he groaned, sinking into the water, unable to keep himself upright. The moment blood hit the water, everything went still. The man running the show laughed victoriously and chanted a spell in a language Killian didn't recognize. His head was underwater for two seconds when Avery pulled him up, clutching the wound on his arm to staunch the blood flow.

"Hold on," he whispered, throwing Killian's arm over his shoulders. Killian's vision swam, and he tried to force air into his lungs, but his arm burned. The white-hot pain couldn't even be cooled by the water. "Hold on," Avery said again.

Killian didn't know what he was holding onto. They moved through the water, and Avery dragged him onto the shore like a sack of potatoes. Blood streamed through his fingers from the laceration he tried to hold together.

The water in the hole turned black, and Killian looked up with bleary eyes. He failed.

Killian wanted to throw up. He hissed in pain when Avery squeezed his arm tighter, reminding him he was still alive. "Gotta get Ryan," he whispered, finding his energy all but gone.

Avery shook his head and pulled him to his chest. "Too late," he said. "I have to get you to Justin so he can stop the bleedin'."

"That man said something about control." Killian found it challenging to keep his eyes open.

"Don't worry; I'll figure it out," Avery promised. "I need you to work with me. We've got to get you to Justin."

Killian's legs wouldn't work. His energy was spent, and he lost more blood than any human should. "Ryan," he murmured.

Ryan was suspended in the air like a doll on strings, and blood dripped into the water below. Everything was still and silent, and then, with a burst of white light, the world roared to life with energies Killian had never seen. *Ryan.* He let the darkness take him.

Killian woke in a black abyss surrounded by stars. It was the night sky—beautiful and untouchable. He held his hand out, and the stars turned to glitter in his palm, sliding through his fingers like water.

"I thought you might like it here," Ryan said.

Killian jumped and turned to face him. His heart raced as he stared wide-eyed at his brother.

Ryan held out his hands and shook his head. "It's just us like always," he said.

"Am I dead?" he asked.

"Not yet," Ryan's voice flashed in amusement.

"Are you?" Killian asked.

Ryan chuckled and shook his head. "Not yet."

Killian didn't understand. "Purgatory then?"

"Nah, you're not there. Trying though. I thought I'd reach you here, try to keep you with me," Ryan said.

Killian whirled around and felt his heart thudding in his ears. He didn't want to be here. There was a battle to fight and win. He stopped spinning and faced Ryan again. "Are you real?" he asked.

"Yeah, at least what's left of me. I think I'm fading," he said.

"Fading to what?" Killian asked. He didn't mean to keep asking, but he was concerned. Plus, he had no clue what was happening. Seconds ago, he had been with Avery.

Ryan shrugged. "Oblivion," he said casually, like it was no big deal.

Killian took a step toward him. There was no pain, just calm. "What now? Malsuims?" he asked.

Ryan smiled sadly. "I heard you. I don't know how, but I did. You were going to let him take you, and I couldn't allow that," he said. His voice sounded too loud in the silent space.

"You can't do this. You have to stay with me," Killian whispered.

They were quiet but had an entire conversation with sight alone. Killian wanted to stay and tell Ryan how hard he had tried. He worked with everyone, let Avery train him, and even asked Avery for help. He did everything right, but they were still apart.

"I'll be with you again, I'm sure. Don't stop fighting for what's important. I need you to stay strong just a little longer," Ryan said.

"I'm a failure," Killian whispered.

Ryan shook his head and threw his arms around him. Crushing Killian in a bone-breaking hug. "Never. I failed you, and for that, *I'm* sorry."

Killian returned the hug and squeezed his eyes shut. He could stay forever. They could live their lives out in a dream. Cross to the next life together.

"I need you to wake up, Kill. You can't die," Ryan whispered. "Please, keep fighting. You have no idea what that will do to me." So it was nothing but a selfish request.

Killian didn't want to be needed. "We're not supposed to save the world. It's supposed to be us."

"Gotta grow up sometime, don't we?" Ryan asked, forcing a smile.

Killian sighed in frustration and ran a hand through his hair. "I'm scared, Ryan."

His brother laughed—a natural, booming laugh—one Killian hadn't heard in years. "Yeah, me too. I'm terrified," Ryan said.

"Then what do we do?" Killian's voice cracked slightly, and he tried to cover it with a cough.

Ryan shook his head and stepped back. "Keep fighting the monsters under our beds."

Killian reached out but was stopped by an invisible wall. "Don't leave."

"Never. Wake up, Kill. For me, wake up." Ryan waved and turned to leave.

Killian opened his mouth to call his name, but the world slowly dissipated in a flourish of stars and lights. He plummeted down when the world fell from beneath him.

The World Falls Down

ANGEL

Justin intervened, as always, because he didn't know how to do anything different. He sent the brown-haired Descendant and the other twin far from her reach and made a point to ensure she knew it was him. His sightless eyes cut through her like glass, and she could feel the rage building within his lithe frame. *Bring it.* She wasn't going to lose to him.

"Nick, make me proud," Justin said, smirking as Angel's eyes sought him out.

She summoned an ice spear and shrieked in frustration, charging. A burst of wind surrounded her, wrapping her in icy claws, and rain and ice mixed in the brewing storm of her creation.

Nick threw himself in front of his brother, raising his hands. The earth rumbled, and a wall appeared before him, cutting off her path. Angel thrust her spear forward, putting all her energy into the tip, and shattered his defenses like mud.

Rock and dirt cascaded through the air like a waterfall, showering them with a musty scent. Vines shot from the hole the wall left behind and wrapped around her wrists and ankles, keeping her still in the air.

One of Nick's bracers melted, and he crafted a dagger, thrusting it forward.

Angel threw her head back and laughed as the fire ate through his vines, snapping them in seconds and allowing her to parry. She knocked the dagger away and slammed the butt of the spear into Nick's stomach as the little energy brat took a spot behind Justin.

Avery was gone. Ryan was dealing with his brother. He would lead Killian to Havoc, where they could call Lord Malsumis to the world and end it all. Then, she would join them, but she had to keep Justin here so he couldn't undo the spells. The minute he interfered, he could end their journey.

Angel flicked her wrist and sent Nick flying with a burst of wind, but two arrows whizzed by her ear. She held her breath and whirled to face Justin as he drew back on a bow and aimed for her. As a young man, he had been a perfect shot, but he shouldn't be able to see her now. She narrowed her eyes as an energy arrow formed on the string, and he let it fly. Red strands of hair drifted to the concrete as she ducked under his third shot.

Nick came flying at her from the side, and she shot into the air, waving the spear down and creating sharp icicles where he stood. He threw himself into a somersault and got out of the way before his armor could be impaled. Every movement drew a horrible clanking and grinding from all the gear he wore, but he would be left with nothing if he chose to fight with it.

Angel snapped her fingers and whispered a fire spell she had yet to use. An arrow graced her shoulder, and she hissed in pain, losing her focus. The spell died on her lips, and the energy dissipated.

Kara threw a shield around Justin when Angel's energy swarmed him like angry snakes. *That brat needs to go.* Angel surveyed the city from the sky, watching it burn. She didn't see the twins, and Havoc sent no word of them having arrived yet, but she also couldn't sense Avery. *It's possible that after he sent her a message about their arrival, he decided to stay out of it.*

A building cracked to her left, and she turned her head as the glass and steel structure toppled toward her. Nick stood at the base, bending and twisting the formation to avalanche in her direction. She sped toward the ground and thrust her spear into the concrete with a thunderous crack. Fire rose through the cracks and spit into the air, hissing like an angry demon from Helwe.

Nick charged the minute she touched down, but when a wave of fire consumed him, he threw his arms up with a pained shout. The fire roared wildly before burning itself out, and Angel smirked as smoke clogged the sky.

Her eyes widened when Nick burst from the putrid smoke, wielding a sword with both hands. *No way.* Angel held up her spear, barely blocking the first blow. She ducked under the second, and Nick's foot planted in her stomach. She gasped in pain, spit flying from her mouth and trickling down her chin. Angel dropped, clutching her abdomen and groaning. It had been a while since she had been challenged like this.

Nick brought his sword down, but she snapped her fingers and shouted a spell she had learned from Summer. Wind as sharp as blades surrounded him, and he turned his back where most of the armor still resided to escape.

Justin whistled, and the wind vanished before it could get started. "Don't try to use my magik against us, Rebecca! I won't let you hurt my brother."

She turned her steel blue gaze to the meddler and snarled in rage. *Keep them busy. Don't let them know the plan.* She couldn't manage the three Descendants alone.

"The boys are coming. It won't be long," Havoc whispered through her head as if sensing her distress.

Angel smirked and wiped the spit from her chin, standing to her full height. Before Nick could gather himself, she flicked her wrist, and he was sent flying into the furthest building she could reach.

Kara yelped in shock, and Angel withdrew a dagger from a sheath on her thigh and threw it at the brat.

Justin pushed her aside, and a gust of wind whipped the knife away. He said something that made the dark-haired girl nod and grip her staff tighter.

Come on, Havoc. Do your part and finish this. Angel floated above the ground, holding her spear before her protectively. She wasted too much energy already; if she had any hope of finishing the summoning spell, she would need to end this now.

She breathed and steadied her nerves as she and Justin faced down. This was it. The time for her to make her mark on this world was now; soon, it would all be for something.

Her Final Revenge

Kara winced when Nicholas ended up inside the side of a building for the third time. Thankfully, he had thick armor, but it quickly got dinged and dented. The man wasn't careful, nor was he observational. He was so focused on ensuring Justin was fine that he ignored his own weak points. Kara tried to fill those in for him, but every time he took a massive hit, she squeaked and covered her face with her hands.

"Don't worry, Little Mouse. Nick has never been good with close-range fighting. He isn't getting injured," Justin said, trying to keep her focused.

Kara nodded and nibbled her lip. She was trying to do her best for all of them. With Tory and Killian gone, Justin had to focus on keeping the army and Angel at bay. She hoped the boys would finish quickly so they could all go home.

"Nick, I believe you're straining the Mouse unnecessarily. Will you get it together?" Justin asked, reading her energy. He stepped in front of Kara and redirected Angel's fire blast into the nearest building.

Rubble flew through the air, blasting a chunk of the structure to smithereens. Kara jumped and looked for Nicholas. He managed to vanish the moment Justin called him out.

Angel had an odd combination of abilities. Kara had yet to ask Justin how she controlled so many things, but she realized she knew nothing about chaos. Maybe it was a perk for them or something.

"Sweetie, step to the right," Justin said, pulling the bow off his back.

Kara didn't hesitate. Angel's spear struck the ground where she had been two seconds earlier. A high-pitched whine left Kara's throat before she could stop it.

Justin ruffled her hair after firing off three arrows. "Don't stress. I've got you," he said.

Kara's heart raced. She was as safe as she could be, so there was nothing to worry about, right? Justin wouldn't let her die.

Nicholas took off his bracers and turned them into swords. Anytime he tried to get close to Angel, she forced him back with her energy, wind, or fire. He didn't make much progress, but he was a good decoy.

Justin fired a couple of arrows, but he also didn't manage to strike her. Angel was evading their attacks, but her face was screwed up in exhaustion. At least she was feeling something, it made Kara feel a little better about the wave of fatigue that washed over her. Kara threw a shield around Nicholas right before Angel could stab him in the neck. The spear rebounded off her shield, but Kara prepared so the pain was minimal. It spiked through her heart, but Kara took a breath, and the pain was gone.

Justin fired another arrow at Angel, and she whirled around to face him with a growl. "You're pushing your luck with me," she said.

Justin smirked. He cocked his head to the side to listen and make sure he wasn't going to get hit.

Despite the chaos hindering his sight, Kara couldn't believe how agile and accurate he was. It would've been amazing to see him in action before he had been blinded. He was probably unstoppable.

"Little Mouse, can you stop daydreaming?" Justin asked, catching the end of Angel's spear in the side. He jumped away and flicked his wrist, blasting the woman back with a wind jet.

Kara held up her staff and chanted one of the only offensive spells she knew. A downpour of lightning struck the ground in multiple places, but she managed to keep the bolts from hitting anyone important. Thankfully, the citizens had been evacuated somewhere out of the way. It seemed out of character for Angel to do, but Kara wasn't going to question it.

Tory appeared next to her, and she clutched her chest, trying not to scream. "Sorry," he set a hand on her shoulder. "I lost Killian and Ryan."

Kara groaned. "How do you lose two people?" she asked.

Tory rubbed the back of his neck. "Ryan kicked our asses. When Killian managed to draw blood, he took off. I was in the middle of getting out from under a fallen beam."

Justin paled and turned his attention west. His nostrils flared, and he stepped away, throwing a shield around them for Angel to beat at. "I need to go. Nick! Your boy toy's gonna back you up," Justin shouted. He turned and set a hand on Tory's shoulder. "I am proud of you," he said.

Kara grabbed the end of his coat before he could leave. "Wait, where are you going?" she asked. "We should stay together."

He smiled and pulled away. "I'll be back, don't worry," he said, his voice soft but uncertain.

She chewed her lip as he teleported away without another word. She wasn't sure she could bear it if something happened to him.

"Find him," Tory said, going after Nicholas and Angel. "I'll manage here."

Kara nodded and bowed her head gratefully. Without Justin's wind barriers to keep the soldiers at bay, it would be up to Tory and

Nicholas to do so. She focused on a single point in her mind and held out her staff. "Mother of the light, guide me to my destination: teleport," she whispered.

A blinding white light surrounded her, and then she was at the tower. It was the only place she could think Justin would go because it was Angel's headquarters. When she didn't see him, Kara frowned. She tried to channel her energy to change her vision so she could search for him there, but a deep voice made her stop.

There was shouting and the clacking of metal and weaponry. Soldiers poured from the tower and marched through the streets, calling out locations and orders.

This was the base of operations, which meant she stepped right into the middle of Angel's plan, whatever it may be.

"Intruder, take her down!"

Kara yelped and raised her hands. This was probably not the best idea, but her panicked brain didn't allow her to think of much else.

"Kara, get down." Strong hands grabbed her and pulled her to the ground.

She shrieked in surprise when a barrage of bullets fired across the top of her head. She wriggled in the stranger's hold until a black shell fell around them.

Avery let her go and jumped to his feet, backing away. "I'm sorry, I'm sorry. Don't attack me," he said. His eyes were wide and terrified, but he didn't look scared of her.

Kara stared, mouthing silent words, and then looked around.

Bullets ricocheted off the shield, and Avery clutched his chest, panting. He was splashed with blood and minor cuts, but he didn't look like he was in immediate danger. Aside from killing himself because of the shields and gun.

"Are you a moron? Put it down," she cried, pulling on his clothes. "This is too much." She didn't even know he was going to be here.

When she mentioned it to Killian, he said Avery wouldn't come and got all grumpy with her. Now, Avery was here and about to die.

"Well, let me know when you've got a plan. I told Cody I'd come to help you in exchange for helpin' Killian," Avery hissed through clenched teeth.

"Why did Killian need help?" Kara snapped, pounding on his back. "Please, put the shield down."

Another wave of bullets slammed into the shield, and Kara did only what she could think of. She threw her energy into Avery's body, hoping it would help him withstand the barrage. When his breathing evened out a little, she calmed. Her heart raced, and she tried to think.

She wasn't much of a strategist, but there was no time like now. "There has to be something we can do," she whispered. "Can't you teleport us?"

Avery smirked and grabbed her hand. "Absolutely. I just needed your permission," he said.

Kara recently read a book about a creature called a vampire. It required permission to enter someone's home; sometimes, Avery reminded her of that creature. He didn't drink blood, to her knowledge, but he was as mysterious and deadly. She slipped her hand into his, and Avery whisked them away.

She looked around, catching her breath as he dropped to a knee.

"Sir, we must retreat," a soldier said. The voice carried down the alley, and Kara looked around. They were behind the tower somewhere.

Shadows draped across them like robes, and Kara shook out her hands, taking a few steps. Avery wheezed behind her, but there wasn't anything she could do to help him. He had to regain energy and pray he didn't do internal damage. Angel's General walked around the corner with two soldiers flanking him.

She froze.

He froze.

No one expected anyone else to be there, and Kara's fingers twitched at her side. There's no way this man was before her. She came to the tower to find Justin, and instead, she was faced with the man who murdered her brother. Her mind swam with a million thoughts and a million different emotions. There was only one consistent thought: kill him.

The man turned and fled further down the alley, and his guards raised their weapons. She had her shield flowering around her before they fired. The second the bullets hit her shield, Kara braced herself and took a steadying breath. She wasn't losing him.

When the guns clicked open to reload, she slammed her staff on the ground. "Charge the ground with my energy: lightning wave!" she shouted. Bolts of electricity zoomed across the ground and struck the two unsuspecting men.

The men fell to their knees, crying out in pain. Kara stormed toward them, allowing her shield to drop, fury alight in her electric blue gaze. Purple electricity ran up and down her arms, visibly bouncing off her skin. This bastard was going down for every horrible thing he did. One of the guards reached for his fallen gun, and Kara kicked it out of reach before stomping the heel of her boot on his hand. The man screamed, cradling his injured appendage.

Kara rounded on the two soldiers. "Get out of here. I only want your boss," she said with nothing but ice in her voice.

Without hesitation, the guards scrambled and took off, screaming for help. They were nothing but cowards. Kara paid no mind as she ran down the alley and into a dead end. The General stood, backed against the wall, holding a pistol and smirking. His one good eye flicked around in terror, and his face was chalky white, but he didn't cry or beg and kept scowling.

"I suppose this is it." His gravelly voice made her skin crawl. "Who do you think is faster?"

Kara pulled a dagger from her thigh-high boot and threw it. She didn't even anticipate hitting him, but the dagger stuck in his thigh, and he dropped his weapon, grunting in pain. Electricity snaked from her hand and jumped to his shoulder, giving him an extra jolt of pain until he dropped to a knee. "You killed my brother," she said, approaching him and kicking the pistol out of reach.

He could probably overpower her, but Kara wouldn't let that stop her. This was her chance to make everything right. When she spoke, he looked up in confusion.

Kara let her Descendant form fade away. She was left as simply Kara McKenzie. A sixteen-year-old girl who used to be terrified of the world. Now, she was willing to burn it for what it did to her family. "You shot him in cold blood because that witch told you to," she snarled. The man trembled very slightly. Kara could all but taste the bitter-sweet fear coming off him in waves. "Do you even remember him?"

The General hung his head and closed his good eye. She wanted to feel good about what she was doing but didn't. Her skin burned with pent-up energy, and she still didn't feel victorious. She wasn't sure how revenge would feel, but this wasn't it. She felt sorrow and fear, but there was no happiness. It was like the weight that sat on her chest since her brother's death got heavier.

"I'm going to kill you," she said, keeping her voice level. If she was going to take a life, she wasn't going to do it out of pure anger. No, she had to be aware of what she was doing.

The man didn't move. He didn't try to fight as she stepped towards him, pulling her knife out of his thigh. Her chest heaved, and she clutched the weapon with white knuckles. Dawson's face came to mind, and that carefree smile was on his lips. That smile was constant. He never found a reason to frown in their darkness.

His blue eyes reflected the very light that shone in his soul. Her grip waivered on the dagger, and tears trickled down her cheeks. *This is for Dawson.* She pressed the tip of the dagger into the man's neck, forcing him to look into her eyes. "Do you have any last words?" she asked.

A trickle of blood slid down the man's stubbly throat. It rolled down pale skin and stained the collar of his uniform. He was Angel's most trusted man. And still, a voice screamed at her that it wasn't his fault. He was being controlled. If the others didn't deserve to die, why did he?

Avery put a hand on her shoulder.

Kara jumped, forgetting he had been with her.

"I get it," he said. "You lost everythin'. Comin' from someone like me, I know it's not a lot, but listen to your heart. I'll support any decision you make, but listen. This will stain your soul in a way you won't understand until it's too late."

She closed her eyes and took a steady breath. Listen to your heart. From the depths of her soul, she knew she wasn't a murderer. If she did, could she live with herself? Someone who hurt, maimed, tortured. No one would miss him. Still, she didn't want to be like that.

Kara let her brother go. She left Haven, knowing she might not return, and she released him. How could she claim to have forgiven herself for his death and then kill someone in his name? That wasn't right. Her hands trembled until she lost her grip on the dagger. It clattered to the ground, and she put her hands to her mouth to keep from gasping. Sobs wracked her body as she poured her grief into her hands. She wasn't even strong enough to give her brother the revenge he deserved. What kind of sister was she?

Avery held out his arms, and she stepped into them, glad he hadn't left her alone. What kind of mistake would she have made if he hadn't ripped her from those evil thoughts?

The General watched her sob without emotion.

When the tears stopped, she returned her gaze to him and stepped out of Avery's touch. "Do you even care? Do you feel anything at all?" she asked, grabbing the man's shoulders and pouring her feelings into him. "Let me show you what it feels like to lose everything," she said.

Kara lived through the worst moments of her life again, giving him her fear. Her brother's dying breath and the blood that trickled from his lips. A fear she never thought would come true. She could never cry enough for her brother, for the pain he must have felt while leaving their world. She went back to those dreaded moments of not knowing what had happened to her parents and where they were. She let him feel the sorrow, the death, and the hopelessness of someone who lost everything.

The man twitched under her fingers before letting out an ungodly scream and collapsing into the wall behind him. Kara hoped he felt everything for the people he tormented, not just her. She removed her hands when his eyes closed. Her fingers searched for a pulse, and she exhaled when she found one. When she dropped her hand, a wave of energy washed over her. It was warm and soothing. She felt her weariness fade, and it spread through her chest.

Avery smiled weakly. "You did it. Your final test as a Descendant. You passed."

"It hurts," she whispered. "Why does it still hurt?"

Avery hummed softly. "I don't think that pain will ever vanish." His voice was the kindest she had ever heard.

She wasn't sure how long they stood like that, but the sounds of shouting and screaming faded when she let him go. Avery walked out of the alley with her, holding her hand and wiping tears from her cheeks. She looked up at the mess across the once beautiful city—bodies everywhere. She thought it was over for a moment, but then there was a monstrous explosion, and a wave of white light pulsed from the back of the city. *Ryan.*

About the author

SLMcGinnis writes Young Adult Fantasy and Coming of Age Stories featuring female leads who grow into the role of strong heroine with an emphasis on mental health in both boys and girls. She promises to make her readers laugh and cry as they connect with their inner child with relatable characters.

This American writer holds an MFA in English and Creative Writing with a minor in Fantasy and Fiction from Southern New Hampshire University. Her love of all things literature encouraged her to leave the safety of the medical field and pursue a career as a college educator with success. As a happy educator in Northeast Texas, SLMcGinnis brings her love of writing to a new level.

She loves writing in her bed in her free time with a cup of coffee and her favorite pillow. She started her writing career as a self-published author and found some success.

She is now represented by Castle Drum Publishing, so she has more time to caffeinate, write, teach, and love on her three dogs and two cats as she suffers the Texas heat.

Follow her comings and goings on her website! slmcginnis.com

Also by

The Lessons of Magik: Book 1 of the Descendants Series
Link: https://a.co/d/1RHwyvC

Step into a world where evil hides behind a beautiful smile and a charming voice. A world in which the impossible is possible, but also illegal.

Kara spends every waking day that something terrible will happen to her family. After all, no one is safe is Angel's city. Least of all, Descendants.

Ryan fights for justice and honor, never taking his eyes off the end game. Even as he searches for his missing mother.

Killian doesn't care about the world, or the people in it. His only goal is to keep his brother alive.

And Angel, well, she just wants to watch the world burn.

Eternally Winter: Book 1 of The Eternally Witches Duology
Link: https://a.co/d/cwk4uS7

Her magic is a curse.
His love is forbidden.
Can they survive in a world where society calls for their destruction?

Jayce and Maya are on opposite sides of a seemingly never-ending war between vampires and witches. They must put aside their differences when they get trapped in an accidental curse cast by Maya's hand. A curse that puts her on the Coven's hitlist as the number one enemy. As her curse grows stronger, Jayce has to show Maya the importance of being true to herself before the Covens can find and destroy them.